MW00462299

IN A CITY FILLED WITH DROWNING, DESPERATE SOULS, DARRAGH FINN, A DRUNKARD, FELON AND ATHEIST, BECOMES THEIR UNLIKELY HAND OF DELIVERANCE.

Christmas morning and a solidly constructed stone chapel that was not there the night before sets in Central Park. That day's front page of the New York Times is blank except for a single poem signed only "df." Then each day, a new poem from the enigmatic "df" appears in seemingly miraculous ways no one can explain and people in need are helped. Is it a sign from heaven, a miracle for today's secular world or somebody's sick joke or computer hack? The powers that be want the chapel demolished and removed from city property, but some see this as a sacrilege and stand in opposition.

"*The Stone Chapel Poet*, McCall's masterfully inventive debut novel, is as vibrant and iridescent as the stained glass windows adorning the small chapel discovered Christmas morning on the lawn of Central Park. Poignant poetry, which appears simultaneously and just as inexplicably to usurp the front page of *New York Times*, becomes the loom weaving together the tattered threads of four desperate lives, shredded by the frozen winds of loneliness. Jaded New Yorker's are left to wonder whether the chapel and the poetry are Christmas miracles or simply unconventional graffiti.

McCall subtly waves his pen and the reader feels the soft kiss of snowflakes, hears Salvation Army bells and smells evergreen needles, transported viscerally to that place in us all where

memories of our favorite Christmases past reside. McCall reminds us that the threads connecting humanity are love and, wherever there is love, there is the intention of Christmas. As Cap Kencaid, McCall's ill-fated fisherman reveals, Christmas, at its best, is not a season but an inexhaustible series of lifelines that can be used to salvage the overwhelmed."

As elegant as it is powerful, *The Stone Chapel Poet* is destined to be an annual holiday refresher for everyone who, as a child once upon a time, knew the undeniable magic of Christmas morning."—*Rick Norman, author of Fielder's Choice.*

"This book had me from the first paragraph. An intriguing story of a Christmas miracle, where the author paints vivid pictures of the characters, and of New York City. I loved it and plan to read it again. Definitely five stars."—*Lisa Stewart.*

"What is the difference between believing in existence and believing in life? *The Stone Chapel Poet* takes us on a mysterious journey that offers an answer to that question, and as it does, H. Alan McCall balances deft storytelling that keeps you turning the page with poignant scenes that melt even 'a fisherman's winter heart.' By the story's end, you'll be reminded that so much of life's pilgrimage begins with a willingness to walk beyond the unseen."—*Dr. Keagan LeJeune, Professor, McNeese State University.*

THE STONE CHAPEL POET

H. Alan McCall

Moonshine Cove Publishing, LLC
Abbeville, South Carolina U.S.A.

FIRST MOONSHINE COVE EDITION APRIL 2017

This book is a work of fiction. Names, characters, places and incidents are products of the author's imagination or are used fictitiously. Any resemblance to actual events, locales or persons, living or dead, is entirely coincidental.

ISBN: 978-1-945181-14-6
Library of Congress Control Number: 2017942170
Copyright © 2017 by H. Alan McCall

All rights reserved. No part of this book may be reproduced in whole or in part without written permission from the publisher except by reviewers who may quote brief excerpts as part of a review in a newspaper, magazine or electronic publication; nor may any part of this book be reproduced, stored in a retrieval system or transmitted in any form or by any means electronic, mechanical, photocopying, recording or any other means, without written permission from the publisher.

Front cover design by John David Eakin, Graphic Works Design, back cover design by Moonshine Cove staff.

For my parents, Norman and Joyce, and for those ancestors gone and those unknown.
Dulce Periculum

About The Author

Alan McCall was born in June 1959, on the Louisiana gulf coast, and is a lifelong resident of the state. He earned a degree in Business Administration from McNeese State  University in 1980, and a Juris Doctorate in 1984 from the Paul M. Hebert Law Center at Louisiana State University. He was admitted to bar that same year and has enjoyed an active civil practice focusing on business formation, property, construction disputes and banking. He has worked at the same law firm since 1985. He is a current member of the Louisiana State Bar Association and the American Bar Association. He has co-authored papers on construction bond liability and insurance coverage disputes, and currently is an Assistant Bar Examiner for the Louisiana Code of Civil Procedure Examination.

Alan has served as a school board member for the Diocese of Lake Charles and is a member of St. Martin De Porres Catholic Church. He lives in Lake Charles, Louisiana with his wife, Carlene, and together they have a blended family of five children. In January 2016, after 30 years as a full time attorney, he began writing the story that would become *The Stone Chapel Poet.*

For more about Alan McCall and what he is working on now, visit his website:

http://stonechapelpoet.com/

There set before you are fire and water;
To whichever you choose, stretch out your hand.

—*Book of Sirach 15:16*

THE STONE
CHAPEL POET

Chapter One

The little chapel stood among the subtle snow drifts like the keep of a forgotten outpost. Gray, wintered trees formed broken walls acres away. The skyline was a subdued dark, hinting at shadows and soaring rises beyond. In the pre-dawn hours, the darkness ruled, with the close clouds hiding the moon. The winter wind moved through these dark canyons, lifting and dropping the falling snow in erratic exhales and long sighs, as if the clouds above were worn and surrendering to the coming dawn, a peaceful surrender, a gentle awakening.

A stone-laid path led to the chapel door, though barely visible beneath the fresh snow. The chapel was close-walled and small, with a single arched door in the front center of the narrow structure. The door itself was lined with four heavy iron bands, dark black, that were bolted to the door's thick planks. Massive, rough, iron hinges held the door's formidable weight. The recessed doorway was framed with thick, wooden beams that each appeared slightly odd in size, as if each were merely squared sections of hard wood tree trunks. A small stone landing spread across the chapel front, on one side of which rested a small bench, and on the opposite side, a halved log made into another small seat. The chapel roof was steep and covered with irregular sized slate plates, most the color of pencil lead. The scattered plates of lighter colors appeared fragile and misplaced.

Thick oolitic limestone clad the chapel's exterior walls. Its color and texture suggested that the stone was quarried from the North Yorkshire Moors, like the stones that gave the historic buildings of Bath, England their distinctive appearance. Timeless stones, rock that did not quarry easily, that preferred to remain buried, but once harvested, seemed to want to last forever, to make their buildings mountain strong and above the reach or hold of God's falling weather. The mortar holding the stones, the cladding's weakest link, was pitted and cracked, old and unwashed, but holding fast like cave art, and still cementing the stones to the walls.

The three stained glass windows on each side of the chapel rested in tall arches sized similar to the front doorway arch. Without the full sunrise or illumination from the inner church, the depictions in the glass were vague and waning, only hinting at the saint or sacrament cast in the art. But the images were grand and true, and the craft of the cuttings and colorings was visible even in twilight, all handmade and timeless.

An age of use, and more so of existence, was all about this chapel. While it had no gated cemetery adjoining its grounds, common to so many old town churches across the villages of Northern England and Scotland, its features suggested that old world vintage. The walls and sills looked aged by long frigid winters and cool, damp summers; its wood beams smooth from the wind more than from its varnish.

But on this morning, of all mornings, a grand surprise waited for those who would pass by this lonesome, dark little chapel. A wonder bestowed for all those who would wander toward its snowy roofline.

Because it was dawn on a snow blessed Christmas morning.

Because this magnificent, frail little chapel rested on the Great Lawn of New York's Central Park.

And because, and mostly because, it was not there yesterday.

Chapter Two

Isla Walson's coffee shop was open late this Christmas Eve, not because of brisk business, and not by choice. She wiped the counter, lazily, not thinking about finishing. Outside she could see a car or two pass every few minutes, and some walking traffic moved across the sidewalk, people bundled in coats and bright scarves, hurrying to get out of the chill. But no one had entered the shop in over an hour. She glanced up at the clock on the wall, near a small, sparsely decorated Christmas tree, and saw that it was near the end of the eve.

She worked behind the counter on Christmas Eve because it was a condition of her new, revised lease. Isla only had one employee, a college student who worked part-time, twenty hours a week. Because Isla had no immediate family to be with, she let Josie, her part time help, have the night off to be with her boyfriend and his family. But someone had to be here until 1 a.m., even on this holiday, as her landlord adhered to the "city that never sleeps" mantra, even in this part of town. And since Isla lived upstairs, alone, she accepted the chore in place of her only employee. It would not be her first Christmas Eve at work, nor did she believe it would be her last.

When her grandfather was alive, the Walson family owned this building, located just off the corner of Essex and Hester Street. The family lived in a three-bedroom apartment on the top floor, and rented out the apartments on the other four floors above street level. Her grandparents used the bottom floor for a small grocery and dry goods store, and a separate entry bakery where her grandmother spent most of her time. Mamma Walson's bakery filled the neighborhood with the aroma of fresh olive focaccia, panfoaccia and tomato pie. Her recipes were memorized legacies passed to her by her mother, who lived all her life in a small Italian coast town, never traveling more than twenty miles from the house where she was born. The Walson's little bakery sold fresh breads daily, and also made breads and pastries for the grocery counter. The grocery was small, but had fresh meats and produce, some times trucked in from area farms and gardens by her grandfather. He devoted his life to the store, working at all of its jobs and needs, from butcher block to stock boy, check-out counter to floor sweep. As her grandfather aged, he spent more of his time sitting at a small table in the front corner of the store, tempting customers with bread samples and fresh olive oil, and stories of his wild days in the Italian countryside, where wine was as plentiful as water, and lawlessness was vivid as sunlight. In the late afternoons he would play dominos with friends, while the store business continued around his humble table. Eventually, he slowed so much he forgot how to score the game, and sometimes just stacked the dominos, as if the little bricks had no numbered markings and were just blocks to arrange in simple shapes. Isla had not realized it at the time, but he had gone full circle, and in many ways, was a child again.

Her grandparents were proud and devoted parishioners at St. Ann's Catholic Church, and a little engraved nameplate showing their name still recognized their gift of a sculptured station of the cross. They were the first parishioners to donate a station, and they chose the sixth station, Veronica wipes the face of Jesus. They never told Isla why they chose that scene, but she imagined that it was selected because of the woman's simple, clear devotion, and bravery that Veronica displayed by publicly comforting a man condemned to death. And when Isla made it to mass, she always sat adjacent to that station, where she knew that her grandparents had sat, as if they could see her there, or know that she was there as much to be with them in silence, rather than to follow the prayers and the hymns of the mass.

Her father inherited the building and the businesses when his parents died, and Isla grew up in the store and bakery, working on small chores under the watchful eye of her mother, but mostly playing with the cookie molds and cake icing tubes, a child artist who painted with sugar and colored frostings. Those had been comfortable years, as time is usually for children unaware of the struggles of business, or the strain of competition for status or wealth.

But time could also be a stark and deep, unforgiving river. Its rogue waves could surprise those afloat on a tranquil morning, and wash a cruel slap of cold across the decks of the day, to down you, maybe even to drown you.

Isla still struggled with witnessing her father collapse with a rag in his hand, washing the store windows, early on an autumn Saturday morning, with the aroma of baking bread just hinting in the air. Isla was only twelve years old when her father fell. Without him, what was left of the Walson family, now only Isla and her mother, went adrift that day, lost and almost invisible, like castaways unworthy of an extensive search and rescue.

Even now Isla could hear the ghost whispers of neighbors and familiar strangers at the funeral home, talking about what took her father's life, the circulatory time bomb they called the "widow maker." She had vivid memories of that day, the church songs, the windy graveyard, and the vacant eyes of her mother. Her memories of her father were much different, more like still pictures and sketches. She could no longer remember his voice, or see him laugh or smile. He was only present in her mind now in poses, in somber stages of life, in distant scenes of work and waves of goodbye. Those were bitter memories to hold, but they were all that she had.

That was twenty years ago. Her mother sold the building within a year of her father's death. She had been smart enough to get a 30-year lease on their top floor apartment and on half of the ground floor of the building, where the family bakery was located. But she gave up the grocery store, knowing that she could only hope to run one of the businesses. The sales price paid off the family bills, and gave her mother a modest cushion, but certainly not a fortune. Over time, the family's prosperity became slow motion atrophy. The savings slowly dissipated, and the impact of the lease's rent escalation clauses became more dire every few years. The combination of time and the decline of the neighborhood slowly crippled the bakery. Isla and her mother worked in the bakery seven days a week, but every year business was a little worse than the last. Three years ago, shortly after a stroke took her mother's life, Isla was forced to sublease the bakery space to a regional chain bakery, Devil's Sweet Temptations, keeping only a corner of a corner of the space for her coffee shop. Really, it was more akin to a coffee counter than a coffee shop. But she had the apartment, and between the small profit she made on the sublease, and her coffee counter, she made do. She was thirty-three, had never been married, and had resigned herself to a life of an imperfectly balanced equation; small expectations equal small disappointments.

The hanging, overhead door bell rattled as the door opened. Isla looked up and smiled, and reached for a coffee cup. She put a splash of heavy cream into the cup, then poured in the black, steaming brew.

"Hey, Jax, I was starting to wonder."

Jaxson Dissy shrugged and smiled. "Crazy night out there. Traffic bad on Broadway, Grand, really bad all around SoHo." He set a bundle of newspapers on the counter and took off his gloves. "But you know you're always my first stop. You're the star shining brightest on the lower east side."

Jaxson Dissy had worked for the *New York Times* for longer than Isla had lived, holding all sorts of jobs in the print room, supervising circulation and delivery, and even running its motor pool and truck fleet. Now, at age 70, Jax was mostly retired. He drove a circulation truck to keep him somewhat engaged, but more than the work, he enjoyed seeing those people he'd grown to know.

Jax had a modest circulation route on the lower East Side, which he could usually finish in 3 hours or so. Normally, he would pick up a load of papers from the distribution center on Pike Street around 4 a.m., but this year, on Christmas Eve, the papers were printed earlier for late night circulation rather than at 4:30 or 5 a.m. on Christmas day. The few hours difference allowed Jax to actually wake up at his home on Christmas morning, for the first time in many years.

"Really, Jax, we're a pretty sad lot, working on Christmas Eve." She handed him the coffee and leaned back against the counter.

"Not just working." He grinned, looking around the shop. "Working alone."

Isla frowned and nodded. "You're a breath of Christmas cheer. Thanks for reminding me."

Jax took off his overcoat and set it on a stool. He yanked off his Jets stocking cap, and his grey, thinning curls welcomed the space. He took a slow sip of the coffee and smiled. "That's professional grade," he said after a long deep sip. "But that's not a surprise. You are a professional brew master."

"You know what they say, aspire to greatness, in all things pointless," Isla remarked as she retrieved a small plate of biscotti from a glass cupboard for Jax to sample. "That way everyone thinks that you're irreplaceable, even when no one really knows what you do to begin with."

"The philosophy of a java engineer," Jax remarked. "Timeless!"

Isla playfully swatted at him with her dish towel. "Where Mrs. Jax tonight? All alone by her fireplace, waiting for Santa?"

"Oh no, she's just fine. We had Christmas at the neighbors before I left. She had her eggnog and fruit roll and my famous winter cream custard. I tell you, that was a big hit with everybody, but I'm not giving up the secret." He winked at Isla, looking for a smile. "Not even to you."

"Understood, Jax, though you know your secret would be safe with me." Then Isla looked over her shoulder at the dark bakery. "Well, maybe not too safe. Those bastards next door at Devil's Donuts would

16

find some way to steal it and make another fortune off me, and off you too."

The watch on Jax's wrist chimed at the stroke of twelve. He looked down at his Timex, and then at Isla. "It's official. Merry Christmas." He reached in a pocket of his overcoat and pulled out a capped container. "Here you go, darling. Fresh winter cream custard. This one just for you."

"And a Merry Christmas to you too, Mr. Jaxson Dissy. And to Mrs. Jaxson too, please tell her for me."

Jax smiled with a rare joy, that shone well in his brown, barrel colored eyes. The happiness of the moment was understood and given back to Isla. A feeling of holiday and spirit and joy, welled up in her from somewhere, a feeling that Isla had not seen or felt or dreamed of in long ages, at least in the last three years of living alone. In that quiet moment, in the first few minutes of Christmas day, Isla was given her sole Christmas present of the year, and she received it and cherished it for the treasure that it was. She was seen, she was remembered, she was welcomed. "Thank you Jax," she managed to say, her eyes a little misty. "Thanks for being here with me, if only for a minute."

As Jax was finishing his coffee, Isla took a knife from the backsplash and walked over to the bundle of newspapers on the counter. Before she cut the binding, she paused and called over to Jax, "Hey, this bundle is messed up. Look at the front page. It's blank."

Jax rose and put on his coat and cap. Then he finished his last sip of coffee, and answered, "No, I thought so too. But they're all like that."

Isla shook her head, "Come on, it's the *New York Times*. You know how many thousands of dollars a word is worth, especially on the front page. This has got to be some mess up."

"Isla, I'm telling you they are all like that. It's not a mistake. And the front page is not all blank. Open one up and see."

Disbelieving, Isla unfolded one of the papers and saw that Jax was right. It was not completely blank. The paper had its regular banner. But that was it, except for one column of writing in the center of the page.

This World

On this world we wander

Like shepherds in the field
Drawn to every distance
To every lamb concealed

About this world we ponder
What treasure can it yield
Its jewels and lucre lavish
Pagan paramour revealed

Across this world we plunder
Breaking bone and earth afield
Defy all hails deterrent
Drunken pride, ambition steeled

If this world we squander
Could its graves and wounds be healed
Crimes and scandals pardoned?
Doom and damnation repealed?

Of this world we wonder
What source the power wield
To fashion our existence
To be our Savior and our Shield
df 12.24

Isla read the column again, then looked up at Jax. "What's the d.f. stand for? Someone's initials? Do you know who that is?"

Jax shook his head. "Nope. But I was thinking that the *Times* commissioned some famous writer to come up with a Christmas message. Probably so."

Isla read the poem again. "I like it. Good thoughts for a Christmas day. Not like the *Times* to white out the front page of the paper though. I still think that somebody, somehow, made a big, big mistake."

Jax wrapped his scarf around his neck and headed for the door. "Isla, with all the writers, editors, interns, computers, software, programmers and obsessive quality control supervisor fact checkers that the *Times* has, do you really think that they would by accident forget to put print on the front page of the paper? I know some of those guys. They're professionals. They're perfectionists. They don't make those kinda mistakes."

Chapter Three
Christmas Day

Jason Dumbarton was on a three-way call with the *Times'* vice-president of operations and the editor in chief. "Whoever screwed this up will be looking for a new job, as of today. And one or both of you may be too. Merry Christmas."

At 7:15 on Christmas morning, after a late night Christmas Eve party and with a pre-breakfast headache, the man responsible for the newspaper with the largest circulation of all metropolitan newspapers in the United States was ill-tempered and moody. He had only been awake for a few minutes, and had just seen a copy of the paper which he retrieved from his apartment's doorstep. Within seconds he dialed JoAnn Taylor, the *Times'* v.p. over plant operations, who was still asleep. After the profanity-filled good morning woke her, JoAnn had patched in Mike Sandoval, the *Times'* editor in chief. Neither had seen the paper at the time of this unplanned, unwelcomed conference call, and both were struggling to understand what was so enraging their superior.

Jason Tobias Dumbarton ran the *Times* Publications division of the *New York Times* Company, and held several titles and positions to cement his power and clout. His tenure was going on four years, and during this short time he had lost more friends than he'd made. He was a dynamic leader, but also a callous realist and ruthless taskmaster. He well knew that paper media was archaic to the vast number of Millennials who accessed most aspects and events of their lives through smart phones or tablets. Their generation was spoiled by the sheer volume of choices of media. Instant access to news, events, sports, music, even television and movie content was not only what this demographic expected, but demanded. Print news in the digital age was difficult business, a high wire act without a net, and with no ambulance at the ready. For that reason, he ruled with a heavy hand, and micro-managed every aspect of the print *Times,* especially its business and content directions.

JoAnn excused herself for a moment and retrieved a copy of the paper from the lobby of her building. Neither Jason nor Mike said anything while they waited for her to rejoin the call. When she returned all she could muster was, "I don't know what to say."

She described the front page appearance for Mike. That portion of the call took a mere four seconds.

Mike thought about what she said, a blank page one except for the *Times* banner and a five stanza poem. His first thought was that someone was playing a bizarre practical joke. He guessed for the right price a few fake papers could be in print, and left on Dumbarton's doorstep, knowing it was the equivalent of sparking the fuse of many, large, dangerous, homemade fireworks. "This is a bad joke. What else could it be?"

JoAnn was not convinced. "So whoever did this also left not just one on Jason's doorstep, but a stack of them in my building's lobby."

While JoAnn and Mike debated whether a jokester had been able to fool the president of the *Times* with a gag paper, Jason Dumbarton paced the dark, wood planked floor of his condo, looking at the city skyline hold the shadows and light of the sunrise, diffused by low hovering clouds. His apartment was on the 44th floor of the One Beacon Court Building, located at 151 East 58th Street. The massive building covered a city block, bounded by 58th and 59th streets, and by Lexington and Third Avenue. None of the apartments had balconies, but his floor to ceiling windows gave him impressive views of the Upper East Side. He could almost feel the cold pressing against the glass, the winterness of the day blatant. But he also caught glimpses of Christmas as he scanned the skyline, twinkling lights, alpine wreaths, elaborate decorations ranging from snowmen to religious themes, in the windows across the way. Of course his apartment offered no such seasonal cheer. His wife of twelve years had a tree adorned in the far corner of the living room, but her interests usually stayed in collectable art, rather than seasonal themed adornments. Her attention to anything else was shallow and waning. He quickly dismissed his wandering thoughts, and continued his reprimand of his two stunned employees. "So Mike, do we need to involve law enforcement? Or do we have anyone in-house I can depend on the figure this out?"

Mike considered the bravado of such a prank, if it was a prank, then responded in a surprisingly analytical tone. "For now we need to keep this a closed system. Let me see if I can find a leak, a breach somewhere. There will be fingerprints, digital or otherwise, and that means there will be a trail. One thing for certain, if this is not a joke, then without doubt this was not an accident. This can't be a mistake.

Too many checks and balances. Someone had to approve the lay-out, had to sign off on all page one leads. I know for a fact that this did not come out of yesterday's page one meeting. So this had to be done after the fact. To bump everything to the inner pages is unheard of."

"Well, Mike, isn't that your job? To oversee those page one go decisions." Jason's deep voice was even but adversarial.

"Yes, but I assure you that I had no input in this. No one ever suggested anything like this as long as I have been here. And I would not have approved of anything like it. It had to be a deliberate act to format page one to a single poem. I'll find out how it happened, and who is responsible."

"So what you're telling me is that a rogue employee took it on his or her self to commandeer page one this Christmas morning, or two, someone hacked into our system and over-rode our print process."

"That is exactly what I'm saying." Mike thought about that answer. This barren lay-out could not have been approved by the meeting of editors. The Page One Meeting is a daily ritual that usually occurs about 4 p. m. every day. The meeting is chaired by the masthead editor, who runs the news desk, and includes about thirty other editors, covering everything from world and local news, sports and entertainment, obituaries to opinion columns. Even on Christmas Eve, with the meeting moved up in time a few hours, the meeting would have been well-attended and would have flowed toward a tentative lay-out just like any other day.

"Get me some answers," Jason said. "By noon today, I need to know which way we are going on this. If we have a cybercrime, a criminal referral will have to be made today. This will not get away from us. Agreed?"

Joann was pacing nervously, thinking that if someone was going to have to take a fall for this, Jason would without doubt burn her to the ground rather than blame Mike. The printing operations were under her supervision. She had to go into survival mode, and discover the root cause of this sabotage. She would have to contact the operations manager at the Queens facility, and also the plant control room coordinator, to understand how this could have happened. What if it had been systemic, happening at other printing facilities located across the country? And why a benign piece of poetry? Surely other, more caustic writings could have been presented on page one of the *Times,* the most coveted space in print newspapers. Without knowing she was mumbling her thoughts, she was snapped to attention by Jason's sharp tone.

"Repeat that, JoAnn. I'm not sure I heard you right."

Startled, JoAnn scrambled to gather her thoughts. "Nothing sir, just thinking out loud."

"Say it. What did you say, what were you thinking?"

JoAnn stopped her pacing and looked out of her window, and her views from her apartment in the Village were neither as lofty nor as panoramic as Jason's. Reluctantly she repeated her impulsive mutterings. "I was just thinking, sir, how many of our readers might like it. The poem, I mean. On Christmas, it's not a bad thought. It's not Robert Frost, certainly, but maybe it's not the worst thing that could have been highlighted on page one. If some renegade hacker wanted to make us look bad, it could have been some racial slur or, some radical, profane hate speech in big block letters."

She was stunned not by any audible response, but by the penetrating, furious silence that seemed without end. Almost in panic she continued, "I'm not advocating that we claim to own the message. It's not a serious alternative, sir, just a wild hair thought. I'm sorry to have even brought it up."

Jason finally relented, knowing that JoAnn was raw nerves and vinegar at this moment. "Not the plan B I had in mind. But duly noted. For the time being we say nothing about this. We do not say the poem is ours, but we do not put it out that we lost control of our process either. Now, one or both of you find out what in the hell is going on at my paper. I don't want to wake up in the morning and find some diatribe that isn't a nice little poem, but maybe some vile manifesto that will bring the wrath of hell to where we all live. Now, I'm going to Mass this morning at the Cathedral, and I want answers by the time I return. This is a career defining moment for you, and I mean both of you."

"Merry Christmas," Mike said.

All he heard in response was the electric click and hiss of the call disconnecting.

"And a happy new year," he said to no one.

***

Claira Vasson's phone also rang just after 7 o'clock on Christmas morning. She was awake, but still in bed. She had no reason to rise this early, as her tabby cat was still curled up sleeping, and she was otherwise alone. This was the first Christmas morning in years that she did not have someone with whom to share the morning. No husband, no son, at least not here in her apartment. Not far away, but to her on this morning, both as distant as another world. The solitude was as chilling as the dawn winter wind. She tried to prepare herself for this loneliness, for the absence of everyone she welcomed into her life, but she realized too late that there was no easy preparation for seclusion, or for a place familiar but now depleted of laughter, missing even the sounds of movement, of the simple background noise of a living, breathing place. She noticed more and more how her home sometimes had the silence of a vacant building. She imagined it was like an empty, dark, ruin of a church, shadowed in a state of abandonment, eons without the sound of a whispered prayer, without even the echo of a chant of canticle intonation. But it wasn't just the silence that was sometimes so profoundly disturbing. It was the feel of the vacancy, of a hurried departure just missed.

Her son was with her ex-husband this Christmas morning, so she was not pressured to get up early to see what presents waited under the tree. Tony was only four, and Christmas was still a magical event for him. Last year was the first year of the separation from Theo, and little Tony woke up at her home on that Christmas morning. But this year was the first Christmas where she suffered the absence of the divided custody. She asked for full custody, all holidays, all summer, with a rare and scripted visit for father and son. But she knew that was a fantasy, that Theo did nothing to justify a virtual loss of his son, and that Tony should not be deprived of all of the childhood memories a boy makes with his father. So this was her every-other-year year. Turned out that she got the odd years and Theo the evens. So today Tony was with his dad. She knew that this sharing of Tony was their routine now, but could not have imagined how wounded she felt to be deprived of Tony's presence on a holiday such as Christmas. He would only have one real Christmas morning as a four-year-old, and she would witness none of it.

The phone cried out again, and Claira cursed in mutters, which sounded like grunts in a brutish foreign language. She debated letting the phone ring, but she checked the caller ID, and she saw it was a work call that she had to take.

Claira worked for the Central Park Conservancy, and held the post of associate park director. This call was from the office of park police, and she was the Park's on-call supervisor this holiday. Probably another mugging, she thought. Or vandals.

"Claira Vasson," she said.

"Yes, this is dispatch officer Warren Hayes. Sorry to wake you Christmas morning, but we have a situation on the Great Lawn."

She yawned as she made her way to her kitchen. She knew Warren well, as he had been stationed with park police for the last several years. His unnecessary identification, with his position and last name, was meant to provoke both her irritation and amusement, as well as to promote his own vanity. Claira recalled the first time she met Warren. He was off duty, but had volunteered to help with a Park summer promotion of the city's National History Museum. He appeared for work that Saturday, helping with a walking tour of several pavilions highlighting a new Native American exhibition, wearing a Bruce Springsteen Born to Run T-shirt, a size or two too small, and faded boot cut jeans that had the words BAD and ASS embroidered on the left and right rear pockets, respectively. As she looked about the shelves in her refrigerator, and turned to her cupboard for an empty glass, she managed to ask, "What kind of situation?"

"Well, I'm not sure how to say this." Warren's pause gave Claira time to pour her juice. "Somebody put a stone chapel on the Great Lawn, not far from Turtle Pond."

Claira paused in mid-sip. "Not funny."

"I know that sounds crazy, but it's not a joke. Do you want me to text a photo to your mobile?"

Claira had already turned away from the kitchen and was heading back to her bedroom to dress. She was trying to picture what kind of pre-fab temporary building could have been assembled during the night, how many people it would take to pull off such a stunt. While those thoughts and similar questions were collating through her mind, she asked Warren, "What's the scene control in place? Do we have perimeters established?"

"Well, we have several officers there now and a tape barricade. But even at this hour, on Christmas, there's a crowd starting to grow."

"Anybody in the structure?" she asked, thinking that this could be something like the Occupy Movement, where protesters would set up shop on public space to make a statement or to provoke attention for a grievance or a cause. Those events, though arguably noble in theory, had gradually devolved into unpleasant demonstrations, where public space was usurped from the public by rule-less occupiers, prone to drug use and eruptive assaults of every kind, not to mention the unsanitary blemish on the property resulting from the absence of hygiene in their communal, frontier living.

"I don't think so, ma'am. The little building was dark when I saw it. The door is not locked, though. Someone could have come and gone."

"Understood. I'll be there in an hour. Send that photo to my cell. And not to anyone else. I don't want it plastered all over Facebook, especially by Park staff."

The awkward, stuttering unsilence of an answer told her she was too late with the last direction. She stood in front of her closet, looking at the mirror on the sliding door, through the mess of blond hair hanging in bangs over her eyes. She dropped her head, and slowly said, "Warren, you still there?"

"Yea well, another one bites the dust. I may have jumped the gun a little with a picture. I mean, you have to see this. It's like a Christmas card. It looks like the North Pole, and Santa could be in there just chilling. It's really way cool. I mean, if this ain't ours, then it shoulda' been."

Claira ended the call exasperated, but not surprised. Not a day went by without some crazy situation developing at the park. Last Halloween, several college students tried to erect a mini Stone Hinge, using large, grey died Styrofoam blocks. They were dressed like what they thought druids would wear, in white, hooded cloaks, and were completely unaware that their solstice ceremony looked more like a KKK rally. The scene had quickly deteriorated into a rancor filled riot, which fortunately did not erupt in physical violence other than several of the mock stones being knocked over and broken.

She picked black corduroy pants and a thick stitched turtle neck sweater, and dressed quickly. She skipped make-up and pulled on her boots. Remembering that it would be close to freezing temperatures all day, she grabbed her coat, and wrapped a green, dark blue and black plaid scarf around her neck as she headed for her door and the subway ride that would take her into the city from her Park Slope apartment. Depending on what she would find at the Great Lawn, she might end up spending most the day away from her Brooklyn neighborhood, and couldn't help but wonder what her son would was doing, and how he would spend his Christmas, just a few blocks away.

Chapter Four

Cap Kencaid missed the icy wet sea wind of Deer Island, Maine. Even though the lobster fishing season was done until next April, he had much winter work to do, both on his boat and in his dock shop. He repaired his own lobster pots, and took small jobs repairing or building pots for other fishermen. Off island, he also had a stand of maples to tap starting in late January or February, depending on temperatures. He was behind in lining up his sales, though he doubted that he would have any problems placing or selling his harvest. He knew several locals who boiled the sap and bottled syrup. He had even tried doing that himself one season, but found that work to be too similar to cooking and kitchen chores for his taste. He would find a taker for his sap, he always did. He just didn't like to procrastinate on anything. Plans worked out better than blind luck or hopeful prayers, in his experience, so he tried to not to take anything for granted.

The sap season only lasted for four to six weeks, but he loved every minute of his time with the maples. It was simple work, and it didn't lead to riches, but it was a part of his winter. He was most comfortable with the trees, or the sea, or the night, or the solitary dawn in his small, smelly shop, any place where he was working alone. That was when he lingered between the tasks undertaken and the daydreams which played like sad songs over and over again in his mind. The early hours, the stormy weather, the quiet wind woods, all were his sanctuary. He was uneasy when he had to deal with others. His abruptness was often taken as rudeness, his self-assuredness taken as pretentiousness. While he didn't really care what others thought or said about him, he had learned it was easier to keep to himself and to the one other person who mattered in his daily life. His mother was the only person he made time for, the only person who knew and accepted him as he was.

But on this Christmas day he was fighting life outside of his elements. Really fighting two lives, fighting for one, and sadly, fighting against another. His mother was dying slowly, a convergence of complications from blood cancer and congestive heart failure. She was hospitalized in New York Presbyterian/Weill Cornell Medical Center for the last twelve days. She had been visiting Cissy, her daughter and Cap's sister, with plans to spend the Christmas holidays with Cissy and her family, before heading back to Deer Island. Cap and Cissy had discussed the visit in detail, because traveling was now too difficult and draining for their mother. Cap argued against the trip altogether, and tried to get Cissy and her kids to travel up to the Island for Christmas. But Cap couldn't convince either of them that the trip was a bad idea, and he relented when he saw the determination in his mother's eyes. It was as if she knew this would be her last excursion, in a way, her last adventure. After this Christmas, she would spend her remaining time in Deer Island, at Cap's house, where she had been living for the last few years. At the time he didn't consider the trip to be the lonely elephant walk to the secret boneyard, but now he saw it for just that. And it angered him, because he was caught unprepared, and had not done what he felt he needed to prepare his mother.

She was in New York City for two days before she needed acute care. Seemingly out of nowhere, her breathing worsened rapidly, becoming labored and shallow. Her legs swelled so much that her ankles were lost under the raised, discolored skin. At 69 years of age, she was weak and frail, and would have been so despite the leukemia that weakened her body and ravaged her immune system. Now her condition was critical, her body's systems bordering on breaking, and any number of problems could start the domino effect of little falls or failures that would cascade into the collapse of everything.

She was in Critical Care/ICU for a week, and was now in a private room on the cardiac floor. Cap saw little improvement in her condition, but the move to a private room made the stay at the hospital easier, as he was not forced to spend long hours in the waiting room. Cap arrived in New York as quickly as he could after Cissy called him. His first impulse was to have her brought back to Massachusetts, where her internist and her other regular specialists could care for her, but when he saw her in the ICU, he knew traveling was no longer possible. And even though he recognized this fact, he and his sister bickered over her care and treatment since he arrived.

Cap was his mother's appointed mandatory. Because she was in and out of consciousness, Mrs. Kencaid could not determine her own care, and even when awake, she was confused and disoriented. The durable power of attorney that Cap held vested him with the discretion and responsibility for her medical treatment decisions. And Cap was a fighter, so he fought his mother's disease and failing health as if she was thirty and vibrant, and with decades of life left to live. Even sixty-nine was not considered old age anymore, not to Cap. Cissy counseled a more passive treatment regime back when the leukemia was diagnosed two years ago, not wanting to subject her mother to round after round of chemotherapy, but Cap refused to consider it. And what Cap said, his mother did. So their mother endured the therapy, and the following sickness. Some days were tolerable, but most were misery.

Now her failing heart was the primary enemy, with a worsening pneumonia a competing villain. And Cap demanded an aggressive treatment of both conditions. Cissy took part in the recent meeting with Cap and the pulmonologist, and the discussion of the likelihood of Mrs. Kenkaid needing a respirator, and the greater likelihood of becoming dependent on it to breathe, was a flashpoint of controversy between them. Just yesterday, Cissy raised the idea of hospice, and the mention of it infuriated Cap. Hospice meant surrender. To Cap, it was not much different than assisted suicide, and as long as he had to make that decision, he would not consent to or condone that course of action.

That was yesterday. Now, on Christmas morning, Cap was alone with his mother in room 822. Cissy and her family were at their home in the suburbs, and he didn't expect to see any of them until this evening. And that was fine with him. Cissy's children deserved some normalcy on this holiday. They invited Cap for Christmas dinner, but he politely declined, preferring to stay at the hospital. Cissy and her husband even offered to stay round the clock at the hospital so that Cap could go back to Deer Island for a few days. But he chose to stay.

Cap would remain as long as he had to, and to whatever end that would arrive.

**

Claira arrived at the Central Park Police Precinct a little before 9 a.m. The 22nd Precinct was still housed in the old horse stable designed by Jacob Wray Mould in 1871, and is located mid-park, at 86th Street. The brick building, with its green accents and stone accouterments, fit the park well, but no longer stabled the police horses. Until recently, the horse squadron had been located at the stables on Pier 76, in Hell's Kitchen. Their new home was the Mercedes House, located on West 53rd Street. With roughly 79 officers and 60 horses, significantly down from its previous high, the squad was still the largest mounted police unit in the country. Units still patrolled the Park, but did not operate out of the 22nd Precinct.

A few officers milled about the Precinct office, and Claira had little trouble finding Warren Hayes. She had met him many times as their work and responsibilities at the park intersected, and his appearance was, as usual, unforgettable. His hair was thinning, but longer than regulation. He folded it over onto itself and made a tiny tail behind his head, like the cropped tail of a Schnauzer puppy. He was muscular and fit, but his movements and mannerisms were clumsy and awkward. He was a massive six feet six inches tall, and sported a faded scar across the line of his chin. If anyone would inquire about its origin, he would mumble some gibberish about 'Nam, even though he was decades too young to have served in that war.

But what made him an unforgettable character, aside from his wicked smile and eyes so blue that they could merge with the sky, was his habit of constantly talking in phrases he lifted from titles or hooks from old rock and roll songs. Warren had Rain Man skills when it came to songs and music. He devoted most of his off duty time to learning and playing classic rock songs with a rag tag garage band named the Tattooed Badges. Warren played rhythm guitar, and could sub in for their drummer if needed. If the band was really desperate and he was really drunk, he might even provide vocals on a few selected songs. Sometimes he even told friends that he was a professional musician, and only got into law enforcement as an aside, for the medical benefits, and for when he had to do "day-stuff." If he had to describe his attitude about life in two words or less, it would be a loud and boisterous "Rock On."

Warren held two insulated coffee mugs, as if he had seen Claira's arrival, and offered her one as she sat across from him at his desk. "There you are. Long Cool Woman in a Black Dress. Except it's too cold for a dress." He grinned like a kid who invented laughter. Carefully he handed her one of the coffee cups. "No sugar and two creams. That's the way I like mine," he said to her as she loosened her scarf.

"Sounds good to me." She wrapped both hands around the warm cup. This would have to do for breakfast this morning, at least for now. She took a slow sip of the coffee, then said, "That hits the spot. Thanks."

"Don't mention it. Now, about our little situation—"

"Any news?"

"Dream on," Warren answered. He stirred his coffee with a red swizzle stick, its end already chewed and mangled, like a used toothpick. Satisfied that his coffee and cream was adequately agitated, he continued, "Nothing new to add. Damnest thing. I can't see how that little church was built overnight. In NYC, that would be a yearlong project, union trade all the way. It's like it's out of some Sci-Fi movie, where we've all been mass hypnotized, because it's been there all along. And we just woke up." He took a slow deep drink of his coffee, then smacked his lips and smiled. "Did you ever see the movie *The Shadow?* That's what happened in that movie. So we know it's possible. Makes you wonder, doesn't it?"

Claira nodded, but not to signal acquiescence, but only to acknowledge that he had finished his thought. "I don't see that as a plausible explanation." She was jaded by the harshness of the city, with its well of cruel and depraved inhabitants, who somehow were also surprisingly adept at technology and the art of the impossible. Her experiences in the last few years would rival anything seen in the fictionalized NCIS television broadcasts. She had no doubt that they would soon discover the methods used to stage this hoax. Finishing another sip of her coffee, she said to Warren. "I'm sure that this prank has a proper explanation. Let's go and see what we see, shall we?"

"Do you mind walking? It's about 4 blocks down off of East Drive."

"Walking is good. But fill up this mug before we leave, please."

"Beast of Burden," Warren said as he took her cup. "The Stones had me in mind when they wrote that tune."

***

The Great Lawn of Central Park is located between the 79th and 86th Street Transverses, north of Belvedere Castle and the Delecorte Theater. Spanning approximately 55 acres, the lawn is famous for concerts and similar events, but is cherished more for the respite its lush summer grass offers to those tired of the sea of cement and pavement wrapping across the rest of the city. While Central Park covers about 845 acres, measuring 2.5 miles long and 0.5 miles wide, it is the Great Lawn at the virtual center of the park that thrives in the spring and the summer.

Claira knew most every square foot of the Park, having worked for the Conservancy since her internship during her last year in college. She had a degree in Environmental Science from NYU, but all of her electives were concentrated on botany and plant science. She immediately pursued a Masters in business administration, specializing in public bodies and non-profit organizations. That background made her an appealing hire, and she had worked for the Conservancy since her one-year internship ended a decade ago. Since then, she immersed herself in everything belonging to the Conservancy. She was familiar with every room of every park construction, and involved in all of the myriad of plans for grounds maintenance, building and gardens restoration, and events preparation. She even served as Park liaison with the State Tourist Bureau, making sure that the bureaucrats did not over sell or over promise what the Park could offer or accommodate.

As they trudged through the snow, she inquired more about this strange, early morning discovery. "Tell me from the beginning, who first reported it, and what was said."

"Well, I had the graveyard shift. I was covering for a buddy of mine, so I was at the desk about 6 this morning. A call came in from one of the park patrols, asking why he wasn't given a heads up about a new attraction." Warren giggled. "That dumbass. He thought the thing was supposed to be there." Then quickly his face became solemn, respectful. "That's how cool it looks, like we put it up. It really is something special."

"Come on, seriously. If this building wasn't there yesterday, it could have only been thrown up in a block of a few hours. It has to be a modular folly."

"A what?"

"A folly."

"No. This isn't a mistake. It really is there."

Claira looked over at Warren to see if he was serious. Satisfied that he was, she continued, "No, not that kind of folly. A folly like the Belvedere Castle. A mock-up. A fake gothic ruin. A façade."

Warren almost blushed, amused by his own naivety. "Oh, now I see." Warren nodded his head. "A folly. Well, I can't say how it was done, but it's solid as rock. I know the difference between stone and Styrofoam. And it doesn't seem to be on skids, like someone slid it off of the back of a trailer rig. Anyway, it's too big to haul around in one piece. No way we would not have seen that delivery truck. And I couldn't find any truck tracks or ruts." Warren froze in his tracks, as if to behold a wonder of the world. "Look, there she sits, right up the path. Goodbye yellow brick road."

Claira also paused in her stride when she saw the Chapel. She ignored the small crowd hovering around the stone building and studied the structure. It was just as it had been described. The photo that had been sent to her phone did not do it justice at all, not in beauty or scale. The Chapel was beautiful, a rustic, stone and beam edifice that looked like it belonged in the Park, or rather, like it belonged next to a cobbled road in the Scottish countryside, a timeless landmark that a village could claim as its vein line to a simple and pious past. After a moment absorbing the scene, she hurried to the Chapel.

A weak and ineffective tape line surrounded the Chapel. A narrow stone path followed from a park sidewalk to the Chapel landing. The snow had stopped its sprinkling, and the path had been dusted by enough footsteps that she could see the inlays of the stones. She slowly knelt, touching the stones, as if trying to feel their depth. After a moment, she rose and continued down the path, with Warren a step behind. As she reached the doorway, she asked him, "You said the door was unlocked. Do you know who's been inside?"

"As far as I know, just me and another officer," he said as he pointed to another patrolman. "That's John Cartwell. He's been here since I called you."

"And you said the door's unlocked?"

"Well, no. It doesn't have a lock."

Claira eyed the small benches that straddled the doorway, and reached for the heavy metal latch on the wooden door. No sound was made by the moving metal as she raised the latch handle. She opened the door slowly and peered inside.

The chapel floor appeared to be fashioned from the same thick stones that were used on its exterior. The center aisle led to a slightly raised altar area, only one step higher than the floor. On each side of the aisle were rows of five rough wood benches, that were finished in a heavy brown stain. The altar itself was nothing more than a wooden table, rectangular, and beside it on its right side was a single unarmed wooden chair. A single cross hung on the stone wall behind the altar and beneath a small stained glass window showing a dark blue night sky, with a lone star shining in the high. She marveled at the stained glass, at the intricate detail. For a moment she could not decipher the glow around this high star, but then could see the hidden message. Somehow, the stained glass cast the radiance in gradually fading brightness. The aura of the star was in the shape of a cross. Claira had never seen anything so captivating.

On each side of the chapel, ornate stained glass windows lit the chamber with small shafts of color. Each side of the chapel had three of these wonderful renderings. Claira was not familiar with the scenes depicted, but each was as magnificent as the next, each simple but intricate at the same time, universal but complex, flowing but distinctive. The beauty of the images was startling. Claira was not a romantic and was not easily swayed, but the visage of these glass windows made her tremble.

Claira found herself walking up the aisle, to the small table that served as an apparent altar. She noticed that the inner walls had candle holders spaced evenly between the windows, and two hanging chandeliers with candles were held high above by thick ropes running through a block and tackle pulley. The candles were all different sizes and with different melted wax runs and falls.

She said to Warren," Did you notice the attention to detail? The stained glass is so beautiful. Look at the candles. Look at the rope holding those chandeliers. Look at the broom in the corner. It looks like it is homemade." Claira removed her coat, while still studying the inner chapel, "Everything looks like a period piece. None of this came from Wal-Mart."

Warren shined his flashlight in the rear corner of the Chapel, and found the broom that Claira mentioned. "Good catch. I didn't even see that."

"Did you look for any identification marking on the glass windows? Sometimes the artists who create the images include their name or initials, just like an artist signs his painting."

Warren shook his head no. "Claira, I am not used to being in churches, and am not used to seeing windows like these. I do have an album of Gregorian chanting, and I have a couple of Enigma albums, but I've never seen anything like this up close."

Slowly Claira walked along the right side of the chapel, studying the windows, but could find no signature of identification. She went back to the altar, and noticed another, smaller door at the rear of the church. While she was examining the altar, Warren shined his flashlight up into the rafters of the chapel, amazed at the size of the beams spanning the breadth of the chapel. The wooden shafts were notched to hold single, hanging candle baskets, in addition to the two chandeliers. He was so engrossed in surveying the chapel's ceiling that he lost track of Claira and where she went in the small church.

He turned back to Claira when he heard her ask, "You didn't leave anything in here when you entered, did you."

"No ma'am. Nothing at all."

"What about Cartwell. Did he leave anything?"

"Not that I know of. I was with him when we checked out the inside. It was darker then, but I don't think he had anything to leave. Why?"

She was standing by the table, a step above the chapel floor, and looking at what was resting there. "Well, this is about the only thing that doesn't look like it belongs here." She picked up what was resting on the tabletop. "Somebody left a copy of the *Times* on the table, dated today. The Christmas edition."

Chapter Five

When Claira walked out of the chapel, she was startled by how much the crowd had grown. Clusters of people stood in a semicircle around the chapel, dressed warmly in brightly colored winter coats, some even wearing red Christmas hats with snowy white trim and a puffed white ball on the end. Others donned stocking caps bearing sports team logos or namesakes, while others chose to let their ears redden in the cold morning air. Most were looking on in silence, but a few queries could be heard in mumbled frustration, such as "When are they gonna let us go in?" and "What time does the chapel open?" and even, "I wonder how long the list is for renting it out for weddings." Claira's amazement at the crowd's acceptance of this chapel, literally from nowhere, was visible on her face. For most people, those self-absorbed in their own moments, anything that was presented to them was their new reality. The old adage of "Seeing is believing," was their operating principle, and visual proof was enough; no further explanation was necessary. It did not matter to them that it was not there yesterday; they either didn't notice it, didn't care, or were open to accept that someone, either in government or in the world of company technological magic, could make just about anything happen.

"Don't these guys have somewhere to be on Christmas morning?" she asked.

Warren Hayes was walking at her side. "Should we get statements from them? See if anyone saw anything over night."

Claira paused and scanned the crowd, not knowing what she was looking for, just instinctively monitoring the crowd for something that was suspicious, something out of place. She had no formal training in police or criminal investigations, but she remembered seeing several movies where the arsonist was present at the fire, watching his handiwork unfold. Could the person responsible for this chapel be in this crowd of people, watching to see the Park's response to this chapel, whether it be considered to be a gift or a trespass? After a moment of processing the faces and the movements around her, she turned back to Warren and spoke in a hushed voice. "Keep it low key. Ask them if anyone saw the construction process, what they thought of the work crew, stuff like that. Just go fishing. Most of these people won't know what we're looking for; most will think this structure is meant to be here. And get someone reviewing all of the park cameras. Every one of them, starting with those closest to the Great Lawn. Check all overnight dispatches. See if anyone called in anything about park traffic last night, anyone had a noise complaint, anything at all out of place, no matter how trivial."

"What do I tell them about when it will be open?" Warren asked, as he could also hear the catcalls from the crowd, wanting to see inside.

Claira considered possible responses for a moment, the said, "Tell them not on Christmas day. Tell them we're here because of reported vandalism, and that we need to get that investigated before the all clear is given."

"Got it. What about securing the chapel? Do we secure it as a crime scene?"

Claira tried to process the possible alternatives. Was it possible that someone in the Conservancy had this done as part of a Christmas program, somehow authorized this to be erected as surprise public work? Or maybe this was some type of prop for a movie, and somehow the right permits were not obtained, and no notice was given. If there were any clues either inside or out of the chapel, they needed to be preserved. Before she could respond to Warren's question her phone buzzed. After checking the ID, she answered, "Hello."

"Merry Christmas Mommy," Tony said, his excitement tingling in every syllable. "Santa found me at Dad's. I was so afraid that he wouldn't know where I was, but Santa must know everything. Dad told me to make a wish and put it in the middle of a snowball, and then throw it as far as I could, and Santa would get my wish. And it worked!"

"Wow, Tony. That's great. Can't wait to see you. I think that Santa left something for you at my house too. And I can't wait to cook you a Christmas dinner."

Tony interrupted. "Mom, Can't you have dinner with me and Dad tonight? Please. Dad said it would be okay, and I want to show you my new Lego set and this dinosaur game with monsters and my Mets hat and glove."

Claira was unprepared for this invitation, and struggled for a response appropriate for her young son. "Well, Tony, I think that you should have some Dad time, and…"

Warren was eavesdropping on the conversation, and nudged Claira in the side. "You should go to dinner with them. Boom, Boom, Pow."

Claira slapped him away, and mouthed her irritation, "Get lost."

Tony interjected, "Mom, please. Dad said it would be okay. Wait, here he is."

Before Claira could protest, Theo said, "Good morning Clair, and Merry Christmas. Hey, I don't want to put you in a spot, but if you aren't already planning something, you could come by for an early dinner. I'll keep it simple, and hopefully edible."

"Boom, Boom, Pow," Warren said loudly, through cupped hands, grinning mischievously, then pretending to shoot an arrow from a cupid's bow at Claira.

Claira turned and tried to ignore Warren, but he started to skip around her, shooting more imaginary arrows in her direction. Claira focusing on her ex-husband, said, "Theo, it's not a good idea. We've talked about this before. I don't want Tony to get any wrong expectations. You gotta back me up on this. It's not fair to him."

"It's just Christmas dinner. It's not a big deal. Come on. It'll be fun."

"Well, it won't be fun for me. Let me talk to Tony again."

"Sure," Theo said, the disappointment obvious in his voice. "Here's Tony, but if you change your mind, you're welcome to join us."

Claira shook her head, not realizing that her eyes were closed and she had her hand raised on her forehead. She did not want to disappoint her son, but she could not pretend they were a family unit again, even for a simple Christmas dinner. She had hardened herself against any doubts and regrets, and would not allow herself to erode her resolve at Tony's first awkward suggestion of a family reunion for a holiday meal.

"Well, Mom, can you?"

"Oh, honey, I want to, but I have to work at the Park. Even on Christmas. I'm at the Park now. So, you and your dad have a great day, and I will call tomorrow and we can have a great time when I pick you up. I'll have us a Christmas dinner just a day late." Small, little tears ran down her chilled cheeks, like drops from a melting icicle, and she wiped them with her gloved hand. "Honey, I love you, but I've got to get back to work. I miss you so much and I love you."

"I love you too, Mommy."

"Oh, I know honey. See you tomorrow." Claira ended the call with her son and glared at Warren, who had lost both the zest in his skipping and the grin on his face when he saw the tears on Claira's face. "Warren, sometimes you don't know when to stop."

Realizing he had crossed the line between friendly ribbing and inconsiderate cruelty, he gushed his apology. "Claira, I'm sorry. I didn't mean to push any buttons."

All Claira could do was nod and wave her hand as she started back to the station. Warren called after her, "Okay, I'll get things sorted out here. I'll catch up to you in a bit. Got this all under control."

As Claira walked through the snow, back toward the station, her thoughts ran back over each word of her conversation with Tony. He had sounded so happy, so eager to share with her the presents he found under the tree at his Dad's apartment. She debated whether she should have been more receptive to the dinner invitation. She did not doubt that it had been Tony's idea, rather than Theo's. She knew that her ex was too timid to voice such an idea, even if he secretly wanted it to happen. When she filed for divorce, Theo had barely contested the petition. He had initially tried to talk her out of it several times, in tearful pleas for another chance to regain her trust. And after her resolve became apparent, he retreated, and pretty much gave in to her wishes on everything, as long as she was fair with his visitation rights. Theo even paid all of the legal fees, court costs, mediation expenses. It was as if once he realized that she wanted the divorce, that he would make sure that he got it for her, as if it was the one last thing that he had to provide to his wife, like it was her dying wish.

The deep voice directed at her snapped her back to attention. She turned, somewhat startled, to find who called out to her.

"What's your connection to the Black Watch?" she heard again.

Claira paused to orient herself to the voice and noticed a man leaning against a park sign directly at her left side, about fifteen feet away. He was average height, and was underdressed for the weather, wearing dark jeans and a dark green suede pullover. His hands were in the sweatshirt's pockets. He wore a pair of worn brown shoes, whose leather was nicked and full of brush burns. Claira eyed him warily, and asked, "Excuse me. Did you say something to me?"

"Why the Black Watch?"

Claira shrugged her shoulders. "I don't know what you are talking about."

"Your scarf. It is the tartan of the Black Watch. The 3rd Battalion of the Royal Regiment of Scotland. The baddest of the Highlanders."

Claira reflexively raised her hand to the scarf, rolling the thick wool between her gloved fingers. "Oh, right. I had forgotten that. This was a gift from an uncle, years ago, who went on one of those Scottish golf vacations. My aunt got a St. Andrews cap, and I got this."

Now he was walking in stride with her, but had not drawn any closer. Claira noticed this, but did not feel threatened. After an uneasy moment evaluating this stranger and whether he presented any danger, she asked, "Have you been in the park long this morning? Did you notice anything unusual? Any big trucks or delivery vehicles of any kind?"

"No, nothing like that. But I'm new to the city, just learning my way around."

Claira noticed an accent in his voice, a brogue, either Irish or Scottish. "You didn't see anything out of place, like a lot of people working on something, a lot of activity, anything like that?"

"No, nothing of the kind. Rather, it's been a quiet, Christmas morning, all in peace."

Claira had hoped for a clue, but she resigned herself to the fact that this man had not witnessed anything of interest. Disappointed, she started to quicken her pace, and said, "Thanks for your time. Merry Christmas."

As she turned her thoughts to the mysterious trespassing on the Great Lawn, and a few thoughts also of her son, she was interrupted by his response.

"The chapel is some wonder, isn't it?"

Claira turned around and looked directly in the man's eyes. He had green, evergreen colored eyes. His nose rested perfectly in a rigid, framed face. He was somewhere between a beard and clean-shaven, the stubble new but highly visible. His black hair had whispers of gray, but in random places and in vague, illogical degrees.

She stared at him for a sizable moment, then asked. "Who are you?"

He smiled back at her. "If you are asking for my profession or rank, sorry to say that I have neither. If you are asking about my business here, I can say with sincerity that I have no pretenses or aspirations, and little in the way of expectations. But if you are asking for my name, then that question is easy. I am Darragh Finn. Quite happy to meet you." He bowed ever so slightly, then simply renewed his perfect smile.

"Darragh," Claira said. "Darragh. That is a very unusual name. What does it mean?"

The man looked down, as if ashamed. After he fidgeted a little, he answered, "There are two accepted meanings. The first is 'Oak'. That is the one I prefer to think Mom had in mind when the naming time came."

Claira stared at him, waiting for the second meaning. After a moment of silence, said, "Well, what is the other one?"

"Rascal."

Claira chuckled. "Oh, I see. So is Darragh your given name, or is it a nickname that you picked up because of your mischievous ways?"

"No, it is my birth name. No middle name, just Darragh Finn. That's the whole of it."

"Well, my name is Claira Vasson, and I work for the Park Conservancy. And I don't know why, but I suspect that you already knew who I was. Why do I get the feeling that this is not a chance meeting with you this morning, Darragh? Is there something that you want to tell me about the chapel? You know something," she said almost accusatory, but not in anger and not without a lean bit of curiosity. Hesitantly, she turned and looked back to where she left Warren, but could not see him in the distance.

Darragh blew into his cupped hands to warm them. His breath was steam-like in the cold morning air, and after a deep exhale, he jammed them back into his pullover's pockets. "I can't help with the questions that you have, but maybe I can help you with the ones you haven't thought of yet." Darragh looked at her as if she was a family member, the way that a brother or sister can talk to their siblings with their eyes, in ways that strangers or even acquaintances could not read. After a moment of seeing her, he continued, "With the important ones."

For the first time since this encounter began, Claira felt conflicted. While this man seemed almost familiar, and did not seem threatening, she could not ignore a twinge of uneasiness, and wondered if she was being played, being set up for some nefarious event about to happen. She had let this stranger get too close to her, and while she could defend herself if needed, those efforts were not guaranteed to prevent her from being harmed if he acted with all of the strength he obviously possessed. She eyed Darragh from head to toe, and while he did not seem vicious, she had seen or experienced all manners of violent wrath from park vagabonds and street criminals, usually desperate and unpredictable, from drug abuse or mental illness, or from the tired, vengeful apathy of hard, difficult living. She carefully pulled her phone from her pocket, and held it in front of her, where Darragh could see. "In about two seconds I am going to have a couple of officers here and then we'll start these questions in earnest. If you have something to say, do it now."

Darragh's voice was reassuring, and his demeanor showed no nervousness or fear. He looked into Claira's eyes, and walked a few steps closer to her. "I can't explain how it got there, if that's what you mean. That, my dear, is beyond me. I didn't put it there. But how it got there is not what's important."

"Not important? Someone built that chapel overnight, or moved it there, in the middle of Central Park, so it just appears out of nowhere and you can't explain how that happened. Then what should I be asking, if not how this happened?"

"The best question to ask is why. The how is not important now, is it?" Darragh nodded and turned to point to the crowd growing in the distance behind him, around the edge of the Great Lawn, where the stone path began and where the chapel rested in the snow. With that answer, he calmly walked away, leaving Claira alone on the snow dusted path.

***

Across town, Mike Sandoval paced the narrow confines of his office located in the *Times* Building. Shortly after his call with Jason and JoAnn, he discovered that it was only the print copies of the paper that had the altered page one. His tablet app allowed him to pull up a digital newspaper, and it had no poem on page one, just headlines and text of reports, just as it normally would. The on-line pages totally conformed to the planned lay-out. In fact, he could not find the poem anywhere in the digital paper. While this was to some degree great news, it made the hard copies of the paper even harder to explain. He had a brief call with Jason first, then JoAnn, advising them of this discovery, while in the cab ride from his apartment to the *Times* Building.

The *Times* newspapers for the greater New York area were printed in a 515,000 square foot plant located in Queens, just off the Van Wyck Expressway, less than a mile from LaGuardia Airport. All of the newspaper articles and columns are prepared at the *Times'* Manhattan headquarters, where Mike was officed, along with the editors and most of the local journalists. After the daily page one meeting, the lay-out of the paper was determined. A digital version of the whole edition of the paper was prepared and approved before transmission to the Queens printing press.

The *Times* used the cold-type printing process. Digital files of each page of the paper were prepared in Manhattan, and electronically transmitted to the Queens Printing Plant ten miles to the east. The cold type printing cycle then took those computerized files of each page and had laser etchings of every page made on oxidized aluminum plates, with a separate plate needed for each of the four colors used in the printing presses. A fifty-page newspaper may need upwards of 2500 etched aluminum plates, all of them prepared in the Queens facility. Once complete, the etched plates are locked into place in the printer, and the ink is fused on to a running stream of paper, only in those marks created by the laser etching.

The creation of a newspaper was mayhem in motion, considering the deadlines involved in getting the news in format to print, the editorial process, and the sheer volume of efforts needed to bring all of the creative processes in unison. The Queens printing plant alone had approximately 340 employees working in the massive building, which buzzed with the noise of the multi-story printing machine and over twelve miles of humming conveyor belts. When running at peak, the printer could produce more than 75,000 copies of the paper per hour, all cut, folded and bundled for shipping.

On Mike's desk was a copy of the digital lay-out of the paper he printed on his desktop printer, as approved and sent to Queens. It was in perfect order. Mike could not find any evidence of any other version of the lay-out sent out from the desk editor to the print plant. After a hurried stop in his pacing, he called for the desk editor to come into his office.

Joe Brensden was the desk editor, also called the masthead editor, in charge of the content of the printed paper. Mike was his direct superior. Joe was aghast when he saw the morning paper, and had been on the phone with Mike, with multiple departments of the Queens printing plant, and with both in-house computer engineers and contract cyber security personnel. Joe entered Mike's office already talking, "This hacker will rue the day he took on the *New York Times.* Damn religious zealots. I swear....."

Mike interrupted him to gain control of the conversation. He didn't have time to listen to Joe vent. "Take a breath, Joe. One step at a time. First, are you sure that no one here sent out another digital edition of the paper? Nothing after your team sent out the approved lay-out?"

"We can't find anything like that at all. Everyone on my team has been with me for years. I know each of them. We will check and double check, but we can't find shit on my side of the wire."

"Then that leaves us two possibilities. One, someone at the Queens plant messed with the plates, or somehow switched out the digital pages before etching. Or two, someone was able to send over another digital lay-out from an un-authorized source."

"A hacker."

Mike finally sat behind his desk. He reached for a coffee mug on the corner of his desk and took a sip, then winced at the cold coffee he forced himself to swallow rather than backwash into the cup. After recovering from that unpleasantness, he said, "Have your IT people go over everything in the screen lab. We need to find the files that the illicit page one etchings were drawn from, and backtrack until we find who sent them. I need to get this pinned down ASAP, because I don't see how we can trust our system to print another paper tomorrow. I have a mind to get to Queens right now myself, and I don't want to do that. You get this process going now and keep me posted on what you find."

"I'm on it," Joe said, still angry. He seemed to view the takeover over of page one as a violation, regardless of the content. He was furious each rare time a typographical error was found in a copy of his paper. This event had him in another level of upset.

"And, Joe, we cannot have this happen again. I will be talking to Mr. Dumbarton in a few minutes, and he will want assurances that we are a go for a clean run in the morning. Whatever it takes. Even if you have to spend the night in Queens and proofread every damn copy of the paper as it comes off of the press."

Joe nodded his response. As he walked out of the office, he was muttering, "Damn religious zealots, with This World this and This World that. Shit. This is no way to run a newspaper."

Mike resumed his pacing in his small office as he tried to think chronologically about the print cycle, and where a hijack of the system could be undertaken. It was going to be a long and busy Christmas day.

Chapter Six
December 26

The reports of the signs came in from each of the five boroughs. Some were calls from early morning commuters, other reports were gleaned from social media, some even by text messages. The alerts were routed to the *Times'* City Desk, where its duty editor reviewed the reports and decided whether to assign a reporter to the story. Not doing so did not mean that the event would be ignored. While the *Times* employed a bevy of its own full time staff reporters, it also accepted submissions from numerous free-lancers, and pulled reports from the associated press wire, so when the unusual became manifest, a network comprised of staff writers and a web-work of journalistic Ronin sprang into action, whether directly or indirectly. They would race to cover breaking news, sometimes along with local and national television journalists, and others working for competing news organizations.

Mike Sandoval arrived at the *Times* offices early, still struggling to make sense of yesterday's mystery. The cyber-autopsy they had performed in the plate lab in Queens revealed nothing. Everything also checked out in the digital records of the paper lay-out. No evidence of a hack was found, no signs of a compromised system in the assembly and loading of the etched plates. They had carefully inspected each and every one of the aluminum engravings used for the print run, and all matched the digital archive sent by the editor to the print station. The editorial committee recommended that the morning paper be printed, and Jason agreed. Despite all of the checking and double-checking, Mike had stayed at the Queens facility until the first of the distribution trucks was loaded, after he had personally spot-checked papers as they ran through the press.

Mike was convinced that his team of sleuths was at their limit of investigative ability, and the next step was to refer the investigation to the FBI, and its cyber-crimes division. He had already researched its complaint protocol, with its IC3 unit, or the Internet Crime Complaint Center, and started the process of preparing a formal referral.

But now he was focused on another tangent, one that his old reporter instinct told him was related to the unexplained events of

Christmas day. He analyzed the common threads in the reports coming in, and phoned several of his best staff reporters and photographers with instructions on what to investigate, what to photograph, and where to go. The City Desk had not yet reacted to the calls questioning the signs by tasking any pool reporters. But Mike made an immediate connection between yesterday's event and these inexplicable reports of this morning. He pulled everything he could find that mentioned unexplained signs in the New York City area, and his desk was now a horizontal bulletin board of clutter. Hurriedly, he stuffed photos and printed emails, along with some of his own handwritten notes, into a file folder, then checked his email's inbox for any updates. There were dozens. He went through the ones which concerned this morning's developing story, then printed additional material that caught his interest.

He answered his cell phone on the first ring, putting it on speaker so he could continue to review and print emails. Mike was waiting to hear from his own photographers whom he had sent to photo-document the signs. Two of them were already at their locations and another was reporting back after completing his assignment. He quickly inquired about the status of the others, gave additional instructions for follow-up, then grabbed the folder and headed upstairs.

Apparently, each borough had one of the revelations, appearing overnight, with no rational explanation. Each was the same five stanza poem, inexplicably written in a prominent, public space, seemingly appearing out of nowhere.

Mike exited the elevator, and hurried down the hall, checking his phone for recent texts. He knocked on Jason's office door and went in before any answer came in response. Jason's executive assistant, sitting outside his office suite, did not even have time to protest.

"Our mystery poet has struck again," Mike said as he entered the plush office set high in the *NY Times* Building at 620 8th Avenue. His voice was booming, his excitement uncontained.

Jason was on a call, gently rocking in his high-backed leather chair, and held his hand up to silence Mike as he entered. He motioned for him to sit, and then wrapped up the call with, "we're moving as fast as we can," and "I'll have to get back to you on that."

The call completed, Jason leaned forward over his desk. "Did our paper get compromised again?" Jason demanded, visibly agitated, as he hung up the phone.

Mike shook his head, almost laughing. "No, nothing happened to us. But I have confirmation that a huge sign or billboard has been found in each of the 5 boroughs, each with the same poem."

Jason leaned back in this desk chair, relieved. "Okay, not us. Then who? Tell me what you know."

"Well, it's pretty unbelievable. Here in Manhattan, there is an entire building wallscape off of Hudson Square. In the Bronx, a wallscape just off of Jerome Avenue. Another wallscape in Queens, on Citi Field, no less. Then there's a billboard in Coney Island, and last a billboard leading to the Narrows Bridge in Staten Island. I have a couple of our photographers out to confirm all of them and get anything else they can find."

"Same poem as yesterday?'

Mike shook his head, and fumbled through the file of papers he carried in. "No, a new one. Here's a screenshot that I got a few minutes ago. It's the wallscape on Hudson Square." He retrieved the 8 by 10 printed photo and slid it across the desk to Jason.

Jason looked over the poem, reading it twice:

MAGNITUDE

How numerous the worlds unknown
Ours an island
A token stone
This universe of magnitude
Seas of stars multitude

How boundless the souls that came before
Their numbers lost
Now legend, lore
A history of magnitude
So vast the lives and deaths accrued

How grievous the wars that raged
The calls to arms
The virtuous caged
The evil malignant magnitude
Of atrocities and servitude

How immense the miracles performed
Answered prayers
Lives transformed

The Sacrifice of such magnitude
To end our earthly solitude

How infinite God's Divinity
Heart of Mercy
Blessed Trinity
Compassion of such magnitude
Deserves devoted gratitude
df 12.26

Jason dropped the photo on his desk and thought for a moment. He had a unique background for a newspaper man. He held a degree in journalism from the University of Virginia, and also a chemical engineering degree from Virginia Tech. He also had an MBA, earned at American University in Washington DC. It was quite the eclectic collection of studies, impressive too, but Jason ended up pursuing those varied degrees because, as he finished one, he realized that a career in that field was of no interest to him. Because his family had generational wealth, he felt no pressure to work. Rather, he studied what interested him at the time. But his unusual background regularly proved useful. It, along with his family's influence, helped him get a job in government, with the Department of Energy, a mid-level management position in which he excelled. After a few years, he moved on to a high profile lobbying position with a national chemical company association. He had a natural talent for public speaking, but was even better at the art of persuasion.

Some of his friends considered him a well-educated and high degreed salesman, but Jason knew better. He was a student of human tendencies, aversions and motivation. He had become extremely proficient at predicting actions and responses, and determining the boundaries of political correctness and compensable grievances. While many people or groups had seemingly complex interests and motivations that guided their decision trees, Jason could navigate those layers of complexity, and manipulate that one, inner, primal hunger, which most people mistakenly assumed was either money or power. Younger people may even assume that the base desire was sex. All a common and useful misunderstanding. The truest of the base instincts was simply survival. And Jason had the ability to trigger that simplest of the uncontrollable animal instincts. Sometimes subtlety, but sometimes with no pretense whatsoever. And once that particular set of fears was exposed, even at surface level, he knew how to use it, to set a trap and to secure whatever goal had been identified. He did not view it always as a zero sum game. Sometimes both parties were happily satisfied with the bargain. But other times, well, it was more like blackmail than negotiation.

Today, Jason was trying to decipher the puzzle before him. The engineer in him looked for evidence and proof, a formula that could be proven, results that could be controlled and replicated, while the journalist in him just wanted to be first with an exclusive story. The MBA part of him was only concerned about owning this narrative, and leveraging it into money.

He looked over the poem again, then asked, "Mike, do you realize the shit storm this is going to cause? There's going to be protests. The atheists are going to raise hell."

"They don't believe in hell."

Jason managed a chuckle. "Yea, maybe not, but trust me, they'll be screaming."

"To what? To the highest heavens?" Mike finished Jason's sentence. "They don't believe in that either."

"I'm happy to see you find this so amusing." Not many people at the *Times* would speak to Jason as abruptly and with such confidence. Mike was one of the few who would.

"Sorry, Boss," Mike said as he rubbed his eyes and yawned. "Had a long and frustrating day yesterday. Both at work and at home. Not much sleep last night either. Even though I saw the papers print clean last night, I was up at the crack of dawn this morning to see it again. Being a smart-ass is my way of coping, I guess."

Jason stared at Mike for a moment and realized why Mike looked as if he had ridden a rollercoaster to work. "Shit, Mike, I just remembered. It's been about a year since Maria passed. Sorry I was so raw yesterday. What has it been, a year?"

"Be a year on the 28th." Mike sighed. "She would have been 13 this year." Mike turned away from Jason's desk and looked at the office's side wall, directly, as if there were a window amid the dark paneling and bookshelves. "Harder on her mom than me. But thanks for remembering."

For a moment, Mike was back in the hospital room, holding his daughter's hand while her exhausted body could do little more than surrender to the disease. Maria had cystic fibrosis, a horrible, debilitating disease that ruined young lives and tormented parents with slow motion suffering. She wanted to see the New Year, her first as a teenager, and somehow Mike knew that she had resigned herself that it would also be her last. But she fell a few days short. Mike bowed his head, and said, "It's rough on me, but more for Jess. You know, this is the year of firsts. First Thanksgiving. First winter without Maria. First Christmas without her. Her Mom is not dealing with all of these days that well."

Jason nodded. "Mike, you've done enough. Take a day. We made a clean print today. The vandal poet hit a few buildings but not the *Times* today. So I'll make a few calls. I'll see you tomorrow." Jason waited for Mike to respond, but when he did nothing but stare ahead, Jason repeated his directive. "That's enough for you today. Go home. Take the rest of the day."

Mike snapped back to attention. He handed Jason the folder he brought into the office with him. "Look through that file when you have a minute. That's my file on the events this morning. This stuff is like urban crop circles. Only we don't have symbols stamped in a grass field, but poetry written on the sides of buildings. The weirdness is not just what happened to our page one yesterday. It's this too."

Mike bent over and nudged the folder closer to Jason. "And that's not all. I'm getting reports of a new building out in Central Park, a little church building that everyone from park police to the professional hobos that live in the Park swear was not there two days ago."

Mike glanced at his phone vibrating in his pocket. He made a quick mental note of the call, then continued by pointing to the file, and said, "Today we have a poem covering a 5 story building's side out in Hudson Square. You know that real estate. How you gonna put ladders or scaffolds up without being seen?" Mike paced in front of Jason's desk, while he continued, "We're not talking about street artists or graffiti bums pulling this off. Not there, and not overnight." Mike nodded his head that the file folder now laying on Jason's glass top desk. "There's a picture in there of a wall at City Field from a security camera. Yesterday it was just a wall. This morning it is a poem a few stories high. The security feed doesn't illuminate enough of the wall at night, but you can see the two day shots. Look at it, before and after." Mike sat across from Jason and leaned back in the leather chair. He nodded to the contents of the file folder, and remarked, "This is some Hollywood level special effects, and it's definitely not on the cheap."

Jason studied Mike and his body language, looking for any sign that this was some candid camera moment or other similar prank. Finally, he looked at Mike intently and asked, "Are you telling me that this is some kind of David Copperfield stunt and no one at City Hall is in on the gag?"

Mike leaned back in the chair a little further. "This stuff makes Copperfield look like amateur hour."

***

A steady stream of customers flowed through the check-out line at Devils' Donuts, some grabbing a pastry or two for a morning meal, others getting a dozen or more to share with co-workers or friends. A few who had time to sample their purchase even made their way to Isla's coffee counter to read the paper and enjoy their sugary breakfast.

Two men in suits and colorful Jerry Garcia neck-ties were finishing their coffee while arguing about yesterday's edition of the *Times*.

"Come on, Billy. Don't tell me you didn't read the paper yesterday. You didn't see the front page?"

Billy was in no hurry to respond, trying to get the last few bites of a blueberry jelly-filled into his mouth without a drip on his shirt or suit. After a careful moment of finishing off the donut and wiping his mouth and fingers with a napkin, he answered, "Look, I didn't see anything but depressing headlines about depressing shit happening damn near everywhere."

Isla listened to the debate rage on, and was tempted to interject. Another customer sat at the counter and drew her away from their discussion.

"Good morning," she said. "What can I get for you?"

"Just a coffee, black."

"You got it."

As she poured a steaming cup of coffee and pulled a saucer for the cup, she could hear the debate between the one named Billy and his friend winding down.

"Look, I quit getting the hard copy about a year ago. I get the digital edition. And I didn't see any missing page one."

"That's not what I'm saying. There was a page one, it just didn't have anything hardly on it, just this cool poetry about the end of the world."

On hearing that last comment, Isla couldn't help but correct that misunderstanding. "Sorry to eavesdrop, you guys, but I saw the hard copy and page one was reserved for a very nice poem and no, it was not about the end of the world." She watched as Billy looked at her bewildered. "It was a Christmas poem. You know, yesterday was Christmas."

"Then you saw it too?"

Isla nodded, "I probably still have a copy around the counter somewhere." Turning to his friend, she continued, "Don't think that I am some kind of literary critic or anything, but I sure didn't think that it was an end of days prophecy, not at all." She left the two to finish their coffee and returned to the gentleman she had served a few minutes before.

"How you doing with yours?"

The customer looked up, and eyed the name tag pinned on Isla's shirt. "Is it Is La?"

Isla reflexively touched the pin and smiled. "No, the "s" is silent. It's pronounced I'La."

"What a lovely name. That's what I thought. A right proper Scottish name." He held up his cup and answered, "Best black coffee that I've had in a while. Not too bitter, but not weak like a cup of black tea." He nodded at her and took another sip. Then he asked, "Are you Scottish?"

"Heaven's no, my family is Italian, both sides. My Mom just liked the name, I guess. Not even sure where she heard it."

"Well, it's a beautiful name, and matches its owner. You know, it means island."

Isla smiled and answered, "I never knew what it meant. Thank you."

The customer grinned and took another sip of his coffee.

"Let me know if you want another."

Before she turned away, the customer asked, "Did you really think that poem in yesterday's paper was a nice Christmas poem? Sorry, but I couldn't help but hear you talking to those gentlemen over there." He lifted his cup and motioned to the men as they walked away from the counter.

Isla glanced back at the two men in the suits and colorful ties, as they exited. "Well, the tall one was the only one of the two who even saw the poem. That dumbass thought it was some occult end of the world thing, and it was nothing of the sort. I take it that you saw the poem too."

"Oh, I know it well."

"Well, what do you think?"

"I definitely agree that it was not meant to be ominous. And occult? No, definitely not occult. I don't know how anyone could get that impression."

"Right. I don't know what that guy was thinking." Isla agreed. "It was a beautiful gesture for the *Times* to print the poem on page one like that. Very respectful of the holiday."

The customer shook his head. "Oh, I wouldn't say that at all. The *Times* had no intention of running that poem, much less on the first page."

Isla looked at him doubtfully. "Seriously? You know, I at first thought it was a mistake too, but I know someone who works there and has been an employee for a long time, and he told me himself that every bundle he delivered was the same. Not a mistake."

The man sitting across from her just sipped his coffee and again shook his head from side to side.

Isla waited for a further response, and when only silence was forthcoming, she said, "Afraid you're wrong about that." She stared at him for a moment, but he kept his head down, as if daydreaming. "Are you sure you saw the same poem I saw in the paper? On the very front page. Everything else blank as those green eyes of yours."

With that comment, he looked up as if caught in some mischief or deception. Isla studied him, as if daring him to hide his intent. He looked around, and while the bakery had several customers about the store, he was alone at the coffee counter. He turned back to Isla, who was still staring at him, but with the faintest of smiles now lining her face. He said nothing. Then he winked at her.

"I thought so," Isla offered. "You didn't even read it. You were just leading me on."

Before she could retreat, he sat down his cup, and said, "On this world we wander."

Isla's mouth dropped and her hand went too late to cover it. "Oh, I'm sorry. I didn't mean to…I'm sorry. I thought that you were talking just to talk. That you were flirting." Her voice cracked, as she was embarrassed by her mistaken impression. She took a step closely to the counter across from the customer, and leaned inward slightly. "So you did read it."

"Well no," he confessed. "Let me introduce myself. My name is Darragh Finn." He offered his hand, and as she slowly reached it for a shake, he continued, "That was one of mine. I wrote it."

Chapter Seven

In a busy hospital, the arrival of a holiday is lost in the repeating clockwork of duty-shifts, the administration of medicines and treatment, and the evolving priorities of triage. The demands for critical treatment, for the precious time of doctors and nurses, find the patients in an unknowing, but rigorous, silent competition. The only thing as equally unremarkable is the departure of that same holiday. And while the scheduling of some tests and procedures is made to wait, the silent stain of illness and suffering, and the associated worry, is constant. What presents as the passage of time is rendered a disorienting slurry of movements, some in real time, but others in slow motion, some others almost still frame. The patients, the poor ones cast in that circumstance, are lost in the complex hurricane of the system, a slow moving storm of unknowing, of fear, of unsure expectations and of the wary disbelief of the science and the mysterious technology of medicine.

The morning after Christmas was no different at New York Presbyterian Hospital, nor in Room 822. There was little joy in the voices in the dim room, little less than even respect for the early new day. The talk, most distilled to accusation and argument, had been ongoing since breakfast.

"Cap, I want to call Father Jacob, from my church parish. To come see Momma," Cissy said.

Cap was seated in the chair closest to the hospital window. The static window had huge drops of water condensing on the cold glass, as if the building was weeping, wetting its tinted window eyes. He was wearing the same gray and green weave sweater he had on the day he arrived from Maine. His hair was untidy, just the way it was when he woke a few hours ago. He had his right hand close to his mouth, as if he were smoking, but there was no cigarette or cigar to be found. He stared back at his sister, and said nothing. The days he had spent at the hospital, either in waiting rooms or in room 822, blended together, and he was no longer sure how long ago his mother was admitted, or when he left his Deer Island home. He was lost in a blurred reality where time was not measured in days, but in eight and twelve hour shifts. He said nothing in response to his sister's question.

"Cap, please. Will you let me do that for Mom?" Cissy asked again, in yet another phrasing of the same request.

Cap stood, and turned his back to his sister, directing his gaze out of the wet window. He stared out at the buildings and the crowded skyline, so opposite from the blue and the sea mist and horizon clouds that lived east of Deer Island above the Atlantic. He slowly drifted back to his boat and his dock and also to the maples, back to a stand of trees that waited for his visits, like lonesome guardians lost on the edge of the forest. But as much as he wanted to visit that peace again, the restful silence of the distant bird songs and the soft touch of the wind, this bleak city held his attention, and would continue its grip, as long as his mother was captive in its metal and glass towers.

Without turning around, he shifted his focus back to his sister who was behind him pleading. "Why, Cissy? You know Mom isn't Catholic. Why do you want to call a priest and impose your religion on her?"

Cissy could hardly speak through her tears. "Well, she used to be. You know that. She was raised Catholic, and I think never really stopped, even after she married Dad. She was baptized a Catholic, and confirmed too."

Cap just shook his head. "She hasn't been to a Mass in decades. Except for a few funeral masses. And those don't count. You know Dad went to services at the Baptist Church on the Island, and Mom always went with him. For as long as I can remember. And after he passed, she went to the same church with me."

"Forrest Kencaid, you rarely go to church, and when you do it is for dinner club or the yearly blessing of the fleet. So who is it now imposing his religion on Mom?"

Hearing his given name invoked by his sister turned Cap away from the window. He looked at her, as she took a few steps closer to him. She whispered, "Because Cap, it's her end time. Father Jacob would say the last rites. He would anoint her."

"This is more for you than her."

Cissy could only blink her tearing eyes. Her upper lip trembled. "That may be true. But I would say it's for both of us."

Cap motioned to the hospital bed. "Not so loud, you'll wake her. She had a decent night for a change, but she could use the rest. So let her sleep."

Cissy cupped her hands to her mouth, and her eyes struggled to hold her tears. "Please."

The room was full of background hospital sounds, the sounds that hid in the corners of the room, but there, beating, moaning, sighing, pleading, trying to talk. The IV pump hummed, its motor turning on and off in regular intervals to control the drip of the medicine. The large lights above the bed made an electric hiss sound, competing with the periodic beeps of the heart monitoring equipment fastened to the wall above the bed. The television was on, but the volume low, too low to discern any words but not so low that a steady stream of murmurs could escape from the small speaker built into the arm rails of the hospital bed. And though the room door was closed, the sound of the activity outside was penetrating. The sounds were loud when you listened for them, but otherwise just there in a distant, haunting way. The kind of way that made you worry about what was watching, or worse, what was waiting in the cascade of the fleeing moments.

Cap reached out and laid his hand on his sister's shoulder. He didn't want to upset her, and he was not being contrary out of cruelty or regular Maine-born stubbornness. He simply believed what he believed, and it was that there was no surrender to death. Yes, it would come, as sure as the north wind brings winter, as sure as water will find its way. But you did not go out half the way and meet it, not with a smile or combed hair, as if waiting at a train station, and surely not with open arms and a travel badge, ready for a spot on the ferry. He pulled his sister to him, and she rested her head against his shoulder.

"I'm not ready for this," she said. "Please Cap. Let me ask Father Jacob to visit her."

"Was yesterday Christmas, or the day before?" Cap asked, the confusion apparent on his lined face.

Cissy lifted her head slowly and studied him, unsure of the reason for that question. She considered some ill motive, some strange type of cruelty, but dismissed the idea quickly. While her brother was rough as sandpaper and hard as rubbing alcohol, he had never been mean or brutal to anyone or anything. She reached out her hand, and found his, and held it. "Cap, I brought you Christmas dinner last night. Remember. Turkey and sweet potato casserole, and cranberry salad. Brought you the *Times* and a boating magazine, and your God-son even had a present for you." She glanced over at the window ledge near where Cap was standing. "Which I see you haven't opened yet."

"That was last night?"

"Yes, Don't you remember, we had a room full."

Cap responded. "Yea, that's right. The whole family was here. Mom slept through most of it."

Cissy managed a laugh. "Yea, and Conrad managed to read Mom that poem that was in the paper yesterday. He did good for the second grade, don't you think?"

Cap nodded in agreement. "There were a couple of words in there that I would have trouble with." He looked over to the hospital bed where their mother was sleeping. Her breaths were shallow but regular, and she didn't fidget or turn as she had done through most of last night.

"Ask him to come," Cap finally said. "But know this, Cis, it doesn't mean I'm giving up on her. And neither are you. No more talk about hospice or any such thing. And you need to do something for me."

Cissy could not answer, except for the sound of her trying to slow the tears. But she nodded her head in agreement. She would do whatever Cap asked, as no condition he could put on the bestowing of last rites could be too onerous or too difficult. She hugged Cap. And he returned the hug miserly. But for Cissy, at that moment, it was as if all the warmth of the world had embraced her. Her bear of a brother, with a fisherman's winter heart and cold tree sap flowing through his veins, had given her a glimmer of a rainbow, somewhere beyond the crying clouds.

***

Isla could not stop thinking about leaving her coffee counter. Her regular part time help was not available on short notice, but she cajoled a friend from the bakery to watch the counter for her. Now she regretted every minute of that rash impulse, and silently argued with herself that she should return.

"We are almost there," Darragh said reassuringly, as if reading her worried mind.

Isla looked up at him. He was not quite a foot taller that she was, but he carried himself straight and broad shouldered, like someone who enjoyed the challenge of physical work. They had been walking for nearly an hour and were still about ten minutes away from the park.

"I don't know what I was thinking," Isla said. "Taking out with a complete stranger across town, on a work day. Leaving my livelihood like I have no cares in the world."

Darragh kept his hands stuffed in his fleece pull-over. His cheeks were a faint red from the chill. He talked while looking over the sights along 7th Avenue, obviously dividing his attention. He ignored Isla's worries about the coffee counter and said, "Lass, we should have taken a cup of your coffee to go. Fend away this chill." He then looked at her with a banter smile, inviting a response in jest.

"Don't think that a hidden compliment about my coffee will set me at ease, Mr. Finn."

Darragh laughed, then bumped her slightly with his shoulder. She glanced over at him surprised both at his gesture and his demeanor, which reminded her of a carefree high school student. She quickened her pace to keep up.

The sidewalk was not at all crowded, and they were making good time walking along 7th Avenue. "Much too pretty a morning to waste what could be a good walk with a ride on those underground trains. But I'll agree with this, though. These large buildings and all this concrete makes the day much colder in winter."

Isla eyed Darragh again, amazed. He seemed to be completely lost, in every decipherable way, in country, in season, even in time. Everything about him seemed out of place. But at the same time, he seemed to be completely at ease. After he convinced her to accompany him on this escapade to Central Park, he insisted on walking. And when she asked if he knew the directions to get there, all he answered was, "North."

Darragh pointed to a colorful sign just ahead to his right and asked, "What is a Hale and Hearty?"

Isla giggled to herself. "That's a yogurt store. You know, frozen yogurt."

Darragh shook his head slightly, bewildered.

"Seriously?" Isla paused and pointed to the counter through the window. The store had large displays colored in yogurt flavors, from vanilla to dark chocolate at the spectrum ends, with colors such as peach and lime in between those two extremes. "Come on. It's like ice cream, only not as good tasting."

"Then why not refrain and find a nice creamy chocolate or strawberry ice cream?"

"Because yogurt is healthy. It's a better choice. You know, for a healthy lifestyle."

"Ice cream is a dessert, is it not? Full of sugar and fruit and heavy, thick cream. It's a treat."

"Well, yes."

"And yogurt is turned cream?"

"What?"

"You know, turned. Curdled. Soured. I understand that you can mix a strawberry or two into the mess, even blueberries. And mind you, it is not a waste. I use it to right the working of the gut when the stomach slips a bit. To kill the green in the gut. Restore the, what is it they are called.... Oh, yes, the active cultures. It's truly more of a medicine than a treat. Why would a shop sell that and nothing else?"

"Because people want a healthy alternative."

"An alternative to what?"

Isla eyed him, frustrated and short-tempered. "I just told you, yogurt is better for you than ice cream."

"So it's a pharmacy." Darragh looked directly at Isla and asked, "Do folk here go to a pub to drink cough syrup?"

"That doesn't make any sense"

"Agreed." Darragh looked exhausted from the discussion. He clapped his hands softly and said, "Off we go."

Isla did not further respond, but eyed him closely, looking for signs of either sincerity or charade. She could not tell whether Darragh was truly that naive. But he was impossible for her to read. He just continued to look at everything they walked past, as if new wonders were presented with each street corner that was passed.

"Up there," Darragh said. He pointed with his right hand, and continued. "The garden is just there. Hurry now."

They walked past the intersection of 7th Avenue and West 58th Street, and continued to the southern edge of Central Park. As they entered the park, Isla asked. "Okay, now that we are here, what are we looking for?"

Darragh turned for a second but did not stop his gait along the sidewalk. "Further on," he answered. "Up ahead by the loch."

"What?" Isla asked. "What did you say?"

"The wee loch up ahead. The water."

"You mean the pond? Turtle Pond?"

Darragh nodded. "Yes, that's it. The pond. Just ahead a bit, now, let's go."

When they finally crested a slight incline of a hill, Isla could see a crowd around a small stone building, forming a rough semi-circle around the structure, about three or four people deep. As they approached the crowd, Isla noticed that three people were entering the chapel, a pretty woman with a police officer and a much older and thinner gentleman.

"When was this added to the Park grounds?" Isla asked, studying the details and lines of the stone chapel.

"Just yesterday."

"It's wonderful. Just beautiful," Isla said, then hesitated and asked, "Wait, did you say yesterday? You mean it opened on Christmas Day?"

"A chapel should always be open. Why would it ever be closed?"

"Well, maybe for security, for safety, to keep out vandals. You know…" Isla's answer trailed off as she was walking along the crowd line, and saw the stained glass windows on the east side of the church. "Wow, that's just gorgeous."

"Oh that it is. You should see the inside of this right wonderful chapel. It's where I wrote that little poem that you liked, the one in the paper yesterday."

Isla looked at him doubtfully. "You wrote it in the church?"

Darragh shrugged his shoulders. "Well, I wrote most of it in my head, over a day or two. But it was in the chapel where I put the words down on the paper, and where I did the final touches."

Isla walked up a few steps, looking for a break in the crowd to get a better look at the chapel's windows. She turned back to Darragh and asked, "Okay, it's a beautiful little building. But why did you need to show it to me?"

"Not just it. Also the lady and gentlemen who we saw enter the chapel. They will either be aligned or will be opposed. The woman I have met, and I have a good feeling about her. She seemed sincere. Wounded, but sincere. You have to aid me in helping them over the next few days."

"Help you do what?" Isla asked, unsure of what Darragh was referencing.

"The stone has been cast. There are going to be ripples now."

"What are you talking about?"

Darragh just smiled at her and nodded over to the chapel. "You'll see. If you look rightly." With that said, he walked away from the chapel, across the white colored field of the Great Lawn, and back to the northern edge of Turtle Pond, and tossed a pebble into its still reflective surface, and shattered the soft, vague image of the stone chapel that laid on the surface of the little lake.

***

"I can't believe that I'm sitting here with you. I don't know what's gotten in to me." Isla looked about the room with a look of revulsion on her face. "I'm leaving," she said as she started to rise from the table.

Darragh raised a hand and gently held her arm. "Please, stay with me a bit. Let me finish this wonderful drink." He took a sip from his tall cup, and then asked Isla, "Could you reach behind you there on that table and hand me that shaker of cinnamon?"

Isla looked at him incredulously. "Do you know what you're doing to me? I own a coffee shop. It's not much, but it's my livelihood. It's what I do. And now I'm sitting in a Starbuck's on 7th Avenue with you, a really strange stranger, watching you drink overpriced coffee while my shop across town is unattended." With that, she grabbed the cinnamon holder from the next table and slapped it down in front of Darragh.

"It's cappuccino. You were the one who told me about it."

"Only because you insisted on coming in here, and only because you either couldn't read the menu or pronounce the word."

"Would you like a sip?"

Isla stared at him. "Are you that dense? Haven't you heard anything that I just said?"

"Aye, I heard what you said, but I wasn't listening."

"What? What does that even mean?"

Darragh sprinkled cinnamon in his drink, then stirred the mixture, dutifully watching the whirlpool that he created in the cup, the dark red cinnamon mixing and disappearing in the white foam head on the coffee. He motioned for Isla to watch the colorful torrent in the cup, smiling. He used his spoon to sample a sip, then smacked his lips and added another sprinkle of the cinnamon. Finally satisfied, he looked up at Isla who studied him, aghast.

"I said, what does that mean?"

"Take no offense, Duchess. I surely meant none, nor abide any. If I have offended you, then I am truly sorry. I simply meant that I was not going to argue with you, or try to convince you to not follow your conscience. I am not going to hold you by force, so if you are determined to leave, then you will find no obstruction with me. So when you asked yourself, what you were doing with me, or why are you here, I accept that you are not talking to me, but to yourself. In such case, I ceased listening, so as not to eavesdrop on another's private conversation."

Isla leaned closer to Darragh. "That is the most asinine thing that I have ever heard."

"I take that tis not a compliment?"

"A compliment? How is calling you asinine a compliment?"

Darragh took another sip of his drink and wiped his lip with a napkin. "I am not sure what asinine means. Does it refer to a part of my anatomy?"

Isla threw her hands into the air. "Seriously? You profess to be this Stone Chapel Poet, yet you have such a limited vocabulary that you can't order a cappuccino, and think that asinine is what you're sitting on. You cannot be that naive."

"And yet you are sitting here with me."

"Not for much longer."

With that Darragh seemed to concede her point. He ran his hand through his thick hair, then asked her, "What do you believe in?"

Isla paused, unprepared for such a question. Her patience with Darragh was exhausted, but a twinge, an intuition, somewhere deep in her mind made her hesitate, prevented her from running away, back to her coffee counter and her solitary life, a life that some days never had her leaving the building that housed her apartment of the fifth floor and the coffee shop on street level. She thought about the question, thought about the rut her life had become, the monotony that her days had evolved into. "What do I believe in?"

"Yes, Isla, what do you believe in?"

She sighed. "I believe in morning and night, in starting one day hungry and finishing it tired."

"So you believe in life."

"If that is what you call it." Isla's mind tacked to the disappointments and loneliness that had become staples for her, events that while bitterly unpleasant had become her daily challenge, her task to perform, without which she would be without purpose. She considered the question again. "I would say I believe in existence."

Darragh shook his head slightly from side to side. "Such distress. What is it about your life that you find so joyless?"

With that question, a flood of memories of her father poured through Isla's mind, like some trigger word had released a long hypnotic trance. She saw her father working in the old store's butcher block, wearing a soiled white apron and cutting meats with a heavy butcher knife, while Isla sat in the corner, wrapping make-believe treasures in the pure white wax paper. She saw him working as a stock boy in the grocery aisles, while she handed him cans of sardines and potted meats, and driving to the country side with her, to purchase fresh fruits and vegetables for the small produce section of the store. Then there were images of him on Sunday, after church, sitting on a park bench with a cup of gelato, watching a little girl swing and play with jump ropes, or laughing at a small six-year-old make faces at zoo animals while her mother held a lemonade and bag of popcorn. Isla's eyes began to mist.

Darragh, offering her a handkerchief, out of nowhere, asked, "Was it something I said?"

"Flashes of growing up, like I haven't thought of in years." She took the handkerchief and dabbed at her eyes, both embarrassed and confused.

"Life can do that, make you forget some magnificent things. Some magnificent moments. But what are those moments that you see? Are they not slices of life? Yours and those that you love?"

Isla studied Darragh, as though she had never seen him before. "Those memories were of things long ago. Childhood times."

Darragh nodded once, then cocked his head to the side, like the pose of a dog at attention, listening hard and thinking. "Are you sure?"

"Yes, those were my memories, of a little girl growing up, of happy times."

"And the memories were of just you? Yes, your childhood, but also the peak of life for your mother and father. Are you looking through your eyes, or theirs?"

"What do you mean?"

"Were their lives not rich with those magnificent moments too? They were yours. But they were also theirs."

Isla did not answer.

"Do you believe in hope?" Darragh asked.

"I believe in concrete things."

"Is not hope such a thing? Something that you can hold on to, with all your heart."

Isla shook her head, but weakly as though she was not convinced in her own belief. "Hope is a fool's errand. Waiting for someone or something that will never come. For a time, I may have had hope, but it's all diminished. It's all gone."

"And what took that away from you?"

"Life did," Isla said after a moment of reflection.

"A life running out of time?"

Isla fell back in her chair, as if she had been deflated. "You could say that. Time ran out on my hopes."

Darragh folded his napkin as she spoke, into a pyramid shape. When he finished, he answered, "I don't see it that way. Now I may have in the past. But not now. I don't think time runs out on you, like you are a leaky vessel losing its fuel and contents as you go. It's more of a question of how you spend your time. Sixty years. That's 720 months, or almost 22,000 days, or about 31,530,000 minutes. That's a lot of minutes for even a less than average life span, at least here in this country. That's a lot of days. How are you going to spend all of that time?"

Isla clinched her teeth, then a second later asked, "Did you just do all that math in your head?"

Darragh ignored the question. "I want to thank you for choosing to share your time with me. It is appreciated. And thank you for this cappuccino. It was delicious." Darragh saw Isla starting to react, then added, "But I'm sure not as delicious had I had this at your shop."

Isla softened her scowl. Part of her wanted to end this conversation, to bid Darragh goodbye, and then extract herself from whatever concerns or worries involving the chapel or the people that he pointed out to her. But she was also curious, maybe more than curious, as if she had somehow become invested in this happening despite her recent exposure to it. She decided to address that one issue before departing. "When we came into Starbucks, you were supposed to tell me why you took me to the Park, to see this chapel. Somehow, we didn't talk about that at all. You went in a totally different direction. So before we go, tell me why you got me into this. What is it that you want?"

"I want to help you by helping you help others."

"Here we go again." Her hands clinched into fists, which she held across her breasts. As if keeping them close kept her under control. "What the hell does that even mean?"

"Humor me."

"I want to. I really do, because I want to know where this mystery train is going. But you are making this unbearably frustrating."

"Do you believe in love?"

"I used to."

"What happened? What changed?"

"Everyone I loved is gone. I'm the last one. No parents. I've never married, no children."

Darragh started to rise, then motioned for Isla to wait. "Stay here. I'll just be a second." Darragh walked over to the register and made a request of the young blond-haired girl working behind the counter. A moment later, he returned to the table and sat back down. He had a single piece of paper in his hands and an ink pen.

Darragh started writing on the paper, and while doing so, asked, "Do you remember growing up in church, going to catechism?"

"Yes, I remember. And I still go to church. Well, sometimes."

Darragh smiled.

"You might know that I sit in the same place at church, by the sixth station of the cross. Where my grandparents would sit."

"The sixth station, Veronica wipes the face of Jesus." Darragh nodded his approval as he continued to write. "Tell me, did you also learn about the golden rule?"

"Sure. Sister Rose, one of the nuns who taught us, would say it all the time, 'Moses had to have ten commandments on the tablets because he was dealing with people already grown up. If he could have started with children, all we would have had to say is love everyone as God loves you.' Pretty simple."

"And do you still love your Dad, and your Mother, grandparents too?"

"Sure. What kind of question is that?"

"Then how can you say that you used to believe in love?"

Isla froze for a moment, then answered, "That's not what I meant."

"Good. I have to go now, but I will see you in the morning. You will be at your shop, won't you?"

"Of course I will. Where are you going?"

"No worries," Darragh said as he folded the paper and handed it to Isla. "This is for you."

Isla reached out her hand and took the folded paper, as Darragh slid his chair under the table. He waved at her, then walked toward the door. She watched him until he was outside, lost in the crowd. She started to protest, to ask him to wait, and even thought about hurrying after him. But she did neither. She closed her eyes and tried to make sense of the morning, and her conversation with Darragh, the bitter, beautiful memories that she had of her parents, the indecipherable logic of Darragh's arguments.

After a minute of reflection, she realized that she still held the folded paper in her hands. She unfolded the paper to find a poem.

LOVELY LOST YOU

Shades on the meadow
Clouds on the blue
Dreaming of heaven
Dreaming of you

Sails on the water
Ships tilt eschew
Reaching for balance
Searching for you

Why are you going
Where birds never flew
Can you still hear me?
Praying for you

Is there a penance
A fine ransom due
Is there a measure
For rescuing you

Doubts and temptations
Rank revenue
Cumber the spirit
The meaning of you

Mourning till weary
Like lost children do
Retreat to sad slumber
And dreaming of you

Stars on the canvas
Sparkle anew
For the promised return
Of lovely lost you
df

Isla read the poem twice. She folded the paper carefully, and found a tissue in her purse to dry her eyes. Her mind was ripe with memories and visions of her parents and her grandparents, little songs her mother would sing or hum while working, the aroma of olive oil and hot bread, the scratch of her grandpa's whiskers on her cheek. She realized that she had not lost them, any more than they had lost her. But maybe she lost herself, or at least became distracted, in a veil of self-pity or jealousy, or by the thousand other excuses she used to explain the disappointments of her life, and ultimately the recipient of her blame.

Holding the poem tightly in her hand, she stood from the table and gathered her things to leave. *Okay, Darragh, you got me. Whatever you have going on with that chapel, you got me.*

Chapter Eight

In years past, those days after Christmas, those last few days of the year, had been days of reflection and restoration for Claira. When in college, she let Christmas be her vacation from the pressures of her classes and jobs. After she graduated, she lost herself in the holiday, almost as if her life played out in a happy story of visits from lost relatives or wonderful surprise presents from a secret admirer, or a compressed rendezvous with a close friend lost in the windstorm of work schedules and distractions. Sometimes she attended several Christmas Masses, for the living nativity scenes, the carols, the simple joy of the simple thought of a savior's birth.

Then she met Theo, and their courtship of three years was a wholesome, gradual escalation of promise and dedications. They had created lasting Christmas memories, ice skating to the carol of the bells, finding a vendor for roasted nuts and chocolate in the falling powder of a white Christmas, even attending the symphony of *Handels' Messiah*. And after they married, she had even higher hopes of yearly Christmas magic. When Tony was born, those hopes were realized, and she knew deeply that each year of her life was better than the one before. No greater wish than that could ever be granted, she firmly believed. How could it; what could be better than to always live in a realm of the best is yet to come?

Though Central Park was always busy, and those days between Christmas and New Year's day were especially hectic with holiday programs and attractions for the children out of school for Christmas break, Claira was able to re-discover herself, to find a new reason why she loved the person she had grown to be. This year, however, was much different. The wounds of the divorce were raw and blistered, and the trauma of missing the holiday with her son was acute, and much more painful than she expected. The trust that she had before placed in her husband and her young family was forfeit. Now, each time she looked inward, she found doubt rather than devotion, regret rather than revelry. But she did not have time to brood, because the spectacle on the Great Lawn pulled her into its orbit. Its mystery needed to be solved, and Claira knew that she needed counsel from others whose expertise could help explain the events that had her baffled. She had recruited help on Christmas afternoon, and this morning, she hoped, would be complete with answers and explanations.

Claira met Warren at the chapel. Even though it was only mid-morning, the day was already warmer and brighter than Christmas day. She still needed a coat and cap to fend away the chill, but it was invigorating, not uncomfortable like the sting of yesterday's cold wind. She waved to catch Warren's attention, and signaled for him to come over to her.

The crowd was large and growing. Most were curious pedestrians, taking a moment to snap a few photographs of the chapel, some even using selfie sticks to picture themselves standing and smiling in front of the little stone church. Others were just passing by, slowing to see the curiosity the chapel had become, but then moving on to the rest of their day. But there were several camps starting to root, little pockets of people who looked like they were going to stay. Park police had to dissuade several people from setting up little pup tents, like campers would deploy around a campfire. Some people carried homemade signs, some with citations to Bible verses, while others had signs that protested anything resembling a church on public property. There were many more supporting signs however, and so far the crowds remained peaceful.

As Warren reached Claira's position on the lawn, he greeted her with a wave and said, "They're out early today. Word is spreading."

Claira nodded. In New York, news of bizarre events spread faster than news of tragedies, so she wasn't surprised to see the numbers of people passing through the park to see the new chapel starting to grow. That's why she wanted to get someone's whose expertise she trusted to examine the chapel, while she still had some level of control over the site. An elderly man had been waiting in the crowd, and was now standing by her side. Claira made the introduction. "Warren, this is Dr. Abner Cole Parson, a professor at NYU. Doctor, this is Officer Warren Hayes. He was one of the first to discover and see this chapel, yesterday, on Christmas morning."

Dr. Parson extended his hand to Warren, and shook it weakly but enthusiastically. "Good morning, Constable," he said. His smile was wide and toothy, as age had shrunken and thinned his face. He had thick, closely cut gray hair, despite his years, and bushy eyebrows that obscured the top of his thick glasses. Warren thought that this little man had to be eighty, but he obviously had a spring of energy left, judging from his extended handshake and the spark in his sunken eyes.

Warren glanced over to Claira and whispered, "Constable," while twirling a pointing finger off the side of his head. Claira shook her head slightly, signaling Warren to stop his inappropriate sign language.

Claira continued, "I contacted Dr. Parson yesterday. Very fortunate to catch him at home on the holiday. We have worked together before on joint projects with the Park and the Natural History Museum. Professor Parson volunteered to look over the chapel and offer his opinion on it, and maybe how it could have been set up so quickly."

The American Museum of Natural History is one of the world's largest museums. Claira had served as Park liaison on numerous Museum promotions and exhibitions, and in that capacity met and worked with Dr. Parson on several occasions. The professor even met Theo and Tony last year, and took to little Tony, spending an afternoon giving them a tour of the Museum's storage floors and vaults, where many of the museum's secrets were kept, waiting to be transitioned to the public space for display. He gave Tony a skeletal model of the museum's *Tyrannosaurus rex* for his third birthday. That was just before the divorce, before Tony had felt the ragged tear growing between his parents.

"Well," Dr. Parson said, "I was a little bemused by Claira's description of the chapel, particularly the stained glass. I'm a Professor of Conservation Sciences in the Fine Arts College at NYU, and a director of and contributor to the Biblical Glass Archive. I have a small space at the Museum, and they let me do a little research on some of their artifacts. I have been trying to convince the curator to let me open an exhibit on historical churches, cathedral architecture and particularly the art of early stained glass. So far, they haven't given me any floor space, but they listen and give me a closet-sized basement office to use while I catalogue my research."

"What's the Archive you mentioned.," Warren asked, "A separate museum just for stained glass?"

"No, I could only so wish. The Archive is a collection of photo-studies of ancient, gothic and medieval stained glass. We have gathered thousands of such studies and have them catalogued in our Archive. You see, historical stain glass is not such a thing subject to collection in one depository. The remaining best pieces are still in cathedrals and historical sites all over the world. And sad to say, some are lost each year. As we cannot collect all of these works in a single space, we have created the archive to virtually do so. Now mind you, if we can save the glass from a threat of destruction or decay, we strive to do so as our funds allow. We actually have several pieces in storage at the University and a few at our museum here, after the closure of the Smith Museum of Stained Glass in Chicago. Several of my colleagues have pieces at their colleges, here and there across the country. But we can do only what we can."

"Oh, I get it, like candles in the wind." Warren waited for a response from either Claira or the Professor, but none was forthcoming. "You know, candles in the wind. Flame blows out. Not gonna last. Old stuff in dangerous places." When the Professor said nothing, and just stared at him, Warren concluded, "So you take pictures of the windows before they get broken."

"More than just pictures," Dr. Parson said, clearly perturbed by Warren's elemental description of the Archive's efforts. "We do much more than that. We photo-document. We measure the artifacts, grade each on criteria ranging from glass density, colorings, fragility, and we map each fragment of the image with precise 3-d imaging. If possible, we conduct computed tomography of the artifact. We conduct non-destructive testing. If we can, we date the glass and analyze the stains to determine the chemical reactions at the glass transition temperatures, and the compounds used and the methods of the staining. We seek to analyze what substances were used in the liquid glass to become suspended in the cooling process. The art of staining glass is ancient and complex. Those practitioners of past methods, in a very real way, were more advanced in some processes than we are today."

Claira said before Warren could respond and further embarrass himself, or her. "Let's get to the chapel and take a look, shall we?"

As they walked through the crowd, Warren told Claira about the morning's developments. "We've had a visit from a couple of reporters already this morning. A guy from the *Times*, with a photographer, and that lady reporter from Channel 2 was here, with a TV crew and everything. They did a spot and left about twenty minutes ago. Don't be surprised to get a call from her. She's really nice."

Claira studied Warren, knowing that his definition of 'really nice' when it came to young professional women simply related to cleavage and big boobs. "Don't tell me you gave her a statement. Did you?"

He looked at her defensively, and raised his hands, as if to ward off an interrogation that might be coming. "I didn't tell her anything, or that guy from the *Times* either."

Claira seemed unconvinced, and stared at him as they walked up the path to the chapel door. Claira paused when she realized that the Professor was standing at the chapel landing, staring at the structure as if he were a Pilgrim finally seeing a quest of the faith. Not wanting to call out across the crowd, Claira hurried back to take him by the arm, and lead him on the way. "Come on now, Abner. Trust me, it's much better to see from the inside," She whispered to him. He moved as if reluctantly, and she wasn't sure he had even heard what she said.

Dr. Parson, finally following them in, took a small flashlight from his pocket as they entered the church. Claira heard cat-calls echoing from the ring of the crowd they had just passed. She glanced over at Warren and shook her head. A couple of park patrolmen kept the on-lookers in check, but Claira knew that sooner or later, they would have to decide what to do with this building. As that thought entered her mind, she closed the chapel door and caught up to Dr. Parson. "Well Doc, what do you think?"

The sunlight was bright enough to illuminate the glass windows, but the professor held the penlight at the ready, and even tested it against the cup of his hand. He did not answer Claira, and acted as though he didn't hear her. He stood in the center aisle of the chapel, and for minutes stared at the windows, starting with the three on the left side of the church, then those on the right wall. Claira and Warren followed his gaze and stood in silence, not wanting to disturb him, but also because they were somewhat stunned by the trance-like fascination consuming him. When Claira could take it no longer, she reached a hand for his shoulder. But before she touched the elderly professor, he spoke.

"Oh my," he said.

Claira and Warren glanced at each other, then she moved to face Dr. Parson. "Well? What do you think?"

He met her eyes and muttered something as he rubbed his chin. He stood in the center of the church and studied the last window, perched high behind the altar. He slowly turned a full circle, eyes darting back and forth over the windows as he rotated, mumbling to himself, occasionally nodding, sometimes also shaking his head as he went. When he finally paused, he looked over the high ceiling of the church, and then let his gaze fall back across the altar of the chapel. After a final delay, he turned back to his right, to face the east wall of the chapel and walked to the window closest to the altar. Once there, he lifted a frail hand to point to the first window. "This first one here," he said. "This is the Revelation of the Star, a depiction we think that traces back to St. Paul's Monastery in Jarrow, England. We have only anecdotal evidence of it now, but I've read about it extensively. The star dominates the frame, not like the other glass windows which have much more detail and activity. This one was meant to be simple with the star dominant. Look at the many nuanced colors that blends. The high star is a sign that calls for reverence, and a light most compelling."

"Do you have pictures of it?" Warren asked.

The professor answered without ever looking away from the windows. "No, son, nothing at all. That Monastery dates back to 686 A.D. We have only the writings of the monks to go by, their crude, colorless drawings, some other historical references and descriptions, and some glass fragments found and saved in archeological quests. The multi-faceted star you see there is an early Jewish rendering of the Bethlehem Star, and it was copied fairly extensively in the early church."

Claira and Warren just nodded at the professor's explanation, and waited for him to continue.

He moved over a few feet to stand before the middle window on the east wall of the chapel. "This piece is called the Journey of Faith. It depicts Melchoir leading the Magi as they follow the star. This depiction is found in the Cathedral of St. Gatien in Indre-et Loire, France. Many hundreds of years old."

"Who is the man with the white beard?" Claira asked, as she pointed to the middle window.

"That is believed to be Melchior, the wise man of Persia, and the oldest of the Magi. The story provides that he was their leader, who led those that followed the Star of Bethlehem. He is said to have presented the gift of gold to the Infant, to signify the Child's kingly reign over the world. The Magi themselves were ultimately enshrined as saints, and were said to be laid to rest in the Shrine of the Three Kings in Cologne Cathedral, Germany. Now, I am not so sure of that, as there are other accounts that the Magi are entombed in the city of Saveh in the Middle East. In the western church, Melchior's feast day is January 6. That is, if you believe in that sort of thing."

Warren seemed eager to jump into the conversation. "I know about that. I remember the Christmas song. I even sang it at our school Christmas play. We three kings, from Orient are, bearing gifts, we travel afar..."

Dr. Parson chuckled and shook his head. "Yes, I see that you remember it well. And it was taught most assuredly wrong."

Warren was devastated that his contribution to the discussion about the stained glass scene was criticized. He defensively asked, "I thought I remembered the lyrics right."

"That's how I remember it too," Claira said.

Dr. Parson shook his finger at them in a gentle, teacher's show of patient understanding. "You are both right, and sadly both wrong. You can't base your historical understanding of these events on a Christmas carol. Like most childhood stories and fables, it has only the thinnest of a thread of the truth holding together a story that can be sung, or can be passed down through generations, not as history lessons, but as events of characters of the faith. Therefore, you are partly right, but mostly wrong."

Warren said, "Okay, where did I go wrong? The three kings did not come from China?"

"Well, again you take the carol too seriously. First off, we do not see them as kings. The Gospel of Matthew refers to them as Magi, not kings. The Latin word *magus*, means sorcerer. Historians view the Magi as astrologers and astronomers. Not kings, as you may have inferred."

"But the Bible story...," protested Claira. She paused to gather her thoughts. "They were kings from three different countries."

"Another common presumption." Dr. Parson replied. "Another wrong premise that made its way into the song. In Matthew, Chapter 2, it is written that Magi from the east arrived and had audience with King Herod in Jerusalem. They told of the star they followed, and asked where the child would be found. And Herod summoned the chief priests and the scribes of Israel, and asked where the Messiah was to be born. And they answered, as the prophet had written, 'And you, Bethlehem, land of Judah, are no means least among the rulers of Judah, since from you shall come a ruler, who is to shepherd my people Israel.'" Abner turned his head to Claira and back to Warren, and smiled in a patient, loving way. "So the Magi set out to find the child, and followed the star that proceeded them, and it showed them the house where Mary held her child. And they were overjoyed and there they opened their treasures and offered the child gold, frankincense and myrrh. But they did not return to Herod and tell him where the child was found. No, the Gospel says clearly in verse 12 that 'And having been warned in a dream not to return to Herod, they departed for their country by another way.'"

"I don't get it," Warren said.

"Several points." The Professor placed his penlight back in his pocket, and leaned against the side of a rough wooden pew. He motioned for Claira and Warren to take a step closer, as if wanting them to understand the subtle details that had been overlooked from the gospel passage. "The Magi did not meet with Herod as royalty. They were not kings. They were not Herod's equal. Herod ordered them to find the child and return to his palace to identify the child, but not so he could offer homage to the child. No, Herod thought the child prophesized was a threat to him and to his hold on power. He meant to kill the child. So the Magi were warned to return to their country by another way. Their country, singular. So some scholars believe that they were all from the same country. I know that some of the magi stories say that Melchior was the king of Arabia, that Balthezor was the king of Ethiopia, and Casper the king of Tarsus, or modern day Spain, but the historical record suggested that they were all wise men, no doubt, but not kings, and that they all came from the ancient kingdom of Persia. Not what you think of as the Orient. Persia is what we call in modern day, Iran."

Claira was entranced by the professor's descriptions. His explanations of the historical context Bible passages captured details that she never considered and had never heard discussed from such an analytical perspective. She was caught between listening to his insights, and struggling to understand how anything he said could have actually been captured in the beautiful glass artwork that was before them. She blinked when she heard Warren calling out to them. He was walking ahead, impatient and curious. "What about this one?" he asked as he pointed to the last window on the east wall.

Dr. Parson took a few feeble steps toward the rear of the church, following Warren. "This one is from a different church. As you could guess by the depiction of the shepherds, prostrate before the manger, this one is called The Shepherd Witness. I think this was first depicted in glass found at the Augsburg Cathedral, Sery les Mezieres in Aisne, France. Again, centuries ago. It is quite spectacular, as it had over fifty distinct colorings and shades assembled rather seamlessly to form this beautiful portrait."

Claira was continuously mesmerized by the description that Dr. Parson gave of the windows. He explained how compounds were mixed in the molten liquid glass to color the glass, and offered ideas of how the dusty browns of the shepherds' robes were made, and the golden amber of the starlight, and the radiance of the hue of glow around the manger. He spoke as if telling secrets unheard for years. "They were artists and chemists and pioneers. One of the old staining techniques used silver chloride, which when heat treated, released silver ions in the liquid to migrate into the glass and become suspended in the plane as the temperatures cooled. The formulas used and the processes were developed over years and years of trial and error, countless pours of glass mixed with secret ingredients, all to infuse the glass with a depth of color."

"Don't we have stained glass made today?" Warren asked.

"Yes, but it's not the same," the Professor said, sounding almost dismissive. "Sometimes it's not even stained glass, but white glass painted over with enamels. And we have chemicals now to use in the staining process, but those glass-smiths of hundreds of years ago used natural compounds. They used organics, and metallic salts. They had secrets that we still do not know the whole of."

Dr. Parson walked directly up to the east wall and closely studied each window, examined the glass carefully, and the outlines used in the design. "Unfortunately, there is no method of dating glass that has general acceptability."

Claira was confused. "Abner, why is that important? Obviously, these windows are just copies. Probably very recent copies at that. Put together just for this chapel. Which was put up last night."

Abner whistled softly, as if thinking both about what Claira's point and the physical presentation of the windows before him. After a moment, he turned to her, "As I said, each of these windows has been copied from an historical relic. I can say with certainty that these windows are not new."

"What does that mean?" Claira was unsure of his point of reference.

"These windows are old. Many, many decades old at least, maybe hundreds of years, though they are in wonderful shape."

Warren looked over at Claira and shrugged.

"Isn't there some kind of carbon dating that we can do? Find out how old they really are? I see that done all the time on TV."

"It's not that easy, son. You're talking about radiocarbon dating. Glass is different. There are some tests that have been tried, like fission track dating and alpha particle recoil track dating. Thermoluminesence dating. Counting the layers within decomposition crusts. These tests have shown some usefulness in selected cases, but work better on materials harvested with the find of the ancient glass. There just isn't a lot of carbon left in old stained glass, and you would have to treat a huge quantity of the glass to even try to run the test."

"Then how do you know this isn't just a very good, modern day reproduction?" Claira said.

Abner smiled, probably realizing that his small audience did not believe what he said or did not understand what they were seeing. "First," he said, gently touching the metal lines between the glass panels on the second window, "Look closely at these lines. New windows use what's called the copper foil technique to frame the glass. These windows are leaded. Next, look at the tracts of the lines. There are no solder joints, which a new window would have. Also, the lead- lines do not deviate in width. The continuous black line indicates an old glass window." He slowly traced the path of the metal line framing a plate of red glass. He took a moment, to catch his breath, then continued "Finally, none of these windows have opalescent glass, meaning that the glass has a translucent white mixed in the colors of the glass. That technique was patented in 1880. Before then, the glass presented a clear of transparent color, usually with a slight texture to the glass. This glass is not opalescent. All of these characteristics point to aged windows, not new."

Claira and Warren stood speechless, not able to grasp how what they were hearing could be true. Before either of them could say anything, Dr. Parson turned to the west wall and gestured for Claira to stand close. "Do you see the pattern?" he asked.

"What pattern? What do you mean?" Claira looked at Dr. Parson, puzzled. Warren just shrugged his shoulders.

"See, we started at the right hand of the altar. Started with the Revelation of the Star. Then the Journey of Faith, then the Shepherd Witness. Now look, this window at the left rear of the church, this is the Adoration of the Magi. See the three wise men, one on his knees, with Mary and the Infant Child. Above, a star and in the background, an angel. This is depicted in 13th Century stained glass in the

Canterbury Cathedral in Kent, England." Dr. Parson turned back and motioned to the windows on the east wall. "Each window is telling part of the story. Look at the other wall again. The high star, the traveling magi, the shepherds coming to the manger. In this window, at the back of the west wall, the Magi have arrived. They have found the child. We are following the progression of events. And we are going clockwise around the church, to end back at the front."

"What's so special about going clockwise?" Warren asked.

"Not big on Sunday school, except for the Christmas carols, big fella," the Professor said with a good natured wink. He turned to look first at Warren, then at Claira. "Old superstition, one never walks widdershins in a church, else you might run into the devil." Seeing that Warren appeared lost, he said. "That means counterclockwise, Mr. Hayes.

"Now this middle scene, I have not seen this in glass. This one is something else." The window showed a woman, Mary, kneeling before the hayed manger, the child asleep. She was clothed in a light honey colored fleece that in the sunlight appeared soft gold, as if threaded with the precious metal. "See how Mary is clothed? That is the Sancta Camisa, the tunic that Mary wore in the manger. In 876, the Chartres Cathedral acquired that relic and it is on display even today. It's located about 80 miles from Paris. But I have never seen the Sancta Camisa depicted so vividly in stained glass."

Professor Parson walked toward the front of the church and finally pointed to the last window in the west wall. "And this is the Notre Dame de la Belle Verriere, also from the Chartres Cathedral." The window showed Mary, dressed in blue, crowned, with her child king. The colors were bright and sparkling, as if a moving spotlight was behind the window, spinning light echoes into the inner chamber of the chapel.

Warren broke the silence by asking, "What about that one up there? What is that one?"

Dr. Parson turned and raised his head to study that window high above the altar once more. "That one I do not know. I may be able to research it, but for now I cannot say."

Dr. Parson went slowly to a pew in right center of the chapel and sat. He almost fell into the seat, as if on the verge of collapsing. Claira was startled and asked, "Dr. Parson, are you all right? Is there something that I can do?"

He slowly removed his glasses and retrieved a handkerchief from a pocket and began the gentle work of cleaning the lenses. He spoke as his hands did their work, "No dear, I am quite fine. Forgive me if I startled you, but I simply did not expect anything like this. Just need to catch my breath." He leaned back in the pew and took several long inhales, then momentarily, exhaling in long, deliberate breaths. After a moment his face reddened and then he continued, "When you told me about this chapel, I expected some modular little building, and some colorful but bland and quite ordinary stained windows. Never did I expect to find anything as spectacular as this."

Claira was standing to his side, still in the center aisle of the chapel. "Abner, the way you talked about those windows, the way each has a name..." Her voice trailed away, thought unfinished.

Dr. Parson finished her sentence, and spoke in abrupt tones, as if arguing with himself. "Each window is a classic work of religious, stained glass art. Each is a relic's depiction. These windows were arranged in a very specific order, a chronological pattern. Not many would know these works. Fewer would know each and every one of them. A couple of them no longer exist. Just stories, bits of history."

"But you know each of them. Someone in your position would have that knowledge. Just google stained glass windows and research the hell out of them and you could come up with the list of them, right? I mean, couldn't someone like you have had these windows made, from their store of research?"

Dr. Parson answered without turning from his stare, without even blinking. "Perhaps. Maybe, but it would be difficult. These windows were made with old, rare techniques. This is not a mass production, by any means. That's just the physical nature of what we have here. There is also the selection of the depictions. I do not even know the source of the Sancta Camisa depiction." He scratched his chin while thinking. He deliberately examined his eyeglasses, and satisfied, placed them back into position on his nose. "I haven't even looked over anything else in this church, have not examined the wood or the stone, or anything else about this chamber. But I know this." He then turned to look directly at Claira, and spoke to her both with his words and the plea crying in his eyes. "Regardless of explanation, whether we find it or not. You must do everything possible to preserve this Chapel. No matter the cost."

Chapter Nine

When the chime sounded from Mike's smart phone, he was just pouring a second drink of Irish whiskey into a short, bowl-shaped copper mug. He pulled the phone from his pocket and saw a text from Jason that simply instructed, "Call me."

Mike sighed. Even though Jason had sent him home to rest and gather his thoughts, the reprieve was so modest that he should have simply stayed at the office. He had taken his time leaving the *Times* offices, going over his email and checking the desk for updates on the wallscapes and billboards. Even when he left, he dallied on the way home, stopping once at a bookstore, and once at a package liquor store around the corner from his apartment. He finally arrived at his quiet and dimly lit apartment, threw his sports jacket across the back of the leather couch, and considered what to do with the rest of the afternoon. And despite his intentions of checking in with the office and taking his wife out for a walk around the neighborhood, all he had accomplished after his return home was to finish the last few shots in an open bottle of Tullamore Dew, and then to open another.

The drinking was becoming more than an unwelcomed, addictive habit. So far, it had not affected his work in any measurable way, but the slow erosion of his competence was occurring, even if he was the only person yet aware of that decline. In the months after Maria's death, sleep had become elusive. Mike found that whiskey was a tool to dim the burning, specter questions and rages in his mind. But predictably, as the time passed, the whiskey's effectiveness dissipated. Now it was merely a numbing device, a salve for the cuts in his soul. A temporary treatment for his daily awakening pain.

Since he arrived home, he had hardly spoken to his wife. She was absorbed with her projects of compiling Maria photo albums and scrapbooks. She'd been working on these compilations for half of the last year. For the first few months after Maria died, Jessie was unable to even look at a picture of Maria without crying. Now, she spent countless hours organizing every photograph of Maria that she could find. Jessie gathered all of Maria's old report cards and school papers and crayon drawings and construction paper projects and arranged them in large, detailed scrap books. She was making one photo album and one scrap book for each year of Maria's twelve short years of life. He kissed her on the forehead, and she patted his hand as it rested on her shoulder. But she said no more than hello. Mike left Jessie working at the dining room table, without any words, just a wave to show that he was going to another room. Jessie smiled and nodded, but said nothing. Mike left the dining room, now Jessie's de facto project room, and stepped in the kitchen to fill an ice bucket with small square cubes of ice. Then he retreated to the silence and the darkness of his home office.

Mike had a dark walnut bar in a corner of his home office. Behind the bar was just enough space for him to navigate among the shelves and a clear fronted cabinet of heavy cocktail glasses, wine glasses and jiggers. The bar lacked running water and a sink, but had three shelves of selected Highland and Speyside Scotches, a couple of Irish whiskeys, his favorite being the triple distilled Tullamore Dew, and a bottle each of vodka, gin and clear white rum. Mike took a sip of the Irish whiskey, took a cube of ice from the ice bucket he placed on the corner of the bar, and put the ice in his mouth. He took another sip of the whiskey and held it in his mouth, letting it wash over the ice. After a moment, he swallowed the whiskey, then let the ice fall from his mouth into the copper mug. He splashed another shot of the whiskey into the mug. He then turned and went across the room to his desk.

The room was lit only by a standing lamp near the bar. Mike had not switched on the ceiling light, choosing to keep the room subdued and dim. The bookcases behind the desk were hidden in shadows, and his two paintings by the German artist Otto Dix on the adjacent wall were all but invisible. Mike walked around the desk, took another long draw from the now cold copper mug, and sat in his swivel desk chair. He turned the desk lamp on, dialed Jason's number, and closed his eyes while rubbing the cold, sweating mug across his forehead.

Jason, not bothering with a greeting, said, "Mike you were right. And where the hell are you?"

"I'm sitting at my desk, but the one at home, where you told me to be. Don't you remember our meeting this morning?"

Jason dismissed the response. "Oh, that's right. Look, I've gone over the file that you left for me. There's a lot we're missing. Every news plug on the northeast coast is carrying a bit about the wallscapes. But they're on the wrong angle, like it's some artsy fartsy college prank. No one's yet voiced any speculation about those walls and our Christmas poem, page one. Those wallscapes are as mysterious as our hijacked page one. But they're missing the unexplained Christmas day appearance. No one has gone to the next level, not yet."

"But Jason, it's poems. For Christ's sake, no one does poetry nowadays. The *Times*, then the 5 building size poems all across the boroughs. I could connect the two while drunk and in my pajamas."

"That's not the only connection that I'm thinking about. I was talking about the park chapel. You mentioned this morning that you thought it may be related to whoever is responsible for the page one poem. That got me thinking. So I've talked to the reporter the city desk sent to Central Park."

"Who did the desk send?"

"Freddie Plant. He hit Central Park, poked around the chapel, and spent the rest of the day chasing down a paper trail for that new chapel building."

"And?" Mike inquired, still cooling his temple and forehead with the cold cup. He knew Freddie well, and if there were a lead to follow, Freddie would tenaciously exhaust every avenue of pursuit and investigate every bit of any direct and indirect evidence. He was the *Times'* bloodhound, a reputation that he was both aware of and thankful for.

"No records at all about the Central Park church. No building permit, no filed notice of the construction contract, nothing in conveyances at all. Also, no record of a construction bond, no bid invitations, no record of any contract award. Every job on public property by law has to have a construction bond filed of record. But not for this build. And there is no record of anything with city planning, or with the zoning office, and no record of stamped drawings. Nothing. It's like the project was purposely and intentionally kept off the books. You know how hard that is to do in this town?" Jason could hear Mike's deep breaths over the phone, but nothing else, so he answered his own question. "It's damned hard to do, and virtuously impossible when it involves park property."

"Freddy is a thorough son of a bitch. If there was anything there, he would dig until he found it."

"Agreed."

Mike asked, "What about the Park Conservancy? Did anyone go straight to the source? What do they say about it?"

"So far, nothing. Not even a 'no comment'. I have a meeting with the director in the morning." Jason paused as if conflicted over an internal debate. Finally, after a moment of silence, he said, "You should attend."

Mike sighed. He would rather have gone to such a meeting alone, knowing that Jason was not one to sit quiet and listen. "Sure, I can do that. Who is the director?"

Jason cursed when the name escaped him. "Damn, I just talked to him. Is it Terry? No, Terrance. That's it. Terrance Greenberg."

"Yea, I've met him once or twice. Nice enough guy. Old money. He is overly concerned with marketing and public relations and his jewelry and exotic cars. The day to day stuff of Park management is not on his radar. Gives me the idea that he's above the routine operations. A big picture guy."

"He'll have his deputy director with him. A woman named Claira Vasson. She's been point on this since Christmas morning." Jason paused for a moment, and Mike could hear the sound of stacks of paper or prints being shuffled across Jason's desk. When he resumed, Jason sounded exasperated, as if he could not find some clue that he knew was amid the clutter of his desk. "He's playing this way too cute. He's not giving me anything over the phone."

Mike considered the possibilities. Only one made any sense. "He's being coy because he doesn't know shit."

Jason chuckled. "Mike, I've looked at over 60 pictures that our guys took this morning. I can promise you this isn't a movie set. This ain't stick figures and facades. No way this was done in the dark of night without anyone in the know. And at this time of year, the Park is crawling with police. A dog can't leave his business on the lawn without his owner getting a ticket."

"And I'm telling you he doesn't know anything about it. Just think for a minute. If I'm right and the chapel is connected to the poems, why would it be surprising that both are for the moment unexplainable? This entire episode is complicated, and surely the answers won't be obvious."

Jason let his silence respond in agreement. After a pause he answered, "Just be at the meeting tomorrow morning. At 10 a.m. 14 East 60th Street."

"See you then," Mike replied. He disconnected the phone and looked into the cold copper mug. The ice was like wreckage on the floor of an all but dry lake bed. "This won't do," he mumbled as he rose and crossed the small room to his small but inviting bar.

***

The park was quiet as Darragh walked the lamp-lit path. He waited for nightfall, then entered the Park at its northwest corner, near Douglass Circle. The residual snow was cleared away, and Darragh paused to study the unique paving pattern of the traffic circle, designed to mimic the shapes and colors used in a traditional African American quilt. The artwork was distinctive, but nothing at all like the plaids and tartans native to his Scottish home.

He had been sitting on a bench near the Frederick Douglass sculpture and the intersection of 8th Avenue and 110th Street, thinking and composing his next poem. Its seeds were in his head now, and growing.

Thinking of Douglass, the champion of the anti-slavery movement, and the difficulty of life as an African-American, born into slavery in 1820s Maryland, had provided some inspiration, as did the Genesis stories he heard as a boy at his family's church in Tain, Scotland. He first learned of Frederick Douglass, the great orator and social reformer, who was once himself a slave, not from his writings and speeches advocating the abolition of slavery in America, but rather from his friendship with the great Irish liberator Daniel O'Connell, who voiced the movement in 1840s Ireland for Catholic emancipation.

While Darragh was no scholar, he understood the irony. In 1845 America, Douglass was viewed by many as inferior, by some mere chattel, in both the south and north of the United States, but while in Ireland, he was accepted as a learned man, treated as an equal, free to move about the country without discrimination or harassment. But as he did so, he would see for himself the rank discrimination and bigotry directed to Irish Catholics, who, from appearances, were just like their Irish countrymen. As Douglas traveled Ireland, he witnessed that intolerance can grow anywhere, in any vast group of hearts and minds, and was not directed only at those who look different, but sometimes also to those who believe differently, speak differently, even think differently. This bias was not fed by the visual only, and fed not by reason, but by a perverted inner sight, and the taunts of a vile, petulant conscience. Such is the fall from grace when men see through the eyes of prejudice and love through a heart of hate.

Darragh walked past the Great Hill in the northwest section of the Park, along West Drive to the North Meadow. He paused before crossing the 97th Street Traverse, listening to the birds settle in the winter-bare trees, and the invading sounds from traffic and the noise of the city. The city was easing into night. He took his time walking through the park, seeing some people walking by, couples arm in arm, some groups of people hurrying to destinations unsaid. He passed the tennis courts, vacant in the cold weather, and walked along the west side of the Jacqueline Kennedy Onassis Reservoir. A horse-drawn carriage passed in front of him, carrying a couple huddled under a blanket, along the 86th Street crossing, the big mare breathing heavy in the cold night air. He crossed the Great Lawn and came to the chapel from the rear. The yellow barricade tape still circled the building, but he paid it no mind, dipped under it and entered the chapel from the little rear door. There were a few people milling about the front of the chapel, but they neither saw nor heard him enter. To the left of the doorway was a small shelf on which stood a single candle in a brass holder. The matches he had used the night before were still in his pocket, and he retrieved them and lit the candle with one strike of the match on the box's rough panel side. He walked to the small table that served as the chapel's altar, and placed the candle on its top. The small flame illuminated the tabletop, which was all that he needed. He took a piece of paper from his jacket pocket, and a pen from his shirt pocket, and sat on the small wooden chair. Without a sound, save his humming of an old song he loved, Darragh got to work.

The poem was written in just less than an hour. Darragh was careful to have the words right in his mind before he wrote them on the paper, leaving no words struck through or letters over-written. When done, he returned the pen to his pocket, and held the candle where he could see the single page more clearly. Darragh read the poem twice, initially silently, but then out loud, thinking about the flow the words, the sounds of the letters together, and the thoughts that their sounds carried when spoken. Satisfied, he placed the poem on the center of the table, stood and stretched his back and shoulders, and then walked to the first row of the rough wooden pews at the front of the little church. Darragh was tired. He had been awake since daylight, and had walked all over the city, learning it by observation, as if he was the first of his kind in a strange new world. Tomorrow would be more of the same. He blew out the candle, slid its holder under the pew, the spent wick still smoking a thin signal of the dead flame. He then laid down on the hard wooden bench, shedding his jacket and using it as a pillow. He fell asleep fast, as he had every night since Christmas Eve.

This night his dreams came to him quickly. He saw a mountain of a man, big and rough, weeping. He saw the shadowed face of a woman, conflicted and torn. Then he dreamed of a little girl dying afraid, in a sad, sterile looking hospital room, with many there with her, family and nurses, and also so many other faces, all silent but talking with their eyes, their demeanor, some even smiling, some holding candles of small but radiant glows, some with arms open in welcome and some with gifts of things he could not describe, but precious and pure. So many faces, so many tears, so many crying, but for so many different reasons. And then he saw the little girl for the second time, and understood.

Chapter Ten
December 27

The 5 Train from Church Avenue in Brooklyn to Grand Central Terminal at 42nd Street was a crowded, 36-minute ride for Claira Vasson. The early hours were hectic, and brought scores of daily commuters to the Church Avenue Station. She was one of thousands of Brooklyn residents who worked on Manhattan Island, and she had made the trip so many times that she was accustomed to the crowd and the jerky train ride into the city.

She sat in a forward car, pressed against a window, and spent the time jotting notes in her leather bound notebook. When her concentration waivered, she would close the notebook and clasp it against her chest, feeling and smelling the leather, recalling the day she received it, wrapped crudely in the colorful comics from the Sunday paper. Tony had surprised her with the notebook a year ago for her birthday. He was quick to tell her that while his dad paid for the present, he picked it out by himself. He even wrapped it, using long strands of tape to bind the book so tight the magic that made her written words wonderful could not escape. He used more of the comics to neatly cover the present, he said, so no one could peek inside and spoil the surprise.

The shop's leather-smith stamped her initials into the leather cover, below an ornate Celtic cross press-carved into the leather. Tony selected the emblem from a dusty ring binder of images that the leather-smith had available, and when he made his choice, the old smith scratched his bald head and admitted that he forgot having it in his catalog because in twenty years, no one ever chose that symbol. The leather binding and cover were soft buckskin, tanned the color of cooked bacon. Tony loved bacon. Now the supple, leather covered notebook was her prized and best possession, a daily reminder of Tony's enthusiastic, unconditional love.

She opened the notebook and re-read for the fiftieth time the outline she made of Abner's description of the Chapel and its stained glass windows. She had added notes and fragments of her own thoughts at varied points in the outline, most punctuated with question marks or word prompts such TIME TO BUILD? METHODS OF

CONSTRUCTION? WHO, and HOW. Those questions were no closer to being answered, she knew, and she would have preferred to be heading directly to the Park in an attempt to find some clue to unlock the riddle of the Chapel. But today she had another responsibility, one that she was not anxious to perform.

After yesterday's meeting at the chapel with Abner and Warren, Claira spent the early evening with Tony, who was still in Christmas mode, his attention darting from present to present, with Christmas themed movies like *Home Alone* constantly on in the background. They had Turkey breast and stuffing for dinner, and spent the after hour talking about Kevin's adventures out-witting Joe Pesci and debating whether he was old enough for an X-Box in his room. Tony fell asleep on the sofa, and did not stir when Claira carried him to his room. Claira quickly cleaned the kitchen and wrote a note for the sitter who would arrive early in the morning, before Tony would awaken. She crept down the hall and peeked in on her son, whose relaxed, regular breaths proved he was in deep and peaceful sleep.

With her son asleep, Claira turned off the television, poured a glass of Chianti, and explored subjects that were prompted by her scan of her notes taken over the last two days. She spent hours reading about ancient churches with famous stained glass artwork, as well as the weight of quarried rock and the process of constructing exterior walls with cut stones. She followed up on some of Abner's declarations about the Magi lore, only to find that he was completely accurate in the description of the glass depictions, but not as precise in his explanation of the Magi story. Well, to be fair, his explanations were not proven to be inaccurate, but rather, were not a completely unchallenged narrative of the star and the wise men who followed it.

She stayed awake late last night, studying background material gathered in her research. Out of habit of wanting to hold paper when reading, she printed several articles addressing the study of some of the original glass artworks, one of which was co-authored by Abner Parson himself. That discovery actually made her laugh aloud. She should have known better than to doubt him in his area of expertise, as he was renowned for his written studies on religious artwork and was accepted as a pioneer in the field of Art Conservation Sciences. But she also printed other material concerning the Magi narrative, and she discovered that the stories and mystery about the Star of Bethlehem were diverse and inconsistent.

A passenger standing next to her dropped his phone, and the curses resulting from its cracked display interrupted her thoughts. Claira yawned and arched back as she stretched her arms above her head. She was both tired and nervous. She was thinking about the meeting she had to attend this morning, and still bouncing among the articles and theories she studied late into the night. And even though those many deviations among most of the widely acclaimed scholarly theories, and the simple Biblical account of the star and the magi, were curiously captivating, she had to remind herself that she did not have the time to indulge her interest. Her presence at the Park Conservatory office meeting was dictated by Terrance Greenburg himself. Unfortunately, her exact role at the meeting and what she was expected to contribute was unclear. Was she to report on what she had seen and what she had learned about the chapel? Or, maybe she was summoned to be blamed for the unforeseen appearance and castigated for the lack of an explanation of its presence. She only knew that Terrance Greenburg called her personally, and told her to expect a frank conversation about the Park's responsibility for the chapel, and its response to the fact of its appearance. Whether she was going to be a fact witness, a cipher in the Conservancy's response, or simply the scape-goat for an unsolved problem was yet to be seen.

While Terrance Greenburg was her direct superior in the Conservancy, she rarely dealt with him on any personal level. She was functionally autonomous in her position as assistant park director, and her reports of park operations, planned budgets and Best Practices reviews were submitted in written form, to be read and disseminated to the board members for their monthly meetings. While she occasionally attended board meetings, she was not a board member, and her involvement at the board level was, at best, as a rotational surrogate, and certainly not as an equal.

She felt the train slowing, and closed her notebook as she prepared to disembark from the train. She glanced about the cabin where a cluster of occupants swarmed to the sliding doors. She waited for the initial rush out of the train, then fell into the remaining crowd exiting into the lower level of Grand Central Station.

As Claira climbed the stairs leading to the Grand Concourse, she sensed that the crowd above her was not flowing as seamlessly as it should. She pushed her way through the crowd of people, and finally reached the open concourse. Immediately, she knew that some distraction was fouling the flow of commuters and her eyes searched for its source.

At its birth, the Station was a simple train exchange and terminal, and the daily schedule was posted on a large blackboard for travelers to see. That original blackboard was now proudly displayed in the Transit Museum, with a chalk written schedule of the fewer and simpler train routes of decades ago. Today, the station used the latest in Liquid Crystal Display technology to advertise the arrival and departure times of the trains from their assigned platforms. The LCD modules were installed above the ticket windows, many of which were closed in favor of automated ticket machines located at intervals throughout the concourse.

Between the extreme of those two technologies, chalkboards to LCD monitors, the station had employed the largest and most complex electromechanical board in the world. Manufactured by Solari Udnine Company of Italy, the huge screen consisted of thousands of flaps that folded and cycled through arrays of letters and numbers to list the train schedules and destinations. When the electromechanical boards were removed in favor of the LCD modules, enough people lamented the loss of what many referred to as the world's largest living sign, that the Transit Authority had the board re-installed at one end of the Concourse as part of its Terminal Birthday Bridge to the Future Promotion. The re-emergence of the board was superbly received, and the Station managers took note that more people would look to the board for schedule updates than would view the LCD modules above the ticket windows.

Claira followed a couple who seemed to be hurrying to the far wall of the station. As they approached the wall, the one with the electromechanical board mounted twelve feet above the station floor, she noticed a movement across the schedules, and heard the rapid deployment of the board's flaps, falling, adjusting, with a sequential fluttering that sounded like playing cards being shuffled by a professional dealer. In less than an instant, all train and track numbers were gone, along with the departure and arrival schedules. In their place was a simple stanza of a poem that read:

> Had temptation been denied
> Would the Garden still be green
> Curious the eyes that hide
> The kingdom from a king and queen

In a moment, the stanza was gone, replaced by the train schedules, as if the poem had never existed. Claira blinked her eyes, as if doubting what she had seen. Before she could turn away from the wall, the board fluttered again, with another stanza replacing the train schedule in a symphonic wave of black, metallic flaps:

> Had avarice been cast aside
> Would enmity never wedge between
> Man and wife, the pain each cried
> No one to blame, or foil demean

The growing crowd standing in front of the electromechanical board was silent, as if anticipating another shift from poetry to platform schedules and departure times. And a moment later, a tremble tickled the board, and the regular train listings reappeared seconds after the synchronized tumble of the flaps.

Claira spoke to no one in particular, and without turning her eyes from the board. "How long has this been going on?"

A young woman dressed in hospital scrubs and an overcoat was standing to Claira's left side and answered, "Not sure. I just noticed it when I was leaving the station. I have been here for about fifteen minutes. If I'm right, there will be two more paragraphs to cycle across the screen."

Before Claira could answer, the board shifted again, presenting another stanza:

> But certain is the human slide
> Toward calamities obscene
> The gravity of sin inside
> The struggle of the mind's machine

"Holy shit," someone behind her in the crowd exclaimed. Claira turned as if by instinct to see who had spoken, and when she turned back the board, the schedule again was displayed.

"One more time," the lady in scrubs announced. And as if on cue, the board rippled again, from left to right, and the train schedule was replaced with the last stanza of the poem:

> Rise tall when the days collide
> Careful judgment will be seen

Baptize in the highest tide
Regain the garden, safe, serene

"That's it," the woman in scrubs said, as if disappointed. "I stayed to make sure I caught it all. I'm pretty sure that it rolled through the entire passage."

"How many times did you see the poem appear?" Claira asked, reaching out to catch the woman's elbow, gesturing her to stay for a moment.

"I guess I read it two, maybe three times. I wanted to make sure that I saw the whole thing. I think that it's so cool. Just like the poem in the *Times* on Christmas morning. And the side of the building downtown." Her face was animated with excitement as she spoke. "I can't wait to see what appears tomorrow. I just hope that I'm in a position to know about it."

Claira was confused by the woman's last statement and asked, "What do you mean by that?"

"You hear all kind of things when you work at a hospital. I hear that the mayor's office is freaking out about it. That they're already starting to cover up the wall paintings. Just think, if I hadn't been here to see the poem on the train board, who knows?" She shrugged her shoulders, then glanced around the concourse, as if suspicious of being under surveillance. She continued in a voice just above a whisper, and said, "This stuff may have been going on for a while, and it's been covered up."

Claira leaned in a little closer to her and asked, "Who do you think is doing this?"

The woman shook her head, as if not sure if she could trust Claira. After a moment of carefully evaluating Claira, from her face down to the leather shoes on her feet, the woman relented. "I think that it's the hybrids," she whispered.

Claira was stunned by that answer, and for a moment, speechless. "What does that mean?" she finally managed. "Do you mean aliens?"

Now the woman in scrubs recoiled a bit and asked, "Aliens? Are you crazy?"

"But you said hybrids, didn't you? What does that mean?"

"It's that underground group that is both very religious and very tech savvy. They are genius level scientists who now answer to a higher calling."

"I never heard of them."

"They're like gothic, but new age. Their base is supposed to be a secret, but I googled them and read that they're running everything out of a closed up monastery in Nova Scotia."

Claira suppressed a smile, seeing that the woman addressing her was serious, almost reverent. "I must have missed that in the news. Where did you read it?"

"Either Facebook or Drudge Report, I can't remember. Listen, if I were you, I'd pull out your phone and take a picture of the poem when it scrolls across the screen again. That way when Big Brother denies that this ever happened, you at least have something to go to." With that, the woman in scrubs disappeared into the crowd.

Even though Claira dismissed most of what the woman said, the suggestion that Claira photograph the monitor with the poem on it was a good one. Claira watched as the poem stanzas appeared on the board, one after the offer, and snapped a photo of each. She then hurried through the crowd that was growing around that end of the terminal, and went out of the station to 42nd Street. She glanced at her watch and saw that if she could catch a cab quickly, she would be just a few minutes late for her meeting at the Conservancy's office.

***

Cissy arrived at the hospital mid-morning. With school out for the Christmas holidays, the family's weekday routine was upset. Her husband was taking a few extra vacation days, but this morning he went to his office. He worked for a start-up computer network company called DTG, the acronym for Digital Thought & Graphics, Inc., and while he could get away with working from home for some tasks, he had a few responsibilities which he could not perform remotely and which could not be easily delayed. A neighbor stayed with the children while Cissy went to the hospital.

Cap was in a waiting room by the elevator when Cissy arrived. He looked up from an old *Sports Illustrated* as she entered the small but nearly empty room. "The nurse is in with Mom," he told Cissy as she sat in e chair next to him. "Getting a sponge bath and fresh linens."

"How was the night?"

"She was up and down a few times. She slept better. I think that she's getting a little stronger. She hardly speaks. You have to prompt her for everything." Cap pushed his rough hand through his hair, trying to rid himself of a robe of exhaustion and frustration. He pulled a cough drop out of a shirt pocket, and let it fall into his mouth. "Doc hasn't been by yet."

"That's good. I want to ask him a few questions," Cissy reached for Cap's hand and gave it a squeeze. "The priest will be here early afternoon. I have a sitter at the house, so I will be able to stay until he visits Mom."

Cap nodded. "I'm not going back on my word, if that's what you're worried about. But you need to consider what kind of message this sends to Mom. I know if it was me in a hospital and a priest showed up to say the last rites, that's a pretty strong hint that the lights are about to go out. How would you like to have that after lunch?"

Cissy bit her lip in a vain effort to steel her composure. Despite her resolve, her eyes puddled with tears. "Cap, there's no right way or wrong way to do any of this. If I had a set of instructions to follow, don't you think I would? I'm flying blind here, just like you."

"That's not what I'm getting at. Hell, I'm sorry I even brought it up. But you wanted me to talk to you, to be honest with you, so there it is." Cap rubbed his brow, exhaustion and disorientation gripping him a little tighter each day. Without raising his head to look at his sister, he said, "Am I right or wrong? Are you? Maybe like you said, there's no right or wrong. There's just different degrees of poor outcomes, and what we do to prolong the glide path down to a hard landing."

Cissy was wiping her reddened eyes with a tissue, but nodding in agreement. "I know. It's not you, it's the situation. It's just a shitty deal. But what's missing from everything that we've said here for the last ten minutes?"

Cap looked at her puzzled, then finally nodded his head. "What does Mom want?"

Cissy's lips quivered, and she nodded in agreement. "What does she want? What choices would she make?"

Cap stared straight ahead, as if watching a battle between ghosts that only he could see. "Then we need to ask her, when she's up for that talk. But until then, nothing else changes. Your priest can see her this afternoon, and you need to get checked and tested for matching, just like I did. Just check in with the nurse's station, and they will get the samples they need to run the test."

Cissy stood and removed her coat. She was wearing a black turtle neck sweater and blue jeans. "You're serious about this?"

"Absolutely. I already had the tests done and I'm a poor match. The doctor told me that siblings have the best match percentages, but all of Mom's brothers and sisters are gone. Children are the next best bet."

"But Cap, Mom is not a good candidate for any more chemotherapy. She's not strong enough. Her body's too weak."

Cap stood and starting pacing the small waiting room, but did his best at keeping his voice low. "That may be true today. But if she gets better, then maybe she can have the treatments. All you have to do is give a blood sample and a little swab from the back of your month."

"I'll do it; I didn't say that I'm backing out of the tests. It's just I don't see Mom coping with any aggressive therapies."

"Her best shot to beat the leukemia is chemo and a bone marrow transplant. All the doctors agree on that. So if she gets this congestive heart issue under control, we need to be ready to get her treatments. Old Stu Waterberg back home has had congestive heart failure for a decade. He's still kicking. Same with the leukemia. With a bone marrow transplant she can go into remission. Mom has a legitimate shot to gain a few more years. That's 2 or 3 more grandkids' birthdays, the same number of Christmas holidays, the same number of summer fishing rodeos."

Cissy hung her head, as if too weak to hold herself erect and broad-shouldered. Without looking back at Cap, she said, "Stu Waterberg is a good fifteen years younger than Mom, and without all of her complications. But you're right, if she has a fighting chance to see a couple more years, then I'm down with that. But I'm afraid she going to spend her last weeks or months here in this hospital fighting in vain. I just don't want to see her suffer."

"Neither do I. But I don't want to give up while there's a chance, either." Cap looked at his watch, then continued. "If we can, Cis. If she can." He put his arm around his sister's shoulder and led her down the hall. "The nurse should be about done now. Let's go see how she's doing."

***

When Darragh walked in Isla's shop, he carried a bundle of six white roses and Starbucks 'tall' sized paper coffee cup. He bounced up to Isla's counter, as she glared at him, aghast.

"Really? You're bringing Starbucks into my coffee shop," she said, clearly not amused.

Darragh's smile disappeared momentarily, but he responded within another heartbeat. "This old cup? It was lying on the sidewalk outside your door, so I picked it up to toss away. But I did bring you a token of my appreciation for putting up with me yesterday, listening to my ramblings and nonsense." He held out the roses, and let his other hand, the one with the coffee cup, slide almost completely behind his back.

Isla eyed him suspiciously, but accepted the flowers and sampled their fragrance. As she turned to the counter to place the roses, Darragh quickly took another sip from the Starbucks cup. But not quickly enough.

"Darragh! You scoundrel. Give me that cup. I have a good mind to shoo you right out of here and back onto the street."

"I didn't want to waste the last bit of it. It's a butterscotch cappuccino."

"I can make that here, thank you." She grabbed the Starbucks cup out of his hand and tossed it into a trash bin. "If I ever —"

"Oh, it was just a bad joke, Duchess. No chain store can craft a beverage any better than you, and rightly so. So forgive an old foreigner for his dry and crude wit and show me to your loo. I'll empty out and be ready for a cup or two of your right dandy brew."

Without a word, she pointed to the restrooms across the store, with the roses still in her hand.

***

When Darragh returned to the counter, a mug of coffee was waiting for him. The roses were on the back counter, in a ginger jar vase, colored in swirls of spearmint green and the white of pillow clouds. He sat at the counter and sampled the coffee. "Just black?"

"Black as your soul," Isla said as she slowly placed a small pitcher of cream before him. "Sugar?"

"Oh, I think that just cream will do nicely. All of these cappuccinos have spoiled me on black coffee."

"Let's pick up where we left off yesterday," Isla said. "I have to say, when you left, I read that poem that you gave me. I was captured in those words. How did you do that? Did you really write that on the spot? Was that just for me, or was that something that you had in your library in that strange mind of yours?" She tapped her temple as she asked that last question.

Darragh placed the cup on its saucer. "Those words had never been written or read before yesterday. And I could not have written that poem without you, to be honest."

"What do you mean?"

"That poem is yours. I offer it to no one else. It is only a reflection of what I saw yesterday, what I saw about you, and in you."

"So you didn't have those words already lined up, some of those verses already worked out?"

"Truly, no."

"How could you come up with that so fast, while I was sitting there watching?"

Darragh shrugged. "I don't know how to explain things that I don't really understand myself. All I can tell you is that sometimes I can just see things. It's like I can take a mental picture of you, but what comes back is words rather than a still image. Yesterday, when you were talking to me, when you started sharing your secrets, I could see so much of you. How could I not give you those words? You gave those images to me."

Isla stared at him, wanting more of an answer. But Darragh only returned to his coffee, sipping, and adding cream almost after every sip. She shook her head, almost imperceptibly, as if debating with herself yet again. "What now?" she asked, at peace with his answer even if not fully convinced.

"What is the name of your church, the one we walked by yesterday?"

"St. Ann's."

"How active are you there? With other parishioners?"

"What do you mean?"

"Well, back home we have the Order of the Daughter of the King, and the Guild of all Souls, where the women of the church band together for ministries, or to pray for the dying, what have you. Any such things here?"

Isla thought for a moment, the answered, "I haven't heard of either of the groups you just mentioned. But of course St. Ann's has a chapter of the Catholic Daughters, and an Altar Society. If that is what you mean."

"Are you in those groups? Do you belong?"

Isla laughed, but from embarrassment. "Look, I'm not as devout as I once was, and never as devout as my mother. But she was a member of both at the church, and so was I. So I guess that I'm on the roll there somewhere, though I don't go to all the meetings. More like I help out the annual bazaar, or at the Christmas programs."

"That will do. Do you think that I could talk to your ladies?"

Isla was shocked by the request. "What do you mean? Like soon?"

"Today or early tonight if at all possible."

"I don't think that will work. That is moving a little too fast. And what are you going to tell them?"

"That something wonderful is going to happen. Or maybe that it isn't unless they can help. I'm going to tell them what I told you. About the ripples on the pond."

"Ripples on the pond," Isla repeated, not encouraged or convinced.

"Yes," Darragh said as he rose from his seat. "All about the ripples on the pond."

Chapter Eleven

Claira was the last to arrive at the Park Conservancy Office, getting there almost fifteen minutes late. She did not realize how much time she had spent at the Terminal, mesmerized by the mechanical board alternating between regular train schedules and the stanzas of the poem, rhymes that appeared and disappeared in tremors, as if an unseen hand wiped away one bumpy tile vision of reality for another. She had been able to hail a taxi easily, but the driver warned her that it would be a slow drive to the Conservancy office. Traffic had been thick and crawling, but she elected to not to call and tell Terrance Greenberg that she was slightly behind schedule. She was not thinking of protocol, or even simple courtesy. She was thinking about a world that was suddenly much bigger than she had previously considered, a world that she could no longer easily explain and certainly, recently, a world that she did not begin to understand. A world, she feared, that was no longer content to remain unseen.

When she arrived at the Conservancy office, she was ushered directly into the large conference room off the antechamber that once had been her office. A year ago she moved to a small office upstairs, next to a pool office of four support staff personnel. At the time, the move did not matter to her because she spent days at a time in the field, and with her tablet and smart phone, she could office remotely with little or no inefficiency. But recently, really during the holiday season, she began to miss her old office, and the sense of refuge that it gave her. Her new office was open, with a glass wall, albeit with hanging shutters, separating her from the pool office of four desks, and all of the noise and commotion that came with four busy work stations. Now that antechamber that had been her office was simply a map room, with large maps and aerial photographs of the park mounted on the walls, and several tables which held scale models of the park, in varying degrees of detail. The walls were still the same color that she chose when the room was hers, Caledon Spring, but its simple beauty was overwhelmed by the size of the frames and prints covering the walls, as if the walls themselves were irrelevant. She did not know why, but the room now saddened her, despite its impressive displays and renderings of the place that became her career.

When she entered the conference room, Mike Sandoval alone rose to greet her. The older man next to him started to rise, but had a pained expression on his face, as if his knees or hips protested the move. She purposely made eye contact with them as she scanned the people seated at the table, to acknowledge their gesture. Two gentlemen in the bunch, Mike, and the old man next to him.

Terrance Greenberg was seated at the head of the large conference table, who in an exaggerated display of annoyance, looked at his wrist watch, a Jaeger-LeCoultre Gyrotourbillion, easily more expensive than a Ferrari, and said, "So good of you to join us, Ms. Vasson, though tardy as you are."

Claira couldn't help but redden a little, even though she expected Terrance to be rude. Being condescending allowed Terrance to project his importance, and diminish, even if slightly, the stature of the recipient of his rebuke. "I'm so sorry to keep everyone waiting. The train station was particularly crowded this morning," she said in apology as she removed her coat. She had already decided not to say anything about poem that flashed intermittently across the display board, at least not unless specifically asked.

"I want to get started straight away, but I suppose introductions are in order." Terrance sat close to the table, so that his hands rested easily on its top. He slowly directed his gaze across all of the faces around him, smiling. "As you all know, I am Terrance Greenberg, and proudly serve as the Director of the Central Park Conservancy. My assistant director, Claira Vasson, you now know from her dramatic entrance. To my left here is Peggy Lipton, my executive secretary, who will take minutes of this meeting. Copies will be available to those who would like. Let's go around the table so we can move on to the substance of the meeting."

The conference table was large enough to comfortably allow five high-back leather chairs along the length of each of its sides. The tabletop was cherry wood, light and red- hinted. The top was covered with a sectioned glass sheet, and was adorned with shallow bowls holding note pads, pens and post-it notes. A credenza of the same cherry wood stood against one wall, on which stood a coffee service, ice bucket, glasses and an assortment of soft drinks on a set of silver trays. On the opposite wall several armchairs were positioned around small end-tables on which rested tall, rustic gold colored table-lamps. The walls were heavy wood panels, stained slightly darker than the conference table, and the color pulled out similar hints from the room's slate floor. Several vintage tapestries of medieval gardens and castles hung on the walls. Claira often wondered how much money those pieces had cost, and guessed that the price was surely more than her annual salary.

Before anyone spoke, Claira made her way to the side of the table where only two other people were seated. Across from her all five seats were taken. She picked a chair four down from the head of the table where Terrance sat, and which put an empty chair to her left and right.

"Peggy, let's start with you." Terrance said, pulling Claira's focus back to the people seated around the conference room table. "Would you break the ice, so to speak?"

Peggy blushed, surprised to have any opportunity to speak at all in this meeting. Awkwardly, she said, "Yes. As Mr. Greenberg said, I am Peggy Lipton, Mr. Greenberg's executive secretary."

The man next to her was in his early thirties, and dressed in a dark blue pin-striped suit, with a French-cut, starched white shirt and a blue and red striped tie. His hairline was receding, but what was left was short and combed to stand spiked. Leaning back slightly in his chair, he said, "Kevin Palanti, Special Advisor to the Office of the Mayor. He apologizes for his absence, but had no time to re-arrange his schedule given the haste in which this meeting was called." He reached into his coat pocket and retrieved a gold card-case, and removed several of his business cards. He handed a few to the woman next to him and asked, "Would you please pass these on?"

Next to him was a middle aged woman, sharply dressed, with understated silver earrings and a thin silver rope necklace. Her dark hair was pulled tightly back into a small bun, and her make-up was delicate but intricate in color and degree. "Janet Olsen, Public Relations, also with the Office of the Mayor." After speaking, she handed the business cards to the gentleman next to her, without offering any cards of her own.

Claira drew in her notebook a crude rectangle representing the table, noting the name of each person and an identifying phrase as they spoke, along with their station at the table. As she jotted down Janet's name, she thought *P.R., that I could have guessed.*

The gentleman next to Janet was an African American, older than anyone else in the room. He wore a blue blazer, shirt and tie, but the top button of the shirt was undone, and the tie loosened around his neck. He had a pencil tucked atop his right ear, and his glasses fell slightly down his nose. "H. T. Washington, City Planning and Permits." After he introduced himself, he looked over to his left, as if passing the baton to the next in line. The few remaining cards of Kevin Palanti were gently tossed to the center of the table.

Mike Sandoval was seated next to H. T. Washington, but before he could speak, the man seated at the end of the table, across from Terrance Greenberg, spoke for him. "Good morning. I am Jason Dumbarton, *New York Times*, and with me is one of my senior editors, Mike Sandoval." Jason spoke hurriedly, as if he considered the introductions to be a colossal waste of time.

Claira quickly wrote their names on her notepad, then said. "Yes, good morning. As Mr. Greenberg said, I'm Claira Vasson, his Assistant Director of the Park. And again, I would like to apologize for getting us all started a little late. Thank you all for coming."

The chair next to her was empty, and the seat next to it was occupied by a young woman typing notes on a laptop computer. She wore a light colored suit, with a peach colored blouse, and her eyes were shadowed with too much liner and make-up. Without pausing, she introduced herself. "Celeste Buck, City Attorney's Office."

The last person seated at the table was dressed in a police uniform but clearly was not a patrolman. His rank was on display on his sleeves. Claira recognized him, and wrote his name on her notepad before he spoke.

"Steven Lombard, Chief of Police."

Claira nodded, and underlined his name.

"Well, now that we all know one another, I suggest we start in earnest," Terrance said from his place at the head of the table. Then, without turning his gaze from Claira, he added, "Ms. Lipton, would you be so kind to bring me a cup of that wonderfully aromatic coffee. You know how I like my second cup." He waited until his secretary rose from her seat, then added, "Thank you." Claira noticed that Terrance offered no one else coffee, which did not surprise her, as he thought of himself first and foremost. Even when well intentioned, his manners would sometimes not overcome his self-indulgence.

Claira could feel all of the stares in the room lock onto her, as if such a thing as visual interrogation existed. She turned a few pages in her notebook until she found her outline, then began. "Here is what we know. At some time shortly after dawn on Christmas morning, Park Police reported the existence of a small stone chapel on the great lawn. At first they thought it was something we originated, and were really just complaining about not being told of our plans. The building is about 18' by 30' in size. Its exterior walls are stone. Heavy wood beam frame. It has seven stained glass windows, three to a side, and a single stained glass window above the altar space of the church. Two doorways, with the rear door being much smaller and without a stone-laid landing. There is a very small loft, accessible by ladder. As for contents, a few rows of rough wooden benches, or pews if you like, and a simple table in the front of the church that could serve as its altar. There are candles spread about. No utilities connected." She paused and set her pen on her notepad, and carefully looked at those seated around her. "This structure was not on Park property on December 24th. I called park police at 8 a.m. this morning, and as of that time, the chapel was still there on the Great Lawn."

"Terrance," Jason said, "We want to carefully consider all of the possibilities that could explain the construction of this little church overnight, if that is indeed what occurred. Obviously, we have to vet each and every fact, each and every source, before we print any details about this, this unusual situation. Do we have your assurance that this is not a publicity stunt, a seasonal attraction? That this is not a park project kept under wraps for some type of surprise appeal for the holiday?"

Terrance shook his head, and seemed insulted that the question was even asked. "This is categorically not an authorized facility. I had no knowledge of this, and I assure you the Board had none either. Claira, do you have any comment?"

Claira turned to her right to look directly at Jason. "I can verify that this was not done with Park oversight or even tacit consent. I have direct supervision of our physical plants assets, new construction, and maintenance. I would know if the Conservancy had this structure built. We certainly did not. And Mr. Greenberg would know if any budgeted funds were used for this construction. The Conservancy did not pay for this."

Jason seemed to smile with that answer, but kept probing. Turning his attention to Mr. Washington, he asked, "What does City Planning say?"

H. T. Franklin pointed to Claira and said, "I have to agree with Ms. Vasson. Our office has no record of any license, permit, or even an application for the construction of this church building on park property. There is no paperwork on file that would identify the contractor, any bonding company, or anyone on the design team, meaning architect or engineer."

Jason glanced at Mike, and nodded in agreement. "We had one of our investigative journalists run the records. He couldn't find anything on this chapel in any city or county office."

"So what does that mean?" Terrance asked. "That we have no responsibility for this construction?"

Jason shrugged his shoulders, and answered, "I have my own opinions about that, but since we have legal counsel representing the City, I would like to hear her opinion."

Celeste Buck stopped typing on her lap-top, and slowly slid it further onto the table. She slowly scanned the room, making eye contact with all present before she spoke. "Obviously, we do not have all of the facts, so my comments are only preliminary. And I would point out that my office is not providing legal counsel to the Park Conservancy, and that you should not infer any attorney client relationship by my presence at this meeting." She turned to Terrance Greenberg, letting that last point register with the Park Conservancy Director. Satisfied that she had prefaced her comments with the appropriate disclaimers, she continued, "With that said, several points. One, whoever constructed this building is guilty of criminal trespass, criminal mischief, and several other possible offenses. There is also civil liability for damage to public property. Two, the building itself is an unauthorized encroachment on public property. If the City, or in this case, the Park Conservancy, has knowledge of the person or persons responsible for the building's construction, notice should be given to cease and desist this adverse occupancy, remove the construction, and remediate and restore the grounds to its former condition."

Terrance gestured to Claira as he spoke, "We have established, I think, that the Conservancy had no involvement with this at all. You heard Ms. Vasson's statement, did you not?"

"Yes, I understand that," Celeste said calmly. "I was simply setting forth the notice procedure for civil forfeiture if notice is possible. Otherwise, the law provides for a notice of trespass to be displayed on the building itself, along with a notice of writ of forfeiture."

"Does that mean that the building would become property of the Conservancy?" Terrance asked."

"Ultimately, yes. There is still a forfeiture proceeding that has to be conducted before an assigned judge, but it is a summary proceeding and fairly straight-forward. There is already a presumption that buildings or other improvements constructed on real estate become component parts of that property, and without a filed declaration of separate ownership, are owned by the owner of the land."

Terrance turned to H. T. Washington. "Are you aware of any such filing? This declaration of separate estate or separate ownership."

"No Sir. I can verify that as of close of business yesterday, no such declaration was filed of record."

"Well then," Terrance said, as he took a sip of coffee. "What other legal issues need we worry about?"

Celeste Buck reached over and closed her laptop computer. "As I said, these are only preliminary opinions. I would of course like to discuss this matter in detail with your attorney, after more facts are determined."

"Yes, yes, that can be arranged easily. Please continue."

Celeste nodded her head slightly in agreement, then said, "It's possible that claims may be asserted against the Conservancy for the costs of construction if any contractors, sub's, or materialmen are unpaid. Any claim for recovery of such costs associated with the construction of the building would be difficult to collect from the Park Conservancy. But that would not pretermit a filing of a claim. Neither the City nor the Conservancy has privity of contract with any architect, contractor, materialman or laborer, so collection claims would be difficult. Without a filed bond securing payment, the construction project itself would not have been covered by a public works bond. As you know, public property, meaning in this case, park property, is exempt from lien or seizure. Even a claim under a theory of unjust enrichment would be problematic, under the limited facts that we know."

"Anything else?"

"If the forfeiture of the structure in favor of the Conservancy is completed, then you obviously have to insure the improvement, for both general liability and property loss. The building would need to be inspected, would need Fire Marshall audit and approval, there are a myriad of ADA compliance issues, also state and local versions of the ADA."

Kevin Palanti interrupted, "What is the ADA? I know I've of heard of it."

"Americans with Disabilities Act," Celeste answered.

"It's the handicap access rules we need to comply with," Claira explained. "We've been working every year to make sure we are compliant. Ramps, wheelchair accessible restrooms where possible, that type of thing."

Steve Lombard twirled his officer cap in his hand, then set it on the table. "I appreciate all of this information. Fascinating. But I have a simple question. How in the hell was this damn thing built anyway? Who was asleep at the switch? I mean, does anyone seriously think that this sprouted and grew overnight, like Jack's magic beanstalk?"

Everyone turned to look at Claira for a response. Predictably, Terrance echoed the same concern. "Yes, Claira, how do you think this was even accomplished? How did no one on your staff see this underway?"

The tone used by the Conservancy Director was ominous, because it demonstrated that Terrance was isolating Claira, and insulating himself from any direct criticism. She knew that she had to carefully present the limited facts that she knew and answer questions candidly, but also that she could be walking a narrow plank with Terrance prodding her forward with a sword at her back.

Claira picked up her notebook and turned a page, not to anything in particular, but to give her a moment to compose her words. "We are looking at the chapel in detail, to see its construction means and methods. It does not appear to be a prefabrication, like some type of kit, but we are still vetting that. We are investigating whether the building could have been delivered on a skid, as a modular unit, then finished on site with pre-constructed roof panels, that sort of thing. We are looking at every lead that we have, chasing down every conceivable theory."

"Terrance," Jason said. "If I may."

"Certainly, Mr. Dumbarton. Please."

Jason shifted his weight in his seat, then continued. "The exercise of how this stunt was accomplished can be dealt with later. And that is important, so you can take steps to prevent this type of practical joke from happening again. But to gain control of this situation, and to establish credibility, I think that there is only one clear choice of action to take."

"Which is?" Claira asked, already fearful that she knew his answer.

"You must remove it immediately. Demo it down if you have to, but it has to go."

Claira exhaled, but fought to keep her composure. She was not sure why, but this man who ran the *New York Times* as his own, private enterprise was clearly driving to one end, being the destruction of the chapel. She likened it to a rush to cremate the body of some reclusive movie star, before toxicology tests or an autopsy could uncover inconvenient truths about the person and the unexplained demise. Better to have unanswered questions to ponder and debate, rather than embarrassing details to explain or justify.

Jason surveyed the room, paying particular attention to the mayor's representatives, Kevin Palanti, and more particularly the public relations officer, Janet Olsen. Both appeared anxious, aware that this was a highly unusual situation, and that public reaction to it would be completely unpredictable. And more importantly, both also sensed that a tipping point was close on the horizon, it only being a matter of time before answers would be demanded. This was his opportunity to leverage the moment, and start a line of dominos cascading to a final fall that would suit his interests. "Think this through with me," Jason began. "What kind of precedent is being set if the building is allowed to stand? Does it signal that any other group, or a person, can stake out a corner of the park and erect something, like a log cabin, a lean-to, an altar, whatever, and the Park is open season for it? It would be like the California land rush.

"Second, how provocative, how contentious, is it to have a church or a Christian chapel on public park grounds? What about separation of church and state? What about equal protection? Are you going to have a synagogue or a mosque on the other side of the pond? What's going to be on the East Meadow? Maybe a Buddhist temple. And what do you say to the secular public? You know some will be offended by such religious constructs. Some always are."

Kevin listened intently, considering that the political fall-out of the chapel could be manipulated by the reporting of the events. It was obvious to him that Jason had already staked out a position, and that the *Times* would not be neutral, but rather result-oriented in its writing and reporting. After a moment more of thought he asked, "Seems like every year The Catholic League gets a permit from the City Parks Department to set up a nativity scene on park property. How does that affect this discussion?"

Jason held back a subtle smile. This conversation was proceeding just as he had anticipated. He waited for Terrance to speak, and when the old man remained silent, he jumped in. "What does legal say about that?" he asked with faux curiosity.

"Apples and oranges," Celeste responded. "The nativity scene is short duration, and must be accompanied by a prominent sign identifying the sponsor of the display. It is clearly temporary, even though a life-sized crèche. Second, other groups can file for a permit for a temporary holiday display. That also happens every year. And despite these distinguishing factors, every year the ACLU or the Freedom from Religion Foundation, or some similar group, seeks a federal court injunction prohibiting the nativity scene, or a court order mandating its immediate removal. Something like this chapel, with no identified sponsor, with no approved application, and which does not appear to be an easily removable display, will certainly provoke litigation. Probably successful litigation, and undoubtedly expensive for all involved."

Claira waited to see if anyone else would object, but no one said anything. She looked to the head of the table, to Terrance Greenberg, who sat back in his chair holding on his coffee cup with both hands, as if relishing a final, bitter sip. She turned back to Jason Dumbarton and said, "I don't think that we should rush to a decision to bulldoze something like this. It's is too unique. And not just the chapel building, but its circumstances. It's like a gift to the Park, and to the public at large. There's nothing ominous about it. Nothing threatening."

She glanced back at Terrance, looking for some level of support. But none was forthcoming. He stared blankly straight ahead, as if denying her presence. She reluctantly continued, knowing that her credibility, and possibly her career, were in jeopardy. "Yesterday the chapel was inspected by a professor from NYU. He is an expert in religious art, and probably has been in more churches all over the world than anyone in Manhattan. He was greatly surprised by the historical accuracy of the things that he found, the age and the detail of the stained glass, even the simple design of the chapel. There is a primacy here, a very prodigious narrative that should be embraced. At a minimum, it should be researched, studied before it is wiped away like chalk drawings on the sidewalk."

"Is that the Professor's conclusion, or yours?" Jason asked.

Claira swallowed involuntarily, and forced herself to take a breath. She was on the verge of losing her temper. As if by reflex, she thought back to the last argument she had with Theo, while he was still her husband. She lost her temper that day, and with its sudden rage, she also lost all of the trust built up over the years of their courtship and marriage. She fought to focus again on the meeting at hand, and the antagonist sitting across from her. Staring at Jason, she said, "He has not rendered any conclusions yet, he wholeheartedly thinks that this chapel deserves a lot more study. And I totally agree."

"Can you tell us the name of the professor?" Janet Olsen asked. "If the mayor is going to release a statement, we would want to hear directly from him before doing so."

Claira did not want to give up Abner's identity just yet. "I will get back with you on that. I think that he is consulting some others with expertise in this area."

Jason laughed loudly, and slapped both of his hands hard against the table. "Could you be playing for more time, to cover your department's ineptitude in not finding this church while it was being constructed, in not knowing what was happening right under your noses?" Jason's tone was sour, accusatory. He looked around the room, waving his hands in gestures of frustration. "I mean, let's deal with what we know. This thing should not be where it is. It's unauthorized. It's a trespass. It's a provocation. It's offensive to probably over a million of the people on this island, not to mention that it is probably an unconstitutional act even if only one citizen perceives it to be state sponsored religion. It's a liability, in more than a few ways. The City Attorney has outlined a host of legal problems that it causes, and that's only her preliminary views based on a scarce few facts that you have been able to gather. The only counterpoint that you make is that 'we don't know.' " He paused, letting the juxtaposition he suggested develop in the minds of his audience. "Seems to me that facts and reason support my position, while ignorance and fantasy support yours."

***

Mike sat across from Jason during the limousine ride back to the *Times* offices. He said little during the meeting at the Conservancy, but was not as constrained when alone with Jason. "You were a little over the top with that Assistant Director. I half expected her to come across the table and blacken your eye."

Jason smiled smugly and laughed. "I'm sure that you would've had my back." He closed his eyes and seemed to drift in thought. Finally, he looked back at Mike and said, "The little pre-meeting I had with Terrance Greenberg worked perfectly."

"What pre-meeting? I rode with you this morning. When did you have a chance to meet with Terrance?"

"I was on the phone with him, late last night and again this morning. I was able to explain to him what the *Times* can do, for the Conservancy, and what I may be able to do for him, personally. This unusual set of events sets up nicely for us."

Mike shook his head. "I'm not following you."

"Whoever infiltrated our firewalls and hijacked our server, overrode our system and commandeered our page one is using a sophisticated technology to overwrite our program and exit without a trace. I've had a friend with some military ties do some investigating, and there is a rumor about a radical development in computer technology. You've heard the term 'quantum computer.' There are a few top secret research groups out there working on quantum computing. It's mostly theoretical, but there a buzz about some real advances. It's called MQS."

"Never heard of it."

"Not many people have. It stands for Magnetic Quantum Saturation. I don't understand much of it, but if it is real, if someone has that technology operational, then it could explain what happened to us. It might explain the wall murals too."

Mike was skeptical. "Is that why you haven't made a criminal referral yet? You're pushing an angle through some of your connections?"

"Something like that," Jason managed to say, smiling, as if Mike had just given him a compliment.

Mike knew better to push that subject. Jason's unusual background was hardly a secret at the *Times*, but the names of friends and connections from his past remained mostly in the shadows. But Mike had other questions that he felt that he could ask. Even though his head pounded from too much drink and too little sleep, he continued, "What does that MQS stuff have to do with Central Park?"

"Just a hunch, a guess. Did you notice that our Ms. Vasson was late this morning, and that she said she was delayed at Grand Central?"

"Yea. So what? She was only fifteen minutes or so late."

"You didn't check your phone before the meeting. There was another poem sighting this morning. Care to guess where?"

Mike considered the question. "Grand Central Station."

"That's right. Grand Central. A new poem, this time at the station in the middle of rush hour. If you wanted to make a splash, Grand Central Station at rush hour would do it. Somehow, the old mechanical display board was hijacked, and a poem was broadcast, alternating with the damn train schedule, on the mechanical schedule board. Funny thing that Ms. Vasson did not say anything about it, don't you think?"

"She could have missed it. Maybe she didn't see it."

"Maybe, but I'm not giving her the benefit of the doubt. We had a poem on our page one. We ran a piece about the wall-scapes in the paper today. It's been all over television. I think that she saw something at Grand Central and just didn't want to say anything."

"But how does that connect to the Park?"

"Maybe it doesn't. Maybe it means nothing at all. But it got me thinking. If there is any chance of a connection between these poems and this new mystery chapel at the park, then I want to own that connection. Now that the computer that runs the board at the train station was hacked, that shows that it is someone outside our operation responsible for the poems. It shows that this was not just an inside job at the paper. It also fits with the MQS tech I'm hearing rumors about. These kind of breaches would not be out of reach if the MQS applications are as next generation as I've been told."

Mike shrugged, biting his lip in concentration, trying to follow Jason's logic. "How does Terrance Greenberg fit in to all of this?"

"Just a tangent. He doesn't want to embarrassed. If we can help him with that, he'll cooperate. Also, if there is some new technology that we can leverage, he wants to be in on the ground floor. Personally." Jason emphasized that last point. "Lots of money to be made. All we have to do is plot the right course, fine tune the way this is all reported, and maybe not disclose all that we learn about MQS."

Mike grimaced at the answer. It always seems to come down to money. Terrance Greenberg was already rich, but like most wealthy people, it seems that more is never too much. The same applied to Jason. Then he thought about the young woman, who seemed to have no idea how to respond to the threat of demolishing the chapel. He considered her plight, then asked, "But this Claira Vasson, I'm sure that she doesn't have a clue about what's happening. Why did you come down so tough on her? The way Mr. Greenberg hung her out to dry, hell, she might lose her job."

"I don't care one way or the other. And I don't care about the chapel either. Whether it's demolished or not. If it's still standing this time next year, I'll renew my weddings vows there for my next anniversary. If it isn't then I'll piss on that spot at midnight." Jason pulled his phone from his coat pocket, just to check the time. Then he continued, "I just wanted to push the issue, because if there is any connection between that chapel and whoever is responsible for these poems popping up all over town, I want that smoked out."

"I get that," Mike answered. "I think that there is a connection. I'm just not sure that you have to leave such a wide path of destruction in your efforts to connect the dots."

Jason exhaled deeply, then shrugged his shoulders. "If that happens, it happens." Then he reached over and flipped the intercom switch to talk to the driver of the car. "Hey, Scotty, let's take a detour. Swing us by Central Park. Go to the 79th street entrance." He turned off the intercom, then smiled as he said to Mike, "Let's go see what all the fuss is about."

***

While Jason and Mike rode to the park, Claira sat across from Terrance Greenberg, who was behind his desk opening the morning mail with a turquoise handled letter opener. She was livid. "What's was all of that about, Terrance? You left me out to there to drown. You used to have my back when I went out on a limb for the Park."

Terrance looked up from his envelopes and said, "Calm down, Claira. There is no cause for worry. Your position is safe as long as I'm here."

"Then why did you let that asshole from the *Times* attack me on everything that I said?"

Terrance smiled, but Claira was not reassured. She had never been close personally with Terrance, but he hired her after her internship and nurtured her career, eventually picking her to be the de facto director of the Conservancy. But this morning, she felt abandoned, and his weak smile seemed simply worn, rather than sincere. He opened the center desk drawer and placed the letter opener inside. After neatly stacking the opened envelopes, he said. "Claira, that was all for show. I will make sure that you will not be mentioned in any negative way in any reporting. I'm sure that the mayor will be calling me at some point today or tomorrow, and all will be explained. You have nothing to worry about."

Claira bit her lip as a coping mechanism to keep her composure. She wanted to believe Terrance, but something deep inside her mind made her doubt his reassurances. Finally, she put those thoughts aside, and asked, "What about the chapel? You are not going to let it be destroyed, are you?"

Terrance's smile diminished, as if he had, for the first time in his life, been asked about some secret, pungent infidelity. "You heard what that city attorney said. That chapel is a festering problem, and it's best to excise it quickly and discreetly."

"But we shouldn't rush to get rid of it. "We should —"

"No need to concern yourself with this any further. We'll see what happens. Now that you know your place is secure with me, I have other appointments to attend."

Claira rose from her seat and headed for the door. But before she opened it, Terrance called out to her. "And, Claira, I trust that you will apprise me of any developments concerning our quaint little chapel."

Without turning to respond, she said, "Yes, sir. I will make sure you know what I know." With that she opened the door and left Terrance grinning as he sat at his desk.

Chapter Twelve

Jason and Mike walked toward a small but growing crowd. Neither had spoken since the chauffer dropped them off at the Park entrance. Jason was occupied on his smart phone, scrolling through both email and texts, and the images that the messages created, while Mike looked inward, where a long and growing list of unread messages awaited, a queue of thoughts unspoken, itineraries for trips never taken. And it wasn't that Mike simply ignored the backlog, rather, he was keenly aware of the burdens that awaited his attention. He simply could not engage either of the binary choices of the flight or fight response embedded in his primal, subconscious, nervous system. Rather, he was paralyzed, frozen, as if standing in front of an opening refrigerator, starving, but unable to choose anything to eat. Simply put, he feared the trials that the days ahead would present to him, and doubted his ability to tolerate the pain.

Mike was a few steps ahead of Jason, and he did not bother to slow his pace or wait for Jason to catch up to him. He needed the time to reflect on the bizarre meeting they had just left, where the decision was apparently made to destroy a small church that no one could explain and no one seemed to claim. A few minutes of solitude, if such was possible in a public park in New York City, was welcome.

For Mike, it felt refreshing to walk in the Park on a winter day. The sky was clear and clean, a blank blue canvas. The cold breeze was erratic, carved and broken by the concrete canyons of the city buildings, but welcome, as something unmade by man, something pure in the heart of the tall city of concrete, steel and glass. The season was not deterred by the city, just as it chilled the Montana prairie, it so marked the buildings of man. But here the winter moved across a space that felt overused, that was worn and blemished. Mike imagined a mountain range where nature prevailed, a forest vast, but kept like a garden, kept for eyes that would appreciate the green and growing things that lived in simplicity, knowing only the morning, the day, and the twilight. As simple, he thought, as life and death. Simple, but foreign and unforgiving, and as humbling as the cruelty of a child's demise. And there was the queue again, the list of questions and the ledger of ordeals. With a tired resignation, Mike accessed the queue, and opened what his mind presented.

Maria was ten, sleeping in a recliner, unable to lie prone because of her failing lungs. She slept in a shallow vein of slumber, just barely under, where little rest was found and where dreams were fragmented, jumbled images of broken promises and incomplete, unresolved stories, where conflicts went unresolved and the characters were neither good or bad, known or unknown. They were just strangers, just mannequins with no names, faces from nowhere, voiceless, soul-less. Mike could not see the struggle in these shattered visions, but could see the restless moves of his daughter, caught in a decaying orbit of exhaustion, too weak to live, and too weak to even sleep.

He thought about the struggle of those living just a few hundred years before, when child mortality was a cruel stain. He knew that in nineteenth century Germany, every second child died in their first two years. And while global childhood mortality fell from 18 % in 1960 to 4 % in 2015, largely due to the decline in poverty and the improved delivery of health care services, Mike knew even in the richest country in the world, and in the largest city in that country, fate or nature or some callous fact of biology cared only about vulnerability and opportunity. Merciless and unforgiving. Mike carried the raw scar of a father who buried his child. And even though he now doubted his faith, and whatever divinity that could sanction such innocent death, he was silently thankful that he did not live in centuries past, where the loss of children was a statistical certainty. Such pain Mike could only perceive as unbearable, and could only result in an agonizing apathy in the debate of God's mercy, forgiveness, perhaps even his very existence.

Mike glanced back at Jason, who was now twenty feet behind him. Jason chatted with someone on his cellphone, not paying any attention to the scene ahead, waving at Mike to go on without him. But Mike was watching closely. Behind him, Jason Dumbarton undoubtedly talked to someone not about the events of the world that needed witness, but rather how to process the news, as if it was raw material, and the *Times* was a processing plant, rather than a journal machine. He remembered a lecture he gave just a few years ago at Cornell University, to a class of senior journalism students, where he explained that in his view, their task ahead in their new profession was quite simple, despite all of the noise and competition of new voices and the growing rancor of social media. Their mission was simply to record events, objectively, and to inform those not present to witness, of the circumstances or the details of these important life episodes and occasions. At base, their task was to document and spread the news. And in that class of over one hundred students, only one of them could answer the question he wrote on the whiteboard in big black letters. 'What is the job of a journalist?' After an hour long discussion, only one young, frail woman, sitting in a wheelchair in the front row of the auditorium, could give him the answer that he wanted. "What is the job of a journalist?" he asked at the end of the lecture.

With precise clarity she said, "To speak truth."

Now Mike was wondering if he could have answered his own question with such simple conviction. Or whether he could give that answer now.

The clamor of the crowd ahead brought Mike's mind back to the present. The roof of the chapel was visible ahead of him, steep and cold as winter rock. Around it a tangle of people moved around its perimeter, some taking photographs, others just looking. On the chapel's north side, a young woman had set up an easel, and was busy with her art. It was too cold for painting, so she was sketching the scene in pencil. A Lucky Dog vendor had set up shop twenty paces from the chapel, though he appeared ready to move should Park Police urge him away. Mike turned and looked for Jason, still on his cell phone, oblivious to the bustle ahead. Mike decided that Jason could catch up, and went toward the chapel and the commotion ahead.

As he approached the church, he saw that a park police officer was standing near the chapel door, and another was milling about the crowd, chatting with the park pedestrians. Mike veered to the side of the chapel, to get a closer look at the stained glass windows. While he had seen numerous photos of the chapel, none were depictive of its force or presence. The little building looked a century old, but no worse for its wear of time. As he studied the windows, he was amazed at the detail and beauty of the artistry. He desperately wanted to get a look at the inside of the church, and to view the windows from the inside of the chapel. He fished his wallet out of his coat pocket and held it close as he approached the officer standing at the chapel door.

He held up his press credentials, and asked, "Mind if I check out the inside?"

The Park Police officer eyed the press pass, and looked conflicted. "We're supposed to decline entry to the public, but you know, there's been a bunch of reporters around here this morning and you're the first to even ask about going in. To tell you the truth, I don't know if that pass gets you in or not."

Mike smiled. "Thanks for your candor, officer. My name's Mike, as you saw from my ID. I am one of the senior editors for the *Times*. It's not often I get into the field to see things for myself. To be honest with you, I miss it. You know, you work for the promotions and you climb the ladder, then one day you realize that sitting behind a desk makes your world a whole lot smaller. So, give an old man a taste of being a street reporter again. I'll be in and out before you can say Gentle Jack Daniels."

The officer grinned, and chewed his lip. "I would like to, really, but I've been written up once already this month and don't want to get busted again."

"Not to worry. I won't say anything that could get you in trouble. Hell, I probably couldn't write anything that an editor like me would let get printed anyway. Too long sitting at a desk reading stories rather than writing them."

The officer keyed a mike worn high on his left shoulder. "Park patrol to dispatch," he said slowly into his microphone. He turned his back crowd, so they could not read his lips or easily hear what he said.

Mike took a few steps toward the bench on the stone landing, but kept this attention on the officer.

"Dispatch," Mike heard from the officer's radio.

"Yea, Officer Brandt at the chapel, Great Lawn at the Park. Press request for entry into the chapel. *Times* editor. Clarify if the facility is open to the press."

"Copy that. Stand by."

The officer looked through the crowd for his partner, who was talking to a young girl who was walking her ten-speed along the sidewalk near the chapel.

Mike caught Jason's attention, even though he was still on the phone.

The answer came through the radio speaker loud enough for Mike to hear. "Negative on press entry. Park office wants the facility closed."

"Copy that," Officer Brandt replied as he keyed the mike's button. "Park patrol out."

The officer shrugged at Mike, and shook his head. "It's not my call."

Jason walked up the Mike and the officer, and for a change was somewhat diplomatic, rather than brandishing his usually George Patton-like sense of tone. "Good morning officer," he said with a smile. "Sorry I missed your explanation. I was chatting with Terrance Greenberg, the Director of the Park Conservancy. He gave us the go-ahead to inspect the chapel, provided we do it quietly and without too much flair. Shall I call him back?"

Officer Brandt dropped his head. He knew exactly who Terrance Greenberg was, and had a good idea of who Jason was too. "Well, I just got off the wire with Dispatch. No admittance is the word I got."

"And I understand that. But you know, this is not city property. The Park is public space, but it is managed by the Park Conservancy, not City Hall, and Mr. Greenberg is the top of the food chain as far as Park business goes." Jason paused and put his arm around Mike's shoulder. "Trust me, we have permission to go in. So, shall I get him back on the phone?"

Brandt looked for his partner, who was still flirting with the English racer, and decided not to force a conference call with the Park Director while he stood at the front door of the chapel. "Look, like I told your editor, Mike, I'm just following orders. But if Mr. Greenberg gives the thumbs up, then it's his call. Just do me this favor. Circle around and go in the back door quietly. Let's not get the crowd juiced up to enter with you, okay?"

"Not a problem, Officer Brandt," Mike answered. "And don't worry. We've got your back on this one."

Jason and Mike took their time strolling around the chapel in a large semi-circle, and a few minutes later, were standing in the chapel.

Mike stood in the middle of the little church, mesmerized by the stained glass windows. He stood silently, as if basking in the colored spotlights of sunlight that flooded through the windows. Jason just scanned the interior of the church.

"This is pretty damn simplistic," Jason said, "like some rustic cabin in the woods, with no power and no water. If not for the stained glass, I bet this could have been put together in record time with a crew that knew what it was doing."

"Jason, look at those beams and the rafters. Those things may weigh a thousand pounds. Same with the stones on the outer walls."

"Okay, you may be right about that. Or maybe it's all press-board and plywood. So what? We just need to flush out who did it, then the how will be revealed."

Mike didn't respond, but rather walked to the rear of the church, examining the windows and the walls more closely. Then he commented, "You know, I don't think that I 've been in a church since Maria passed."

"I'm not sure that I would call this a church. Yea, it looks like a little church, but it has no congregation. It has no priest or pastor claiming it."

Mike turned and spoke directly to Jason. "Are you sure that you want to push for a tear down? Why rush? I'm starting to feel the same way as Ms. Vasson."

Jason shook his head, and turned to leave through the rear door. "Take a few photos if you want, but let's go. I want to follow up on whatever happened at Grand Central, see if it connects to my dark computer theory."

Mike sighed, knowing the argument had ended, really even before it began. "I'll take a few pictures just in case we can't get a photographer inside before it's too late."

"Fine, just hurry."

Jason left the church, and Mike stood alone, his mind unkempt and disordered, worried about what he was going to do next.

***

Warren Hayes waited on the museum steps, not paying attention to anything about him. He was thinking about a Gibson Firebird guitar, with a special edition in-laid rosewood fretboard and custom Lolar pick-ups. He had placed the guitar on his eBay watch list, and there was one other active bidder at the moment. Warren had the high bid by five dollars, but someone listed as 'ToneLord" had jumped his bid twice in the last hour. Warren had already exceeded his budget limit by more than two hundred dollars, and was livid at the thought of losing this item. It wasn't just the guitar, though it was unique. Warren was captivated by the duel that the bid site created for him. It was as if it was a matter of honor, and because of that, he was determined to win this contentious battle for the guitar. He would not allow someone named ToneLord to intercept such a rare find of a working musical instrument.

The Firebird was a studio edition, ebony black, and was listed by a Nashville guitar shop, selling on consignment for a private owner. That meant that the true owner was probably a professional musician, which only made Warren covet the guitar all the more. A call to the

Guitar Shop confirmed Warren's intuition, and he also found out that if he was the successful bidder, he would be given the owner's gig bag and a few other treats to sweeten the purchase.

He and ToneLord had been bidding on the instrument for the last three days, and the listing was drawing to a close. They pushed out two or three other bidders on the first day, and now it was down to the two of them. And while Warren knew that another bidder could jump in at the last minute, it had happened to him before on a twelve string Rickenbacker, he had a feeling that today, it was just the two of them. Warren was fixated on his smartphone and did not notice Claira standing in front of him.

"Something's got all of your attention," she said to him. "Anything to do with the chapel?"

Warren glanced up, annoyed by the interruption. "Oh, no, just in an EBay War at the moment. Only 26 minutes left. Looking to add to my guitar collection."

"Well, I'm sure that Abner is waiting for us in his office. Let's go."

They went in the cavernous main museum building, passing through the Theodore Roosevelt rotunda, into the Akeley Hall of African Mammals. Claira turned left and went to the far end of the concourse. "His office is in the basement. We have to use the staff elevator down this hall."

When they reached the elevator, Claira keyed in a four-digit code that unlocked the elevator control. She pressed B-2 and stood back as the door slowly closed in front of her. Warren stood to her left, focused on his phone.

The elevator door opened to a hallway that was cluttered with bookcases and shelves. She hurried to the small room at the end of the hall that served as the office of Abner Parson. The office door was open, and he was sitting behind a small desk piled high with books, files and loose stacks of paper. Smoking a small, thin cigar, he had music playing in the background.

Claira knocked on the open door as she entered. "Hey, Abner. Thanks for making time for us this afternoon."

Abner parson looked up from is desk, his glasses riding low on his nose. He wore a white button-down collared shirt, thread bare at the color, with a knitted gray wool tie, loosely tied with a 4 In Hand Knot. His Gatsby eight-piece cap sat perched on his desk lamp, with the lamp-light half smothered by its dark brown patches. He looked up and smiled as they entered.

"I take it from your call this morning that your meeting went poorly."

Claira sat in a chair across from Abner, while Warren retreated to a small sofa that covered the entire side wall of the small office. He moved a stack of large print photographs, most of old churches and windows, and sat among the other papers that covered the sofa.

Warren spoke before Claira could answer. "Hey, Professor. I didn't know that you smoked. That's gotta be against the rules in this place."

Abner chuckled and held out the cigar as if on display for Warren and Claira. "Yea, well, this is one of my poor choices in life that follows me still." He slowly turned the lit cigar over in his hand, admiring it. "This is Don Diego Privad #4, my personal favorite. I have a smoke eater ash tray here, that and the fact that hardly anyone else comes down to the second basement, my addiction is benign and unnoticed. Besides, this smoothing cigar helps me think."

Claira eyed Warren and Abner with annoyance. "You boys can talk about cigar clubs some other time." She placed her purse on the corner of Abner's desk and retrieved her notepad. She opened it to the page where she wrote the names of those at the meeting, and said, "Abner, they want to remove the chapel. The lead guy from the *Times*, Jason Dumbarton, was at the meeting, along with a city attorney and others from the mayor's office. Even the Police Chief was there. You would not believe the traction all of that separation of church and state bullshit had with the rep's from the mayor's office. And my boss didn't argue against it." Claira's voice wavered as she finished, "I think the decision was made before we even met. I think the meeting was just a pretense."

"When will this happen?' Abner asked, dismayed.

"As soon as possible. Maybe tomorrow." Claira turned to Warren and asked, "Have you heard anything about the chapel? Anything about scheduling removal, crowd control, anything like that?"

Warren looked up from his phone, obviously still distracted. "Nothing specific. I talked to my buddy who was there this morning. He said a couple of suits from the *Times* had special permission to enter the chapel. They only stayed a few minutes. Went in the back door and looked around a little. Other than that, nothing new. Just maintain a soft perimeter and crowd control."

Claira shifted back to Abner and asked, "Abner, did you follow up on any of the things that you noticed at the chapel? Have you changed your feelings about it at all?"

Abner sat back in his chair and puffed his delicious cigar. "I was there not an hour ago. At the park. I'm sure that I stared at the chapel like an archeologist would gaze at a newly discovered pyramid. I looked at the stone walls and the slate roof still holding hints of snow on its edges. At the stained glass ornaments." He paused, as if visually recalling each moment of that visit, seeing each detail again is mind.

"Claira, I have lived a long life, and have seen many wonderful things. Many wonderful things. And I have also seen waste, and stupidity and cruel disregard of culture and history. I have studied many profound legacies left to us by ancestors more faithful and more attuned to their destiny than anyone I know."

Abner pointed his bent fingers toward the Park, as if he could see it from his subterranean office. "That chapel out there, just a few hundred yards from this building. It's beyond my science, beyond what I can explain. That church is a thing displaced. Is it a trick? Some kind of fakery to incite a reaction? Maybe. Is it a provocative offense to stir up controversy, to fuel a debate about the secular and the diminishment of the church in the state? Maybe yes to all of that. There has always been a friction between science and faith. In my very unique chosen field of study, I walk that tight-rope almost daily. I can only tell you that despite what logic tells me, and what my training tells me and what scientific method compels me to think, I believe that something profound is happening here. Something very profound."

Claira nodded in agreement. "Professor, I am sure we'll find out how this was done We need more time." Looking over at Warren, sitting on the sofa, glued to his phone, she asked, "Well, Warren, what do you have to say on this subject?"

Warren looked up from his phone and eyed both Claira and the professor. With a shrug of his broad shoulders, and the innocent expression of a child, he answered, "Hell, Claira, you know what I think. That little chapel is a Stairway to Heaven." He paused to glance at his phone, then placed it in his shirt pocket. "It would be tragic to let it get demolished for no good reason."

"Yes, tragic," Abner said.

With that, Warren stirred in his seat on the sofa, slowly turning his head, straining to listen. "Wait a minute," Warren said. "I know that song, playing in the background. That's 'Wish You Were Here.' That's Pink Floyd."

"Yes it is," Abner said, as he blew a smoke ring into the air. "London Philharmonic Orchestra. Performing the songs of Pink Floyd. It helps me think." He laughed. "And smoke."

"Damn doc, I never thought of you as a Floyd fan. I have to say that I'm impressed." Warren then pulled out his phone and checked on the status of the auction. "Victory!" he said.

"So you won the right to buy a guitar?" Claira said, wanting to get back to talking about the chapel.

"Yes I did. ToneLord had no chance."

"I tried to buy Cubans once on line," Abner said. "Almost got caught up in a sting operation. Damn government overlords telling me what cigars I can smoke."

"Doc, you shouldn't be confessing stuff like that in my presence. I am an officer of the court, you know." Warren talked without looking at Abner, still busy completing his purchase.

"Guys, let's get back to the chapel," Claira said. "What are we going to do?"

Abner placed his cigar on the smoke-eater ash tray, and answered, "I have an idea or two. Are you both willing to help?"

Claira stood and placed her leather bound notebook back into her purse. "Of course I am. But I have a feeling it will take more than the two of us."

Abner turned his gaze to Warren, sitting on the sofa and typing hurriedly on his smart-phone. Claira followed with her eyes. Sensing that both Abner and Claira were staring at him, Warren stated, "Hang on a second. Just logging out of PayPal."

"Warren," Claira started, but was interrupted by Warren raising his hand, silencing her.

"Officer, are you going to tow the police line on this?" said Abner. "We could certainly use your help."

"Professor, have you ever heard of Molly Hatchet?" Warren asked as he finished his on-line purchase.

Abner thought for a moment. "Yes, that name is familiar." He took a moment, then continued, "If I recall correctly, Molly Hatchet was a 19th century prostitute somewhere in the deep south that routinely decapitated her clients."

"Well, I'll be. That's right." Warren shot up off the sofa and walked up to Abner, giving him a congratulatory slap on his shoulder. "But I was thinking about the band that took her name as their show moniker. They really had one hit record, but it was a great one, and it's looping in my head now, the music, the lyrics…It's what we are doing now, the three of us."

"Oh, God Warren…don't…" Claira started to say.

Abner looked back and forth, between Claira and Warren, confused.

Finally, Warren shouted, "Hell, yes I'm with you. You got my vote when you told me all the stories about the stained glass." He leaned over Abner's desk, and started to whistle, snapping his fingers, shifting his head back and forth in mock singing. After a moment, he seemed to finish his imaginary song, and said, "This makes up for all the catechism I missed."

Abner smiled, and started to laugh with Warren. "That's great, Warren."

Claira sighed, her exhaustion and confusion beginning to overwhelm her. Her mind drifted to Tony. He had no trouble at all with believing in the unbelievable. He had the advantage of childhood, and did not have to disconnect the logic circuits of his mind to grapple with events or circumstances that posed impossibilities to her. His mind was not bound by teaching, not tied to the conventional dot connecting the way Claira was taught to think. What would he make of the chapel? Would he see it as a criminal trespass, or as a wonderful presence that did not need explanation to be accepted? She let her head fall into her hands, and considered that more than anything she needed her son, his simple joy, his ripe expectations for each minute of the day.

Abner turned to Claira, searching her for enthusiasm to buttress his resolve. But she was spent, he could see. He rose from his desk and went to her. He leaned over and held her hand, waiting for her to lift her eyes and see him. When she did, he saw the redness in her eyes, the effort to hold back the emotions and fear that gathered just beneath the surface. "Claira," he said softly, but contritely, "We may not have the best of chances, but we will give it a go anyway. We are never judged on our outcomes, but our efforts."

Claira just nodded. He rested his hand on her head, and brushed her hair with a gnarled finger. Then he turned to Warren, who had become engrossed with something on his iPhone.

"Warren," the professor asked, "You've got me curious now. What was the name of that song you were talking about? The Molly Hatchet song?"

"It's just one of the best songs ever. It's called 'Flirtin' with Disaster.'"

Abner's smile slowly subsided.

"Yes," Claira said. "How apropos."

Chapter Thirteen

The train lumbering home was crowded, but not full. Claira sat in a corner of the car, against the forward bulkhead, her head down, her shoulders relaxed and rounded. Her coat was unbuttoned, but wrapped around her tightly, kept in place by her arms folded across her chest. Her eyes were opened, but unfocused, as if that could disengage her mind, and save her from the heavy cloud of qualms behind her eyes, the veins in her conscience, the psalms of her soul.

The pressures of the days since Christmas had finally broken her confidence, and she felt alone and overwhelmed. Both her family and her career seemed in jeopardy, and she felt that she was only passively involved, as if she could do nothing about the script playing out before her, that her role was chosen for her among a mysterious and appalling cast, with iron words written to say and hear, and iron conflicts to torment her because they could not be bent. She seemed to be only a supporting character as a divine tragedy unfolded. But were her words from scripture, or a sour and forgotten script? Was her doubt the subject of a parable story, or the object of a perjured and septic mind. She feared that she knew that a mournful ending waited ahead, and her only choice was whether to walk to its bitter conclusion, or run.

City night was arriving, with its dark skies holding stars beyond sight, overwhelmed by the electric light pollution of the city. The chill of the winter night seeped through the train window, like the wake of a slow, icy flood. She could feel the cold's reach with every breath of its frigid air. And while she had always loved the winter, it being her favorite season, now it seemed different to her. There was no wonder or brightness left. It was just relentless.

Claira missed her usual train home and called her apartment to tell her sitter she would be an hour or more late. Tony had already had his supper, and was busy coloring and watching cartoons on a network devoted only to that. She thanked Connie, a sixteen year-old who lived in the building, for working a little late. Since that short conversation, she had kept her eyes closed, thinking, and processing the events of the day.

127

Claira had learned to ignore the background noises of the train ride, the random conversations and one-sided telephone dialogues, the strains of the train sounds and the metal echoes. So numerous the trips she made, she had ways to measure the passage of time. She knew the number of pages she could read, the number of songs she could listen to on her IPod, and back when she was pregnant, the number of prayers she could recite, in the duration of the train ride. But today she did not count, did not listen and did not pray. Instead, she desperately tried to cope, to understand.

Some sense pinched her to attention, shallow at first, not a sense of danger, but one of differentness. Something was different. When she opened her eyes, she nearly jumped out of her seat.

Sitting next to her, so close that he was nearly touching her, was Darragh Finn.

"Jesus," Claira said, barely able to control the volume of her voice. "You scared the granola out of me."

He had wedged himself in an open seat between Claira and a portly man dressed in a suit and vest, who spilled over onto the empty seat. Darragh looked at her meekly, as if unsure of his offense, and said simply, "Good to see you again."

"Have you been following me?" Claira asked, agitated. She was both suspicious and curious of Darragh. And a part of her was actually relieved to have found him again, on the off chance that he could reveal something useful about the chapel.

Darragh shook his head. "Not following you, looking for you."

Claira gathered her purse and her notebook which rested on her lap, and clasped them both against her chest, as if her notes and written thoughts of the chapel were exposed to some danger of appropriation. She glanced around, trying to gauge the train's distance to the next stop. "Looking for me. Why?"

"I think you have some educated guess about that," Darragh too looked around the train car, but more out of curiosity than apprehension.

"Our meeting in the Park, that was not an accident, was it?"

"No, not an accident. But before we get to that, will you tell me something?"

Claira straightened in her seat, unsure of what to expect from such a vague hypothetical. She studied Darragh's face, looking for a hint of whether a game was being played at her expense, but found no clue leading to anything that made any sense to her. On the contrary, he looked more like a penitent parent seeking forgiveness and understanding from a disciplined child. As if he was sorry for asking a question that he was bound to ask. "That is a question that deserves no answer," she stated. "Without any context, how could you expect me to agree to that? It's not as though we have any history together."

Darragh's diminished smile showed his disappointment. "That is true. We lack the comfort of familiarity. But you could indulge me nonetheless, an old man who means no harm, no ill will."

Claira considered his request. "You can ask, but I reserve the right not to answer."

"Fair enough," Darragh turned toward her more, careful not to disturb the obese man next to him who was beginning to snore. Looking into her deep brown eyes, he said, "You are yoked to some heavy burden. That much is clear. Would you tell me, what is the weight that you carry about?"

Claira repeated the question to herself, stunned by the frankness of the inquiry. "That is a question that will go without answer." She paused to consider a further response, then added, "Even if what you asked is true, why would I tell you, a complete stranger?"

Darragh was not bothered by the rebuke, and sought to explain himself more clearly. "Please understand, Ms. Vasson, that I am not a provocateur. You said it yourself, our meeting at the Park was not by chance."

"What does any of that have to do with me, personally? Nothing. Why should I answer any personal question? You have no right. No right to ask me such things." Claira felt her emotions swell, her heart rate accelerate as her systems began to spike with anxiety.

Darragh reached out and touched her right hand, gently, and with a parent's resolute devotion. Instantly, Claira's tension receded, though slightly, as confusion also clouded her senses. "Let me ask it another way," Darragh said, as he patted her hand. He glanced about the train car. No one was bothering to pay them any attention. Innocuous conversation among strangers had little pull, and the weary passengers on the train were occupied with their concerns. "Do you have faith?"

Claira lowered her head, feeling as though tears were imminent. "I was raised in a Methodist family, but have fallen away from the church." She sniffled.

"That's not what I asked. Not what I mean. I am not interested in your attendance record or your accounts for giving your tenth share to the mother church. I only asked if you have faith, that's all."

"If you would have asked me that a year ago, I would have said yes, without hesitation. But now," Claira paused as her voice left her. "Now, I would say that what faith I have is broken."

"Are you an atheist? Or Agnostic?"

Claira's quick response showed that she was offended by the question. "Or course not. I never said that."

Darragh laughed. "You are surprisingly nimble to defend that which you think is so broken." He patted her hand one last time, then released it. "Your faith is much stronger than you think." Darragh looked up, sensing that the train was approaching its next stop. He asked, "Here?"

"No, not this one. Mine is the next stop down the line."

"That is a beautiful portfolio you have there." Darragh motioned to the notebook held tightly between her arm and chest.

Clutching it a little tighter, Claira nodded. "My son gave this to me for a birthday. Just last year."

"Do you know what that symbol is?" Darragh asked, pointing to the leather cover.

"Well, it's a Celtic Cross, isn't it?"

"Yes, but not just a generic version. If your son selected that one in particular, he has a keen eye. That is the Kildalton Cross. It is old country Scotland. Very old, and very special."

Claira's mind immediately jumped back to Abner's discussion of the stained glassed windows, the reverential way he talked about the depictions, the solemn way he looked at the images. She sensed the same from Darragh as he eyed the image of the cross on her notebook. It was eerie and reassuring, frightening and enthralling. "What do you know about it?" she asked, as she laid the notebook on her lap, exposing the entirety of the cross.

"The Kildalton Cross dates to the 8th Century and comes from the Isle of Islay, off the west coast of Scotland proper. The monks at Iona created it. The detail here is poor, given the size of the cover, but the arms and the trunk of the cross display images of the Virgin and Child, and very special Biblical scenes, Daniel and the lions, Cain and Abel, Abraham and Isaac."

Claira was studying the images contained in the planes of the cross, as if only now noticing those fine details. "How do you know so much about it?"

"Hard not to hear about it growing up in a church family in Scotland. Iona Monastery was founded by St. Columba, one of the patron saints of Ireland, and a pioneering missionary in Scotland. When I was a boy, I thought that one or two of the nuns from my church were actually there when the Kildalton Cross was first conceived. They looked as old as the prayers they made us lads memorize. Sister Tess, especially. She was as hard and sharp as sword metal." Darragh laughed, as he recalled the old nun and her teaching way. He blinked, and with a smile still on his face, he gestured to the notebook and said, "You should be proud to have such a fine, historical emblem on such a personal gift. And you know, I don't believe in coincidence."

"Meaning what?"

"Meaning that your son's eyes were guided. That you were meant to have that."

Claira nodded. She ran her hand over the notebook, then gently placed it in her briefcase. "He was three when he picked it out for me. For all I know, he was guided not by a heavenly hand but by the old man at the shop."

"And then who guided him?"

"Don't get all creepy on me, okay." Claira glanced up, then continued, "This is my stop. My apartment is just a few blocks up the street."

"Is there someplace that we can go, a pub or something, so we can finish our talk?"

Claira shook her head. "I have to get home. I have a sitter with my son, and I'm sure that he's waiting up for me." She stood, as the train approached the station landing. "But I tell you what, you can walk with me to my building, and we can talk along the way. But on one condition."

"Which is?

"That I get to ask you some questions too. This isn't just a one-way street."

"By all means. By all means."

***

The sidewalk was sparse with people once they cleared the station. Darragh volunteered to carry Claira's briefcase, and before she could object, he had its strap slung over his shoulder. "You lead the way."

Claira started walking, and Darragh followed right at her side. "Tell me what you know about the chapel," she said. "No bullshit. Tell me what you know."

Darragh nodded. "I know it's perfect. It's what I pictured, what an old stone church would be back home, the kind that my grandparents or their parents would attend."

"How was it built? How did you put it there?" Claira's questions spilled out her, as if she had finally found a source of true answers, though she also knew somehow that the man next to her was not a clear revelation.

Darragh looked at her and smiled, then answered, "You mistake me for someone of great power or great wealth, someone who can spend a fortune to make a thing so. I am neither." He shrugged his shoulders, like a witness who just missed some event unfold, and can only describe what was found, not what was done. "I can't say how it was built, no more than I can say how any wonder of the world occurs. How does a flock of geese migrate from Canada over thousands of miles to the same pond in Louisiana every year of their lives? How does the body heal itself after trauma? How does an infant imprint its mother before birth?"

"We're not talking about miracles. Everything you just mentioned has a scientific explanation. Evolution. Biological, genetic memory. Maybe those things were explained as miracles centuries ago, but science has caught up with the mythology."

"Science and faith are not mutually exclusive."

Claira shook her head. "Maybe, maybe not. When I was a young girl, considering what to do with my life, I had to do a report on Marie Curie. The first woman to win a Nobel Prize. You know, she was raised in a Christian faith, but as she become one of the world's greatest scientists, she became agnostic. She believed that nothing in the world should be feared, but only understood. She was fascinated with the idea of unlocking the mysteries of nature, the world all around us. She is quoted as saying, 'that through science, we will come to understand more, and fear less.' "

"So she became an agnostic because she could not prove the existence of God?"

"Well, not exactly." Claira struggled with the question, unprepared for the debate. "The point is that she came to look at science as the higher pursuit. The quest to understand the why of something, the physical and natural laws that compel a predictable outcome. Faith in God is beyond any material phenomena that can be measured, tested or studied. There is no proof of God's existence, one way or the other. So she expressed neither faith nor disbelief."

"Well, isn't that the point of faith? To believe without seeing. The doubting Thomas scripture comes to mind."

"Not to an analytical mind."

"Anyone else?"

"What?"

"Do you have another famous scientist who rightly postulates against religion?"

Claira thought for a moment, then answered, "You must already know this, but a significant majority of scientists are not religious. Dr. Stephen Hawking, for example."

Darragh nodded. After a moment, he asked. "And I am sure that you know this, but who is considered to be the founder of the scientific method?"

"Francis Bacon," Claira answered without hesitation.

"He who said, and I quote as best I can, 'that God never wrought miracle to convince atheism, because his ordinary works convince it. And while a little philosophy inclines man's mind to atheism, the depth of philosophy brings the mind back to religion. For while the minds of men look upon causes scattered, and it may sometimes rest in them, and go no further, but when the mind beholds the chain of them, confederate and linked together, it must fly back to Providence and Deity.'"

After a pause, Claira simply said, "You carry around that quote in your head?"

"It is a pretty good quote."

"Bacon did not live in modern times. Perhaps his slant to religion would not have been so strong had he witnessed what science has brought us today."

"Or maybe more so. The world is not a calm and fearless place now, is it? Despite the wonders of science. And technology."

"Bacon could not have imagined what technology has made ordinary. Your example is much too dated."

"Einstein then."

"Albert Einstein was not a devout Jew. He believed in science."

"And he fought vocally to separate himself from those who he considered to be fanatical atheists. He referred to them as the ones unable to hear the music of the spheres."

"Wow," Claira said with a laugh. "The music of the spheres. I never heard that one before. Music of the spheres." She paused to let her smile fade. "As a scientist, we are trained to question, to test, to study, to explain. There is not much room for blind faith."

"So you dare not to believe?"

"What does that even mean? And what does that have to do with the chapel?"

"It has nothing to do with the chapel. And it has everything to do with it." Darragh slowed his pace, causing Claira to stop and turn. "I will tell you all about my life, my story, where I came from, what I am doing here, but first you have to be honest with me. Is that a fair bargain?"

Claira studied the man before her, looking past his grey-streaked hair and quixotic smile and wide shoulders, past all of that to the subconscious parts of him that were projected, the virtues, the candor, the trustworthiness, all qualities that some people had, but most painfully lacked. She sized him up in mental weighing of merit. "It's a bargain."

Darragh started walking with her again. "Claira, forgive me for being forward, but why do you have trust in me, and no trust in your husband?"

"Did Theo put you up to this? How dare you? How dare you bring my personal life into this? How could you do that?"

Darragh voice was gentle, defenseless. "I only ask because I must. Otherwise, you would not consider what I said. You would not ask that question to yourself."

Claira's breathing was rushed, the cold visible in her exhales. The tremble of Darragh voice was perceptible, the sincerity of his words palpable. "What does that mean? That I haven't thought about what happened to my family every day? What it has done to my son?"

"Have you really thought about it, or have you buried the seeds of doubt so deep that nothing good will grow soon?"

Claira shivered, and stopped in her tracks. "Why did you say that? Tell me, why did you say doubt?"

Darragh hesitated before responding, as if letting the words of her questions hang in the air with her breath. "Because that is what has broken you. You lost trust. You let doubt rule your mind."

"You don't know what you're talking about. You don't know anything about me and my family."

"Then tell me. What offense did your husband do to you? What did he do to break your love?"

Claira's eyes flowed tears. She wanted to run away, to slap the man bruising her with these questions and run away, never to see him again, never to have to hear questions that she had banished, never to have to think about her wounded history with her husband and her child. But the questions were all around her now, swirling in her mind, and holding her back as if headwinds, slowing any escape. She reached for her briefcase nonetheless, and rather than strip it from Darragh's shoulder, she hit his chest, but each blow was getting weaker, and her words poured from her heart. "He betrayed me. With a woman from his past. He betrayed me."

"How?"

Claira paused. "How do you think?"

Darragh put an arm around her, and at first she resisted, struggled, and struck him again. "Just say it, Claira. What do you know he did?"

Her jaw clenched. "He was contacted by an old girlfriend. Tony was just a baby. And he took money out of an account he had, almost twenty thousand dollars and gave it to her. Most of our savings. He never told me anything about it. Not one word."

"Why?"

"Because she was his first love, and she asked him for it. And he didn't tell me."

"That is only part of the reason."

"What? What are you talking about?"

"She was very ill. She needed a treatment that her insurance would not approve. She had no money. She was desperate and alone, and she, as a last gasp for help, called a love from her past, called your husband, and, there is really no other way to say it, she begged."

Claira pushed away from Darragh and shouted her response as more tears fell. "How? How can you know that?"

"Because you know that. Deep down you have always known." Darragh spoke gently.

Claira felt those words pelt her like frozen, bitter drops of rain, flying at her from angry and menacing clouds. She dropped her head, wounded and ashamed. "Even if nothing physical happened between them, she could still reach him. Somewhere inside him, he heard her and gave in to her. But he didn't tell me. Why would my husband not tell me about it?"

Darragh gently put his hand under her chin and lifted her head so she could see him. "Because he didn't trust you. He didn't trust that you would understand. So he took a chance that you would not find out about what he did."

"You said it, he didn't trust me." She almost shouted the words, as if those words proved his guilt and her innocence, as if they justified her actions.

Darragh nodded, letting her continue.

"You're right, he doubted me. Why wouldn't he trust me?" But even as she cried those words, she felt the conflict spring in her. "Why would that girl even call him, why would she do that? She ruined my marriage. Why?"

"Who can say? But I will tell you what I think happened." He paused, as she buried her face on his shoulder. "I think that she was like most people, most young people especially, when she got desperate and scared —"

"She called her old boyfriend, her white knight."

"No, she did what terrified people do every day. She prayed."

With that, Claira looked up at Darragh, deeply into his eyes. He nodded his head.

"She said a prayer, and then another, and another, and then a plea. And you know what happened then?"

Claira shook her head, but she knew. She knew before Darragh said another word.

"Her prayer was answered. And the answer was what your husband did for her."

Claira's tears released, in the pain of guilt and envy, but also in warm waves of acceptance, and emotion. "Why wouldn't he just tell me? Why would he doubt me?"

Darragh guided her down the sidewalk. "It's getting late. And I have to go. But ask yourself. Why would either of you doubt each other?"

Claira sniffled and wiped her eyes. "You can't go. That's my building right up there. You have to come in even for a minute. You promised to tell me about your story. I feel like I have confessed my heart and soul to you. You can't get away now. You're going to meet my son, Tony, and then you're going to tell me who you are. And how you did what you just did."

Chapter Fourteen
Princetown, Devon County, England
A Long Year Ago

The thick, granite walls were cold to the touch, like grey, glacial ice, and served the prison well, as a prison unto themselves. The barracks and the guard towers and the other buildings rose above the circling stone walls, for the town and the world to see, but the thick rock walls were the prison, where time retreated to the past, and the ghosts of the moor held their silent, somber court. And like the other granite tors perched in rough rises on Dartmoor, the walls of the prison were the stoic sentinel, rather than the manned towers and platforms, guarding not just the bodies and souls of men, but also their quiet deliberations and desperate prayers, and their vain and often futile bargains with heaven, whose gates were well more than a world away.

Darragh Finn walked along the perimeter walls, occasionally touching the edifice, as if testing the cold stone boundary. His companion kept pace, but he walked with his hands clasped loosely behind him, with an at ease demeanor and simple stride. Darragh broke the silence as they paced along the high stone wall. "Sometimes I think I hear whispers of the history here, the sounds of resignation...."

"Two centuries plus," his companion said.

Darragh nodded and looked at the man at his side, dressed in an unbuttoned coat, showing the black shirt and white collar of clergy underneath the heavy garment. "Less than a decade of my days here. Just under six years. But there's been more than a few that have never left these walls behind them. That prison cemetery is 'right about full, now isn't it." Darragh pointed to the fenced yard ahead of them, silent and waiting.

His companion smiled and shook his head slightly. "Aye, so it is. That's just the marked graves. Many more times two of unmarked, unremembered." He paused to insure Darragh's attention, "But there is always room for one more."

Darragh laughed. "I could have been there." He grew silent, thinking about his close look into the abyss, and the price paid for his return. He looked at his companion, his receding gray hair and grey eyes proud of his age. "Those earthly arms are not mine to feel just yet." He raised up and pointed over a low stone fence at the rear of the prison grounds, and said, "But there's a good spot I would pick, in the shade of that solitary veteran tree. There in the corner."

"That big yew tree?"

"Aye, the yew tree."

The clergy man laughed and slapped Darragh lightly on his back. "And what did Luke say about such things?"

Darragh grimaced as they walked slowly into the winter wind, toward the prison cemetery, his hair rippling, and his smile subsiding. "You know, just because you are the Curate Deacon of Dartmoor Prison, your reach is not as an inquisitor and teaching headmaster. Curate means one tasked to cure souls, not to test them on their lessons."

The Deacon raised his eyebrows at Darragh's response, but unclear as to whether from amusement or disappointment. "Your point being?"

"That you shouldn't put me to the test, not on the day before I leave these walls, hopefully for good."

"You mistake my question for a test. My intention was not to challenge your intellect, or even your memory. Rather, something much more important."

"Being what?" Darragh stopped and picked up a smooth pebble, rolling it between his fingers, as if it were some talisman or relic of some other forgotten sorcery.

"That which you cannot study for or memorize."

Darragh waited for the Deacon to answer further, but when no further words were spoken, he finally prompted the Deacon to continue. "What then?"

"Character."

Darragh sighed. No point to argue with the Deacon. He was too coy and too patient. Resigned to the conversation's path, he thought over the context of their discussion, and then realized what the Deacon had in mind. "Luke, you said. Despite your declaration, this sure feels like a quiz." Darragh took a final look at the pebble, then tossed it to the fence circling the prison graveyard. He watched it bounce once on the frozen ground, then sharply into the fence. "Luke is my weakest gospel." Darragh eyed the Deacon slyly, then continued, "But you well knew that." He thought for another moment, turning his gaze back to the prison cemetery. "Well, when you arrive to where you were invited, do not presume to sit in a place of honor, but take the lowest seat. Better not to be embarrassed, and asked to surrender the favored place in favor of someone more worthy." Darragh paused, as if not sure his answer was complete. Then he added, "Which in my case, most anyone would be more worthy," Darragh said as he smiled.

"Luke, Chapter 14," the Deacon replied. "But you act not because of fear of embarrassment, but rather out of a spirit of humility."

"So no big yew tree to shade my gravestone?"

"No yew tree."The Deacon laughed.

"What about the nice hedgerow, there, a couple of good spots from which to choose." Darragh pointed to another section of the cemetery, then studied the Deacon's face for his answer.

"Perhaps, perhaps not."

Darragh considered that response, and after a moment relented, "Best to reserve me a spot in the boggy area at the edge of the yard. Where the latrine drains. Seems appropriate."

"A man who knows his station in life, and afterwards too." The deacon laughed again and reached to shake Darragh's hand. "I am going to miss you and these wonderfully deep conversations."

Darragh agreed. "I will not miss this place," he said, as he gazed about the yard of the prison, its grey walls and grey buildings close and quiet, as if listening to his laments. "But I will miss the moor, I will miss the relic church St Michael's, will miss my job in the brewery making jail ale. I will miss some of the people who are not here by choice. But I will miss you the most."

The Deacon nodded. He gazed around the prison grounds, as if humbled by its grey, earthly strength. "Darragh, are you sure that you have your course ahead charted? That you are confident in this task?"

Darragh scratched at his short beard, greying slower than the crop atop his head. "Deacon, sir, it may be a fool's errand, a gargantuan waste of time, but it is a calling that I can neither explain nor ignore. But even more than that, it's a debt that I owe."

"I believe you. Had I not, I would surely say. But you have restored my faith in what I am called to do." The Deacon shook his hand a final time, then slapped his shoulders in the Highlander's bid of farewell. "I hear you, laddie. And I believe in you, sure as the moor wind is cold and the Dartmoor night is the blackest of dark. Take care, now and again."

Darragh watched the old man walk away, doubtless headed to the administration building to finish his day's paperwork before departing the prison. As he watched him walk away, he thought about the steps that he would walk tomorrow, about where those steps would lead him. He was scheduled to depart at eight in the morning. A free man again, after six years of incarceration. Six years that transformed him, turning the essence of a feeble spirit into a pilgrim constituent. As he stood in the cold, for the next few minutes before he would be ushered back into the barracks, he stared at the mist rolling in from the south of the moor, and remembered his first day's arrival at his hilltop home, the Down Wing of the prisoner barracks.

***

The Arrival, Six Years Earlier

HM Prison Dartmoor was a Category C men's prison, noteworthy for its conversion from a military prison in the early 1800s, to an active criminal penal facility. It was also notorious for its overcrowding, poor sanitation, and for its location on the highest moor in southern England. Originally opened two centuries earlier in 1809, the prison stood adjacent to the town of Princetown in Devon County, occupying approximately 50 acres of fenced and guarded land.

Darragh looked at the countryside from the prison bus window, being a modified Serco van, with all of the enhancements designed for security rather than comfort. Darragh's thoughts were lost somewhere between the land that he saw and the shadows in his depressed and desperate mind. Before today, he had never been south of Edinburgh, Scotland, and had spent almost all of his life in Tain and the lands of surrounding Ross County in the north Highlands. He learned to love the beautifully desolate mountains of northern Scotland. He grew up there, hunted there, worked on farms and on docks on the North Sea coast. Most of England was a poor substitute for the Highlands, but Dartmoor was vaguely familiar to his highland home. Old and twisted trees dotted the harsh terrain, and tall grasses in random patches flowed in the direction of the wind. He closed his eyes, and tried to remember the voice of his sister, his only living relative, and who was his only loyal supporter. After he was sentenced to HM Prison Dartmoor, she learned all that she could about the prison's notorious past and its remarkable location. She told Darragh that she would try to visit, but until then, knowing about the place where he would work and live, would serve as her constant connection to him, faint though it may be.

He could hear Jenny's voice as she talked about Dartmoor. "Just think, Darragh, the prison is there in the middle of a vast park, a grand place for a holiday. Surely, we can find time for a visit, and see the park where you get to stay at her majesty's expense."

His sister was right about Dartmoor's rugged appeal. As far as he could see from the bus window, the hills rose and fell in clean, unspoiled tracts, as they had for centuries. He thought about her descriptions of the moor's countless bedrock outcroppings, large tors, and open rolling hills, as well as wooded areas and rivers. Dangerous peat bogs called featherbeds were scattered around the moor. "These are nature's vile traps, and have been the death of prison escapees for centuries," she said. "So no jailbreaks for you, Darragh. Be warned."

The moor countryside was also littered with Dartmoor kistvaens, stone crypts dating back to the Early Bronze Age. There were also menhins, or standing stones, either as monoliths or stone circles, and stone piles called carins, used in the lost past as trail markers and guideposts. He suspected that he had seen some of these relics as the bus climbed the moor, but simply did not recognize them, as the distance horizon seemed to extend forever from his gaze, across rough landscape flowing backwards into memory and time.

And Jen was right about another thing. All of the physical wonders of the moor were amplified in the folklore and folktales of a headless horseman, of witch imps and pixies, spectral disembodied hands that seek to wreck motorists who drive near the town of Postbridge, and prowling devilish hounds that patrol the dark moors after sunset. And there was also the infamous Beast of Dartmoor, a phantom panther that hunts in the mists and the forests of the moonlit moor. He could hear the passengers behind him, fellow inmates, telling tales of beasts and witches and curses in both a reverent and respectful tone, either believing, or afraid to disbelieve in any open or vocal manner, for fear of a curse or some evil retribution.

As the bus turned along a long curve in the road, the prison came into view. And it was as Jenny had described, a walled enclave that centuries ago could have been a fortress castle. All the chatter in the bus ceased, as the passengers saw their destination just ahead.

***

Darragh stood in a line with six others, his fellow passengers also sentenced to Dartmoor Prison. They were in the first building inside the walls, in a large first floor room being processed into the prison. The walls were unremarkable, a pale color that would be forgotten quickly. Two guards were standing against each of the side walls, and a fifth was seated at a desk facing the new arrivals. The man who sat in the very back of the bus was two in front of him, at the head of the line. He was tall and slightly overweight, but strong and formidable, with a shaved head and tattoo of crossed swords on his neck. He wore a short cut mustache, more gray than not, and closely cropped hair.

"Name?" a guard said, sitting at a small intake desk in the lobby of the administration building.

"Pontius Pilate. I got sent here because I kinda' messed up that whole Jesus scenario." He spoke the word 'scenario' slowly and with emphasis, as if the guard would have trouble with a four syllable word.

"Name?" the guard asked again, his voice curt and absent any bemusement.

A fellow guard standing alongside of the line of prisoners took a few steps to the head of the line, and rested his nightstick on the man's shoulders. "Straighten up, mate. Got no time for lip."

"Stacey Talbot Dower. But me' mates call me STD's."

The guard sitting at the table looked down at his clipboard, and wrote a note in the margin of the paper. "Yes sir. We have a special place for you. G Wing. Now take your bedding and your prison issues, and go to the end of the hall, where Officer Frye is kindly waiting. Next."

Mr. Dower walked slowly toward the waiting officer, smiling with mischief, as if he had succumbed to a particularly heavy bottle of single malt and had just soiled the Queen's personal washroom. All of the guards paid him particular attention, as if they sensed in him a wild animal tension, while the remaining prisoners seemed harmless and mild.

The man in front of Darragh spoke without being asked. "George Falwood," he said evenly, as he was familiar with the process.

"Yes sir. George W. Falwood. So glad to have you back." The guard looked up and nodded to the inmate, showing a sizable gap between his upper front teeth.

"The pleasure is all mine, I must say. Couldn't wait to get back."

"How's the misses and that little sprout of yours?"

"As good as could be expected. I suspect that one of them would prefer to have me about the house. Maybe not both, though."

The guard laughed. "You will be missed," he said as he wrote a note on his paperwork.

"If you say, then it must be so."

"G Wing," the intake officer said. "Next."

Darragh waited for the man in front of him to collect his bedding and prison clothing, then stepped up to the front of the desk. "Finn. Darragh Finn." He answered without any emotion, as neutral a tone as he could manage. Darragh wanted to show the guards and prisoners both that it was just another day to him, just another place to be. He wanted to mask the hopelessness that blackened his nerve, that made him doubt his own dignity and worth.

The intake officer looked him over, then glanced back down to his clipboard. "Here we are. A first timer." He checked off some space on his notes and said, "D Wing."

"Hey, wait a minute," STDs called from across the room. "Why does the new man get Down Wing? I'm back on Granite. No f'ing way that's right."

A standing guard warned as he approached the far wall, "Not another word, mate."

"What's the difference in wings?" Darragh asked.

The sitting guard looked up from his notes and answered. "You must have a lucky clover behind those green eyes of yours, son. D wing. You get a cell to yourself. A wee tiny one, but yours alone. Our guests in G get to share accommodations. But I don't make the reservations, I just read out what's on my log. Next."

Darragh gathered his linens and clothing and walked over to Mr. Falwood. Before Darragh could speak, Falwood said, "Dartmoor Prison has six prisoners' wings. A is the Arch Wing; B is Burra Wing. Both of those are for vulnerable inmates. That's where they put the perpetrators of sex crimes."

"Why do they call them vulnerable prisoners?"

Falwood eyed him closely, as if to see if whether Darragh was asking a serious question, or if the question was just part of larger game. "Cause that is where they generally put the sex predators," He repeated. "The guys convicted of sex crimes. They don't mix well with the general population. You cross paths with them once in a while, but they even have different meal times and such."

Darragh glanced back at STDs and then asked, "What about him?"

Falwood laughed, but it soon morphed into a cough, which seemed painful and ominous. Finally, he answered, "Ol' Mr. Pilot there is not a pedophile or a rapist. He is just an angry, misunderstood drug trafficker who likes guns. Now where was I?"

"You were telling me about the wings, and what to expect."

"Right. E is the East Wing, and it's for those who hold jobs around town, day passes, that kind of thing. It's the Resettlement Wing. G Wing, my assigned quarters, is the mainstream population. Call it Granite. You're in D Wing, Down Wing. It's mainstream, but also has space for vulnerable prisoners. Usually they try to put a newbie like you who has no history to speak of on the Down."

"That's five," Darragh noted. "What about the sixth wing?"

"Yea, that would be Fox. F Wing. That's the enhanced mainstream. They get a few privileges, like their own clothes rather than these prison rags, video games, better jobs. That's the goal to shoot for, if you're gonna' be here a while."

"I'm looking at up to ten years, probably a little less. Should I be worried?" Darragh asked in a whisper.

Falwood studied him from head to toe before answering. "Dartmoor is mostly white collar criminals and lesser felonies. Not too many gents like STDs over there. He's a real cocker, that one. You're big enough to send a message, not easy meat. Keep your head down and your mouth shut. You might skate right by trouble and not even know it."

"Thanks for the advice."

"Look for a guy goes by the name Xanadu. He's got a little book that can help newbies. But it's gonna cost you."

"How much?"

"Not sure the going rates nowadays. But get one. It's worth keeping all of your teeth. Plus, I found it to be a fun read, if you can get past all of the blood, gore and sex."

Darragh shuddered. "What the hell kind of book is it?"

Falwood, coughed out a small, weak laugh. "Well, it's like a farmer's almanac for inmates. It's the Hitchhiker's Guide to HM Prison Dartmoor."

***

144

Darragh hardly slept in his first night in the prison. The hours were haunting. The wind made noises, or carried noises, that were not like anything from in the highlands. These were what the inmates called the spirit winds of the moor. Some would say that these winds carried the sounds of those wrongly imprisoned, the cries and moans of their lost loves, lost youth, even lost souls. But others would say the wind carried nothing clean or pure, not from place to place. Rather, these were winter moor winds, made for the evil done before and during the condemned's time in chains, the high winds of hell, and that some spirits did not ride the winds, but rather were bound to these winds for eternity, to circle the granite rocks and woods of the high moor, in eternal, echoing pain. That was the curse of Dartmoor Prison, a whirlpool of cold air and rushing gusts locked in a vague path all around the prison, that brought the souls back to Dartmoor, a tortured, false escape and the inevitable train wind return. For if Dartmoor did not receive its cut of justice during the prisoner's days of life, then it was sure to be taken in his nights after death. At Dartmoor, rehabilitation was possible, but retribution and punishment was a certainty, either at the hands of men and their system of justice, or at the call of those unseen. The wagers made were contract, and the accounts were settled, one way or another, a spoken breath of contrite payment, or a bitter last breath in default. For the new prisoners, their fate was to hear the wind songs until their sleep grew deep, and if cursed, to hear the wind songs even in their dreams.

Only time would tell whether Darragh would find peace in his slumber, or if not peace, at least a respite from the drudgery of the day.

The next morning was welcome, just as an end to the dark. He dressed when told to, and made his way to the galley for breakfast without a word spoken. After filling his tray, he looked over the room for a place to sit, and chose an empty table in the center of the galley hall. He sat at the end of a bench, and stared down on the food on his tray. His breakfast was black pudding and sausage, with a single slice of buttered bread and thin, cut down milk to drink. His stomach turned at the sight of the pudding, even though in the highlands he ate it many times. But today it looked like ruin, like a serving already passed from wholesome into rot. As he flipped the pudding with his spoon, he sensed someone standing next to him. Before he could look, he heard a course, grating voice. "Hear you are looking for me."

Darragh looked up and saw a short man, maybe 5'6", but with thick, toned arms and coal black hair combed straight back. His nose was scarred, with a burn or something worse, and one eye seemed to sag lower than the other, as if its socket was bent or broken. The man sat down across from Darragh. "Well," he said as he lined up his tray and took a sip of his coffee.

"Sorry," Darragh said, careful not to look the man in the eye. "I am new here. I'm not looking for anybody or anything."

"That's not what Falwood told me."

"Oh, Mr. Falwood," Darragh sighed in relief. "Forgive my manners. George did tell me to find the man who wrote the Prisoner's Guide to the Galaxy."

"What? What did you call me' book?"

Darragh saw quickly that his joke was either misunderstood or was not at all funny to the scarred man sitting across from him. "I'm sorry, a poor attempt at humor."

"No, it was funny. Can't you see me laughing?" The man's glare was hateful, the sagging eye looking like it was being pushed out of its broken socket.

Darragh was stunned, looking into the fallen eye and the scarred face that was as unnerving as a grotesque mask. He worked up enough courage to respond. "Now you having a go at me? I pulling my first day here, and I don't mean to make an enemy of the first man I meet at my first breakfast here inside these cold walls. I'll have plenty time to do that later." He paused, then added, "My name is Darragh. Darragh Finn."

"So do you want to know about my book, or not?"

Darragh considered whether such a thing could possibly have any utility, and then whether he would insult the man if he did not at least seem interested. "I am definitely interested, but I am of limited resources at the moment. Sorry, what's your name again, I must have missed it."

"Everyone here calls me Xanadu. It's my clan name. I explain all about the clan system in my book. I self-published it a couple of years ago. Dartmoor has a desk-top publishing center, mostly used by prison solicitors trying to practice law. I went a different way. I write self-help books, prayer books, and works of erotic fiction."

Darragh smiled at Xanadu, hearing the man describe his catalogue of works. "What's the name of the book about the prison?"

"Dartmoor Demijohn." Xanadu lowered his head, as if that helped quiet his voice, and glanced around to see if any guards were milling about. "You know, demijohn, the large bottle wrapped in wicker. The book is like a large jug, but full of info rather than wine. But it's, shall we say, a black market item. Not sanctioned by the warden or by Her Majesty, if you know what I mean. Cost you a carton of smokes, or three flapjack bars, or five chocolate bars. Very much worth the price of admission, I must say."

"Can you spot me a bit, while I build up my currency?"

"Sorry mate, no Royal Bank of Scotland here. I don't do credit."

Neither Xanadu nor Darragh noticed a tall man standing off to the side of the table, listening to their conversation. He got both of the men's attention when he said, "Mr. Finn, when you finish that fine meal, report to one of the guards at the south door. He will escort you to my office." Turning to Xanadu, he said, "And you, sir, thank you for the sheet music. Spot on rendering." The man turned and pointed at Darragh then said, "Put a Dartmoor book in this man's hands, and I will see you have two flapjacks and one Cadbury. And don't haggle about the price, like you do when I hear your confession. My last penance to you was a bargain." With that, the man turned and walked away, stopping once or twice at tables along the way, for quick words with other prisoners eating their breakfast.

"That's one tall son of a bitch," Darragh said. "Is he the warden? Am I in trouble already?"

"At Dartmoor trouble is never far away." Xanadu took another pull on his coffee, then said. "But that's not the warden. Don't think for a minute that the warden would be buying one of my books for you. No Sir!" He nodded back to the tall man walking out of the galley and said, "That man handles all of the funerals here, last rites, and the occasional exorcism. He is the Curate Deacon of the prison. The closest thing we have to a holy man behind these walls."

**

The Deacon's office was little more than a kitchen pantry. The room had a small table in place of a desk, and two mismatched chairs, one on either side. The walls were painted a dull white, but where marked with water stains and other ugly signs of neglect. A small cross hung above the door, and other than that, nothing adorned the dreary walls. The only other items in the room were a small two drawer wooden filing cabinet, and a floor lamp standing close to the table.

The guard knocked on the open door's frame and said, "Here's the first one of the day. Not too long father, we need to stay on pace." With that, the guard retreated down the hall a few paces, then stood at ease against the wall.

The Deacon motioned for Darragh to enter. "Darragh. That is a fine name. One that I haven't heard spoken in a very long time. Come in, sit down," the Deacon said to Darragh, as he thumbed through a file on the small table.

Darragh sat on the small wooden chair. He said nothing, waiting for the Deacon to look up and acknowledge his presence. But the Deacon continued reading, and without glancing up at Darragh, said, "Good morning, sir. Make yourself comfortable. Tell me about yourself."

Darragh glanced about the room, cautiously. After a moment, he responded, "I shouldn't be here."

"So, you're an innocent man. Just like everyone else here at Dartmoor," the Deacon finally said as he closed the file and looked directly at Darragh.

"No, that's not what I meant. No doubt about my crimes. I just shouldn't have been caught."

The Deacon smiled. "Burglary, wasn't it?"

"I come from a long line of burglars, hard drinkers and sheep-stealers," Darragh said proudly. "Had I not mixed the first two recently, you and I would not be having this conversation."

"What are you saying, Mr. Finn? That you should not have tried to burglarize the Glenmorangie Distillery? Are you showing some sign of remorse? Or, are you only admitting that you should have not engaged in your larcenous crime until you were sober?"

Darragh accepted that question as a challenge, and composed his response carefully. "In truth, I admit only to a more literal correlation. I was hammered on highland single malt at the time I burgled the distillery. One of the best drunks of me' life. A fine Macallan 24-year-old. Had I not fallen asleep in the truck, on the farm road to my barn, I would have rightfully appropriated 4 barrels of Glenmorangie 18-year-old, a score of cases of cask strength 12 year, a few keen rare old distilling manuals, probably worth more than the small batch whisky, and just enough petty cash to see me through a pub run weekend."

The Deacon smiled, impressed with both the deed's description, and the apparent joy in Darragh's voice as he relived the adventure. He rubbed his head as Darragh described the perceived injustice that triggered this bit of larceny, being only a dispute over a cutting of Maris Otter barley, a very vocal disagreement between the distillery brew-master and Darragh, on whose family land the winter barley was grown and who was owed the price for the harvest. Darragh easily proved ownership to the crop, and insisted on payment by an in kind tender of their private reserve bottling, while the brew-master insisted Darragh be paid in pounds sterling. Not surprisingly, Darragh lost that argument, and was not paid in kind. When he was paid by a bank note, Darragh decided to appropriate the in kind method of payment he had requested, and to keep half of the cash for his troubles. Neither the fine people of the Glenmorangie nor the county judge viewed his leaving of the other half of the payment, in a wad of pound notes tied in a roll by a sprig of twine, in the distillery's barrel cellar, as a viable defense to the theft. Especially not when he laid bare the petty cash box in the distillery office.

"Ten years seems a harsh term for the crime you describe."

"Yes, well, I had a few choice words for the judge, and also had a history with the prosecutor. Seems his wee sister never moved on from me, on accident mind you, breaking her heart, on one or two occasions." Darragh slapped his knees and said, "Had I been born a century sooner, they would have written grand songs of my escapades. Now a days, you get only this prison issue and a six to ten-year long term in Her Majesty's Dartmoor."

"May I ask why you took the petty cash from the office, but left half of the money you were paid in the barrel room?"

"I am a man of my word," Darragh said proudly.

"You do know that the value of the malt that you took greatly exceeded the price of the barley harvest."

Darragh gave a small nod, "Wouldn't be much of a burglar if I didn't, now would I?"

The Deacon leaned back in his chair, balancing it on its two rear wooden legs. "Mr. Finn, I would like to discuss your trials and tribulations in much greater detail, but our time is short this morning. My job, or at least part of it, is to orient you to Dartmoor Prison. You will see, this is not a high security prison, but it does have its rules, some onerous, some a mode of inconvenience, but all quite serious and all absolute. And there's also the matter of the prisoner's book of rules. You would do well to learn all of these rules straight away."

"Yes sir."

"And if you acclimate well, your time can be both productive and restorative. You can choose to enroll in open university courses. If you pursue electronics, carpentry or brickwork, you will emerge from Dartmoor with a guild level trade. You could also work in catering, farming, industrial cleaning, painting and decorating, or even desktop publishing. There are occasionally openings in the town brewery for prisoners with trustee status. So you see, there is no reason to be idle here, no reason to diminish."

"Sounds lovely. I feel most qualified to work as a taster of ale and a sampler of pies."

The Deacon chuckled. "We will have to see where best you fit. Now the other task assigned to me is to be mindful of the spiritual needs of the inmates. I take this charge very seriously indeed. I hold services every Sunday here on the prison grounds. We have study every Thursday evening. Once a year, a memorial service is held at St. Michael's, the church ruin outside of the prison walls. It is obviously not open for the entire prison population. To go there is a privilege. And a fine service we have there. Very fine. My office is generally open, just ask for a time to meet, and the guards are told to honor your petition. I am generally seen around the galley, should you feel bashful about the guards and tell me of your need to talk."

Darragh rose and said, "Thanks. Except for my sweet sister, everyone else I know has thrown a stone at me' door."

The Deacon disagreed. "You only think the world has given up on you. It hasn't. He hasn't." The Deacon's eyes shot upward.

Darragh's eyes followed the Deacon's, as if he truly expected to get a glimpse of the Lord, smiling down from a window in heaven.

The Deacon continued, "As I am sure you have heard before, the challenges in life make you stronger."

Darragh shook his head. "I'm startin' this day, the first of many, and I confess I slept not much last night, with the sounds of these prison demons and ogresses wailing outside my building. And I may have just said a little prayer, seeing that I was right scared after hearing all of the mates on the bus go on about prison ghosts and spirits. But to be clean with you, Deacon, I am not a religious man. I put more faith in me' liquor to ease my soul than in any church prayers and hymns of God's glory. I've put more money on the tavern bar and in the piper's purse than ever in any church tithe. And I've on more occasions spilled pints on accident, than I ever spilled tears for anything that I've done or threatened, by long ways." Darragh paused to read the Deacon's eyes, but found nothing, just the stare of a man who had heard too many confessions of sins and hellish deeds to be moved by Darragh's weak claims of bravado. Darragh continued, "To find me captive in a church would be a rare find indeed. So you have a high challenge with me, if you mean to save my poor soul. But maybe one day." Darragh extended his hand to the Deacon.

"Aye, sir, maybe one day," the Deacon agreed, as he shook his hand and then watched him walk down the wall. "One day indeed."

***

The Deacon made good on his promise of payment, the candy bars and fruit granola planks called flapjacks must have changed hands, because on Darragh's third day at Dartmoor, while standing in line for breakfast, Xanadu eased in behind him in line and slipped him a copy of his prison book. It was the size of letter paper folded in half, and was about one hundred eighty hundred pages long. Xanadu cautioned him, "Don't be an ass and try to read it here. Just slip it in your shirt, and save it for your cell."

Darragh did as he was counseled, and did not even look at the book until that evening. He expected a short collection of lists and outlines, full of poor grammar and no punctuation, but Xanadu's book was well planned and written with a both an ominous tone and reoccurring touch of humor. The book's cover was laminated, and showed a well-drawn demijohn, the jug empty, and wrapped in a cracked and tattered wicker weave. The pages of the book were thick bond paper, and the chapters were written in a modern font, with diagrams, pictures and drawings spread out among the pages. The table of contents listed fifteen chapters.

Darragh scanned through the pages, jumping from one chapter to the next. Some of the book was a first person narrative, almost autobiographical, while others sections were compilations of stories, or chronologies of events. He was captivated by some of the gruesome events depicted in a few of the chapters, and made to laugh by the dry wit in some of the other writings. He hid the book in his pillow at lights out, slipping it through a small cut into the down of the pillow. He slept fitfully, dreaming of failed escapes and cruel punishments, and torture at the hands of other prisoners. The writing was that good.

***

Darragh's head flew violently sideways. The punch connected with the side of his head, high on the jaw-bone, below his left temple. The strike's force both spun him around and lifted him off his feet, and he landed on the hard ground of the recreational field, seemingly falling faster than gravity could justify. Quickly, a semi-circle of prisoners formed around the spot where he lay, with voices taunting, frantic, some urging him up, and others cautioning him to stay down.

Darragh reached for his jaw, and carefully padded it, feeling a knot already rising under his beard. For a few disorienting moments, he was unsure of what happened, then a voice made it clear.

"It's Monday. And on Monday, this field belongs to Granite," STDs yelled. He held a scarred soccer ball, pinned between his hip and hand.

"Sorry if I got in your way," Darragh said in a stutter. He rocked on the ground, somewhere between a prone and sitting position, as if trying to balance, but unable to sit up and incapable of finding comfort. His eyes searched for his attacker, unable to focus. "No offense. Nothing done on purpose. I've been here a just a week. I didn't know about that rule." He rolled over onto his knees, and struggled to get up. He barely had time to close his eyes when he caught a vague glimpse of a boot streaming toward his face. The kick sent him back to the ground, blood sputtering out of his nose and mouth. STDs chuckled as he held his follow-through, keeping his right leg high in the air, posing for all to see, as if just sending a soccer ball screaming for a winning goal.

"Learn the rules, City baby," STDs said as he jogged to the middle of the field, where a few other inmates were passing another soccer ball.

As STDs retreated to the soccer game, Falwood and Xanadu rushed over to Darragh and helped him up, and slowly and deliberately, guided him to a small bench at the edge of the soccer field.

Inspecting the wounds made by the kick, Xanadu pulled a small towel from a pocket and started to dab at the blood.

"You gonna need some ice on that," Falwood said. "Let's get you to the infirmary, tell them you got kicked in a soccer game."

Darragh shook his head, trying to orient and re-boot. "What the hell just happened?"

Xanadu was standing next to the bench, where he could see the soccer field. "You broke the rules. Granit gets the soccer fields on Monday. You were trespassing."

"There's no such prison rule," Darragh argued back. "Rec hour is open time, and the yard is open for all of us."

Falwood, shook his head in disagreement. "Them's the Warden's rules, right. But there's also the Book Rules. That's one that you broke."

"But I didn't know about that rule."

"It's in the Book. Not knowing is no defense," Xanadu said.

"Yup, it's in the book," Falwood said.

Darragh looked at both of them in disbelief. "You mean that Demijohn book? The one that Xanadu wrote?"

"That's the one."

"Chapter 5, the rules of etiquette. I also touch upon that rule again in chapter 8, Work and Play. It's an important safety tip if you want to keep all of your teeth."

"That bunch of made up rules about the soccer field is real? You're not serious, are you?"

Xanadu looked over at Falwood and laughed. "About as serious as that size twelve boot you just tasted."

Darragh struggled for words to protest. "But how does that happen? Who enforces the rules?"

Xanadu threw his hands up, frustrated. "What's the purpose of getting that book if you don't bother to read it?"

"I read it, most of it anyway. I just —"

"You didn't take it seriously," Falwood said.

Darragh spit blood. The side of his face was swelling either from the blow of STDs iron-like fist or what had to have been steel-toed boots. He had ringing in his ears and he was fast developing a headache, the kind that made him think of his brain as a putrid bottle of juice, fermenting, swelling its closed plastic vestibule. He crouched over and emptied more blood from his mouth, then asked, "Why didn't the guards intervene? They could have at least stopped the kick to my head."

"It's in the book," Xanadu said. "They will give the population one minute to deal internally with any rules violations, provided that no piercing or cutting weapons are used."

Darragh looked over to Falwood, hoping for a sane response.

"That's what the book says," Falwood agreed.

Xanadu motioned to Falwood, and the two helped Darragh to his feet. They starting him walking, but his compass was faulty and he weaved off course every third or fourth step. "Take it slow, little steps work best," said Xanadu.

The three guards casually gathered at the edge of the rec field, watching, but not showing much interest. Falwood waved, and said, "Got his bell rung. Can we get some ice for that egg rising on his noggin?"

None of the guards said a word. They just stared at the trio wobbling toward them from across the field.

"That was wicked bad luck in the soccer game today," Xanadu remarked as they neared the guards.

"Never have seen such a collision going up for a header, not even in club play." Falwood had one of Darragh's arms over his shoulder, leading him toward the infirmary building, after the lead guard on duty nodded permission.

As they were leaving the field, STDs paused in his game and waved over to them. "Bad luck mate. Soccer is a contact sport," he yelled over to them. "Don't let anyone tell you different." His mates on the field laughed and hooted, egging STDs on. "Maybe your bud Xanadu has an extra tampon, help with that bloody nose." More laughter, more curses.

Wincing, Darragh turned his head toward STDs and called out. "My bad. Next time I'll know better."

"How's that?"

"Cause it's in the book." Darragh gave the thumbs up sign as he staggered, with help, to the infirmary.

* * *

After a week, the bruises around Darragh's check and left eye were nearly gone, and their black plum color dissipated across his face and the line of his beard. He missed just one day of work in the gardens, although he was sore and his neck felt like it could only turn with the effort of broken gears working through a tortuous and dangerous friction.

He stuffed another hand full of weeds into a grass sack, and slowly stood, only to see the Deacon standing next to him.

"You're moving like a man hung over," the Deacon commented.

Darragh slowly lifted the sack and swung it over his right shoulder. "The Highlands don't have enough whisky to lay me out like that bastard's boot."

"Leave the sack. Walk with me a pace or two."

Darragh shot a look over at the yard guards, watching like sentinels from the garden's gate.

"No worries about the blue bulls. They know not to bother with me when I'm with a prisoner. Let's walk."

As they slowly walked down the rows of carrots and winter vegetables, Deacon worked a toothpick with his right hand, mining the spaces between his teeth. Finally, Darragh asked. "Is there something that you are going to tell me? Maybe a pardon came in from the queen? Maybe you all have found out that I have royal blood in these veins. The prison surgeon had plenty to test."

Deacon laughed. "Hardly. I do have a suggestion for you. No more wood shop in the afternoon."

"But that's the schedule that they gave. Garden in the morning, carpentry in the afternoon."

Deacon eyed him carefully. "Do you want to be a carpenter?"

"No, but I don't have anything else to do, and I sure don't want to work in the prison laundry. Them's my only two choices."

"Well, I have done some rearranging. Now in the afternoon, you can go to the print shop. You would like it. Your friend Xanadu runs it with vigor."

"I am not a writer and don't draw that well either. I'd prefer to work with wood, if I have to choose."

155

"Would you now. You would prefer to be in the shop with prisoner Dower. He's just itching for another reason to crown you again. You must have made an impression on him."

"Where did you hear that?"

"Where indeed." Deacon raised his arms and turned slightly, looking over the prison grounds, as if it was his given kingdom, by grant of the Crown. "Don't doubt that I hear many things inside these walls, some idle, some much more immediate."

Darragh thought about this news, his being on a short list of prey. "How would moving me help? Wouldn't it just make STDs more determined, like I was pulling a string to dodge him?"

The Deacon nodded. "Quite true. But you are not the only occupant being reassigned. There are a few more being moved. Mr. Dower will, in all probability, not think twice about it."

"Well, why not reassign Dower. Or better yet, just put his ass in lock-down."

The Deacon frowned, and said, "That would most certainly get his attention. That brute actually is a fair to better carpenter, when he isn't beating the daylights out of someone. Better to go along to get along. And since I pretty much run the work schedules, I know that is it not unusual for a newbie such as yourself to change work rotations after a week or two of orientation. That's all this is, just me tinkering with the schedule."

Darragh clapped his hands. "When do I go to print shop?"

"No time like the present. Be there for the afternoon turn."

***

Darragh sat at the computer keyboard and stared at the screen, having just deleted the few paragraphs he'd written. He looked over to Xanadu, who was sitting at his desk. "I've been doing this for three months, and have not written anything worth reading. I'm no good here, I should go back to the wood-shop and take my chances with STDs."

Xanadu, not looking up from his book, said, "I'll give you a tip, the same one that I got when I was at Strangeways. You're failing because you're trying to do two things at once. Do only one."

Darragh looked back at him confused. "What are you talking about? What two things?"

"You're thinking and writing at the same time, and you're failing at both. Do them one at a time."

"What?"

Xanadu closed his book and rose from his desk chair. He pointed to his head and said, "You got to think first. Think about the outline of what you're writing, think about the flow of the words, the points or ideas that you are describing for the reader. You can't just sit there and write with nothing in mind." He sat on the edge of his desk and folded his arms across his chest. "Think you can do that?"

"No one has ever accused me of being a very good thinker. Maybe I am over my head here. Maybe I should just ask the Deacon to put me on some shit detail in the laundry."

Xanadu grumbled a few inaudible words.

"If you're going to give me a cussing, please let me hear it loud and clear."

"What I said was don't quit. That's really the whole secret. You can't quit. When I was in Strangeways, I saw too many scarecrows who couldn't do the time with their eyes open. Every one of them died, or drifted to a place just as bad."

"What's Strangeways?"

"It's hell. Her Majesty's Prison Manchester, but known to the rats and inmates as Strangeways. Not like Dartmoor. Strangeways is max security, and houses murders, rapists and terrorists. Hell in a brick shit-house."

"You said eyes open. What is that?"

"When a prisoner gives up, and stays high, juiced up all of the time. That's eyes closed. A lot of that at Strangeways. And worse things too."

"Like what?"

Xanadu pointed to his face. "See this? I got this at Strangeways. It's called a buttercup. A cocker about the size of STDs thought I ratted him to a guard. So one day he boiled a stick of butter and threw it in my face. Lucky I didn't lose my eye."

Darragh was aghast. "That's horrible. How did he boil it? Where?"

"Used a bunch of cigarette lighters and an old tin can. He had a couple of goons hold me down. Basted me like a Christmas turkey." Xanadu almost seemed to grimace when he described the assault. But then he looked up, and said, "I wrote about it in my book. I just changed the names to protect the innocent."

"So when you said, write about what you know, you mean what you really know."

"Yea, well screw it. Past history. Come back here tomorrow with a poem or a story. Write me something from yourself. If you can't do that, then you're outta here."

***

The next day when Xanadu got to the print shop, Darragh was leaning against the windowed wall, smiling. Xanadu circled to his desk, and saw a piece of paper on his chair. He glanced up to Darragh, who took a step forward, eager to see if what he wrote would be acceptable.

Xanadu picked up the paper and read the words, just under his breath, softer than a whisper.

Drake

He was gone before noticed
 while in sunlight, hopeless
eclipse
A shadow on the world

He talked in chords, lyrics
Coded clues of mystic gimmicks
Light echo
Reflection of life longer than it was

He walked in ancient footprints
On borders dark and immense
A pilgrim
A scout of solace and solitude

He was a simple sojourner
Past marathons and tearful mourners
A lighthouse lamentation
A beacon cast out to sea
df

"You did this alone? By yourself?" Xanadu's voice was rich with contempt.

Darragh hung his head, disappointed. "Yes, no one else has even seen it."

"Tell me about it. What is the subject of the poem?"

"It's about a young musician, a lad named Nick Drake. He was talented, but tormented, and died so young, either an overdose or maybe suicide. But his songs lived well beyond his days, and he is more famous now than when he was alive."

Darragh moved closer to Xanadu's desk, nervous. "You said to write about what I know. I always thought Drake was great. He's about my favorite musician. So last night I thought about him, his life and death. And when I woke this morning, those words were there, in my mind, so I wrote them down before I forgot them."

"It's good. No one at Dartmoor will give a shit, but it's good."

***

"It's been what, two plus years?" Deacon asked.

"Yea," Darragh said. "It's been a blast."

"I never see you at Sunday services. Nor at weekly study."

"Aren't you supposed to keep your eyes looking at heaven, rather than the seats in the church room? How would you know who's there?"

"I see well more than you know, son." Deacon sat down on the bench in the rec yard, watching the other prisoners mill about the grounds. "Don't be proud about your lack of faith. Trust me, it's no virtue."

"This is not a place where virtue grows. Hell, it's just the opposite."

"So tell me then, what do you believe in? Surely, it is more than yourself."

Darragh laughed and ran his hand through his thick hair. "I get it. You look at me and see an idiot farmer, and are surprised that I don't wear a rosary around my neck. Well, my good deacon, I may be lacking in school lessons, but I am not uneducated."

"Apparently not in the subjects that count, son. But show me, impress me with your wisdom."

"Ah, I've got no time for these silly games."

Deacon shook his head. "Son, you've got several years of time to give me." He pointed to the prison walls and smiled.

Darragh studied the Deacon. The old man was determined to talk God back into Darragh's life, but Darragh was just as determined to remain unbridled to the shackles of religion. But the Deacon did make one point, being the intolerably slow crawl of time in the vise of the prison walls. So if he wanted to compete in a debate, then let the games begin.

"I want some chocolate. Say five bars."

"For what?"

Darragh leaned in closer. "For the thrill of the debate, the competition."

The Deacon considered the price, then answered, "I'll tell you what. If you give me an educated debate, and I alone be the judge of that, then I will get you the chocolate."

"Five bars?"

"Yes, five good Cadbury bars."

"Fine," Darragh said, leaning back a little as if to better define his space for the competition. "Tell me, Sir. Do you know the writing of the Scottish philosopher David Hume?"

Deacon raised his eyebrows, surprised. "You've read Hume?"

"I have. And I subscribe to his ideas. Especially methodological naturalism and his arguments regarding experience."

"Meaning what?"

"In a word, that all human knowledge is ultimately founded in experience."

"You are talking about philosophy. What about religion?"

"Taken as a whole, it is pretty clear that all religious beliefs trace to one thing, and that is the primal dread of the unknown."

"Your point being?"

Darragh pointed to Deacon as he talked. "Please, no personal offense is intended here. But it seems to me that religion is not based on faith, but rather, simply, fear. I fear death, because of pain, because of not finishing what I've started, but really because no one knows if there is anything after death. It is the fear of the unknown."

"That's where faith comes in."

Darragh shook his head. "Only if it is another name for fear."

The Deacon scratched his chin. "What about the argument that the sheer complexity of the universe, the grandeur of its size and reach, implies that there is a Divine design to its works."

"Hume was not impressed with that argument. Consider the concept of Experience, that human conduct is based on experience. One then can never truly perceive, through experience, that one event will always cause another. I respond to your offering this way; I have not experienced God through observation or otherwise, nor have I observed, through any point of reference, this universe or any others. I cannot say that either exists in the way you envision them. Further, it is folly and conjecture to link them together as cause and effect. And surely one is not proof of the other, any more than saying that a volcano is proof that hell exists at the center of the earth."

A bird flying above cast a shadow on the ground, and it moved across the yard, silent and sure. The Deacon watched it as he considered Darragh's response. "How do you explain the experience of miracles? History is replete with them. Do they not inspire you to faith?"

Darragh laughed. "I knew that was coming. I again go to Hume, and his theory of minimal astonishment. No miracle has ever been proven, documented, because it can't be. There is no evidence sufficiently pure and unassailable to unambiguously prove a miracle."

"But doesn't the event prove itself?"

"Onus probandi," Darragh said. "Burden of proof. The event cannot prove itself."

Deacon stood and paced around Darragh, who remained seated. "What about the parting of the Red Sea, documented in the Bible."

"For the sake of argument, I will accept what is written, though I do point out that the Bible is full of narrative that is not literal historical accounts, but rather allegorical. But assume Moses did cross with the tribes of Israel, he did it in the shallows with the benefit of wind set-down. Meteorologically speaking, the Red Sea has parted many times."

"You sure know and use some big words, for a burglar."

"So that means the game is done?" Darragh smiled.

"Not quite, Darragh. Let me skip over the ample number of miracles, like the Shroud of Turin, the burning bushes, the power of Jesus to heal, to walk on water. What about the Resurrection of Jesus, the miracle of all miracles?"

Darragh frowned. "I am going to anger you, and that was why I did not want to play this silly game. For all that you say about the events of Easter, the resurrection, others have written that he was not dead, but unconscious, that his body was moved, maybe resuscitated. We could go on like this all day. Let's just end with this. You believe in something that has not and cannot be proven or experienced, and I believe only in matters of fact."

"Fair enough, Mr. Finn," Deacon said as he extended his hand. "You will get your chocolate. You have smarts upstairs but so little wisdom. Maybe one day I can convince you otherwise."

"That would take a miracle," Darragh laughed.

The Deacon left Darragh sitting on the bench, as he slowly walked out into the prison yard, following the trail of the bird that flew by not that long ago.

***

While time passed slowly in the prison walls, it did pass, and Darragh did inch closer to a day of release. He had unpleasant days, illnesses linked to the cold and damp winters and injuries caused by his encounters with STDs or others like him. But for the majority of the time, Darragh made do, working afternoons in the print shop, and splitting his mornings in the gardens and, if the brewery ran, on a work pass to help with the beer and ale runs.

Five years had passed. Falwood died in year four, of a vicious lung cancer that spread like spilled ink across his organs, ruining everything that let him live. Xanadu left six months later, paroled, though Darragh believed that he did not truly want to go. The Deacon still prayed for some of the prisoners, ones who did not pray for themselves, though Darragh did not know if he was in that number. And his nemesis, STDs was still his tormentor and his reason for vigilance.

Garden duty in March was an exhausting shift, fighting the still chilly rain and the mud that held your weight like setting concrete. The crew was clearing the field, and even cleaning a new patch of ground. This work required shovels and pry bars to move the rocks that the earth held just below its surface, so the guards were more vigilant.

The crew had been working for an hour trying to dislodge a granite rock for a new section of the garden. Darragh dug around its base, using a shovel to feel for its bottom.

"What's wrong, you little cocker, can't find a way to handle a rock like this one?" STDs worked on the other side of the field, but came over to Darragh's rock at the direction of one of the guards.

"This one's in tight. And it's a heavy bitch too."

STDs got on his knees and felt around the rock's base. "You're right about that, cocker. This one ain't moving without a tractor."

A crowd of four other prisoners drew close, drawn to the challenge of the rock. Twice as many shied away, wanting no part moving anything that big.

162

STDs stood, and slapped away mud from his knees. He raised his hand above his head and circled it. When one of the guards, the one named Percival, approached, STDs said, "This bitch is going nowhere with just us pushing on it. We need the tractor, and I don't mean Little Fergie."

Percival nodded. "It's coming. Fergie can do it. Sargent Benty will be here in a minute. While you are waiting, gather some of that plank wood and lay a path."

Darragh tossed aside his shovel, and started placing the wood over the mud ruts, with three other prisoners. STDs held his shovel across his shoulders. "Very nice, ladies, I can see that you've crawled around in the mud before." STDs laughed.

The Model TE20 tractor was old and light, but was the only piece of equipment kept on the prison grounds. Percival took Benty's place behind the wheel, and drove the tractor slowly, never out of second gear, and positioned the old machine ten feet behind the rock. He said to no one in particular, "Hook 'er up."

One of the prisoners went to a wheelbarrow which held an assortment of tools, and after a minute declared, "No chains in here. Don't have any chains."

STDs watched the preparation efforts amused. "Sorry to disappoint, but that little Fergie's never going to move that granite. You need an excavator."

Percival disagreed. "We got a whole bunch of excavators, you included. If we got the manpower to dig around the rock, loosen it up, I can drag it away. It can't be rooted too deep. It just popped up within the last few years."

"We still got no chains."

Percival jumped off of the tractor, leaving the engine running. He walked over to the wheelbarrow and used his baton to dig around the assortment of tools. "Here we go lads," he said grinning. "Use this rope around the rock, and this strap to hook to my tractor. This will do."

Darragh had been listening and watching. "Captain, that's a tie strap. Don't think that's good for static pulling."

"You got an engineering degree I don't know about, Finn? I've cleared more rocks from these fields that you morons can count."

"Hook'em up," another guard said. "Day's a'wastin'."

STDs tossed the rope, strap and hooks to Darragh, saying "Since you've already soiled you pants, cocker, you do the honors."

Darragh had enough rope to wrap around the rock three times. He tied the ends with a square knot and closed the ends with a back-up overhand knot. He left just enough slack in the loops of rope to secure the strap's hook. Once done, he slid himself out of the mud around the base of the rock, and trailed the strap until he reached the back of the tractor. He secured the other end of the strap by hooking its end into the mount on the tractor frame. Once done, he whistled, took a few steps back, and twirled his right hand in the air.

Percival took his time finding first gear, and slowly eased off the clutch. The strap went taunt, but the rock did not move. After a moment, he engaged the clutch.

"Didn't budge," one of the guards said.

Percival strained to see behind him. "Did the wheels spin? Did I lose my traction?"

STDs laughed. "I told you that little Fergie was too old and too light."

Darragh scratched his head, not knowing who to believe. "What if a few of us got a pry-bar under the back end while the Captain is pulling with the tractor? Maybe leverage will help get it going."

"Good idea," Percival said. He pointed to two prisoners who had done nothing but watch for the last hour. "You two drummers, double up on that pry bar behind the rock when I pull."

"It's never gonna work. That toy tractor couldn't pull a loose tooth from my mouth, Boss." STDs laughed as Percival glared back at him.

Percival put the tractor in first gear and pulled the strap tight. "Okay, now get that bar underneath the rock. Work that bar."

STDs eased up behind Darragh and said, "If that cub scout knot of yours comes undone, I'm gonna make you eat rope, cocker."

Percival pressed the tractor, gunning the engine, still in first gear. The boards under the wheels were holding, and the Fergie was stressing to move the rock. Then a hum sang in the air, like a massive guitar string being tuned. The strap seemed to turn, to roll a few degrees, then with a bang the coiled rope exploded.

In the instant before the coils of rope failed, STDs sensed the impending calamity, and jumped in front of Darragh, and with a thrust of his muscled arms knocked him to the ground. The five-pound hook attached to the end of the strap, propelled by the tension stored in the nylon mesh, shot toward the tractor like a projectile, which would have killed Darragh had he remained standing.

Darragh knew instinctively that Stacy Talbot Dower, or as he preferred, STDs, had just saved him from either death or a grievous injury. And before he was back on his feet he saw that not only had STDs saved him, but he had also taken his place.

Darragh could not tell who was screaming, the prisoners, maybe even the guards. More than one person was shrieking, crying. Some others just turned away or fell to their knees. Percival yelled for medical help, and someone ran toward the prison infirmary, either a prisoner or a guard.

STDs was flat on his back, the metal hook embedded deeply in his neck. His chin was split open, holding bits of broken teeth and bone. Blood bubbled up out of his mouth, and spilled from the wound in his neck.

Darragh knelt beside him, and reached for his right hand. "What did you do to yourself, Stacey? Why did you do it?"

STDs eyes fluttered, searching. When he found Darragh's face, he said, "One good deed. Me Mom said I was meant for one good deed."

Darragh yelled for help, for anything that could stop the blood. He looked back and found Percival, also on his knees at STDs feet. Percival stared at him, almost through him, and shook his head."

STDs fist clenched around Darragh's hand. "Tell the Deacon what I did," he managed to say in wet, red sputters. Then his fist relaxed.

Chapter Fifteen
December 28

Claira woke roughly, suddenly, as if pulled from her sleep by the sounds of approaching explosions and screams, a timpani of terror. But as she opened her eyes, all was silent, in her room and even the street outside. The riot she thought she heard was phantom. A dream, or a haunting. Her dream vision was nonspecific, but she knew that it concerned the Park, and more specifically, the chapel. Without any details that she could remember, she could only sense that her subconscious mind had broadcast her concerns for the chapel like a silent movie dream, acted out in strange dress rehearsal episodes, dreams of possibilities, or hopeful outcomes. Or maybe an omen, a premonition of something much more ominous. A nightmare, or a warning.

After a moment she oriented herself. She was in her bedroom, alone. The dawn was just breaking, light peeking around the edges of her covered window. Instinctively, she felt her neck. Her silver chain was still around her neck, on which hung a small solitaire diamond, a gift from her father on her wedding day. The necklace was covered by the Giants jersey she wore as a nightshirt, white with red numbers on the front and back. Number 56, a vintage Lawrence Taylor jersey.

Her apartment was too quiet. She leapt from bed, not bothering for her slippers, but wrapping herself in a long robe. She glanced at the alarm clock on her nightstand, only to verify that the time was around 7:15 a.m. She had overslept, letting sunrise find her still in bed.

She first peered into Tony's room. He was fast asleep, breathing deeply, content in the warm deepness of pleasant slumber. She edged his bedroom door back to shut, and started down the hall to her kitchen and den.

She didn't know what to expect. She remembered listening to Darragh talk for what seemed like hours, telling her vivid stories of his past, his rises and falls, his good and his bad. She half expected to see him asleep on her sofa, but the den was empty. She reached for a lamp's light switch and gave the room a little more light, and let her also peer into the kitchen. He was gone.

After a moment to straighten the pillows on the sofa, she retreated to the kitchen. Before she opened the cupboard for a coffee cup, she noticed two pieces of paper on the table, folded in half. Still standing, she reached for the papers, and slowly unfolded them. The first page simply read, "C. There is little difference in what you know and what you choose to believe. But that little bit of difference defines you to everyone in your life. It is like the sound of your voice, or the taste of your tears. So unique, but so much more familiar to the ones you love. D.F."

Slowly, she shuffled the pages to read the second sheet of paper, and after a moment of reading, her hand covered her mouth, and then felt the warm fall of her tears. She managed to sit at the table, and read the words on the page again.

DOUBT

When doubt descends on painter's plans
The pallet meekly molds and grays
No vivid view of mortal man
No rebel rendering of future days

When doubt descends on tinker's thoughts
Gears or circuits may not be built
Cancer's cure may not be sought
Better static stain than failure's guilt

When doubt descends on children's camps
Their games and goings grow rote and stale
The wick too wet to spark their lamps
The wind too weak to fill their sails

When doubt descends on soldier's speech
No questions asked in death's debate
Heavy hands halt reason's reach
Martyrs fashioned a flagrant fate

When doubt descends on pious prayers
Faith's foundation starts to fray
Tribes again become lost heirs
Bleating lambs who've lost their way

When doubt descends with all its might

Grit and turn into the storm
Steady for the coming fight
The pilgrim's quest yet to perform

Claira read the poem three times, each reading a little slower than the previous. She then folded the two sheets of paper and placed them on her table, under a small vase that needed fresh flowers. Rising, she slowly went back to her bedroom, retrieved her phone, and dialed a number saved in her contacts. Her call was answered on the third ring.

"Hello,"

"Hey, Theo. I need to talk to you. Do you have a few minutes this morning?"

His voice hinted that he was both surprised and worried. "Is everything all right? Is there something wrong with Tony?"

"No, nothing like that. But we need to talk. Something happened to me last night. Well, I'm not saying this right." Claira paused to find the words. "It would be better to talk in person. Can you come by on your way to work?"

Theo's delayed answer proved that he was confused. "Yea, okay, I guess that I can be there in a bit. Do you want me to grab two Starbuck's on the way?"

"Well. Sure, I guess. Only if you want to."

"Clare, baby, what is it?"

Claira started to lose her voice. "There's so much happening to me right now. More than I can handle by myself. I used to be able to tell you anything and everything, and you could hear it all, even the little details and secrets that I tried to keep hidden. You could always talk me off the ledge, defuse my runaway anger, you could make me laugh even when I cried."

"Well, yea, until I couldn't."

"Theo, I'm sorry I doubted you. I can't say it any other way."

For what seemed like a season, there was no reply, no words for her to hear, not even the sounds of breath, or the timid sounds of the heart in the throes of confusion. Finally, Theo found his voice. "Clare, what are you trying to tell me?"

"I don't know how to say this. I panicked when I doubted you. For the first time in all of our time together, I ran away from you, when I should have run to you."

"Clare,"

"Just run. Get over here, as fast as you can."

***

Mike had been awake for hours, listening to the dark thunder of his memory. He started drinking, for real, at midnight, and finished half a bottle of Irish whiskey with little more than a few cubes of ice. He may have fallen asleep for some miserable interval of time, or maybe he just drifted in the dark night-shadows between sleep and self-inflicted insanity. But at some point in the whispering night he realized that no bargain had been struck, that he was marking the year since his daughter's death with a silent vacuum violence, an internal and benevolent storm that was ripping him apart, from the inside out. About 4 a. m., he had made a pot of coffee, and mixed the whiskey with the bitter brew in place of cream. He sat alone in his dark home office, soaked and battered like driftwood, alone with his quiet pain. His throat ached with the hurt of an open burn, and his eyes were weary to the point of betrayal. He was empty of tears, barren as a desert dune.

As he sat in the twilight room, he tried to forecast the insults of the day. There would be calls, or messages of some kind, from family and friends who would offer some sympathy but who would falter, not knowing what to say. There would be the pulling, desperate desire to open Maria's bedroom door, to peek inside as if a yearlong nightmare would end, as if time would unwind, and she would be there in her bed, just sleeping. There would be Jessie, unpredictable, careening from memories to tears, sinking into the faces of Maria, frozen and reflected in the chronology of pictures assembled over the passage of this terrible year.

And then there would be the ride to Green-Wood Cemetery, and the slow walk through the hills, with the stone monuments and the trees in the cold, where other people would make their calls to their fallen, to their lost, maybe only to names, names on stone because all else was forgotten. Would that ever happen to him? Years from now, would he forget his daughter's smile, or the feel of her hair on his skin, the sound of her voice and her sneezes and giggles, the music of her love? Would he grow numb, or would his anger just grow him cold, like a winter tree petrified, to live as rock with barren branches and the cruel reality of displacement from the birth of any other season. Or would that tragedy befall his wife, already rankled with the dissonance of despair. Or would it ensnare them both? He had wanted to be the strong one, the base of the rock for Jessie, an anchor until she could forgive for her loss. But he knew that his strength had been exhausted, and his footing long washed away.

His cell phone buzzed. Mike ignored the intrusion, and sipped on his cold, whiskey laden coffee. He had no intention of going to work today. The mystery of the chapel and the poems, and for that matter, the troubles of the rest of the world, would have to wait. This was a day to remember, the almost merciful end of the Year of the Firsts. No longer would he have to experience each event as the first without his Maria. Her loss would always still be with him, but it would not be cruel testament marking a birthday or a holiday or an event at school or even something as simple as the days she praised life in the words of her diary.

Not that he would ever look at that book again, with its Maria handwriting and Maria flare of hearts above the lower case "i's" and "j's," and Maria words that were sprinkled throughout, like "Quazy," her combination of 'queasy' and 'crazy', to describe the way some of her medicine made her feel, or "Slad," her word for sad and glad, the way she said she felt when she said her prayers. Mike asked her what she meant by that term, one day when he was alone with her in her hospital room, and she smiled and explained that she was glad to be at peace with whatever would happen, but sad that her Mom was so far from finding that feeling. And he was too, very far from that feeling, on that day, and every day since, though he never let Maria see that in him.

The phone buzzed again, and this time he looked to see who had called. The display showed Jason's name and number. Mike tossed the phone back on his desk, and as it landed, it sounded again, this time showing that a new text message was received. Mike finished his spiked coffee with one long swallow, then read the text. "Call me. We have a break on ID of the poet. Park under siege by kids."

***

Isla was firing with adrenaline, and even though she'd walked miles around and through the Park, she felt as though she was combusting with nervous energy, like a flameless fire, like the blood chemistry of fear and fight. Darragh had inspired her with a purpose and a reason, something that she abandoned long ago, but now newly found, now a precious part of her heart. She was both hungry and hesitant, and in all manners, alive.

170

She arrived at the chapel at daybreak, as she was instructed, and found Darragh idly chatting with a park officer on the chapel landing. When Darragh saw her approaching, he waved to her and said, "I was just explaining what a wonderful day is in store for the park visitors today. Are we set with our volunteers?"

Isla ran up to greet him. She caught her breath and said, "Yea, well, I don't know what we got. There will be some, for sure. But there just wasn't enough time to spread the word."

Darragh nodded in agreement. "We'll make due." He gestured to the officer standing at his side, and said. "Isla, this is my new good friend, Warren Hayes. I've been telling him about you, and your wonderful coffee shop and your wicked ways with cappuccino. Warren, here she is, Isla Walson."

"Wow," Warren exclaimed. "You look like a young Joni Mitchell. You know, 'Free Man in Paris,' 'Court and Spark.' "

Isla's face showed her confusion, but before she could speak, Warren continued. "Okay, you probably don't remember Joni Mitchell, but back in the day, she was top of the line great songwriter and artist. She could write songs that just pulled tears from your eyes, the kind of music that everyone would say, 'wow, I wish I had written that.' You have the same features. Way past pretty, real close to exquisite."

Isla blushed, and turned to Darragh, for either rescue or reassurance.

"Well, no time for more introductions, or in your case, Warren, more unbelievable efforts of flattery. We need to —"

"Wait a minute," Isla said. "How long have you two known each other?"

Warren answered her with a huge, inspired smile. "Oh, I just met Mr. Finn this morning, 'bout an hour ago. But turns out we have some friends in common. Well, at least one. Claira Vasson. The lady that pretty much runs this Park."

"And what does she say about the chapel?"

"She says that she needs all the help she can get to keep it in one piece." Warren fiddled with his cell phone, then produced a picture of Claira taken on Christmas day when she had first seen the chapel. "Here she is." He offered the phone screen to Isla.

Darragh waited until Isla returned the phone to Warren, then asked, "Back to our volunteers. How many are coming?"

Isla held out her hands and shrugged. Yesterday afternoon was frantic. Isla contacted her friends in the Altar Society and the Catholic Daughters chapter at St Ann's, and had begged them to meet her at her coffee shop. There, she introduced them to Darragh, who, through a captivating advocation, solicited them and each and every group they could organize to come to the Park the next morning and show their support for, and possibly save, the chapel. He urged them to call their friends at other churches. Now they would see what response would heed their call.

As Isla stood in the cold with Darragh and Warren at the chapel entrance, the volunteers started to arrive. At first there were ladies that Isla knew from St. Ann's, Mary Pishnick, the president of their Altar Society, and Evelyn Stout, the church pianist and music director, who brought with her several of the choir members. Then Joan Weber came with her twins, dressed in their boy scout uniforms, whose troop was sponsored by St. Ann's chapter of the Knights of Columbus. Soon after, other members of that troop arrived, eager to join their friends in a mission that they did not quite understand. Then just familiar faces arrived, ladies that Isla saw then and again at church, but who she did not know by name. There were eight or more altar servers, dressed in their white albs and rope cinctures serving as meager belts.

Warren moved close up to Darragh, and pulled him to the side of a group of assembling people, all marveling at the beauty of the chapel. "I just got a text from Claira. The demolition crew is going to get here between 8 and 9 this morning."

"Well, they don't waste any time, do they?"

Warren was bewildered. "I don't even know who 'they' are. But I do know that for some reason this chapel is some kind of big threat to the politicians. I've seen all kinds of civil disobedience, and I'm with you on keeping the chapel standing. But I can't let anyone get hurt, and I can't let this get out of control."

As the crowd of volunteers grew, Darragh's apprehension started to regress. "Isla, get your friends from St. Ann's over here close. I want them to see what we are standing for this morning. Why they answered our call. Inside, on the altar, there are copies of a paper I want to hand out to everyone who happens by. We'll start here, around the chapel, and if we can, we'll cover the Park entrances too."

"Sure." Isla eyed the crowd growing around the little church, and asked, "Will you have enough of those papers? Looks like we have about twenty or more from my church here already."

"Trust me," Darragh said, smiling, "we will have plenty."

***

Preston Browne was riding in the passenger front of the dual cab F-250, a heavy duty truck whose back bed had been modified to carry two lockable tool storage compartments, and which was pulling a trailered Ingersoll Rand PowerSource 600 generator. He was an imposing figure, a college football player in his youth, who still carried his weight so well that his 260 pounds were proportioned over his 6'6" body in such a way that he appeared skinny. Preston worked for Empire Bostick Construction Group, a highly successful regional commercial and industrial construction company. Somewhere in traffic behind him was a tractor trailer rig bringing a Hitachi Zaxis 1400K Long Arm Demolition Front Excavator, and a Caterpillar D9T Bulldozer. His work crew consisted of 8 men, and they would be arriving in flatbed trucks with ground mats and covering, as well as the rest of the equipment they would need for the demolition job. He hoped that the waste trailers were not too far behind, but did not expect them until mid-day. That should not be much of a problem, since it would take several hours to off-load the heavy equipment, secure a construction perimeter, and finalize the demolition plans with the supervising city permitting officials. He lamented the fact that the days of his working youth, when demolition could begin as soon as the wrecking balls was in place, had passed. Now, he spent as much of his time processing paper, getting environmental audits and site assessments, as he did in busting walls and concrete. But it did not matter, as the efficiencies of the equipment he had with his crew made up for the bog of bureaucratic licensure. And his pay was the same, maybe even a little better.

As his truck approached the Park at 72nd Street and Fifth Avenue, he noticed two groups of children, both boy scouts and girl scouts, passing out papers and singing Christmas carols. "A few days late," he commented to his driver.

"We got kids singing every night in my neighborhood," the driver said. "They gonna sing all the way through the twelve days of Christmas. But it usually slows down after New Years."

Preston went back to his job notes. He walked the site late yesterday afternoon, and took a few pictures of the site and the stone chapel. He did not think that the job would be that involved, considering the fact that the chapel had no electrical or plumbing issues to worry about.

He talked absently to his driver. "You know, somebody paid a small fortune to build that little church. And the City says it's got to come down. What a waste."

"Somebody screwed up big time. I think that they built it in the wrong place, and now nobody wants to admit the mess-up."

"Too bad," Preston said as he scanned through his file notes. "Pretty windows. By tomorrow, it'll be just a pile of broken colored glass. What a waste."

The driver interrupted Preston's concentration over the work roster and his outline of the job assignments. "Hey, Preston. Looks like the P.D. let us down on crowd control. East Drive was supposed to be wide open for us. That hoard of people looks like the crowd I saw last year for the summer pops festival."

Preston looked up and saw large crowds of people on both sides of East Drive. Just ahead, a mass of pedestrians clogged the street, as they moved across the Park toward the Great Lawn, where the chapel sat on the snowy meadow. The F-250 slowed to a stop, and as he watched the migration scene unfold before him, a small girl approached the side of his truck, followed closely by her mother. Preston rolled his window down.

"Excuse me sir, my name is Alice and I'm a member of the Harlem Youth Gospel Club. Sponsored by Northside Neighborhood Fellowship Church. Please take one." She extended her little hand, and smiled a smile of a child's subconscious joy.

She handed Preston a sheet of paper, folded in half. In a child's handwriting, across the front of the folded page, were the words. "Save our Chapel." As Preston stared down at the page Alice said, "Please excuse my handwriting. I wrote that with my mittens on. It's a little sloppy, like my baby brother would do." She giggled.

Preston eyed her carefully, then asked. "What's all of this about, little miss?"

"Some bad men are coming to bust up a little stone church. It's so beautiful. I went through it this morning. It has pretty colored windows and when you sing inside the church it sounds like angels are singing with you too. Well, I got to go, I have to hand out some more of the papers, then Mom said we can get lunch and go back and see the chapel again." Alice smiled at Preston as if she had known him all of her young life. Then her mother leaned over and whispered to

174

her, and the smile disappeared, as if taken by the wind. Alice stared up at Preston, and asked. "Say, are you one of the tear down men?"

Preston looked down at the little girl defensively. She looked as if her eyes would explode in tears. He glanced around the truck, knowing that the sign on the truck's door and the trailer carrying the heavy light plant were giveaways to his goal and intentions. "Honey, I'm not here to do anything bad. Someone built that church in the wrong place, and I'm here to move it. That's all."

"But it's not in the wrong place," Alice protested, her lips quivering with emotion.

"But honey it is. They built it in the wrong place."

No, it's not. It's in the perfect place. Have you even seen it?"

"Well yes, but the man who built it wants me to move it."

Alice looked up at her mother, whose eyes were intense with building protest. Turning back to Preston, the little girl said, "That's not true. I know, because I know who built the chapel."

Preston just nodded. "You do now. Tell me who built it, and maybe this is just a mistake, because I bet we're out here today for the same man."

"I don't think that you're working for him."

Preston managed a small laugh. "It's gonna be fine, Alice. I promise. Just tell me who you think built the chapel."

"God built it," she said loudly, then slowly starting shaking her head. "And I don't think that you're out here working for him."

Preston was shocked by the answer, and quickly looked up at the girl's mother. She stared at him with a tight jaw, clinched like a fist. He started to speak, but Alice's mother cut him off. "Mister, don't you ever defame that Name, don't you defame His house."

Preston was speechless. As Alice was led away by her mother, she turned around and waved excitedly at Preston, smiling a wide birthday smile and skipping to keep up with her mother.

The driver said, "Damn, Preston, that was some real spiritual shit she just put on you. They ain't happy about us tearing down their church. What are we gonna do?"

But Preston was busy reading Alice's paper and didn't answer. Carefully, after a moment more of reading, he folded the paper and handed it to the driver. "Call in to the home office. I have a feeling we're not going to get anything done today."

Claira somehow knew the call was coming. And when the sound came, an old fashion ring of a bell, she knew its source without checking the caller I.D. She keyed to accept the call and said, "Yes."

"Ms. Vasson," Terrance Greenberg screamed. "What in the hell is going on at the Park? And where are you?"

"I'm at the Park now, sir."

"And?"

Claira pressed the phone closer to the face. "It's very loud, sir. I'm having a hard time hearing you."

"Why isn't the Great Lawn cleared of pedestrian traffic? I have a crew assigned to start work this morning."

"Cleared, sir? Not sure what you mean. I'm not aware of any plans to close parts of the Park." That last statement was a lie, but Claira considered it white and barely a misdemeanor sin.

"Well, we had to move fast and get control of this mess," Terrance was seldom at a loss for words, but Claira had thrown him off guard with her response. "You would have seen the work orders and schedule on your desk when you arrived. But this thing has turned into a disaster. Where have all of these people come from? Why are all of these children there, passing out a poem? Someone told me that there are hundreds of them, out there all over the park, and that it's not just kids passing out the poem to save the chapel, but parents, clergy, what have you. Now it looks like whoever is responsible for these poems popping up all over the city has also involved my Park with this unfortunate crusade. You need to get down there to this chapel as quickly as possible and evacuate the Great Lawn. Before it's too late."

Claira was standing twenty feet behind the chapel, looking at its back door. A steady stream of people was exiting the chapel, all of them looking amazed at what they had just seen. The line included people of all ages, grandparents to toddlers. As they filed out of the chapel, some drifted to one side or the other to look again at the stained glass windows. Others just seem to wander off a small distance, then turn and behold the chapel as it stood in the old snow, with happy people all around its meager frame. She turned her attention back to the phone conversation and said, "Sir, I don't think that's possible now. There's too many people here, and they all seem to admire this chapel. What do you expect me to do? What do I tell them?"

"Tell them any damn thing, but close that whole section of the park. Seal it off. I will get the Chief of Police down there himself to clear the area."

Claira shook her head in disbelief at his rage. "Mr. Greenberg. Terrance. Listen to yourself. You are talking about alienating thousands of people. You're going to cause a huge disruption in the Park, during the Christmas holiday. If you could see all of the faces here, all of these happy people, sir, I don't think that you would be so resolute in your decision to demolish this chapel."

Terrance could say nothing in response for a moment, but then concluded what Claira knew would be obvious. "You don't agree with my decision. And you are there doing nothing to support me. I fear to ask whether you had any hand in this insult, this insubordination. Are you complicit in this riot against the Park?"

"Terrance, there is no riot here. You should get here and see for yourself."

"Claira, don't think that I did not notice your lack of an answer to my question." His voice was sharp and bitter, full of disdain.

"Sir, I have always been grateful for the opportunities that you gave me at the Conservancy. And I always will be. But, with respect, you did not ask me a question. No sir. It was rather an accusation, and I can tell from your tone that no matter what I say you won't believe me."

Terrance lowered the volume of his voice, knowing that her assessment of him was accurate. "Forgive me, Claira. This whole situation is upsetting to me, and I'm sure just so to you also. Just tell me that you had nothing to do with this outrageous conduct, and of course I will believe you."

Claira thought of the late night conversation with Darragh, and the oral history he shared with her. Then she recalled this morning, and the poem he left for her, and the new poem that she read when she got to the Park. But her mind kept circling back to her talk with Theo, and the revelation that Darragh had forced her to confront, the truth that she needed to see again and believe again, for her Tony, for her family, and maybe more so, for her own sanity. "Sir, all I can say is this…" she barely managed.

"Go on, Claira, answer me." Terrance was back to his political self, trying to coax out of her the answer that he wanted to hear.

"Sir, all I can say is this. Guilty as charged." With that, she hung up on leaving Terrance yelling over a disconnected line.

Mike walked into Jason's office a little before noon. As he reached the front of Jason's desk, he said, "I just got the message. Well, I got it a little while ago."

Jason ignored Mikes' superficial apology for being late. "Have you seen the news feeds this morning?" Jason keyed a button on a remote control and the flat-screen television housed in a bookcase on the side wall flashed to movement. The screen showed the chapel, ringed by a large assembly of on-lookers. The next clip showed a line of people as they entered the chapel, as if it were an attraction at Disney-World. "Damn near every channel has a lead about the chapel in the park. Look, there's an army of little kids out there, cub scouts, brownies, altar boys, youth choirs, you name it. Freddie reported to me that there's a handful of them at every park entrance. That's almost fifty entrances, with kids and their parents, handing out a new poem and asking for support in their push to keep the chapel. I think they're accepting donations for some kind of defense fund, which they have no permit to do, but they're doing it anyway."

Mike listened without interruption as he slid into a chair at the front of Jason's desk. He swiveled the chair to better see the television monitor. When Jason finally turned off the video, Mike rotated back to face Jason. "What new poem? Are you saying that all of these kids' groups have this one in print?"

"Exactly. It's everywhere. You can't go into the park without some kid shoving one into your hands. Thousands of copies of it. Freddie says that every once in a while, someone goes into the chapel and comes out with stacks of copies of the poem to be passed out like a flyer for lunch specials at a local diner." Jason worked through a file that was cluttering his desk and retrieved a copy of the new poem. "Here is one of the hand-outs that Freddie sent over."

Mike reached for the paper, and read the latest poem.

THE BIRTHRIGHT

Awaken in a system caste
Born into a princely claim
Bestowed with blessing unsurpassed
Royal blood and regal fame

Linage of a privileged class
Comfort in ancestral name
Destitute the others vast
Who lack a noble sovereign flame

What birthright brings the poor outcasts
What legacy is suffered shame
What limelight guides the ones harassed
What repose lies for those defamed

A fading light is sure forecast
Disease and darkness cannot be tamed
Inverted bowls of sand contrast
Time returns from where it came

Paradise lost and kingdoms past
Seven deadly sins to blame
A pension won for all who ask
The infant King has so proclaimed d.f.12-28

"Wow," Mike said after reading the poem. "No doubt now that the chapel and the mystery poet are connected."

"Yea, well he won't be a mystery man for much longer. We got a lead on this guy. Freddie had a P.I. run surveillance at the park for the last two nights. Same guy comes and goes in the chapel both nights." Jason handed Mike a photograph, 8 by 10. "Don't have a name yet, but Freddie's running with it. We'll have a name to match the face soon."

"You still think that this guy is some kind of computer hacker? This latest poem, they're just handing out copies, looks pretty low tech compared the other ones."

"Whoever this guy is, he's got some big resources behind him. That's four different poems since Christmas, all with a different delivery method. And the first three are still difficult to explain, especially the one that took our page one on Christmas day. I'm still pissed about that, but I have to give it to this guy, whatever he did is an impressive piece of work."

While Jason droned on about his suspicions and his admiration of the skill by which these events were controlled, Mike re-read the poem, trying to understand the theme that linked the poetry together. Aside from the religious overtones, Mike sensed that there was something else the poems had in common, some other connection that had yet to be seen or understood. When he realized that Jason had stopped speaking, and was apparently waiting for an answer, Mike looked. "What do you want me to do?"

"I need you at the park. See the scene for yourself. Meet up with Freddie and his surveillance guy. Then I want you back here, heading the article we're running tomorrow about this poetry being the product of religious fanaticism, and the chapel a seizure of public property by some religious zealots. That's our lead for tomorrow's page one."

Mike winced. He had some inkling of Jason's perspective on the chapel from the meeting at Greenberg's office, but did not see it to be a vendetta campaign to malign the appearance of the poems. "Jason, do you really think that is where this story is going? I don't see anything ominous here."

Jason's response was cutting. "What are you talking about? Our paper was attacked. Grand Central was hi-jacked. This is not a game, not some innocent stunt."

"What about all of the people out at the park today?"

"They're out of context. They don't know what we know. They don't see the big picture."

Mike's thoughts were clouded by the memory of the journalism class and the succinct reminder of the journalists' creed. To speak truth. But he also understood that foundational precept was rarely followed in the agenda driven world of ratings and profits and market share. Jason interrupted those thoughts, "Mike, we are not in the business of observing and reporting. Any fool with a camera and recorder can do that. We are in the business of telling the public what the news is. We have the expertise to see things and understand things that people skimming over headlines cannot see."

"So you're saying that we have to think for them," Mike said, appalled.

"No. We write the news. They can think about what we write."

Mike just nodded. He was too tired to argue, and his mind too distracted to focus on the subtleties of Jason's argument. He rested his face in his cupped hands. Through that facemask of fingers, he said, "I was going to take the day. Have to go out to the cemetery. It's Maria's anniversary."

Jason's voice was blunt in its absence of empathy. "Sorry. I forgot about that. Why don't you run by the park, just for an hour or so, and then go to see Maria. Call me when you are done. In the meantime, I want to track down Terrance Greenberg. See what he knows."

Mike slowly rose from the chair. Without speaking, he stared at Jason. Without either a nod or a shake of his head, he turned, and as he left the office, said, "I'll be in touch."

***

The Greenwood cemetery gates soar like gothic church spires, and were designated a New York City landmark in 1966. The sprawling cemetery grounds contain wooded dales and manicured pathways, decorative ponds and waterways, aged family crypts and mausoleums, and the solemn intrigue of decades of memories carved in stone, names and dates, family crests and epithets, and the hint of promises made and promises broken whispering in the air.

Located deep into the grounds, Mike's maternal grandparents rested in the Sandoval family mausoleum, as did his parents and his Maria. Fives vaults remained empty, though two were promised to Mike and Jessie.

Mike walked past the Hillside Mausoleum, now like the Cemetery Gates, a tourist attraction. He paused and peered down on the lawn below the hilltop, garden-like, with its headstones and obelisks spiraling out from the oval sidewalk. He continued on, and climbed Battle Hill, the highest point in the cemetery, where Minerva's bronze statue gazed out to meet the stare of the Statue of Liberty, standing resolute on its pedestal in New York harbor. He wondered whether Maria would slowly fade in his memory over the tumbling of time. Who would remember her in a generation, who would utter her name? She would never have children to love and hold her memory. She would never grow old enough to mark places in the world with her gifts, her thoughts and pieces of work. Was there another life that she was now living? Was she happy and at peace? Was she waiting to greet him one day, whether soon or distant? He felt ashamed that he could not answer those questions. But he was more angry than ashamed, and that anger had no release.

The Sandoval Mausoleum was in a much older section of the graveyard, that saw little foot traffic. As he approached the tomb, he noticed someone sitting on a worn concrete bench just ahead of his family crypt. He paid little attention to the man, and raised a bouquet of twelve white roses he carried to his face, as if to memorize the fragrance rather just smell it. After unlocking the heavy metal gate of the mausoleum, he pulled it open. The hinges creaked a protest, but relented. He entered the small alcove between the rows of vaults, and stood before the stone that marked Maria's place of rest. And in this shadowed silence, he said nothing, and he cried no tears. But he vented his mind, silently screaming rough and accusing prayers, if you called tantrum pleas with God a form of prayer. And he listened for some response, some explanation of defense of his child's suffering and death, but found none forthcoming, save for the distant movement of ghost prayers of others, echo words that moved through the cemetery like the scrape of dead leaves ahead of a cold autumn wind. And they too were unanswered, as far as Mike could tell.

An hour later, as he left the alcove and shut and locked the metal gate, he noticed that the man on the bench was still there, slightly shivering in the cold. The man looked at him, the way an artist would study a subject whose portrait was underway. Mike slowly recognized the man. It was the same face that he had seen in the photograph Jason showed him, the man seen entering the chapel in the middle of night.

Mike, feeling threatened, turned to face the man directly. "You're here for a reason. What is it?"

"Only to take a moment of you time. If you don't mind, that is."

"How long have you been following me?"

"I haven't been following you, if that is what you think." Darragh took his hands out of his pockets and held them aloft for Mike to see. "No reason to be alarmed."

"What is it you want?" Mike said, his back still against the mausoleum door. "Is it something to do with the chapel? The poems?"

Darragh shrugged. "I'm here only for you. Not those other things."

Mike tensed. If this man was not here because of the park chapel or the poems, what else could it be? Was Jason right? Was some fortune in play because of some technology? Mike took a step forward and asked, "Who are you?"

"My name is Darragh Finn."

"If, as you say, you are not here because of the Central Park chapel, or these poems popping up across town, what is it?"

Darragh leaned back on the bench, looking over the cemetery grounds. "Very strange place, this Green-Wood Cemetery. It's beautiful. But it has the feel of a tourist attraction. A place people come to see while on holiday. They come to see the sculpture of Minerva at the gate, and the statues and the gardens." Darragh's thoughts seemed to leave him, and he said nothing more, only looked at the gravestones in the distance, as if captivated.

"And the chapel."

With that, Darragh turned to face Mile.

"The Green-Wood Chapel," Mike said. "It was built around 1922, and it surely is used for funerals. But it is also rented out for weddings, and gatherings."

"Is it now?"

"Where else but New York would a graveyard book weddings and have a tour trolley motoring around the grounds. With a guide telling all sorts of bits of history here."

"It's like your Central Park, but with about half a million permanent residents nesting in the coolness of the ground."

Mike smiled at the comparison. "Never thought of it that way."

Darragh stood and stretched. "I know about your daughter. I am truly sorry for your loss. And I know that I am a stranger, but if I may, I have something for you. Something that I wrote."

Mike studied him. This man wasn't asking for trust, but neither was he giving any justification for anything that he'd done, or at least was a part of. Mike looked back at Maria's crypt with great grandparents that she never knew. He turned back to Darragh. "Why would you do that? Why would you write anything for me? You don't know me, not anything about me."

"Mr. Sandoval, you are right, what you just said. But indulge me for a moment. Walk with me."

Mike hesitated for a moment. His suspicions had not been sated, or his apprehension abated. But he was also aware that this man was a puzzle piece. He took a few hurried steps, then fell in stride with Darragh as he followed a curved sidewalk.

"Your family vault?" Darragh asked, pointing back to the mausoleum.

"Yes. It goes back to my grandfather. He had the foresight to buy it when a family could afford to be buried here. Sounds funny to say this about a cemetery, but it turned out to be a very sound investment."

They walked a moment without speaking. Mike broke the silence. "You wrote the poems, the one in my paper, This World, and the one on the buildings. At Grand Central."

"Aye, I did."

"How did you do it?"

Darragh smiled. "Am I talking to Mike or to the *Times* newspaper?"

"Is there really a difference?" Mile waited for a response, but continued. "You came here to see me. I did not track you down. So what is it, Mr. Finn?"

Darragh reached into his pocket and retrieved a folded paper. "Here is why I came to this place on this evening. To give you this. A poem that is not going to be anywhere but in your hand. You will not see it on display for the world. This is for you, you alone." He handed the paper to Mike, and turned to walk away.

"You know that the Chapel is going to be demolished tomorrow."

Darragh slowed his pace, but did not stop.

"That was a great effort to mobilize supporters today. But it's not enough. Tomorrow there will be security to make sure that the construction crew does its work."

Darragh turned to face Mike. "And you agree with that?"

"Not really, but it's not supposed to be there. How did you do it? Maybe if we knew, the decision to remove it would be changed."

"You don't really believe that, Mike. If something that beautiful is given freely, should it be destroyed because its manner of being is not known?" Then he turned and continued his slow, steady stride.

Mike said nothing. He looked at the paper in hand, and part of him wanted to rip it to shreds, to refuse to be pulled into any more of this mystery. But he slowly unfolded the single page. And he read the poem, over and over again. When he finally looked up, Darragh was gone.

Mike folded the paper and put it in his pocket, and ran back to the Sandoval family vault.

Chapter Sixteen
December 29

Claira's phone rang at a quarter to 5 in the morning. One glance told her the call was from Warren, and she knew that he would not be calling this early with any good news. She prepared herself for the worst and answered, "What's up, Warren?"

"Park units are already mobilizing near the Great Lawn. I'm going there in a few." He waited for a moment, as if debating whether he could say more. He continued, "C, I got a bad feeling about this. 'Bad Moon Rising.' "

"What are the orders?"

"Set a perimeter. Crowd control. Give the contractor space to work."

"Who's pushing this? Is it Terrance Greenberg? Or is this coming from City Hall?"

"I'm not sure. I think it's both, maybe, with a little push from that guy at the *Times*."

Claira considered those possibilities, which if proven true, meant that their ability to do anything to stop the demolition was almost nonexistent. "Who's going to be on site and in charge?"

"Well, you won't believe this, but Chief Lombard is going to be there himself. He'll be Dean on the Scene," Warren said with a laugh.

"Where are you on this, Warren? How do you feel?"

There was a long pause, then he said, "Like the great Joe Walsh once declared, 'The Smoker You Drink, The Player You Get.' Yea, that about sums it up."

Claira was exasperated, considering the early hour of the morning, and her response was short and conveyed her state of mind, "What the hell does that mean?"

"Well, obviously, that makes no sense at all. Just like this situation with the chapel and the poems and the Wise-men and the Silent Night Star." Warren let that sink in for a moment then asked, "You got that?"

"When you put it like that," Claira answered, "I see exactly what you mean. We have to find some way to slow all this down. I'll be rolling out of here in a few. I'll see you there."

***

The plan was to have the Great Lawn sequestered before sunrise. The park police blocked the 86th Street entrance at 5 a.m., with the intention of limiting traffic to the construction trucks and crews. Both the East and West Drives in the area of the Great Lawn would be closed to all traffic, except for construction crews, support vehicles and police units. Officers were stationed at all of the east and west park entrances between 79th Street and 97th Street. Their instructions were to be a visual deterrence. They would not prevent pedestrians' entry into the Park, but their mere presence would dissuade some from bothering to go to the chapel. And if events started to boil over, units could converge from every direction.

Inside the Park, forty officers were assigned to the immediate chapel area on the Great Lawn, with instructions to keep a hard perimeter of fifty yards from the chapel.

Steve Lombard met with the mayor and his advisor's the previous evening. Lombard himself did not see why the chapel had to be removed so quickly. He even counseled against such aggressive action. He laughed when, after telling his wife about the meeting, she called him Old Testament Isaiah, the lone voice crying out in the wilderness. He replayed the meeting in his mind as he sat in his car, in front of the 22nd Precinct Building, just off of 86th Street, mid-Park.

***

"Look, I get that you want the building to go for a load of reasons, all well and good, but I just think that we wait a few days." Steve looked around the mayor's conference table, a large metal frame holding a blue tinted glass which looked five inches thick, but found no support. They were seated in the same large office as the mayor's desk and chair, with the conference table partitioned from the rest of the office by a large aquarium holding a handful of colorful fish he could not name. He finished his plea by adding, "Let the people put their Christmas trees away for God's sakes."

"Pun intended?" asked Terrance Greenberg.

"What?" asked Chief Lombard, missing the point completely.

Mayor Ben Creavy finally spoke. "Steve, Mr. Greenberg has a valid concern that the longer that chapel is allowed to stay, the harder it will be for anyone to demolish it. I get that. It's like pulling off a bandage, quicker is better than a slow pull."

"Thank you, Mr. Mayor," Terrance said.

Steve Lombard stared at Terrance as if he were the suspect of a major crime. "Look, my men will handle this situation with professionalism and will get the job done. But guys, I gotta tell you, my wife was eating this stuff up all day from the television. We go to St. Patrick's every Sunday, and all of her ACTS retreat lady friends were burning up Facebook about this chapel. Then you have the kids out there, and their parents. Altar servers holding little novena candles. It was on TV at the top of every hour. They had choir groups singing carols all the damn day." He looked over the table, with the mayor sitting at its head, surrounded by his advisors, including Kevin Palanti, Janet Olsen, and the Assistant City Attorney, Celeste Buck. Across from him was Terrance Greenberg, and next to him was *Times* president, Jason Dumbarton. He addressed them all, while staring directly at Terrance Greenberg, "You do know that there will be a backlash. It's not like I'm seizing a dumpster that everyone wants to see go. It's a little church, and it's just a few days after Christmas." He scanned over the rest of the faces listening to him, sensing that none would say anything remotely supportive. "Am I the only one who sees those optics here?"

"That's why we preempt that problem," Jason said, his voice booming, his hands darting about for emphasis, "They won today. They beat us to the punch. Tomorrow we quarantine a section of the park before anyone gets there. Let the contractor get the job done. They'll be finished before the New Year, and all of this will be forgotten."

Steve ignored the newspaper man, and looked directly at his superior, the mayor. "Sir, with respect, we don't even know who 'they' are."

The mayor nodded, but moved on from his chief of police. "Mr. Greenberg, do you have anything to add?"

"Only, this. We missed our opportunity yesterday, dare I say possibly with one of my own administrators sympathetic to this mysterious cause. But after good counsel and much deliberation, I feel that our best course of action is to regain control of our own grounds, and to protect the Park from any other usurpers."

The mayor nodded. Terrance always talked in long words rather than short, his way of exhibiting his sense of refinement and class. It was a boring and transparent habit as far as the mayor was concerned. Still, he knew that it was the Conservancy that really dictated whether the situation would be dealt with aggressively or with a more patient and deliberate response. His biggest concern was that a crowded Park could hemorrhage into a disruption of city services and safety. After deciding to take a middle of the road position, which would assuredly make some constituency upset, but which also gave him the greatest numbers of others to blame for any turmoil. After leaning over to hear a whisper from Celeste Buck, he straightened in his chair and said, "Look, this is not a city issue. That chapel was put on Park property, and if the Park Authority wants it removed, then city government will facilitate. They have the demo crew hired, not us. It's their call. But gentlemen," he paused with a chuckle, "if this turns into an old fashion shit show, then I'll pull the plug on this operation until everyone's nerves calms down." He tapped the table top and looked over at Steve Lombard. "You got that, Chief?"

"Loud and clear, Mr. Mayor," Steve Lombard said, while thinking, how could it be anything but?

***

Steve Lombard entered the 22nd Precinct Building and went straight to the captain's office. Joel Nunnally was sitting at his desk, running over a list of officers and their assignments for the morning. Nunnally started to rise when the Chief entered, but Lombard motioned to him to stay seated. Lombard went straight to a Keurig single cup coffee machine on a side table, grabbed the first module he saw in the basket, and started a cup brewing in the machine. "Fill me in," he said.

"Chief," Captain Nunnally said, while the machine hissed a stream of coffee in a dark blue mug, "We're ready to go. The teams have been briefed, they know their assignments. We went over engagement rules twice. The teams assigned to the Great Lawn should be just about in position. Street access has been secured and the work crews know where to go and where to park. So far so good."

Lombard took the mug from the machine as soon as the last drop fell into the mug. He drank the brew black, and after a long bitter mouthful, said, "Good to hear. I want to be on scene at first light. When does the heavy equipment arrive?"

Nunnally looked at the clock on his desk. "It's a little after 6, so in the next thirty minutes or so."

"Any issues so far?"

"There were a few stragglers in the park early, but they seemed to disperse without much protest." As he talked, the intercom sounded his name. He picked up his phone and dialed dispatch. "Nunnally here, you paging me?"

Lombard took another long sip of coffee, then put the cup down on table and left it. He turned to listen to Nunnally's side of the conversation.

"How many?" Nunnally asked. After a moment, "I've got the Chief here in my office. I'll be back to you in a bit."

"Trouble already?" the Chief asked.

"Well, seems there's a few people in the chapel who refuse to leave. One of them is talking about constitutional rights and freedom of assembly and is recording video of every move our offices make."

Lombard's face was stoic, but his nostrils flared as he spoke. "How did that happen? We were supposed to have the chapel closed to the public last night."

Nunnally shook his head, and answered, "Sorry sir, but park patrol says that the chapel was secured. Somehow they must have sneaked in through the back door."

"Your guys couldn't guard a henhouse in broad daylight." Lombard turned and headed for the door, shouting back to Nunnally as he left the office. "Tell the park officers to stand down until I get there. I don't want this to be a live feed on every national morning show. Tell them I'm on my way."

***

Isla stood just inside the chapel front door. Dressed in dark jeans and a black wool coat, her hands were cold from removing her gloves, to be able to use the buttons on her phone. She needed to be able to snap photos quickly, shoot video as well as navigate through the board of apps and other icons. Behind her, sitting at the altar table, was Darragh. He awoke and started writing right after they slipped into the chapel with Warren's help. He was so deep in concentration that he didn't appear to know that she was present.

Outside, a cluster of four park officers stood in front of the chapel, three behind the senior officer, who was calmly trying to coax Isla from the doorway. "Ma'am, you are not supposed to be inside the church. Please step outside so we can talk this through."

"We can talk just fine right where we are," Isla said.

"Okay. Do you understand that this is private property? You need to please vacate this structure."

"This is public property, a public park."

"Yes ma'am, it is. But you have to understand that not every building on the park grounds is open to public access without any restrictions. Let's be reasonable here."

"Let's cut the crap. You want me out so a bulldozer can make match sticks of this church."

"Ma'am, I don't know anything about that."

"Are you an atheist?"

"Ma'am?"

"Are you?"

The officer looked at his fellow officers behind him. The youngest was trying to suppress his laughter at Isla's quick retorts. Turning back to Isla, the lead officer took a step forward. "No ma'am, I am not. I'm not sitting in the front row every Sunday, either, but I go when I can."

"Don't get any closer. I'm posting this. Do you want the world to see NYPD dragging a helpless woman from the threshold of a chapel doorway? Are you going to shoot me with a Taser?" She tapped her chest and said. "I've got a pacemaker. You better not electrocute me."

"Ma'am, I don't believe you have a pacemaker."

"Oh yes I do. And it's an old, cheap one that's very delicate. I can't even be near a microwave. I have to use the stove to warm up my TV dinners. And the stove top to pop my popcorn."

"How many others are in the church with you?"

"We're full up. Mostly nuns and baby orphans." She glanced behind her, then back to the officer. "And some very religious amputees."

***

The construction crews arrived just before dawn. The trucks entered the park grounds by the 86th St. transverse and made their way to the staging area. The grounds immediately around the chapel were cordoned off, but a small and growing gathering of pedestrians was around this expanded perimeter. Preston Browne jumped from his truck's passenger seat and put on his hard hat and coat. He walked up to the cluster of park officer's. "Are we good to go this morning?"

Sargent Denny Mitchell, the lead officer who had been talking to Isla, said, "What time are you guys going to be ready to start?"

"Shouldn't be long. As soon as we off load the equipment and put down a few mats. Say nine o'clock."

"That soon?" Sargent Mitchell frowned.

190

"What's the problem now?"

Sargent Mitchell saw the Chief of Police approaching, and felt immediate relief. "You talk to the Chief about that. Seems that there are a few people in the chapel."

"Fan-freaking-tastic," remarked Preston, as he turned and headed back to his truck to get instructions from his office.

***

Darragh walked up to Isla, who was watching the milling of the officers outside the chapel, through the door that was ajar. He could see a group of the officers huddled together at the foot of the stone pathway that led to the chapel. Others were aligned like a noose around the chapel grounds. They faced the growing crowd, but were not interacting with them, or doing anything to engage the growing mass. "They won't wait much longer," said Isla, while Darragh stood beside her. "Do you have a plan to get us out of this?"

Darragh shook his head. "No plan. Just waiting to see what happens, and respond to that as best as we can."

"Well, yesterday we had the support of altar boys and church choirs. They won't make the same mistake again. They won't let them get close enough to the chapel to be in the way. I can see some of the same people that were here yesterday, off in the distance, but they can't get much closer to us." She pointed to a cluster of girl scouts dressed in their uniforms, singing and passing out cookies.

Isla noticed something unsettled about Darragh, as if worry had found him for the first time in his life, as if it were an illness, a virus for which his system had no defense. He paced from the chapel doorway to the table, and back, not talking, or even looking at her. It was as though he were alone, his mind seeing a different reality, a different perspective. She moved to the center aisle, and reached out for his hand when he approached. "Darragh, what is it? You've got me a little rattled, pacing like that. Are you okay?"

Instead of answering, Darragh went to the doorway and stared out at the crowd in the distance. Between the crowd and the chapel he saw heavy pieces of equipment, earth moving machines, and a crew of men preparing their machines and rigging for a busy day of destruction. A large skid was being unloaded from another truck, a debris container from its looks. Two of the younger workers were driving stakes into the ground and running a plastic mesh fence between the poles. A windscreen. Behind them another crew was linking together sections of hurricane fence. This fence was in twelve foot segments, and had a standing footing. With the sections connected, a worker would hammer a hook-shaped spike into the ground, so that the hooked end held the fence footing in place. Darragh turned to Isla, his face flushed and worn with disappointment.

"Remember our afternoon at Starbucks?"

"Sure.

"We talked about you, didn't we? About wonderful things."

"Darragh, you made me see things that I had blocked out of my mind, out of even my heart."

"What I have learned, I think, about miracles, is that some people will never believe, will not see, what is right before their eyes."

"What are you saying? I already believe that this chapel is a miracle. I don't know how, but that's what I believe. And the way your poems appear, the way they are shared, that's another miracle. I just realize how fortunate I am to witness two miracles. How many people live their entire life and never see one?"

Darragh sighed. "Miracles happen all of the time, but most people are so blind that they go unrecognized. Remember when you told me about the stations of the cross, about the sixth station?"

"Sure. Veronica wipes the face of Jesus."

"Veronica was not her name. It is the name that the church chose for her. 'Vera' means true, and 'eikona' means image or icon. So you get Veronica. Her veil has the true image."

"You mean Veronica was not a real person?"

"No, she was real all right. Her name was Seraphia, and she showed bravery and love by wiping His face. She could have been killed for that act of kindness by the parade of soldiers that followed the procession. But the sudarium she used did capture the image of Jesus."

"What is that word, sudarium?"

"It means sweat cloth. It is a Latin word. And what you never hear, what no one talks about, is how the image on Veronica's Veil matches the image of the Shroud of Turin. The images are super-imposable. But so much effort is directed at disproving the authenticity of those relics that it is as if the burden to prove them as real now rests with the church. So no one talks about them, or for that matter any other miracle." Darragh squeezed her hand. "Do you see the seed of evil in that?"

"What do you mean?"

"The moment that you attempt to prove the occurrence of a miracle, you suspend faith, and when that happens, you open belief to a question of doubt."

Isla nodded in agreement. "Then this chapel is a reminder. And what you have been doing, to remind people of what they have forgotten. Like you did for me."

Darragh sighed, "But some people do not want to be reminded of anything."

Isla looked out the open doorway at the crowd of people growing around the perimeter of the chapel. "Those people, a lot of them believe. Or they want to believe."

Darragh looked into her eyes. "Isla, what do you believe?"

She let her eyes answer that question, in her tears, and then in emotion that swept through her like pulse of energy. She squeezed his hand in return, then said, "I believe that we have to hold on to this chapel as long as we can."

"Until your horsemen arrive?" Darragh asked.

Isla giggled. "You mean the cavalry. Don't say 'horsemen,' that makes it sound too biblical."

"Right. It is coming; don't you think? The cavalry?"

"I'm sure that it is," Isla said, as she silently wondered the same thing.

***

Claira arrived at the Park and made her way to the Precinct office. She waited at the front desk for Nunnally, but after five minutes she started for the door. As she was almost out, she heard her name and turned back around.

Nunnally was standing at the interior door, holding it open until she reached it. Before she could say a word, he cautioned her. "I have been briefed by Mr. Greenberg. I will say that he is none too happy with you right now. In fact, he told me if you showed up here that you had no authority to speak on behalf of the Conservancy and that you should go immediately to the Conservancy office."

"Then why are you bringing me back to your office?"

"Because Chief Lombard has already been here this morning, and is out there in the Park now. And because I heard Warren Hayes talking about this chapel over the last several days. So I want to know what is going on here. Can you explain that to me?"

Claira looked at him. "Look, if you're trying to keep me here until I get arrested or get served with some type of restraining order or held up by other Conservancy personnel, I promise I will not make that easy for you." She turned and started to back-track down the hall.

"Ms. Vasson, please. Trust me even if you don't like me, okay."

Claira considered the circumstances, and the fact that if she was going to be arrested or detained, that could happen anywhere in the Park, at any time. She followed Nunnally to his office.

He offered her the seat across from his desk, and then circled around the small office and fell into his chair. Nunnally was overweight, and even at the age of forty-three had degenerative conditions in both knees, which the extra twenty pounds he carried did not help. He looked like he was constantly suffering some level of pain. He leaned back in the chair, and rubbed his bald head.

Claira said, "I have no reason to not like you, although I don't appreciate the way you look at me or other ladies with whom you work. So let's just get that out of the way right now."

Nunnally was shocked. No one had ever spoken to him like that or about that subject, and he immediately started worrying about his career, worrying about what would happen if anyone made such complaints to the HR department about him. The level of discomfort that stayed visible on him grew in intensity. "I don't know what...I mean, I'm sorry if I offended you in any way, and —"

"Enough said. What do you want to know?"

Still flustered, Nunnally could not make eye contact with Claira, but managed to ask, "What are you and Warren planning to do about the chapel?"

"Excuse me?" Claira answered, although now it was her voice that sounded stressed and defensive.

Nunnally lifted a newspaper from his desk and tossed it in Claira's direction. "Have you seen the *Times* this morning? Big write-up about the chapel being illegally placed on park property. It goes on about separation of church and state and how this is an unconstitutional endorsement of religion. The ACLU is quoted about a suit that is going to be filed in federal court today. And those poems? A hacker up to no good, who is suspected of identity theft and a host of other cyber-crimes."

Claira stared at the paper but did not retrieve it. "That's horseshit. And you know it."

"Don't lecture me on what I know or what I should believe. But I'll tell you this. You cannot win this fight. And Officer Hayes needs to be very careful, as his future is on the line here."

Claira's intensity flashed. "What are you implying?"

"Look, I like Warren a lot, he's got a good future with the department if he doesn't mess it up. And I know you two are buddies. I just got the feeling that he might go afield on this one and not see this the company way."

Claira's denial was reflexive. "I don't know what you are talking about. I haven't been talking much with him lately, with the holidays and all. I've been really busy, as you might expect."

"Then a friendly word of advice. Keep an eye out for him. Like I said, Chief Lombard is out there today and I sure would not want Warren to do anything crazy."

"Neither would I. Neither would I."

***

Chief Lombard walked up to the front door of the chapel with three officers at his side, Denny Mitchell included. When he reached the stone landing. "This is Chief of Police Steve Lombard. I would like a word."

Both Darragh and Isla appeared at the doorway. "Yes sir," was all Isla said.

"Should I come in?" Lombard's request sounded ominous, like a doctor's diagnosis of death.

Isla shook her head. "Let's talk just like we are now. I wouldn't feel that good in close quarters with you and your men in this little church."

"I assure you that I am only here to talk. To discuss this situation. Nothing else. That is, nothing else at this time." Lombard's face was like stone, passionlessly threatening.

For the first time Darragh spoke. "You can come in, but have your men wait outside."

Lombard peered through the door, trying to see who else was inside and what were the conditions of the occupancy.

"Chief, we don't have anything to hide. We'll leave the door ajar." Isla looked over his shoulder at the officers wearing vests and other tactical gear. "Trust me, we are more worried about what your men plan to do, than you can possibly be about us."

Lombard nodded, and whispered something to the officer at his right side. Officer Mitchell stood at the rear, and looked content to have been relieved of the responsibility of communicating with the chapel's occupants. Lombard gestured to him, and pointed at the hurricane fence now surrounding the chapel. His message delivered, Lombard climbed the shallow steps of the chapel landing and entered. Inside, he said, "You cannot be here."

Darragh motioned for him to sit on one of the benches. "Have you ever seen anything like this?" He pointed at the stained glass windows, the wood beams reaching high across the sanctuary. "Why would anyone want to destroy such a thing?"

"That is beside the point." Lombard's voice seemed to carry in the little church, like thunder in a canyon. "Look, I was at the first meeting the mayor had about this chapel, and bottom line, the Park powers-that-be did not put it here and do not want it here."

"So what happens next?"

"You two walk out of here with me. You do that, and no charges, no arrests. There will be a lot of questions, but nothing that, shall we say, has any resonating consequences."

"But if we stand our ground?"

Lombard yawned. "This is early, even for me." Turning directly to face Darragh, he said. "Son, this isn't 'your ground.' That's the whole point now, isn't it? If this chapel were on your spit of land out in the country somewhere, then all is well. But this isn't your land, is it? This is Central Park, for God's sakes."

Lombard rose from his seat, and started for the door of the chapel. "Come out with me and walk away, right now. If not, I assure you that we have responses for any contingency that can arise. Let's not go there, shall we? Let's end this the best way possible, for all involved."

Chapter Seventeen

Cap was the last to arrive in the physician conference room. Cissy sat on the far side of the pecan-shell colored table, just ending a phone call. Her eyes were red and weeping. As Cap sat across from her, she cupped her forehead in her left hand, not wanting to meet his gaze.

A doctor dressed in a green striped shirt and a solid green silk necktie, and a white lab coat with "Dr. Fastel" stitched in red, sat at the head of the table. He opened a folder that was placed on the table in front of him, and said, "Good morning, Sir. You must be Cap. My name is Jacob Fastel."

Cap offered his hand, then said as the two shook hands, "Morning Doc. I know that I've seen you around the floor. But I did not know that you were treating Mom."

"Well, I am not one of her primary physicians, though I am an oncologist and I am familiar with her conditions. Your sister asked me to meet with you this morning. And to state the obvious, everyone here consents to a discussion of confidential medical information. We don't want to run afoul of HIPPA."

Cap nodded, and after a moment delay, so did Cissy.

"Well then, after a review of the test results, neither of you are candidates for a cell donation to your mother." Dr. Fastel glanced over at Cissy, who seemed to be day dreaming, and after an extended moment of silence, continued. "Mr. Kencaid, as you know, you are not a compatible match. Your sister, Cissy, is a compatible donor, but..." his voice trailed to silence, as Cissy reached for his hand.

"What Dr. Fastel is trying to say is that I have stage one Non-Hodgkin's lymphoma, and I need to start treatment very soon." She had raised her head to speak, but once finished, her head fell back into her hand.

Cap slumped in his chair, deflated by the news. "What does that mean? Is she going to be okay?"

"What it means is this," Dr. Fastel said. "As strange as this sounds, your sister is fortunate. Her condition is treatable, and her prognosis is very good. Frankly, your insistence on the testing for donor compatibility was fortuitous, because we were able to catch her condition at an early stage. Had it not been for you, and considering that she is currently asymptomatic, we would not be intervening and treating this disease at such an early inception."

Cissy looked at Cap, "I just found out earlier this morning. The kids don't know yet. I'll have to figure out the best way to tell them I'm sick. Conrad is going to be so afraid. A second grader shouldn't be worried about his mom dying." She un-balled a tissue that had been in her hand, and wiped her eyes again.

"I don't know what to say," Cap said. "What is it that I can do for you?"

Cissy just shook her head.

Dr. Fastel closed the file folder on the table. "Mr. Kencaid, I will be treating your sister, and I assure you that we will take excellent care of her. I am optimistic. As difficult as this is for you both, for the family, I must also advise that your mother's condition is grave. She is not responding as well as we hoped. Her systems are compromised, her renal system and lung function as well. If we intubate her, there is a significant risk that she will become dependent on the respirator, and that we will not be able to take her off of the machine. She is near comatose, has little strength left, but is not suffering."

"What are you saying, Doc, that there is no hope?"

Dr. Fastel cleared his throat. "What I am telling you is that your mother is very weak. Once her organ systems begin to fail, it creates more stress on her body than she can tolerate. As I stated earlier, her condition is grave."

"Well, I'm not going to say pull the plug. I'm not giving up on her."

"Cap," Cissy said, trying to compose herself. "That is not what Dr. Fastel is saying. No one is saying to stop the medications, but if she gets to a point where she needs a respirator ... Mom would not want that." She dabbed her eyes with a tissue, and hung her head, as if ashamed.

"Are we there yet, Doc?" Cap asked stood, pushing his chair back against the wall of the little, bland conference room.

Dr. Fastel remained seated. "Mr. Kencaid, all I can say is that she is very close. She could barely open her eyes last night when I checked in on her. I have consulted with her critical care physician, and if she slides any further she will need to be admitted to ICU."

Cap looked at Cissy, who seemed on the verge of tears. "You need to head home and be with your family. I'll be with Mom, and will give you a call this afternoon." He turned to Dr. Fastel. "I get it, Doc.

But I'm not one to give up. Miracles happen all the time, don't they?" With those words, Cap left the conference room, and headed back to Room 822, where his mother was asleep.

***

Warren, in uniform, walked the perimeter of the now fenced chapel grounds. He saw Claira hurrying across the lawn, and waved to catch her attention.

"Walk with me a bit," he said in a soft voice, when she reached his side. They turned, and made their way through the growing crowd. Once past the gathering, he brought her up to speed on the morning's developments. "Your boss has got the crew ready to work. The only thing slowing them down is that there are a couple of people in the chapel. One of them is Mr. Finn, and the other is a lady he's got helping him."

"Who is she?"

"A local. Her name's Isla. She's only known Mr. Finn for a few days, but like with you, he made a lasting impression." Warren retrieved her photograph on his phone and showed it to Claira. "I met her yesterday. She's the one who spread the word and got so many people out here."

Claira considered the desperateness of occupying the chapel, but also how much time that act could delay the demolition. Two people would be a delay, but not a deterrent. More importantly, she did not know what reaction would be provoked, and she did not want to see anyone hurt. She studied the barricade that circled the chapel. "But today, they got the fence put up." She peered over to the chapel, and saw the assembly of policemen in front on the little church. She pointed to them. "What are they getting ready to do?"

"Well, the Chief of Police has already been in there to talk to them. They won't let this drag out long. They will go in and remove them."

"How much time before that happens?" Claira looked at her phone, scanning through recent messages.

"My guess is soon. Thirty minutes. Maybe less."

"That's not going to be enough time." She started to move to the front of the chapel. "Maybe if I plead with the Chief, maybe he'll rethink this."

Warren reached for her shoulder, turning her toward him. "I'll slow things down a little."

"Warren, what are you going to do?"

199

"Rage against the machine," he said as he kissed her forehead. "Now get going."

***

Claira made her way to Chief Lombard, showing her identification several times and explaining that she was the Assistant Director of the Park Conservancy. When he saw her approach, he excused himself from a cluster of officers and said, "This is not a good time, Ms. Vasson."

"Chief, we shouldn't be escalating this situation. Look around. There are reporters here, news cameras. Look at all of these people here. You know that every one of them has a smart phone, which means everyone has a camera. Do you want videos of your officers dragging people out of a church on Facebook and YouTube?"

"Ms. Vasson, are you speaking for yourself, or for Mr. Greenberg and the Park Conservancy? I got the word that you had a major disagreement with your employer, and I'm not even sure that you still have that job. As much as I tend to agree with you, and that's off the record, I am going to do the job the City of New York is paying me to do. So if you will excuse me."

Out of the corner of her eye, Claira caught a glimpse of Warren, walking through the barricade and toward the chapel. His stride was brazen, purposeful. Whatever Warren had in his mind, his determination was plain in each of his of his long, confident steps. She turned back to Chief Lombard and said, "You know better than this. You can be better than this." With that, Claira disappeared into the crowd, as if summoned. Chief Lombard watched Claira fade into a cluster of people surrounding the chapel fence, then noticed Warren as he entered the chapel door. Lombard pulled Officer Mitchell aside and demanded, "Who in the hell is that, and what in the hell is he doing."

***

Isla and Darragh greeted Warren after he entered the chapel.

"Man, it's getting a little tense out there. How you guys doing?" Warren asked as he looked over the chapel. Its charm captured him again, as if he was seeing the stained glass windows and the wooden pews and the candle chandeliers for the first time.

"We're waiting for the cavalry to arrive," Darragh said with a smile.

"The cavalry. I like that." He smiled at Isla. "I'm the cavalry."

Isla giggled. "Sorry to say, but I don't think of a one horse parade as the cavalry. We're about 49 soldiers and fifty horses short." After brushing a mix of ice and snowflakes from his shoulders, she looked in his eyes, past the blue strands of color, the way that you can only when that person is no longer a stranger, when that person is known and trusted. "But we're glad to have you anyway."

"You got my stuff?" he asked, smiling, reaching for her hand as the last of the snowflakes fluttered from his shoulder.

"Yep, right over there in the corner." Isla pointed to the items that she and Darragh had brought with them when they arrived in the middle of the night.

"Warren, are you all right?" Darragh asked, "You don't have to do this. We will buy time another way."

Warren ran his hand through his hair, then smiled. "Nah, I'll be fine. I always get a little stage-fright. You get a load of how many people there are out there?"

***

Warren came out of the chapel carrying a battery powered Roland CUBE 50-watt amplifier. He set it on the split log bench on the chapel landing. Darragh placed a second speaker next to it. Warren adjusted the headset he was wearing, placing the microphone and earpiece into a comfortable position. Isla handed him his guitar, a 2011 Gibson Les Paul custom, Rattler Burst, which he slung it over his shoulder and plugged it into the Roland with the fluid movement of a performer.

He peered over the crowd, most of whom had not noticed the officer with the electric guitar. He strummed a few cords, then ran through sections of the E minor scale. Satisfied, he said, "All right, guys. I'm Warren Hayes, NYPD, presently at least, and also one of the founding members of the Tattooed Badges. I'm not what you call a religious man, but this chapel is something to savor, not destroy." He strummed a couple more chords and adjusted the volume on the Roland. "Here is a Bart Millard song. Key of E."

Isla looked over to Darragh and grimaced. She did not know what to expect from this gentle giant, and his lack of nervousness made her nervous. Darragh nodded, then glanced at the officers huddled by the barricade, and the crowd behind and around them. Warren got everyone's attention, and for the moment, at least, none of the officers charged to the chapel.

Warren started the song, playing an open E chord and seamlessly changing to E major 7 and A suspended 2. The notes from the guitar carried through the December air, like a crystal canticle of an open air cathedral, a song of solemn refuge. The soft clamor of the crowd, grew quieter, and the faces of the old and the young in the crowd all looked for the source of the sound. Even the work crew milling around their equipment and tool boxes stopped to listen. Warren repeated the intro, then with his eyes closed, began singing the amazing words of the song, 'I Can Only Imagine.'

As Warren's voiced the lyrics, the crowd noise eased, the hush becoming contagious, the call to quiet sincere. Warren sang each word clearly, each note bright and clean.

Without missing any notes, Warren turned to Isla and Darragh and winked.

Darragh nudged Isla, "The laddie has a right good voice." He pointed and smiled.

Warren strummed through the intro chords again, ringing a few notes as he worked to the second verse. As he started singing the next verse, the voices of many in the crowd joined with him, as if it was a favorite and practiced hymn. Others in the swelling crowd swayed with the flow of the song, some bowed their heads for a moment, some gazed skyward.

Claira was in the crowd, and was stunned by the precision of the music, the purity of the artistry, the passion in the song. She stood behind the barricade, in a throng of people, captured by the unexpected melody and the lyrics that asked them such personal questions, so reflective and tirelessly tranquil. Claira had seen Warren and his band before, but he rarely sang lead on any of the songs, and was usually relegated to playing rhythm guitar on the edge of the stage, and occasionally joining in a chorus. It was a role he seemed to love, more of loyal support than front man. But hearing him today was a revelation. *Damn, Warren, where did that come from?*

***

Chief Lombard pointed his finger at Mitchell's chest and demanded, "Is that son of a bitch one of yours? What kind of stunt is this?"

"Chief, Officer Hayes is the real deal. He's a good cop, sir. Been knowing him for more than a decade. I didn't know he could sing like that, though."

As they argued, Warren finished the song to a loud retort of applause. Lombard fumed, but could not help but notice that the crowd was spellbound by Warren's performance, cheering and asking for more. Someone from the crowd yelled out, "Sing a carol, a Christmas carol."

Warren looked toward the Chief, whom he'd met a few times, but didn't know him. But he could tell from the animated discussion between the Chief and Officer Mitchell that his rendition of the Mercy Me song did not particularly move his Chief of Police. He turned his attention back to the crowd, and said. "A Christmas carol, someone said. I know a couple, so let's see. How about this one." He started the chord progression, Am to C to G to Em, and then after the introduction, began the lyrics of "What Child is this?"

The crowd joined in the chorus, louder than for the first song, their voices blended with Warren's, and Claira thought all of the Park grounds would be filled with this music.

Isla sang along, and when the second verse started, joined Warren on the landing of the chapel, waving, encouraging the crowd to raise their voices higher. She let her eyes run over the faces in the crowd, twice the size from yesterday. *Maybe all of these people can make a difference.*

Darragh stood in the doorway, pensive. He knew that their time was running out.

***

"I want you to move as soon as this song is finished. Move with purpose. Now listen, I don't want any rough-necking. Don't bust any chops. You get around them, cuff them, and walk them around and out through the back. Do not come back down here through the barricade gate and into the crowd. Got it?" Chief Lombard pointed at the rear of the chapel, where he had another squad of officers waiting.

"What about Officer Hayes?" Mitchell asked.

Lombard grimaced. The brotherhood of officers created strong, loyal bonds, and asking an officer to cuff another in blue for anything less than some horrendous felony was unthinkable. Warren may have stood with the wrong side this morning, but he did not cross any line that deserved such a public betrayal. The chief hung his head, staring at the snowy ground. "I'll deal with him. Now let's get ready to go."

From his makeshift stage, Warren could see the squad's response move developing, and also knew that there was nothing he could do to prevent it. With the crowd singing in unison, he moved close to Isla and urged her to flee, but she refused. He glanced at Darragh, locking in on his eyes, and saw that Darragh was not going to budge either. He moved to the edge of the small chapel landing, and as he finished the last chord in the carol, he took his guitar from his shoulder and set it against the bench holding the amplifier. Before he could turn, eight officers surrounded them. They moved quickly, like soldiers in a drill. The crowd was livid, yelling in protest.

One officer roughly spun Darragh around and pressed his face into the chapel wall, pushing harder than was necessary and rubbing Darragh's face against the cladding, the cold stone scraping away enough skin to draw blood. Without easing up, the officer slid his baton under Darragh's chin, and pried it up, leveraging the flesh against unforgiving stone and mortar. Darragh made no sound, no scream of either protest or pain. But the insult was obvious, a broken nose, a semi-circle cut below his left eye, the size of the bottom of a cola bottle. Then the officer's elbow crashed into Darragh's head, forcing it across the stone wall, leaving another trail of blood, and the sound of something breaking. Another officer pulled Darragh's hands behind him and had him cuffed before Warren could intercede.

Lombard came to Warren's side and warned him. "Stand down, Officer. You're in deep shit already, so don't make me put the bracelets on you too. You get to walk away with your head high only out of respect for the uniform. And that's the only reason."

Isla yelled at the short wide-bodied officer who still had his weight pressing Darragh's ruined face into the stone chapel wall. "What's your problem. No one is resisting. No need to bust us up."

The officer turned to her and smiled, reeking from the sick enjoyment of the pain he inflicted.

"Turn and face the crowd," Isla said. "Smile for the cameras. Smile so everyone can see who bloodied up that church wall." She pointed to the red streaks on the cold stone wall. "Keep laughing. This is your fifteen minutes of fame. Tomorrow it will be infamy, and it will last a lot longer than the sick pleasure you're getting now. You small, pitiful bully."

Lombard turned when he heard Isla's admonition, and the expression on his face showed that he too was dismayed by the choke hold being applied to Darragh. He motioned for two other officers to stand Darragh up straight, and pointed them to the back of the chapel.

Then he faced Isla, who stood looking at him with contempt and disappointment.

"Is your thug squad going to bust my head too? Loosen a few of my teeth? All because I'm standing at a chapel door in a public park, singing a carol and giving thanks."

"This ain't thanksgiving, bitch," the wide-bodied officer leered, a lewd smile still covering his face, like a crude tooth line on a cheap Halloween mask. He released Darragh to the other officers, but stayed near the chapel door.

Before Lombard could say anything in response, Warren took two steps forward and landed his right fist on the officer's chin, spinning him back into a slow pirouette that landed him on his knees. "You just caught the midnight train to Georgia, farm boy. Next time you talk to a lady, show some respect. Don't dishonor the uniform defaming her."

Isla studied Warren. He seemed to be bigger, his presence flexed, the need to protect her honor and name a projection of his virtuous self. She said softly, "Thank you, Warren."

Lombard threw himself into Warren, yelling, "Stand down, Officer, Stand down."

The Wide-body officer spat blood.

Two officers were at Warren's side, but hesitated, not knowing what to do. Isla took a few steps forward, to the edge of the landing, and yelled to the crowd. "This is your chapel. This is your church. This is your park, and this is your ground. What is it worth? It was given to you and should not be taken away. Tell them that you received it, that it has passed from them to us. Tell them that what is given cannot be taken away." As she spoke, a female officer held her hands behind her and cuffed her. Isla did not resist.

She turned her head to Chief Lombard, and as she was being led away. "You don't realize what you're doing. All because of a metal badge and an order from your superior. For that you will betray what you know is right. Because you were ordered to. What's next? No room in the inn? Would you pull the child from the manger, and send the shepherds away, back into the shadows of the night? Would you obey that order too? What do you have to see, to believe?"

Warren followed her around the chapel grounds, with two officers, each at his side. He was not cuffed, but they hurried him along.

The crowd again yelled their disapproval. Lombard eyed the growing mass of people, and turned to stand at the side of Officer Mitchell, was picking up Warren's guitar, and carrying it and the

Roland inside the chapel. "We need to get the fence line manned with more personnel. See to it."

With that Lombard turned and walked toward the barricade, hoping that the line would hold.

Chapter Eighteen

The sound was persistent, like a heartbeat, a deep and distant pulse. And like those life sounds, it was soft, a faded sound, a tremble that was not forefront, but rather behind the curtains, just offstage, just out of sight. Again the sound. Another, and another. A sound of no origin, a sound out of time. A calling? Was the sound calling him, or warning? Was the sound to be trusted, this wooden heartbeat? Or was it ominous and ill, the sound of life failing, of the hull bending and breaking, the sound of falling, or worse, sinking. He had heard this sad noise before, many times, in many strange earth voices. The sound of the ebb, the pull of ocean, and all that is in its arms, back out to the black twilight sea.

The sound called him again, and this time he relented. He turned from the lighthouse that beckoned, and went away from the place of his dreams. Cap opened his eyes, and then heard the knock again. A gentle tap on the room's door. "Yes, come in."

The door swung open slowly, silently. In the dim room, Cap strained to see the visitor, but he could not tell who the man was. A few more steps, and out of the short dark hallway. Cap rose from his seat by the window. "Yes? Who are you looking for?"

"Yes sir, sorry to bother you. Hope that I did not disturb your rest. I am looking for Captain Kencaid."

"That's me." Cap strained to focus on the face standing before him. "Do I know you?"

The old man shook his head. "No sir, I don't think that we've ever met. Jaxson Dissy is my name. Most folks just call me Jax. Well, most folks don't call me at all, just a few friends." The man laughed at his own rambling, then offered his right hand to shake.

Cap reached for the old man's hand, though puzzled. He searched his memory, looking for placement of the face before him. A friend or neighbor of his mother? Doubtful, because Cap knew most everyone on Deer Island. An old black man with long grey curls walking the streets of Deer Island would not be unnoticed or forgotten. Maybe someone from a church or prayer group? That had to be it. Some ministry had sent the man, maybe to pray with him and his mother, or maybe to talk about hospice, or some other such foolishness, like punting on third down. Cap gave the man's hand a squeeze, and was surprised when the squeeze came back reflected in the man's grip of Cap's weathered and sea-salted hand.

"That's a man's shake. You can say more with a strong grip than in two minutes of hellos and how are yas." Jax smiled and released the muscles of his hand.

Cap did the same and returned the smile.

Jax handed Cap a vase of white and pink roses that he held in his other hand. "Please take these. I understand that your mother is very ill, and I hope that this might just brighten the room for her. I've been in the city all my life, and I learned to appreciate flowers as a thing that you just don't see enough of."

Cap took the vase and set it on the window ledge. "Thank you. Very kind." He turned back to Jax and waited for some further explanation, but when the silence between them became intolerable, he continued, "So, are you from some hospital ministry? Some outreach group?"

Jax shook his head. "Forgive me. I should have explained all that, but frankly, I am at a loss for words myself. Do you mind if I sit? I have a hell of a story to tell you."

Cap looked over to the hospital bed, where his mother was sleeping. She was awake an hour ago, and was able to call his name and ask for a sip of ice water. But she had hardly moved since then. The doctor ordered a nasal feeding tube two days ago, to keep her caloric intake up, and she tolerated the tube with little complaint, which worried Cap. Did that mean she was too weak or tired to complain? Had she given up? Or had she reached a point of unawareness? He turned back to the old man standing at the foot of the bed. He looked neither uncomfortable nor energetic about this strange visit. Rather he looked meek, but assured that whatever he was doing here was a good thing. "Okay, sit a minute and tell me this story. But low, as you can see, she's resting."

Jax smiled and walked over to a seat by the window. Cap sat in the recliner that folded out into an uncomfortable single bed. Once they were both seated, Jax leaned over, close to Cap, and asked, "Any chance that you have been reading the newspaper, say since Christmas day?"

***

Preston huddled with his work crew, making sure that everyone had their duties assigned and that the sequencing of the work was in order. The heavy equipment was staged to the right rear of the chapel, and the waste bins to the side of that works-space. Their instructions were to send a strip crew in first, to remove the table and the pews, and any other items of fixtures or furniture. The candle chandeliers would be lowered from the ceiling and saved. The biggest debate focused on the stained glass windows, and whether the crew should try to remove the windows intact. Preston had studied them carefully, and concluded that the windows could be preserved, but it would greatly slow the demolition job, and that even with care, one of more of the windows could be damaged in the deconstruction process. But it was not his decision to make, and ultimately, the order had been given to him by a faceless voice over the phone. No extra effort to save the windows.

Preston climbed to the seat of the Zaxis 1400K Excavator and fired up the engine. While the pews and altar table were being hauled out through the back door of the chapel, he moved the big machine slowly to the front of the chapel, and used the claw arm of the excavator to start digging up the stones of the walkway leading to the chapel landing. He was thankful that the engine's diesel roar drowned out any sounds of protest from the crowd, and he kept his head down, purposely not looking at the crowd, so he could not see agitated disappointment at the fall of this humble, little church.

***

Claira was not far from the barricade when the demolition work started. She tried again to reason with Chief Lombard, but the effort was futile. She did not hear her phone sound, due to the rancor from the crowd, but luckily felt it vibrate. She pulled the phone from her coat pocket and answered, "Where are you? They've started."

"We're getting there now, so be ready to raise some hell with me," Abner managed to say. She could tell that he was talking to some other people with him. She strained to see him in the crowd, and then noticed that a small part seemed to be opening in the multitude of people. Through it pushed Abner, his frail posture and body seeming to be overwhelmed by the mass of bodies. He walked with his wooden cane, but hurried with no limp, and his face was animated with a youthful fury when he saw the movements of the excavator and the work of the construction crew to empty the chapel. He marched directly to the barricade, and confronted Chief Lombard.

"I presume that you are in charge of this desecration," Abner said. "This needs to stop immediately."

The crowd echoed a myriad of sounds around the chapel grounds. An amalgam of voices could be heard, recited prayers, songs and chants, and yells of condemnation and anger at the work of the demolition crew. But the volume of those voices seemed to decrease when Abner spoke, as if the crowd somehow knew that a champion had come forth to challenge the guard at the castle gate. Claira made her way to Abner's side, and rested her hand on his shoulder.

Chief Lombard looked at him dismissively. "And who might you be?"

"My name is Abner Parson. Dr. Abner Cole Parson. I am a professor at NYU and I am the Director of the Biblical Glass Archive. I also represent the Natural History Museum. You need to look at these documents, and stop this demolition."

Chief Lombard looked at him suspiciously, but before he could speak, Claira said. "Dr. Parson has inspected the windows of the chapel. He has an office right across the street at the museum and has been retained to opine on the value and historical significance of the chapel windows."

"What do you mean, historical significance? The chapel is only a few days old. It would only be historical in the lifespan of an ant."

Before Abner could respond, a man in his early thirties pushed his way to the barricade gate, and handed an unsealed envelope to Chief Lombard.

Without looking at the envelope, Lombard asked, "Who the hell are you?"

"I am an attorney for the Catholic League of New York. That envelope contains copies of the licenses the City issued for the League to display two nativity scenes, for the period December 17th to January 2nd."

"So," Chief Lombard said in response. "I saw the display, and it's set up about three or four blocks from here."

"The license states that two displays can be present, at the 85th Street park entrance or adjacent to the church building."

Lombard removed the license and read it carefully. Once finished, he looked up and answered, "This license refers to St. Ignatius Loyola Church. That's on Park Avenue, again, about three blocks from here.

The young man never lowered his gaze, "Yes, but you need to review the licenses more precisely. One grants a license to the

Catholic League to set the display in the area of the 85th Street Park entrance. That would include this area of the Park."

"Nice try counselor, but I'm not buying." Lombard considered most attorneys to be manipulators and villains. "You gotta be on the entrance, not in the middle of the Great Lawn on the grounds of the park."

Unfazed, the young attorney said, "The second license allows the display to be placed adjacent to the church. It does not specify the church or otherwise identify what church. It does not specify 980 Park Avenue; it does say that St Ignatius Loyola Church can display a nativity scene adjacent to the church. The application, a copy of which is attached to the license, simply refers to the nativity scene to be in the 85th Street area of Central Park, adjacent to the church."

Lombard took the papers again and read the application attached to the license. "Wait a minute. It looks like this one application was submitted for two displays. But the church that it refers to has to be St. Ignatius."

"Chief, it does not say that."

"So what you are telling me is…"

Abner interrupted the discussion and handed Chief Lombard another folded paper. "Chief, I have here a Conservation Directive from the New York Historical Society." It was printed on heavy bond paper, showing the legend of the Historical Society and an official seal of a notary affixed to its bottom right margin. "I too have friends in high places, Chief Lombard."

Lombard took that document from Abner's hand and read it carefully. It was not a court order or filing, but it was on the Society's letterhead, and made reference to cease and desist directive. Lombard was confused. "Wait, is that even legal? Only a court can issue an injunctive order. Do you have a court order, or not?"

Before Abner could respond, the attorney said, "What I am saying is that the license clearly allows the placement of a nativity display adjacent to the church, in the 85th Street area of the Park. Therefore, this church is a recognized structure by the City of New York, part of this licensure, and that this present activity of demolition is in derogation of my clients' rights."

Claira interjected herself into the discussion. "Chief, you need to stop the demolition while all of this is sorted out. On behalf of the Park Conservancy, we are required to honor the licenses duly granted. If a nativity display is licensed, then we will not contest that grant.

211

And frankly, I cannot think of a more appropriate spot to have a nativity display. Have you even looked at that those wonderful stained glass windows? Everyone one of them is a part of the nativity story."

Preston could not hear any on the arguments raging just a few feet from his position. The diesel engine of the large excavator pulsed in the noise of internal combustion, and rendered everyone arguing at the barricade gate mere silent movie actors. More than half of the stone pathway leading to the chapel was removed. He reversed the excavator, and looked up to see whether the crew was finished with the emptying of the contents from the chapel. The foreman gave him the thumbs up. Preston revved the engine of the excavator and started turning the excavator into position to reach into the side of the chapel, between the first stained glass window of the west side of the chapel and front corner of the little church.

Around the chapel fence line, four flags fluttered in the occasional puff of wind. They were large, seven feet by four feet, and were hoisted atop poles that were twenty-five feet above the ground, anchored in heavy concrete block bases. The fields of the flags were white, and each had a different Christmas theme, one a wreath, a Christmas tree, and snowman, and Santa Claus in his sleigh. The breeze periodically curled and folded the flags in lazy rolls, but mostly they seemed content to dangle in the insufficient breeze. Claira noticed the flags, and wondered for a second who placed them on the Great Lawn. *Another strange intrusion.*

Then Claira was snapped back to attention when a tall man, dressed in matted black robes, approached the barricade gate. Abner greeted the man, as if they had known each other for years. Abner then led him to the front of the assembly, immediately in front of Chief Lombard.

"Who are you?" Lombard asked, though without the sarcasm and disdain he had displayed earlier in the morning.

Abner spoke for the man. "May I present Father Casim Vanke, the Bishop of the St. Thaddeus Monastery, also known as Qara Kelsia, the Black Church, the first Christian church established in Iran."

"Are you an Iranian?" asked Lombard. "Are you saying that this guy came here all the way from Iran?" He ignored the attorney, who was still clamoring on about the license and the scope of the authority it created.

The bishop looked at Abner, then back to Lombard. He nodded and answered with a heavy accent. "Armenian. West Azerbaijan Province, Iran."

"Horseshit." Lombard directed his stare back to Abner, but the old professor offered no reprieve or no effort to calm the growing storm of words.

"This man has traveled around the world at great personal cost and also at considerable risk." Abner said. "I contacted him the day I saw this chapel, and windows which show in elegant detail priceless depictions of the Bethlehem Star and the Nativity of Mary. As you know, or I presume that you know, the conditions in his home country. He comes from a country not known for its religious freedoms or tolerance. He came to see this miraculous chapel, drawn to it like the Magi of the gospel who followed the miracle of the star. Are you going to destroy the reason he travelled here, right before his eyes?"

Before Lombard could answer, someone in the crowd declared, "I came here from Montreal, just to see this Chapel of the Holy Star." His accent was heavy French, and his voice seemed to quiver with disappointment. "Surely you are not going to ruin this beautiful shrine?"

Lombard shook his head. "I am not doing any of that. This is not my decision; do you understand?" He was talking not to Abner or the Bishop, but to the crowd.

A voice further back in the crowd pleaded, "We drove all night from West Virginia. My daughter is sick. Please let her see the chapel. It's all that she talked about since she saw this on her Facebook page." Then the pleas were acknowledged and echoed by tens of hundreds of other voices in the crowd of people, the intensity growing, the urgency building.

The young attorney cautioned the Chief of Police directly. "The licenses I presented to you vest rights in the licensee, rights that you are duty bound to protect as an instrument of the city government. If you seek to defer that obligation, I have co-counsel seeking a restraining order prohibiting any destruction of this chapel until cause is demonstrated in district court."

For the first time all morning, Lombard felt overwhelmed. He knew the decision to tear down the church was not a popular one, but the Park grounds were managed by the Conservancy and its directive was his charge to see fulfilled, despite his personal reservations. But he sensed that this had become more than just a protest of an unpopular decision. It had become exactly what the Mayor wanted to avoid; chaos, a building, growing, malignant disorder, or in common parlance, an old-fashioned shit-show.

Claira was about to speak, when a scream from deep in the crowd grabbed everyone's attention. Claira turned to the sound of the scream and saw an old woman dressed in a light blue coat and scarf scream again and point to the flags. "Look," she old woman yelled. "Oh my Lord."

Claira, Lombard, Abner, and everyone at the barricade gate turned their gaze upward, and saw the flags defy the will of the wind.

Instead of hanging limp in the slight breeze, they now stood straight on their hoists, flat and straight as if made of plywood rather than cloth. The Christmas symbols were all gone, and in their place written words.

AGNOSTIC

Where reigns God on this good earth
While kings sleep and children play
Through languid days and craven nights
Where crimes of wagers detest their birth

And in a moment, the flags fell into the cloth existence again, showing their original Christmas symbols, tethered banners slightly moving in the breeze.

Then a gust of wind, or the breath of heaven, or something beyond the arguments of men, moved the flags again into the panel existence.

To deny his presence until proof is shown
Is to barter blessings for meager pay
To bleed all color from glory's sight
To find life only in flesh and trust in stone

Then the words were gone, as the flags settled limp on their lanyards, holding the wreath and the trees and images of Christmas again on the cloth. The crowd stood mesmerized by the flags, a silence that was like the loss of voice. Everyone focused on the flags, waiting for the next move of the wind. Then the flags became rigid again, and new words appeared on the white fields of the flags.

What cost your soul to disbelieve
No hope for infants, asleep they sway
No forge of faith for the sinner's fight
No tears of promise for those who grieve

Claira reached for and held Abner's hand, and he held her hand tight, glancing at her only for a moment to smile, to acknowledge that he too was a witness. Then the flags softened and fell, only to become mysterious placards again, in a count of heartbeats, in a passage of breaths.

What form of miracle need you convince?
What new passion for your doubt betray?
Witness wounds and thorns and mercy's plight
The wardrobe of the shrouded Prince

When the flags lost their bones again, and collapsed back into cloth, a murmur was heard in the expanse of the crowd. Then silence, waiting. And the wind moved again and more words came into being.

Where reigns God on this good earth?
In humble shepherds afield they pray
In weary widows who still shine their light
In hearts of sinners, who still know their worth
There reigns God on this good earth.
df 12-29

The flags became just flags again, nothing but cloth and stitching. But even those people in the large crowd who could not see the flags transform knew something remarkable had occurred. Videos of the event were already circulating, and word of what happened was spreading, both with the people present in the Park and those elsewhere.

Bishop Vanke muttered foreign language prayers under his breath, the words hushed but reverent. His hands clutched the crucifix that he wore around his neck, on a dark, twined chain.

Lombard was speechless. He looked at the flags, then to Abner and Claira, as if they either caused the flags to shift from one banner to another, like a device in a magic act, or could otherwise explain what had happened.

215

Abner pointed to the excavator and yelled, "Chief, you need to stop this now."

Preston did not notice the flags and the poem's appearance, and raised the claw arm of the excavator high, its rusty, rigid bucket teeth ready to penetrate into the wall of the chapel and tear out a section of the little building. But before he directed the metal boom to crash through the chapel wall, for some reason he could not explain, he glanced at the fence line. And there he saw Alice, the little girl who gave him yesterday's poem. She stood along the fence, wearing the same musty and worn coat, tears rolling down her face, her mother at her side trying to console her. Preston hesitated, restrained by the thought that what he was doing was premature, and wrong. Not wanting to provoke the little girl into any further despair, Preston froze, the excavator arm raised high and vibrating, as if wanting to fall, to satisfy a desire to slice into the church, to shatter the wall and window, in a callous insult to the people who admired the chapel. But Preston held the metal hand at bay, refusing to release it to its murderous designs.

In the next moment, he saw his foreman running up to the excavator, franticly waving his hands, and indicating to him that he needed to kill the excavator engine. A police officer was also trotting up to the excavator, waving him down from the cab of the machine. Preston then slowly backed the machine away from the chapel wall, lowered the metal arm and curled the menacing bucket inward. He looked over to Alice, who waved at him, now only sniffling and fighting her sobs, but happy that he had turned the monster machine off and lowered its cruel robotic claw. With a smile on his face, feeling good about the apparent reprieve, Preston waved back to Alice, and gave her the okay symbol with his right hand.

Lombard directed two of the officers to confiscate all four of the flags. While he was doing so, Abner made his way through the barricade with the Bishop. The officers still at the barricade gate voiced a weak denial of entry, but Abner used his cane to motion them to move out of his way, and they passively complied. After what they had seen with the flags, they were not keen interfering with anyone associated with the chapel or who was obviously some type of clergy. Abner and Casim had to navigate around the trench that had been cut by the excavator, and once they passed it, several members of the construction crew busied themselves with placing of hazard tape around the hole. Four volunteers, from either the Catholic League or

St. Ignatius, began the placement of the figures for the manger display in the front left of the chapel, statues of shepherds, animals, and Joseph. A rough, wooden box was filled with hay, and waited to be set in place. The four worked happily, to the encouragement of excited voices in the crowd. After a moment on the chapel landing, Abner and the Bishop entered the church, and closed the door behind them.

Claira debated on whether to call her office, or go there in person. A very real possibility existed that on this day her employment would be terminated. But her musing about her future was interrupted by a tap on her shoulder.

She turned to see Mike Sandoval. He wore a leather jacket, unzipped, over his white shirt and tie, with a green wool scarf around his neck. His face was unshaven, and his eyes were raw and red, as if acid burned. "I hoped to find you here."

Chapter Nineteen

Cap sat in the corner of the hospital room, slumped in the chair, his eyes closed, his thoughts adrift. The old man, Jax Dissy, had stayed with him for most of an hour. The tale he told, about a prisoner turned poet, a rogue Scotsman on a mystic mission in the great lost city, to reach out to random souls in need, was fanciful, delusional, and anything but perceptual. But the old man was cogent, persistent, and cited the poem on the front page of the Christmas morning newspaper as evidence of the veracity of his story. Cap just smiled, and eventually asked the man to leave. But as he did so, the old man gave him two envelopes, one for him, he said, and the other for his mother.

Initially, Cap tossed the envelopes on the window ledge, having no curiosity of their contents. He then called Cissy, to check on her, and to tell her that Mom woke up to take a few sips of water and ask what day it was, before falling back to a restless sleep.

Cap turned off the television, preferring the near silence of the room to predictable repetition of the television programming, whether it be news, game-shows, sit-coms or old movies.

Cap thought about what Jax's story, that this poet chose to speak to him, and that he had words for Cap and his mother. Jax said that he shouldn't believe all of the negative reporting in the newspaper about the Stone Chapel, and "...that it is not some stunt, nor the work of religious fanatics. The chapel and poems are not some type of hellish lake of fire, wake of the flood sermon, or the work of some self-promoting fake prophet. It's in the park if you want to see it, there if you want to believe."

The envelopes rested on the window ledge next to old newspapers and a grocery sack of pretzels, crackers and packs of beef jerky. Cap glanced at his mother. She was sleeping, breathing shallow, in wet breath sounds that scared him, covered to her chin in blankets warmed in some machine somewhere out in the hallway. His thoughts shifted to his sister, and the worry she had to have for her family and herself. Everything came up snake eyes this Christmas. What further insult could there be? He looked over at the envelopes, rose from his chair and picked up the first envelope, the one that Jax had said was his, and slowly opened it. He removed a single page of paper, with a hand written poem neatly in the center of the page, and silently read the neatly penned words:

WAVES

The gulf sends back the daybreak
Waves on the surface and the floor
The gulls call glory's for flight's sake
The waves wane as one upon the shore

The days count on to heartbreak
Each breath softer than the one before
Waves of years wane now to heartache
Tides of tears and sorrow pour

Wave goodbye and let tomorrow take
The hearts of sons and daughters to restore
The call to home is never a mistake
Enough is never less nor is it more
df

"Son of a bitch," Cap muttered to himself.

Cap looked at the poem again, not reading it, but looking at it as if taking its picture, seeing it as a whole, and not words to be read from left margins to right.

"You shouldn't curse like that," a soft voice said.

Cap turned, startled, to see his mother awake, trying to sit up higher in the bed.

"Mom," Cap said as he came to the bedside. "Take it easy. Let me help you with the pillow."

She raised her head, and Cap slid another pillow behind her. She managed a smile, and reached for his hand.

"What can I do for you?" Cap asked.

She rubbed her eyes, and reached for the tube that slid up into her nose.

"Best not to touch that. You've been in and out so much, the doctor had to put that in to make sure you get enough calories. You've already lost enough weight on this hospital food diet. So, as soon as you start getting stronger, that tube can come out."

She blinked her eyes and nodded. "Cap," she said softly. "Where's Cissy?"

"She's at home with the kids, with the family. But she been up here almost non-stop. They all have. They'll be back to visit later, or for sure tomorrow."

"What's wrong with her?"

"Mom, what do you mean? There's nothing wrong."

"I know that something's wrong, not sure what. She's been crying all day, upset."

"Mom, there's nothing wrong. She was here just a while ago, and had to go home. But everything's all right."

Mrs. Kencaid closed her eyes, not to sleep, but to consider deeply, to think about what to say. She opened them again, and motioned for Cap to come closer. "Come sit next to me and talk."

Cap tossed his poem on the window ledge and slid the chair closer to the hospital bed. "I'm here."

"Well, son. You gonna think less of me, but I had this dream, a dream where Cissy got sick, but you were there and the kids and their dad, everyone there and she got better, and wasn't sick no more."

"Mom, that's just a dream. It doesn't mean anything."

"It does. And I wasn't in the dream. I was nowhere there, and I wasn't with her when she came home. It was like I was just watching from a long ways away, but I could see everything so clear, and I could hear every word. So she's gonna be okay."

"Mom —"

"Shh..." she said in a raspy small voice. "Remember what your dad would always say about the sundown, about the clear late nights on the water?"

"Yes, I remember, the darker the night, the brighter the stars."

"Yes."

Cap held her hand tighter.

She looked in his eyes, a little tear now on her cheek. "Cap, I'm afraid. I see the dark, and I'm so scared. But I'm so tired."

Cap shook his head. "Mom, don't talk like that. You're gonna be fine. We just need to get you stronger, and —"

"Son, I know that I'm spent. Just don't leave me alone. I don't want to go alone."

"It's okay, Mom, you're not by yourself. I'm here with you. I'm not going anywhere."

Mrs. Kencaid closed her eyes again. She seemed to drift to the edge of slumber, but resist the fall. "Forrest, is that man still here? The flowers?"

"No, Mom, he was just a friend visiting, just came to check up on you. He brought you some roses. Reds and whites." Cap pointed to the vase on the window sill holding the long stemmed roses.

"Cap, I'm so afraid. Read to me. Please read the words to me, I can't read myself."

"What words, Mom? What are you talking about?"

"I'm so afraid. Please read it to me."

Cap put her hand in between his palms and held it tightly. He looked at the window ledge, where the second envelope sat. How could his Mom know about that envelope, about Jax Dissy, or about Cissy's diagnosis? She must have heard them talking. But that could only explain the poem and the Jax's visit. Cap had never said anything about Cissy's illness, and Cissy would never have told her mother that she too had cancer. "Okay, Mom, let me see if I can find it." He released her hand, and quickly went to the ledge and tore open the envelope. He read the poem, the one meant for his mother, his eyes sinking into the written words. He held the poem in his hand, and then looked over at his mother. Her eyes were shut, and she had slid down from the pillow that he had placed behind her head.

"Cap, please don't leave me," she whispered.

"I'm here Mom. And I have your poem. Written just for you. Don't worry. Don't be afraid. Do you want me to read it?"

"Please, Forrest."

The hint of a smile crawled across Cap's face. "Mom, you know I don't like that name."

Mrs. Kencaid did not speak, but gave an almost imperceptible nod. Then a small grin. "Forrest," the words escaped with a breath.

"Mom, this is your poem. I'll read it to you. It's called "The Dark.""

> I am not trustful in the dark
> My faith is weak and starts to fray
> Would I listen and build an ark
> If a voice from heaven is heard to say
>
> I'm like a prism in the dark
> The black provides no light to bend

No rainbow flows from a single spark
Without a star I can't ascend

I have no vision in the dark
Only a flame to light the path
Still I know I must embark
And walk beyond the unseen wrath

I find no comfort in the dark
But I trust in the promised dawn
And to shadow protests I can remark
The shepherd's staff will lead me on
df

"The dark," Mrs. Kencaid said softly.

"Yes, Mom, that's the name of it. Did you like it?"

"Forrest, I'm not afraid any more. Don't you be…"

The paper fell from Cap's hand, and floated to the blanket covered bed. The panels and monitors on the room's walls started flaring, and a moment later a nurse hurried in. There was a flurry of activity, and another nurse called a code over an intercom.

Cap went to knee, beside the bed, still holding his mother's hand. "It's fine, Mom, it's all right. The dark's all gone now."

One of the nurses asked Cap to move, so she could slide in the crash cart next to the bed. Cap stood, and lifted the poem from the bed and said. "It's okay, DNR. I have her durable power of attorney. DNR."

The nurse studied him carefully, and asked, "Mr. Kencaid, I know that any resuscitation directives are yours to make. Are you sure that you want a DNR? Will you sign that order in her chart?"

"Yes"

The nurse turned to her co-workers and said, "No code. DNR." She turned to Cap . "A doctor will come and examine her and call the time of her passing. I'll be right back with the order for the record."

Cap nodded, and sat in the chair next to the bed. He held his mother's poem, and read the words again. "Just like dad always said, Mom, the darker the night, the brighter the star. Find your star, Mom, and ascend. There's no dark, not anymore."

***

Mike Sandoval arrived at the Park in time to see the spectacle of the flags. Unlike a lot of the people next to him, he didn't fumble with his phone or camera, trying to catch each image in photographs. He was reflective. As he read the words of the poem, he thought of the poems that presented themselves in equally wondrous ways since Christmas morning. He stood silently, reading the words, and somehow he could remember the words, the entire poem. It was much more than memorization. His recollection of the poem was perfect because he comprehended the meaning of the poem, so the words became easy to recall, even obvious. For some reason he could not explain, the words of the poem remained in his mind when the flags fell loose again on the flagpole, simply became what he knew without effort, like a melody, or the way he could see the richness of his favorite color with his eyes closed.

As the people in the crowd considered what they saw, Mike made his way to the barricade gate. He found who he was looking for, still where he spotted her from his distant approach. He tapped Claira on his shoulder, "I hoped to find you here. Mrs. Vasson, could I speak with you for a moment."

Claira's eyes answered the question. Her gaze was cold, unblinking.

"Please."

"Why would I spend a second talking to you? Don't you think that you and your boss made your position crystal clear at the meeting at the Conservancy office? The *Times* has been pushing its twisted version of what the Chapel means, and how it's a criminal act. I saw what your paper wrote about the poems, and the slanderous description of the man who probably wrote those poems. So why would I ever talk to you?"

Mike struggled with his response. "This would be off the record. I would... I will not record anything, and will not quote you, and will not report on which we speak."

Claira looked at him with suspicion, and did not bother to hide her distrust. "Sorry, I have to hurry to the office to be humiliated, castigated and fired." She turned and started to walk away.

"He came to see me last night. He wrote a poem for me, a very personal poem."

Claira stopped. She closed her eyes, as if counting votes in a razor thin election of whether to ignore Mike or to listen to him for a least a minute longer. Mike said nothing more, and waited for her to decide whether to trust him. She turned and said, "Who?"

"Mr. Finn. Darragh Finn."

Claira took a step closer. "You met him?" Claira was surprised at that claim, but for some reason it rang true, as something that Darragh would cause to happen. As if testing Mike, she asked, "Then did you see what happened to him this morning? I don't know how bad he was hurt, or even where he is."

Mike ignored those questions. "How does he do it? How does he make all of this happen?"

His dodge of her questions did not go unnoticed. Claira looked at Mike, and shook her head. "He doesn't do anything. He doesn't have any super powers, if that's what you thought." She felt her voice catch on her exhaustion, as though the effort to compose her words was beyond her store of strength. She let her head droop, her voice trail. But she found the will to continue. "He has one thing that most of us, most people, sorely lack. And that is faith. He writes about what he feels, what he sees, what he dreams. And he told me that he sees what to put on paper, and if he writes it and he leaves it in the chapel, and the next day it gets published or disclosed to the world in some amazing way. This whole series of events, of poems, is an effort to give us all what he has so much of. Faith."

"But why here, why now? Why did he come to me?"

Claira yawned, her exhaustion overcoming her. She turned her head toward the stone chapel, then back to Mike. "I can't say. I guess that in some way you needed whatever he told you. As for all of us, just look around. You think of this city as the center of a cosmopolitan and nuanced society. But maybe he sees something else. Maybe to him this is a dissipated place, with scores of people existing rather than living. When you look at it that way, isn't this a desperate place, with countless desperate and lost lives? What better place for a miracle?"

Mike nodded. "So what happens now?"

"Who knows? I think that Darragh was planning to give us a poem each day until the New Year. Now, I don't know what happens, if he can't get to the chapel. I imagine that it ends here and now, for better or worse."

"And the chapel?"

Claira shrugged. "I would hope that after this morning, the City, the Park, someone will recognize what a waste it would be to lose it, and worse, to lose it by our own hand."

***

Jason pushed the accelerator to the floor. His Aston Martin DB5 hugged the closed oval track, fighting the tension of each high-speed turn. The track was closed to the public, so Jason did not have to worry about sliding into another vehicle, or having one slide into him. He pushed the car as far as its 4.0 liter inline-six engine would allow. The engine only generated 282 horsepower, low by the standards set of some modern cars, but a super car for 1964. Jason loved the car, as it was the same make and model featured in the James Bond movies, *Goldfinger* and *Thunderball*. He paid handsomely at auction for it, and had it shipped to him from Cardiff, Wales, another expense which he did not mind, considering its choice condition and its pedigree, 38,000 kilometers, original engine and drive train, vintage upholstery and dash. The previous owner had a blue tooth stereo installed, but it was housed in a component box in the trunk. Such foresight, Jason had thought. That decision not to alter the original dash got another eighteen thousand dollars at auction.

After five more laps, Jason slowed the vehicle and steered the sleek silver car into the pit. He removed his helmet as he climbed out. "She was humming today, Stan," Jason said. "Despite the cold weather." He tossed the helmet to the track mechanic, and poured himself a cup of coffee from a large silver thermos which sat on a work table in the pit.

Jason came to EPCAL oval track located in the old Grumman Navy yard in Riverhead, Long Island a few times each month. Collecting vintage cars was his favorite hobby, but he was not content to park the cars in a garage and spend his time waxing the hoods. He took a long sip of the coffee just as his phone rang. "What's happening?" Jason asked as he answered the call.

Mike was used to Jason's lack of pleasantries. He responded in kind. "No go on the demolition. A couple of people managed to get in the chapel overnight and stall. One arrest, a woman. The man in there with her was busted up pretty good. The work crew was able to dig out the stone path leading to the chapel, but the crowd was huge and they wailed when that started. By the time the police got the people out of the chapel, enough commotion had been stirred up that the

Police Chief and Mayor decided to pull the plug."

"Damn it. What else?"

"Another poem popped up today, this one on a set of flags on the Central Park Lawn. I saw these myself. The police confiscated the flags, but I don't see how any computer program could have done it. I think that theory of yours about some revolutionary software platform is off base."

Jason said nothing as he considered that possibility. "You say the flags were taken by the police department. Well, then we'll find out what kind of technology was used to pull off this stunt. So that's a good thing. And I put Freddie in touch with a digger. If you have ever had a picture taken, this guy can dig it up. So now we know all about the mystery man from the church photo. He's a felon from Great Britain. Just released within the past year. So we've got a story roughed out now to shine a little light on his bizarre behavior. It'll be a real expose."

Mike winced at the glee with which Jason discussed the failures of others. For all Mike knew, Jason thought of him as weak, broken, because of his inability to overcome the loss of his little girl. He considered whether to tell Jason that the man hospitalized at the hands of the park police was the same man that Jason planned to dissect in the morning paper. He doubted that anything he could say would change Jason's mind, but decided to try. "Boss, I'm pretty sure that the guy who was in the church this morning is the same guy you're talking about. From what I saw, he's pretty bloodied up, maybe even hospitalized. So maybe we tone down any run about him until we get a little more fact checking done. Get the police report. Check out his condition, what charges filed, maybe even get a statement from him."

"No use. I'm sure that he's lawyered up by now. We'll run with Freddie's story, and then if we have to we can run a clean-up piece in a day or two. Call in and get a draft of Freddy's copy, and see if you can polish it."

"And what about the chapel? Are we running any story on it?"

Mike could hear Jason mutter to himself. Finally, he talked in intelligible words. "Maybe. I'll call Terrance Greenberg. We'll go from there."

***

Joel Nunnally followed Warren into a conference room at the Park Precinct building. Closing the door behind him he sat at the head of the table.

Warren said, "I want to see her."

"You're not in a position to speak of wants. You are looking at being written up, at a minimum, for insubordination. That's if you are lucky. You could be charged with aiding and abetting, obstruction of justice, conspiracy, beings how your guitar just happened to be inside the chapel. You want me to continue?"

"Are you going to let me see her, or what?"

Nunnally jumped from his chair, almost knocking it over. Warren did not flinch at the eruption, but followed Nunnally closely with his eyes, as if trying to see what he would say before he spoke. "Son, I'm trying to help you here. This is beyond what the union can clean up for you. This is well past not following a simple order. You could be charged. The mayor could have your head on a spike out by the Brooklyn Bridge, if he wants it."

"Captain, I appreciate your concern, but I wasn't drunk. I know what I did. Probably would do it again, too. So, are you going to let me see her, or what?"

Nunnally shook his head and chuckled, but in an ambiguous way. Warren could not tell if the Captain was concerned, but shocked at Warren's lack of remorse, or if he was looking forward to seeing how badly Warren would burn. Nunnally rested his hands on the chair back, and leaned over the chair, as if preparing to preach to Warren. Nunnally's temper was lost, and spittle flew from his mouth as he spoke, in a mist of bubbles and mini-drops, almost like a tiny spray from a can of air freshener. "Officer Hayes, you're in some deep shit here. Do you know how deep?"

Warren leaned back in his chair and smiled. "As the late great Johnny Cash might say, six feet high. And rising."

**

The mayor watched the video on the wall mounted monitor in his conference room. He could see the crowd of people all around the chapel, swaying while some police officer sang from the front step of the church. He pressed a forward button, then stopped at what appeared to be a sign on a flagpole, stenciled with a poem, but it then explicably went limp and lost all of the words in favor a Christmas tree. He went further still, and stopped when a civilian was brutally

227

rammed head first into the stone wall of the chapel by a smiling and laughing officer. On that frame, he paused the video, and looked at those seated around the conference table. No one spoke while he made eye contact with each one. Then turning to his left, where Chief Lombard sat, he said, "Steve, how in the hell did you let this happen? This was supposed to be low key, low profile."

Lombard made no excuses. "Two people snuck in the chapel last night. My officers responded with restraint, except for one. We were very fortunate with the crowd control; they were almost too cooperative. They raised hell with their voices, but nothing else. It was almost like they were there to witness. And unfortunately, we did not disappoint."

"How bad is that man injured?"

"Not sure yet, Mr. Mayor. He has a concussion, a fractured orbital rim under the eye, possible closed head injury, some cuts and abrasions."

"That sounds bad. What do you mean you're not sure yet?"

Lombard looked down at the table. "Not sure if he will need surgery."

Kevin Palanti, the mayor's special advisor, opened an I-Pad and checked his email. "Looks like he is in surgery now. Not sure for what."

Lombard put a cough drop in his mouth, tossed the paper wrapper on the table in front of him, and said, "Sir, it gets worse. The officer who shoved the civilian into the wall. His name is Astor Rebane. He was assigned to desk duty four months ago for excessive force. He was not supposed to be on Park duty. With all of the publicity about the chapel and the growing crowds, he just slipped back into the detail, and no one caught it until it was too late. Turns out that he posted a bunch of anti-Christian rants on some social media page."

The Mayor, looking at Janet, asked, "What's the worst we can expect? From a PR standpoint."

"Atheist with a badge brutalizes unarmed man at chapel doorway. A headline like that for sure. And that's before we know how badly this man is injured. Let's hope the surgery is successful."

Kevin asked, "That video we saw. Where did we get it?"

Lombard looked at him. From the body camera of an officer. But it's safe to assume there is other content out there. I would guess that every third or fourth person has a photo or a video of some portion of the morning at the park. So we're talking about thousands. And it gets stranger. There is a parade of clergy and what have you, call them pilgrims, coming to visit the chapel. From Iran, from Eastern Europe, all parts of the States, from the four corners. A new nativity scene has been set up next to the chapel. The NYU Professor I talked to this morning is giving lectures on the lawn of the Park about these wondrous stained glass windows. The crowd is eating this stuff up. It's like holy ground now. Half my officers cross themselves every time they walk past the chapel."

The Mayor looked over to Celeste Buck, from the city attorney's office. "Celeste, you have not said a thing. What's your take?"

"I counseled you previously that this was not our problem, as it was not our property. Those facts have not changed, but new facts have been added to the equation. We cannot deny, as the Chief has surmised, that there is video evidence of an officer possibly acting inappropriately. Our own video can arguably demonstrate that. Had the officer not been suspended from active duty, his action may be defensible. But given what you have said at this table, he was not supposed to be there due to his propensity to be too aggressive. And he is there anyway and does what again what he was suspended for. If he has a bunch of derogatory material on his social media, it could even be a hate crime. There is certainly serious exposure here to a civil judgment." She paused to see if anyone had any questions, but no one said a word, as her summary was frightful enough. After surveying the table, she continued, "On the issue of the unexplained chapel appearance, the windows, and the poem or poems associated with it. Sir, if I may, I am taking off my attorney hat now, and just talking to you as a citizen. I can only say that I believe we are seeing something…." She could not finish her thought.

"Miraculous," Lombard said.

She blushed and nodded, then made sure not to make eye contact with anyone at the table.

The Mayor tapped his fingers on the table, a habit of his while thinking. "Options?" He finally asked. "What do you think?"

"I suggest that we communicate directly with the Conservancy about their lack of control at the Park." Celeste finally said, but answered with her head pointed down to the tabletop. "Put them on notice that we view this as their responsibility, wholly or partially. We need to be compartmentalized, find every letter, email, or other written communication about the chapel. No doubt, we will be named in any civil suit, and we need to protect the city's position, even if it turns out that we are not aligned or not completely aligned with the Conservancy."

"What about making a press release? Janet, can you draft some statement, some talking point for me to consider? I want to be ready to get out in front of this."

"Sure, I have a few ideas in mind."

"Kevin, I want to monitor the medicals for this man. By the way, do we know his name?"

"It's Darragh Finn." Lombard removed his glasses, and rested them next to the paper wrapper from his cough drop. "A Scottish national. Has a record, burglary of a whiskey distillery. Just released from a prison in Dartmoor, England."

Kevin perked up and asked, "Can we make something of his criminal past? Maybe make him a little less sympathetic."

The Mayor shook his head. "That's a dangerous play. No way we can spin that we knew about his past when he was confronted at the chapel. Right Chief?"

Lombard agreed. "We did not know anything about that this morning. And that doesn't explain why Astor Rebane would be back on patrol. We can't very well say we called him to the Park to deal with a Scottish tourist with a past of burglarizing a distillery."

Kevin said, "Look, I'm just thinking out loud. I wasn't suggesting anything…"

"Agreed," the Mayor said. "Anything else?"

Janet said, "What about talking to Mr. Dumbarton? He was at the meeting at the Conservancy. Perhaps we can get some guidance from the *Times*. Perhaps the courtesy of being of advised of what story they plan to run. That way we can coordinate our response. Make sure that nothing is out of context, you understand." She smiled as she made that last comment.

"I'll consider that," the Mayor said.

"One more thing, Sir" Lombard said. "This Mr. Finn. His initials, D.F. There's a lot of talk out there that he's the poet, the man who writes these poems that have been popping up since Christmas day. In fact, I was told directly that he is the writer."

"Who told you that?" the Mayor asked.

"That little spitfire girlfriend. The one that was in the chapel this morning with him and Officer Warren Hayes. Her name is Isla Walson. What are we going to do with her?"

"Where is she now?"

Lombard picked up his glasses and placed them back on the perch of his nose. "She's still at the Precinct office. But we don't know what to do with her. Claira Vasson, the Park Assistant Director, insists that the Park Conservancy will not press any charges, that there is to be no further efforts to demolish the building. Her boss has been vague and noncommittal, like he is a deer in the headlights."

"What is the connection between this woman and Mr. Finn?" asked Kevin.

"What?"

The Mayor said, "You said that she's Finn's girlfriend. What's the connection between those two?"

Lombard shrugged and shook his head. "No, not his girlfriend. Officer Hayes' girlfriend. Or that's the impression I got, the way he took up for her. And that's another thing. What are we going to do with him?"

The Mayor rose from his seat. "Steve, you figure that out and give me a recommendation in the morning. No one talks to the press. No one has any comment yet. I'm going to get Mr. Greenberg on the line, and Jason Dumbarton will be the second call. And for the time being, I don't want any work crews out there tearing anything down. Not until I get some answers that make even a little bit of sense."

Chapter Twenty
December 30

Claira could not escape, neither from the black-caped, pursuing visage, nor from the dream itself. Part of her knew that she was within the erratic borders of a nightmare, but the aspect of her mind that felt fear did not care. That part of her wanted to avoid injury and pain, real or unreal, wanted to survive another second, another moment, to awake again in a real world or even in another dream, and that back corner of her mind was in control.

She ran from the blackness behind her, a thing that she could not identify. And it was close. In one moment it sounded like the slap of large, sharp feathers against the wind, in another, like the boom of wet sails filling and cracking at the fist of a storm. It was close and relentless.

She was in a place totally unfamiliar, a landscape of burnt forest. Smoke spiraled up in places, and the look and smell and taste of ash was everywhere. Large trees, their trunks black and ruined, still stood in clustered groves, but more were on the ground, splintered from their fall, some burning, some just a smoldering mess. Some were so charred as to be like old iron, spent in rust and ruin. What little grass remained was straw, waiting to burn. Beyond were the bleak rocks of a bald mountain. Already burned, already purged. But she ran, either away from the flames, or maybe the sin, she could not be sure. She was not thinking, not of choices and outcomes. She ran from the sound and the feel of a horror behind her, pacing her, herding her, as if she were prey, surrounded by predators, so confident with the assurance of the kill that the hunt was prolonged, either for practice or sport.

She stumbled as something touched her neck, just below her hairline. Onto her knees she fell, curling into a fetal ball shape on the charcoal floor.

She stood, but fell again, tripping over a mound of rocks. She looked at the thing that had made were fall. A stack of rocks, covered in soot so thick as to be invisible against the black, burnt ground. But the rocks were smooth, and while broken, parts were held together. Her trembling hand reached for the mound, and the soot brushed away, showing the lines of dirty joints of mortar. She rose to her knees, and could see the broken stones all around her for what they were, the chunks of fallen stone walls.

Behind her came the screams of something being crushed and cracking, the sound of the green break of living bone. Fear overwhelmed her, but she turned to see her pursuer. She saw a gargantuan figure, dressed in something like robes or a cape, matted black, alone on a hill above her. Another figure drove a giant metal beast, breathing fire, as it crushed the colored faces of saints under its evil weight. She looked closer at those faces, so thirsty for light, and saw them splinter and drown in the dust. The sound of glass breaking, a church falling, the sound of history closing.

She opened her eyes. Above her prone body, inches from her face, was the black sleek face of the thing, without the pulse of living tissue, but with black rigid ears and an inhuman nose pointed out from the cover of a synthetic skinless face. She screamed.

The thing above her giggled. And laughed.

Claira recoiled, and felt the pillow under her head press downward, catching her forced fall. The giggles, the laughter, rang in her mind, so familiar.

"Mom, did I scare you?" Tony asked through his cackle of giggles.

Claira felt the sheets, the comfort of her bed, and focused on the face above her. The black mass of her dream melted away, and sitting next to her was Tony, wearing his batman mask, laughing at her, and at her terrified reaction.

"Mom, did I scare you? Did you pee the bed?"

Claira sat up and lifted the mask from his little head. "No I did not pee the bed. You're the only one in this house who does that, mister." She ruffled his hair and hugged him, tighter than ever before, as if to cleanse her from the remnants of the dream.

Tony giggled, put the mask over his face, and then squirmed to the edge of the bed. "Wait till I tell Dad that I scared you."

Claira pulled a pillow behind her and rested back against the headboard. She looked at Tony, then glanced to the bedroom door as she heard steps coming down the hall. She looked back at Tony and smiled.

Theo entered the bedroom holding a cup of coffee and a plastic sippy-cup of juice. He handed the juice to Tony, who tried in vain to drink it without removing his mask. Then he handed the coffee to Claira, and asked, "How did you sleep?"

She looked at him as though guilty of something, then nodded. "Okay I guess. Crazy dreams."

"Not anything crazy about us, I hope." Theo's expression held the tint of worry.

Claira shook her head, and reached for his hand. "No, nothing like that. I'll tell you later. It was about work."

Tony now had his mask pulled up, resting on top of his head. "Mom, I have a question for you. What would you rather have? Typhus or lice?"

"What? Tony where did you get that? What kind of question is that?" She glanced over at Theo, who was trying to hide the smile on his face with his hand.

"It's a pretty simple question, Mom. It's an A or B question. Typhus or lice?"

Before she could say anything, Tony boiled over with laughter.

Claira shot glances at Tony and Theo, helpless.

Tony jumped up and down on the bed. "It's a trick question, Mom. Do you get it?"

Her expression answered no.

"Mom," Tony said almost exasperated. "Here's why it's a trick question. You get typhus FROM lice." With that, he jumped and landed on the bed in a sitting position, giggling all the way.

Claira reached for Tony and pulled him closer to her, but shot a look at Theo asking if he planted that crazy question in Tony's mind.

"Don't look at me," Theo said, throwing his hands up in surrender. "He asked me the same thing an hour ago. He got it from a Batman cartoon. Can you believe that passes for kids' consumption now? A cartoon Joker joking with Batman about typhus."

Claira rolled her eyes and then kissed Tony on the top of his head. Without looking up she asked, "What time is it?"

"It's about seven. I've got the paper on the kitchen table. You're all over it, but not by name. Front page has a column about Mr. Finn, basically calling him a fraud and a felon, and that he has somehow pulled a fast one on the Park Conservancy, and on the people of New York."

Claira dropped her head and hugged Tony, then shooed him from the bed. "Not surprised." She rolled to the edge of the bed, and grabbed her robe. "They've been building up to that for the last few days. Did it say anything about yesterday? About how he was injured? About his condition?'

Theo shook his head. "There's a mention of him fighting with the police, resisting arrest, threatening them. Nothing about his injuries."

Claira could tell that Theo had something left to say, but he was looking for the words. His face said it all. His lips trembled, as if still in gear, but the engine of his mind was slipping.

"What is it?"

Theo looked at her, with an expression of amazement. "You'll see. You need to read it for yourself."

Claira tied the robe of her belt and followed Theo to the kitchen, with Tony padding right behind her, holding his sippy-cup.

"Mom," he said between sips. "Can I ask you a question?"

"Sure honey, anything."

Tony smiled up at her and finished his juice. He wiped his mouth with the sleeve of his pajamas, then asked, "What's typhus?"

***

Isla turned on the lights to the coffee shop at five in the morning. The bakery counter would be dark for another half hour, but she had her pots of coffee brewing and a display of muffins and pastries ready for sale. She walked over to the door, turned over the sign saying the shop was open, and unlocked the deadbolt.

Before she could completely turn, she heard the door open. Startled, she wheeled back around to see Warren standing in the doorway, not in uniform, but wearing a NYPD baseball cap.

"Good morning," he said.

"Warren, you gave me a fright. What are you doing here so early?"

"Well, I just wanted to check on you. I tried yesterday, but they held me most of the day. By the time I got out, you were already gone."

Isla went to the counter and pulled two cups from a shelf. "What do you take? Sugar and cream?"

"Lots of both."

Isla poured the coffee and added in the cream and sugar for him. "I was debating what I was going to do today. First things first, I wanted to check on Darragh, but I don't know where to start. Then I was going to try to find you." She sipped her coffee, waiting for his response.

Warren took a long swallow of the coffee, and embarrassingly, smacked his slips. "Man, that's good." He sat the cup in its saucer and studied Isla as she leaned away from him, her back to the cupboard counter behind her. "You were going to try to find me?"

Isla nodded. "Well, I figured that you could help me out with Darragh, how's he doing, where's he at, that kind of thing."

Warren's smile faded, and disappointment crept over his face. "I guess that I can help with that. I need to find out about him too."

Isla could see that she had let him down with her response. And that frightened her. But she was more frightened about denying her feelings. She pulled a saucer and napkin from the cupboard, and served Warren a large blueberry muffin. "Here you go," she said as she slid the saucer to him. "On the house, with the coffee and all the refills that you want. After what you did yesterday, your money's no good here, for as often as you want to come back."

Warren froze. He looked down at the counter, as if unsure of his place in the room, empty though it was. When he lifted his eyes and met hers, he said, "No one has ever done anything like that for me. Thank you. I really mean that."

"It's the least I could do, after you rescued me yesterday, at least for a moment."

Warren reached in his coat pocket and pulled out the paper. "Your picture is on page five," he informed her. "Your name is not listed, but you are called the rowdy, rouge trespasser." Warren laughed at the reference.

"Oh Lord," Isla murmured, as she read the article that started on page one, and continued on page five.

"That's not the good part. Wait to you get to the op-ed page. And before you cut to that, could you freshen me up a little?" Warren smiled as he extended his cup for a refill.

***

The article about Darragh Finn, and his mysterious involvement with the stone chapel, was brutal and descriptive. He was portrayed as a charlatan and a thief, and the article was sprinkled with anonymous sources indicting him as a cruel opportunist trying to profit from the generosity of the public during the Christmas week. More than one unnamed witness speculated that the entire ruse was an elaborate scheme to lure as many people as possible to a confined area of the park, so that their identity information could be electronically stolen, everything in their phones, their tablets, their laptop computers, all swiped in a digital vortex of some new technology, and that the chapel was just the bait to lure them close enough for the trap to be sprung in an invisible, electronic assault on their lives.

But the pictures in the paper did not coincide with the treatment of this man in the text of the article. The photographs of the stone church perched in the snow on the lawn of the Great Lawn of Central Park somehow betrayed the accusations of the article. The crowd's joy was too apparent, the chapel's simplicity too pacifying. But more telling was the opinion column written by Mike Sandoval, which was on page one of the editorial section of the paper. Next to a small picture of him was a photograph of a drone view of the Great Lawn, where the little stone chapel sat in the purity of the snow, surrounded by thousands of people, a great crowd of curious, humble patrons of a park sanctuary in the rigors of the grey city, of hopeful ones, faithful ones, and maybe more than some being desperate ones. They were captured in this photograph. All gathered to see the chapel, to read its priceless picture windows, to hear the whispers of those who believed just a little more than they do, to be reassured, to be, in some small measure, restored. And below that photograph was his narrative, a testament in print.

The Catharsis of Despair   Mike Sandoval, Editor

There have been any number of essays considered and written by minds and writers much better than I, many great and enlightened works of philosophy and religious thought, on the concept of despair. The common definition of the word is "the complete loss or absence of hope." And how desperate that state of being sounds to be. For what dire circumstances can eradicate all hope, erase all of the wellspring of faith? Daresay none, not in the modern society of man. But just a lifetime ago, even less, there were the stains of Auschwitz and Treblinka, the killing fields of the Khmer Rouge, the criminal neglect of the souls in Darfur, Sudan. And before that, how many battles posed the poignancy of man? Did the victims of those loathsome days hold any flicker of hope as they suffered, as they died? Are the sins of the sword not stoked by the same embers of greed, the same cinders of lust and hate, as are all the wars for castles and cities, for rivers and treasures, for the sons of the country, for daughters of the home? And the tales of the conquests and the legend of the bounty live in songs and poetry, while the victims hear no toasts, nor whispers of farewells. And yet hope and faith survive these sadly banal blights, in the perseverance of the few survivors, and in the forgiveness of the lost and the lame.

Can despair then exist, any more than a mere moment in chronological time, or as a punishment, or a penance, for wrongs of the present, or crimes of the past? The poet Miller Williams penned a book titled *Why God Permits Evil* but in its pages I found neither answers nor clues. The German philosopher Freidrich Nietzsche famously declared that "God is dead," that the Christian God was not a credible source of moral principles for the actions of man. Does that idea serve as the rubric for a secular view of the world? I thought not, ever loyal to the seed of hope that no natural or human storm could subdue.

But then I lost my daughter at the age of twelve, to a hereditary lung disease that laid claim to her, but not to me. When she was first diagnosed, I had such high hopes, hope for a cure, hope for a normal life for her, hope that she would soon forget the suffering of her childhood as she grew to a parent and had kids of her own. As the texture of her few years wore thin and torn, I hoped for a miracle, and in her last days I hoped for a rescue, a climatic deliverance from death's dark door.

When I lost her a year ago, I found that despair did exist, not as a state of mind, but as a torture of time, a hard weight of an increasing number of numb days, where I have spent my time losing my sobriety, my family and my faith. Was Nietzsche right, was God dead? Or perhaps he never was, and we trek alone through an illusion of accidents and the random cruelty of an animal world.

This Christmas was only an irritant reminder to me of her last one, in a hospital room with an IV tree and bows and wrappings of bandages and breathing tubes. An anniversary of heartache and bitter, broken words of pain.

And then a poem appeared, on Christmas morning, in this very paper, a mystery still, of how it came to be, which asked for reflection on this charmed and cruel world. A small stone chapel also appeared, on the lawn of Central Park, as if shuttled out of time, this little church had no lights or utilities, but windows of colored glass telling the story of a guiding star. The story of the first faith, the highest hope. A story which I ignored. Then another poem appeared on the sides of buildings, and I looked to see, but for selfish reasons, I looked only to find the secret behind the trick, to discover the clever device behind the magic act. And the next day, another short poem somehow became in the hub of Grand Central Station, then on the next morning another poem was passed from the hands of an array of children, all gathered in the park, little lambs of the flock. And finally, yesterday, another appeared on the fields of white flags washed clean by a holy wind.

Each day brought a curiosity, and I again lost interest, succumbing to the absence of feeling anything good. Had I looked, truly looked, I would have seen that each of the poems were graceful lyrics, words of reminders, the melody of living well. But in my dark, uncaring pain, I thought little of these events, as curious as they seemed, for I had settled on the view that either God was dead, or He never even was.

And as I sought to mark the passage of a year from my Maria's death, by visiting her grave, a man found me at the cemetery, a strange man who spoke few words and who seemed to be hopelessly lost and joyously found. And he gave me a piece of paper on which he had written a poem, a poem for or about a little girl he never met, for a broken shell of a father and husband, who for a solid year had raged against his world, his faith and his God. An anonymous man, this stone chapel poet, was the author of these wonderful Christmas poems, and sadly is the man that was beaten and battered yesterday at the doorway of that sacred little church. From what I know, because of those physical insults, he will not be writing a poem for today, not for people of this needful city. So I am going to give you, my readers, the poem that he gave to me.

THE CROWNING

Crown the little dying one
She suffers sleep and cries no more
Drowns her brittle sighing breath
She wakes covert and startled, soars

Down her kitten crying smile
Her mother deep in memory's store
Frowns upon her painted face
She needs mementos to adore

Renown the simple days that pass
Her father walks an empty floor
Now mysterious and forlorn
Her vacant room he does deplore

Find they will her smile again

And see her as she was before
In dreams and certain rest ahead
Their missing love will be restored

Crown the little dying one
She sleeps abreast and hurts no more
Her gown of glitter angel's breath
She lives anew on Eden's shore
df

I read those simple words in the shadow of the crypt where my Maria rests, and my hope was restored. So if you ask me, does despair exist, my answer is a certain yes, as I have toiled in bleak, despairing days, this past year of them, to be sure. But what is lost can be found, what is absent can be present again.

Before these past few days, I would have said that I never witnessed a miracle, though I prayed for one so hard that my body and spirit hurt. But now I have seen a miracle, a miracle that sowed its seeds back into my barren, desert life. And I am not referring to the mystic chapel or the revelation poems on the buildings or words on signs or flags. The miracle that happened to me is cast on a single piece of paper, words that do not name my daughter but capture her with such precision and detail that I see her in each letter and line.

As this Christmas week draws to a close, I can thankfully say that I have learned a lesson about miracles and hope and the faith that has held this world together for thousands of years. The kind of hope that inspires men to follow the arc of a star until it rests over a rural crib. The kind of faith that asks no proof but sings of promises made and fulfilled. And as my last words to you, I say simply, follow your faith, and hold on to your hope. Merry Christmas and Happy New Year.

Chapter Twenty-one

"What in the hell were you thinking?" Jason said, but did not pause long enough for one to be forthcoming. "You deliberately went behind my back. You sabotaged me."

Mike sat behind his office desk, which was covered with boxes being filled with his personal items accumulated in his office over the years. He did nothing to acknowledge Jason's anger, and continued packing. He carefully placed a framed photograph of Maria with her favorite player from the New York Giants, Benjie Grovin, the star running back, into the biggest of the boxes. He remembered the moment captured in that photo. Benjie had come to the hospital with a few of this teammates. Maria was not on the general pediatric floor, and she would not have met Benjie or any of the other players that morning, but Benjie had got off the elevator on the wrong floor, and by chance knocked on Maria's door. Her eyes fired with excitement when he stepped into the room, and he knew immediately that his finding her room was not an accident or a coincidence. They formed an almost immediate bond, and he visited her twice more before she died, bringing her gifts of autographed footballs and jerseys, and a Giants cap that she wore on the day she died.

After that moment of reflection, Mike covered the photograph with thick packing paper, then looked up at Jason, who was standing across from him, leaning over Mike's desk. Mike cleared his throat, and said, "Jason, I did not sabotage you, or the paper. I wrote an opinion piece, as is my prerogative. Frankly, it was something that I had to do, to lay bare a year's worth of stagnate thoughts and feelings."

Jason stood straight and retreated a step. "You went behind my back. You know what we planned for the page one story. Your piece countered all the points in the story. You're done here."

Mike managed a dry, small smile. "Hence the packing of my office," He said as he motioned toward the boxes on is desk.

"Your insubordination and treachery will not be forgotten. Don't think that you will land on your feet when you walk out of these doors."

Mike sighed, his frustration unmasked. "Let me ask, what do you call straight news? In the page one run, there was not a single word about Finn's perspective, no attempt to get his response or his side of the story. It was a hit piece, and it was well-written, factually based and concise. But it was a hit piece nonetheless."

"Then you admit that every word was true."

"True, that he has a criminal record. True, that he was recently released from prison. That he was at the chapel yesterday, and he somehow got in the chapel before the demolition crew arrived, all true."

Jason nodded his head with each word, his arms folded across his chest, like a bidder at auction as Mike continued. "The statements from the unnamed witness, the unidentified sources, about some new gadgetry to steal the saved information and data on everyone's cellphones, all fabricated. The accusation that he is some kind of mass identity thief, also pure fiction. The best lies have tendrils rooted in some truth."

Jason's face reddened. "He is responsible for this paper being subverted on Christmas morning. He hacked our print room, our network. He is a cyber-criminal, in addition to his felonious past."

Mike rose from his desk. "Did he now? Can you tell me how?"

Jason had no answer.

"I seem to recall that you did not want to refer anything out to law enforcement when you thought that there was some new computer tech that you could get your hands on. One of your DOD buddies whispers to you about some new software, and you see dollar signs. All I know is that he sought me out, when I was adrift and drowning, and threw a life-line to me." Mike paused as he placed the lid on the open box. "You know that I had the authority to print my column. But had I taken it to you, had you seen it before deadline, would you have approved it?"

Jason turned away at the question, choosing to stand at the window and stare down at the street below. "Who knows? But you should have taken that chance."

"No, sir. I am the editor, not you. And as much as I know you disagree with that reality, as editor I have the right to submit my copy. But as editor, I could have also required a re-write of the page one on Mr. Finn. I could have rejected the story for twenty different reasons. But you know and I know the story was outcome driven. It wasn't about reporting, or journalism, or running with an exclusive. You had a conclusion in mind, and narrative that you wanted made public, and your story was printed to support that preordained result. But I did not reject it, though I regret looking the other way on it now. So don't lecture me on the subject of journalistic ethics."

Mike stacked two of the boxes and then picked them up. "I'll send for the rest of my things. Jason, thanks for the opportunities that you gave me. I have accomplished things I thought were beyond my abilities while I worked here. But I need to do something else with my life now, and I am not sure that this is the place I need to be."

Jason stuttered. After a protracted pause, all he could manage was, "Well...."

Mike walked around his desk, and when he reached the office door, turned to Jason, "Well. A well is a hole in the ground. Usually a very deep subject. Maybe one day we can discuss that." With that, he left Jason alone in his office, and greeted and thanked many of his shocked co-workers, who had no idea why he was leaving.

***

Cap arrived at the Park mid-morning. After his mother's death, he checked into the Pierre Hotel on 61st Street, one block from Central Park. He and Cissy agreed to have their mother's memorial service in Deer Island, and he would head north to Maine in the evening. But before he left, he knew that he had to see the stone chapel.

He walked slowly along the winding paths, letting his eyes wander, his mind linger in memories. His mother had a gift for gardens, the proverbial green thumb. Cap liked the strength of trees.

In the distance he saw a gathering of people. He approached the crowd and slowly made his way through the people. Then he saw the chapel. *Mom, how I wish you could be here to see this.*

Unlike the days before, the chapel was not closed to the public. A long line of people curved along the path, now repaired, that led to the chapel door. He made his way parallel to the chapel, and saw people exiting through the back door. The line was moving slowly, but steadily. He retreated and got in the line, behind a father with two young boys, both wearing stocking caps and bright blue overcoats.

As he approached the chapel entrance, he saw a nativity scene, with a little girl standing next to the manger while her mother snapped a picture. At the chapel entrance was an elderly man, who welcomed the people as they entered, and passed out a simple program that gave brief descriptions of the stained windows. He wore a Museum name tag that simply said Abner, and he smiled as he handed Cap a copy of the two-page leaflet.

Cap took his time going through the chapel. The windows were vibrant, iridescent, more than he expected considering the overcast day. The movement of people, both inside and outside, made little shadow ripples in the light pouring through the windows, and made the depictions seem to show movement and life.

As he exited the rear door, he heard a reporter talking into a television camera. "The crowds arrived early this morning at the Great Lawn, eager to see the chapel. And in a startling reversal, the Director of the Park Conservancy issued a statement saying that the Chapel has indeed been a project long planned in conjunction with the Museum of Natural History, and that the misunderstanding about its dedication as a park attraction resulted from contractual nondisclosure provisions in the construction contract. And as you can see from the park patrons this morning, they are sure glad those issues have been resolved. From the Great Lawn of Central Park, I am Stacey Kelly reporting for Channel 2 News."

As Cap circled back to the front of the chapel, he saw a familiar face. He made his way to the man and tapped him on the shoulder, saying, "Mr. Dissy, good morning."

Jax turned and smiled, and held out his hand. "Mr. Kencaid, good morning." The two shook hands, and Jax said, "So sorry to hear about your mother's passing. My condolences."

"Thank you. My sister and I appreciate it very much."

"Let me introduce someone to you. This is Isla Walson. Isla, this is Mr. Cap Kencaid. This is the man I visited yesterday, in the hospital."

"Pleasure to meet you. And thank you for taking the time to come to the Park this morning."

Cap nodded. "I'll be heading out later today, but I had to come by. And let me ask, do either of you know where I can find the man who wrote those pages that you gave me, Mr. Dissy? I would like a word with him before I head out."

Isla's face darkened. "He had surgery yesterday. He's still in the hospital."

"Can you tell me which one?" Cap asked. Isla looked at Jax, as if seeking permission to answer. Jax said nothing but gave the slightest shrug of his shoulders.

"Weill Cornell," Isla said. "Upper East side."

"Thank you," Cap said as he excused himself. "I know that one well."

Chapter Twenty-Two

Cap asked the nurse at the floor desk where he could find the room of Mr. Darragh Finn. "Room 615," she said without looking up.

As Cap made his way down the hall, he noticed a man in uniform sitting outside Darragh's room. Cap pulled an ink pen out of his pocket, and the letter sized papers he received at the chapel. He folded the papers length ways, and wrote a few notes on the paper. Cap did not hesitate, and walked up to the guard and asked, "Can I go in for a visit?"

"Name?" the guard asked.

"I'm from hospital ministry. You can call me Brother Ken."

"What's your business?"

Cap smiled. "The Lord's business."

The officer handed Cap a clipboard and instructed, "Sign in and be out in ten minutes."

"Certainly," Cap said as he signed the visitor log. "Have a blessed day."

Cap knocked once and opened the door without waiting for a response. He entered the dim room, and let his eyes orient to the gloom. "Mr. Finn? Are you awake?"

"Aye," a broken voice whispered.

Cap moved closer to the hospital bed. Darragh was blanket covered to his mid-waist, and wore a hospital gown. An IV tube was placed in this left arm, and an oxygen saturation monitor and an automated blood pressure cup were respectively on his right index finger and arm. His head was heavily wrapped in bandages, one eye completely covered. "Mr. Finn, my name is Cap. Cap Kencaid. I understand that you wrote the two poems that were given to me yesterday, to me and my mother. Is that right?"

"How is she?" Darragh managed to say.

"Well, she died, right after hearing your poem for her. I came here to ask you; why did you send those poems to us? How did you even know us?"

Darragh moaned as he turned slightly in the bed. "They were needed, weren't they? I hope that you or your mother weren't upset with them."

Cap shook his head. "No sir. In fact, my mother found peace with hers. The other one made me think about things too. But you didn't answer my question. How could you send them? We're strangers, neither of us knew you."

Darragh talked with his one uninjured eye closed. "I can only tell you that someone's prayer was answered, yours, your sister's, maybe your mother's. I offered a small comfort, a small thought."

"Are you some kind of psychic?"

Darragh managed a laugh. "No, nothing like that. I can't tell the future, nor can I start fires with a wink or a nod. But I can sometimes be pointed to someone in need."

"I didn't pray for anything." Cap looked at the man laying before him, in obvious pain.

"Prayer is not like ordering take-out on a phone app." Darragh shifted in bed again. "And you don't always get what you ask for." With that, he managed a weak laugh.

"What's so funny?"

"You are, Mr. Kencaid. You are not at all what I asked for, or what I was expecting."

* * *

Terrance Greenberg wore a dark blue suit, with a white carnation in his lapel. He sat at his desk sipping coffee, and did not bother to stand when Claira arrived.

"Good morning, sir. Sorry if I'm a minute or two late.

"Not at all, Claira, sit down. Have you heard our press release of early this morning?"

"Yes, sir, I did. I have to say that I did not see you reversing course on this, but I'm happy you did."

"Well, I have been talking to the Mayor's office, and I have given considerable thought to this situation. How can I say, earlier I was given faulty advice, and I dare say I was even misled. But that is behind us now."

"So the plan is…?"

"Our plan, Claira. Our plan. You are very much needed and a part of this enterprise. I know how much that you look up to Professor Parson. He will have an important role with the chapel from now on. The museum will coordinate with us, and will have direct involvement with the church building. As part of the museum complex, we can largely avoid all of the separation of church and state disputes that the city attorney's office was worried about." Terrance paused to pour himself another cup of coffee, but did not bother to offer one to Claira. "You will continue here, won't you, as a vital piece of our team?"

"And all I have to do is —?"

"I am not asking for anything, not anything at all. We just have to be honest with ourselves, and admit that someone here had that chapel built for us, and that we simply weren't aware of those plans as we should have been. But that speaks to the great level of competence and expertise that we have here, in house I mean. Our people have vision. I have already told our entire staff, that I do not even want to know who planned and administered the construction of the chapel, and that it is enough to know that it was done by someone within our organization for the betterment of our Park, of our Conservancy." He paused to smile and wink at Claira, "And if that person is sitting across from me now, such a visionary, then I do not want to know. It is enough that we can tell the public that the chapel is our gift to the city, to the people of New York."

"Sir, I —"

"Don't be modest, Claira. And enough said. I am just so glad that you are back with us and that, shall we say, my, our misjudgment from earlier in the week is forgotten. You know, I have long considered who would be a worthy successor at my desk, not that I am ready to leave any time soon. But your handling of this entire episode," he paused, looking for the words to say. "It has been…epic."

Claira stood, sensing that the meeting was over. "Happy New Year, Mr. Greenberg."

"Quite right. Happy New Year."

***

Warren walked up the stairs to his apartment. The day had not gone as badly as he feared. He still had a job, though he was on administrative probation. He would be on desk duty for a month, maybe longer.

After he left Isla's shop, he was coached by three different supervisors from his department, each telling him with varying degrees of tact what he had to do, which was to agree to file a report which could be used to charge Darragh Finn, as well as Isla Walson, with criminal trespass, obstruction and conspiracy. He resisted, and after several verbal lashings, was told to take the rest of the day and to think long and hard about his place in the department, his future with the force, and most worrisome, the forfeiture of his pension.

He thought about going to Isla's, but convinced himself that any more contact with her now was perilous to both of them. He didn't think that she was in any danger of being charged, especially not after the Park's belated acceptance of the chapel, but it was clear to him that Darragh would be charged with something, and that meant that the prosecutor's office might try to hold charges hanging over Isla's head as a means of coercion. That was standard operating procedure for a prosecutor. Hell, he was also being coerced, by his own department.

He checked his mail box, and found a bevy of junk mail. He made his way up the stairs and to his apartment. After tossing the mail on this kitchen table, he went straight to the refrigerator for a beer. He removed a can of Coors, popped open the top, and went into the den and crashed on the sofa.

He had a dilemma to solve before tomorrow morning. As always, when Warren was surrounded by quiet, when he tried his best to think, a tune or a phrase of lyrics would pop in his head, sometimes as an inspiration, other times as an inopportune distraction. He was listening to Bruce Springsteen and the E Street Band earlier in the day. But as he took another long swallow of his beer, an old Merle Haggard song entered his thoughts, and he found himself remembering a lyric about what he was gonna do with the rest of his life. That was exactly the challenge before him, to see the many paths to the rest of his life that were being presented to him, and to select one, knowing that he could only go one way, that is, there was no going back to try again if his choice was a poor one.

Warren finished the beer, and pushed his head back against the pillowed sofa. A thousand doubts cycled through his mind, the threat of losing his job and pension, balanced against the revival he felt standing on the chapel steps, singing to the largest crowd he'd ever seen. And then there was Isla.

After a minute more of worry, he stood and went to his guitar case holding his Gibson, knowing that a few minutes of strumming would help clear his mind. When he opened the case and removed the guitar, he noticed a folded sheet of paper in the velvet pocket on the inside cover of the case. He set the guitar down, and removed the paper, slowly unfolding it. "Hello, Darragh," he said as he read the words left for him by Darragh Finn.

Chapter Twenty-three
December 31

The morning was busy at the coffee shop, with a constant flow of customers asking for coffees and cappuccinos to go. Isla worked the counter alone this morning, but expected her part-time help to arrive around noon. Even so, Isla nearly doubled her normal morning business. *The year is ending on a high note.* A few of her patrons asked her about the Chapel, or whether she had really stood up to the threats of the demolition crew. One lady even asked her if she had actually laid down in the path of a bulldozer. But mostly she noticed some of her customers talking in whispers among themselves, nodding and pointing to her as if a celebrity. Isla was grateful for the brisk pace of customers, but did not like being a spectacle.

The events at the Park and the interrogation at the precinct office the day before exhausted her, and she overslept her alarm by a few minutes. But even tired and occupied by the flow of customers, she found herself glancing at the doorway, expecting to see Warren bounce in for a visit. As the morning passed without any word from him, she wondered if she misunderstood his concern for her. She scolded herself for letting her imagination free, because she was disappointed so many times before, and wanted to guard against that reoccurrence on the last day of the year.

A few minutes before eleven, a friend of hers who worked at the bakery came over for her break and asked for an espresso, double.

"Wow, usually you take a cup of French roast with sugar. You must need a jolt."

"Yea," Sharon said as she looked around the counter. "Mind if I sneak a smoke?"

"Not if you agree to pay my fine. You never know who's watching."

Sharon stuffed her pack of Virginia Slims back in her purse with a frown. "Yea, you're right. I'll make do with the coffee."

"So you have big plans for the night?"

Sharon looked over to the bakery counter, then back at Isla. "Well, we're supposed to go to Times Square, and then to a party at my cousin's place in Chelsea. What about you?"

"No plans. Hopefully I'll have a quiet night."

"Aw, Isla, you can't be alone on New Year's. Why don't you tag along with us? It'll be fun, and you know, my boyfriend's got lots of friends. Who knows, you might even meet someone tonight."

"What, so I'll get a kiss at midnight?"

"Well, who knows, maybe more if you play your cards right."

Isla playfully slapped at Sharon with her dishtowel and shook her head, and then glanced to the door when she heard it open. When she saw a middle aged woman holding a list in a gloved hand, her spirit sagged. She looked back at Sharon and said, "I think that you have another customer. She looks like she's here for a take-out order. A big one."

Sharon finished her coffee. "Yea, back to the grindstone. But call me if you decide that you want to join us. Who knows, you might just get lucky."

***

Warren was back in Nunnally's office, answering the same questions he endured yesterday. When he glanced at the clock on the wall he saw that he had been in the office for two hours and under interrogation for over an hour. He yawned, leaned his head back in frustration and said, "Captain, if you're trying to make me comfortably numb, you've done it."

Nunnally did not understand the Pink Floyd reference, but was not amused nonetheless. "You must have had a hell of a drunk last night to come here with a piss on my shoes attitude. I would have thought that you would have done some serious soul searching. Figure out what you want from this department, a future or a jail cell."

Warren sat up straight and looked directly at Nunnally. "Captain, I've answered all of the questions that you've asked, more than once, and none of the answers are going to change. Now, it's like this. I did think about things last night. And I had a moment of clarity, right in the middle of Bruce Springsteen song, "Thunder Road." That one's my favorites, from the *Born to Run* album. Anyway, I realized I can't control what you or the department or the mayor's office or even the F, B and I are going to do, any more than I can control gravity or make the F barre chord an easy one to play. And then I had a cold one, a Coors, and I read something that really put everything in perspective. I love my job, and I'm good at it. But it's not my life.

Once I realized that, your threats don't seem all that persuasive anymore."

Nunnally looked as if he had been chastised by his church pastor. He composed himself and asked, "Who do you think you are, Dr. Phil?"

"Dr. Zhivago." Warren could not help himself, and Nunnally was such an easy mind to play with.

"What?" Nunnally asked startled.

"Z,h,i,v,a,g,o. Zhivago. Dr. Zhivago."

"Who in the hell is Dr. Zhivago?"

"Only the most famous doctor, philosopher, poet and protector of loves this side of St. Petersburg."

"How do you say his name?" Nunnally asked.

"Dr. Zhivago."

"What kind of doctor is he?"

"The best kind. A healer of the heart, I suppose."

"So he's a cardiologist? Do you have a heart condition that the department does not know about?"

"Nope, I'm fit as a fiddle."

"Then why are you going to a cardiologist?"

"Who said anything about that?"

Nunnally pointed to him. "You did, you said that this doctor Zhivago was your doctor."

"No, you asked me if I was going to see Dr. Phil."

"Then you said, Dr. Zhivago."

"Yep, that's what I said. Dr. Zhivago."

"Never heard of him."

"He was trained overseas, I believe. And captain, if you don't mind me saying, I've noticed how you fidget in your chair a lot. Is it hemorrhoids?"

Nunnally stood abruptly. "That'll be enough of all that. You're on thin ice, and the sun is rising. I've got one more question for you. Where is your friend, Darragh Finn?"

Warren paused for a moment, as that was the first new question that he had been asked all morning. So that was the mystery behind the interrogation. They had lost Darragh Finn, and suspected that Warren helped him escape or at least knew his present location. Resting back in his chair, Warren said, "I would imagine that he is still at the hospital recovering from surgery to fix the fractures around his eye. Where else would he be?"

Nunnally eyed Warren suspiciously. "Darragh Finn left the hospital sometime early this morning. Whereabouts now unknown. He apparently had help. Someone posing as a hospital minister came with a wheelchair to bring Mr. Finn to the hospital chapel. He never came back to his room."

Warren smiled.

"Do you know anything about that situation?"

Warren shook his head. "No, sir, I don't. But it tickles me that he used the ruse of going to a hospital chapel to give his guard the slip. Should have been wary of the old chapel ruse with this one, considering that he's been sleeping in the brand new old stone chapel in Central Park all week. One of your boys?"

Nunnally nodded.

"Whoa, Lombard's going to want a pound of flesh with salt and pepper for that screw-up. Glad I've been here all morning. Couldn't have a better alibi if I would have planned it."

Nunnally sank back in his chair, waving a dismissal to Warren.

Warren rose and made his way out of the office, but turned when he reached the office door and asked, "Captain, is there anything I can get for you before I go. You don't look so good. Frankly, I've never seen a whiter shade of pale."

***

The afternoon business at the coffee shop was steady, but waned as the afternoon grew older. Isla planed on leaving at 6. For a brief interlude around noon, she had been tempted to call Sharon and agree to join them for the party. But she decided not to and saw her evening as an early dinner, a movie, and a hopeful fall into sleep sometimes before the birth of the new year.

She was cleaning one of the Bunn coffee machines when she noticed several of her patrons turning to stare away from the counter. She paid little attention to them, but stopped moving, maybe even breathing, when she heard a chord progression from an acoustic guitar. She turned, slowly, as if trying to find the sound of the music with hearing rather than sight, and found Warren, standing just inside the door, smiling, as if he was being paid to be there.

He played an introduction to a song that she heard before, one that was familiar, but she couldn't place. Not until he sang the first verse.

Isla stood behind the counter, her hands on her cheeks, as if holding the smile on her face. Her eyes were filling, but holding their drops. Her heart seemed to tremble between its beats, both curious and delighted.

Sharon came running from the bakery, laughing. "Isla, he's singing a Genesis song to you! "Follow You Follow Me." That's one of the best songs ever!"

Warren's guitar provided a complex series of simple, beautiful notes, and his playing was unrehearsed and spontaneous, flawless, subdued and tender. His voice offered the lyrics as a ballad prayer.

Everyone in the bakery was still-frozen, watching and listening. The sounds of the street seemed to fade, unable to enter.

Without any interruption in playing, after finishing the Genesis song, Warren shifted the melody, and said, "I can't top Phil Collins, but after everything that happened yesterday, this one I wrote for you."

I saw you stand
Against the forces
I saw your tears
When trouble was deep
Still you stayed
Despite the choices
Saying prayers
I saw you weep

Take my hand
I will not tremble
Take my fear
So I will sleep
Take my doubt
I will not stumble
Take my heart
Away from trouble
Take my love
To the distant oceans
Take my love
Whenever you leave

Warren repeated the chorus and finished the song, then took the guitar from his shoulder and leaned it against the wall. He walked to the counter and held out his arms.

Isla looked at him, astonished. "Warren, you came to serenade me. On New Year's Eve. With a perfect song." She felt a tear track across her face, but she let it run its course and fall.

"It's New Year's Eve, and who knows, maybe after yesterday, one or both of us may end up in the pokey. So let's go out with a bang."

Isla shook her head slightly, but visibly. "I don't know. You seem to be big trouble, like double feature trouble. And I'm not sure, but are you asking me out on a date?"

"Yea, there's a few things you need to know."

"Like what?" Isla asked, taking a step closer to him.

"That I'm Bad to the Bone."

Another step closer. "And?"

"I was Born to Run."

"Anything else?" Isla said, now standing directly in front of Warren.

"I Ain't As Good as I Once Was."

Isla put her arms over his shoulders, and her eyes looked into his, searching, learning. "That's good enough for me," she whispered, as she kissed him for the first time.

***

Warren and Isla had dinner at her favorite restaurant, Ibiza Garden Café, a Mediterranean themed wine bar and grill located on West 15th Street. They talked for hours over a meal of beat salads, Turkish dumplings and seafood pasta, and easily finished a bottle of Gadea Anejo, a mahogany colored Spanish wine, with a slices of cheese cake for dessert. As they finished the meal, Warren looked at his watch. "Just about 10:00. What's next?"

"I've done the Times Square countdown before, but if that's what you want to do, then I'm game."

Warren shook his head. "I've got a better idea." Warren handed her his credit card, and said, give this to the waiter when he returns, I've got to make a call.

Warren was back in less than five minutes. They left the almost empty restaurant and felt the cold night air whisk by them. He hailed a cab and after they climbed in the back seat, said to the driver, "Columbus Circle."

Isla eyed Warren and asked, "What's the plan?"

Warren just grinned, fished some money out of his pocket for the driver and said, "You'll see in a minute. Working park detail does have its perks."

A few minutes later they were at Columbus Circle, where a horse drawn carriage waited. Warren said to the coachman, "Thanks Tommy. I know you're busy tonight. Glad that you could work me in."

"Are you kidding? You've had my back more times than I can count. So what's her name, this angel with you?" Tommy bowed slightly to Isla, and tipped his cap.

"Tommy, this beautiful lady is Isla. Isla Walson. Isla, this is Tommy Moreland, but his friends call him Tommy Mustang. He's the best coachman in the whole park."

Tommy slapped Warren on the shoulder. "No more talking. Warren, let's get you two up on the carriage, and let's take a ride." Tommy helped Isla climb into the carriage, and after Warren got aboard, he went to the front of the carriage and retrieved a thermos and two mugs, and handed them to Warren. "Here's some hot chocolate, perfect for the night air. Miss, there's a blanket on the seat next to you, help yourself if you feel a chill." He climbed aboard, took the reins in his hands and gently eased the horse into a steady walk along Central Park West.

Isla held Warren's hand and leaned against him. "Warren, this is so perfect. It's almost too perfect. I can't believe that I'm here with you. Last week I had such a dark view about my future. But now…"

Warren squeezed her hand and answered, "I know, last week seems like a year ago. These past seven days have been the strangest but also the best days of my life."

"And it has a lot to do with Darragh. He started all of this, and got busted up for his trouble."

"I don't understand all of the threads connecting all of the events around the Park, and the people too. But it seems like Darragh does."

"You know Warren, today was the first day since Christmas day that we haven't gotten a new poem. And I know yesterday the poem came from the editor at the paper, but it was still Darragh's words. It just seems like we're missing something, that we should have gotten one every day until the new year."

Warren looked at her smiled. "The day's not over yet."

Isla looked ahead and could see Belvedere Castle before them.

Warren finished his hot chocolate, and then asked Tommy, "How's the crowd tonight at the Park?"

Tommy chuckled. "See for yourself. It's like they moved Times Square to the Great Lawn for this evening. It's packed."

Tommy directed the carriage up West Drive, and pulled over when they got close to the crowd. "You two have a wonderful evening. And happy New Year."

Isla thanked Tommy and let Warren help her down from the carriage. They walked together through the crowd to the Stone Chapel.

They worked their way to the spot where the barricade gate had been erected. Spotlights now illuminated the chapel. The nativity scene was also highlighted, and seemed a tranquil living portrait of the peaceful manger that became a holy nursery. A group of carolers stood beside the scene, and sang carols, their faces red from the frosty air, but their voices clear and crisp.

Warren looked at his watch. "Eleven thirty."

On the chapel steps, he recognized Abner. He stood next to Claira. Warren made his way to the front of the chapel, and introduced Isla to them both. Then he asked, "What's the plan?"

Claira answered. "Nothing really. We're a little in the dark, not knowing if Darragh is going to be able to be here. There's a sense in the crowd that another poem is suppose be presented today, but they don't understand that Darragh was knocked out of commission."

Warren turned and glanced back to the crowd, then said, "Darragh snuck out of the hospital today. There's an APB out for him, and from what I learned this morning, there is some pressure remaining to charge him. We all know that it's crap, but I think that it's best if Darragh remains incognito. But he left me a poem, that I just found yesterday, and even though I know it was written for me, it's also written for everyone. I have it with me, and Claira, I think that you should read it to the people here."

Claira looked to Abner, who nodded agreement without even seeing the poem.

Warren reached into this coat pocket and handed Claira a single sheet of paper, folded over twice. Abner strolled over to the carolers and spoke in a whisper to their leader, who nodded and gave Abner a wink.

He then returned to the chapel steps, and as soon as the vocal choir finished the carol, Abner picked up a microphone connected to a portable speaker, and addressed the crowd. "Good evening, good evening, ladies and gentlemen, and thank you for coming here on this beautiful night, this beautiful New Year's Eve. I know that you all have been drawn here, that you have been compelled to come here, some because of curiosity, some because of a thirst to fill an empty feeling in your lives. I am happy to say that this wonderful little chapel is now an accepted and protected part of the Park and of the Museum of Natural History. And unfortunately, unfortunately, our resident poet will not be able to attend in person, but he has given us a poem for today. At this time, I would like to introduce to you Mrs. Claira Vasson, one of the Directors of the Central Park Conservancy, who will share with you this New Year's Eve poem. "With that Abner stood aside, and handed the microphone to Claira.

Claira looked over the vast crowd, and then back at the chapel behind her. Turning back to the crowd, she said, "Wow, so much has happened in the last week. It's stunning, when you think about it, what all has transpired, and what you have accomplished as citizens and people with an open mind and with a joy of recognizing something that is truly beautiful, and truly unique. With that, I will share with you this poem, written by Mr. Darragh Finn, the man some of us are calling the Stone Chapel Poet.

The Composer

Should my life be measured to music
What notes have I written or sung
Do they flow like words of a poem
Do they translate to multiple tongues

What chorus my opening sonata
What dance dare my minuet
Did my vocals violate promise
Vice and vanity my dire duet

Or should I blame another composer
For missed rhythm or lyrical crime
For insults to instruments given
For transgressions standard in time

Like song my life will find ending
Like drums my thunder will fade

Will I be an opera tragic
Will I shutter my symphony afraid

Brave then a voice a cappella
A carol to judgment abate
My composer does rally for mercies
And return to Eden's estate
df

The crowd was hushed and motionless as she finished the poem. Claira folded the paper and handed it back to Warren.

Someone in the crowd shouted, "three minutes until midnight." Warren checked his watch, and looked at Isla and nodded.

A murmur grew in the crowd, a subtle sound of words just barely spoken. Another minute passed, and the crowd sensed the coming new year. Another minute, then a voice started a countdown, and others voices sounded in, and when the counting reached ten, many more voices.

"Nine, eight, seven,"

Isla grabbed Warren hand, as she counted, "Six, five, four,"

Claira looked over to Theo and Tony, who had defied his sleep and was yelling in the countdown, "Three, two."

And then the spotlights grew dim, and in the high above, in the clear but light-polluted sky, a single star seemed to glow, to spin a radiance that was like a private fire in a giant diamond. The star seemed to draw to it an edge of darkness, as if it was framing its beautiful light with the darkest part of the night sky. And the starlight seemed to ignore the glow of the city lights, the aura of the buildings, and seemed to shine just for the people in the park, those around the chapel.

In the next instant, the sounds of bells or song fragments or whistles seemed everywhere. Everyone in the crowd was getting a message, all at the same time.

Isla's phone gave one pitched ringtone to signal the arrival of a new message. At the same time, Warren's phone sounded a guitar lick from a Neil Young tune, and Claira's pinged once in a note of electronic music. She checked her phone and found this.

COME

Come the rain
The little seeds
To heal our stain
To hear our pleas

Come the wind
The whispers will
To comprehend
To be fulfilled

Come the sun
The warm array
The night undone
The dark betray

Come to me
Let me behold
The spirit free
The secret told
df

Warren glanced over at Claira's phone, and saw the same poem that he had received. He looked at Isla and asked, "Did you get the poem?"

"I did."

Claira studied her phone. "Mine came across as an email. And it says from DF."

Abner nodded that he too had received the poem, and then pointed to the crowd. Everyone seemed to be checking their devices, comparing with their neighbors.

Abner turned on his wobbly knees and went into the chapel. He found a pew in the dark and sat. Warren and Isla came in behind him, and as they approached, the outside spotlights came back on, shining enough light into the chapel that they could see Abner sitting on the last row, looking at the stained glass window in the peak of the chapel roof. "That was the one window that I could not identify," he said as he pointed to the window. "Look at it; it is still radiant. Now I know what that window depicts. It's not an ancient event at all. It is meant to depict what happened here tonight. It is our star, the New Year's star that fell on this chapel tonight."

Claira walked up behind them. "I believe you."

Isla wrapped her arm around Warren and stared up at the window, which seemed to have the sun behind it, even at the stroke of midnight.

Abner stood and reached for Warren's hand to steady him. "Officer Hayes, you are seldom at a loss for words. What do you think about all of this? What do you say?"

Warren put his arm around Isla's shoulder, and answered, "As the great Steve Winwood said, 'We're Back in the High Life Again.' "

Chapter 24
January 1

"What color would you say that is?" Darragh asked, pointing to the icy chopped water of Eggemoggin Reach.

"Blued white," Cap replied. "Like that every winter."

Darragh smiled. The reach seemed daunting, formidable, in the snowy gusting wind, but also serene, inviting.

"Would you take me out on the water?" Darragh asked without looking at Cap, keeping his eyes on the spirited sea.

"That reach is not for day sails, not in the winter. But when you're mended, we'll see."

Darragh turned from the window. "And when will that be?"

Cap shrugged. In truth, he didn't know. He acted impulsively, without any sort of plan, and maybe that's why they had been able to get out of the hospital and all the way to Deer Island. Cap was opportunistic, and when he saw a tiny window that could lead to Darragh's escape, he grabbed it. He pushed a wheelchair to Darragh's room, telling the guard that they were going to chapel. Maybe because it was the second time Cap had been to Darragh's room, maybe the guard was just lazy, or maybe because they had a little intervention from above, but Cap was able to get Darragh out of his room just as the night's darkness was ending. Once off the floor, Cap retrieved a duffle bag he had stashed under a waiting room bench, and gave Darragh a hooded, quilted flannel jacket, overalls, and a cheap pair of slip-on boots. The hood gave enough cover to hide Darragh's bandages. They departed the hospital through different doors and at different times. Cap went straight back to his hotel, and Darragh used the money from Cap to take cab rides all over the city. After an hour and a half, the fifth cab left Darragh a block from Cap's hotel. Cap picked him up, and they were then on the way to Maine, driving against the north wind but with the tow of the sea and the harbor pulling Cap back like migration.

Cap gave Darragh a sprig of beef jerky and said, "I just got off the phone with a friend of mine, a doctor. He agreed to help us out, and to look after your wounds and bandages. As long as nothing goes sideways, you should be fine."

261

Darragh nodded, but otherwise did not answer.

Cap got two heavy shot glasses out of a cabinet, and brought them to the kitchen table where Darragh sat, still looking out the window to the foamy sea. In his other hand he carried a bottle of Aberlour 15-year-old, select cask reserve. The sound of the bottle uncorking turned Darragh's head. Upon seeing the whiskey and the shot glasses, he said, "Hello."

"Yea, I thought that we'd start the new year with some holy water," Cap said with a wink. Cap poured the shots.

"To the angels of your life, your mother, your sweet sister, and the rogue one charged to be my guardian," Darragh said, raising his glass in a toast.

"And to the stone chapel and what it brings with it," Cap added, and let his glass touch the edge of Darragh's.

Darragh finished his whiskey in one swallow, while Cap took only half of his. "I'll be moving on when I'm able," he said to Cap, as he slid his glass over for a refill. "You should think about coming with me."

"I'm home here, on Deer Island. I'll be tending to Mother's things. She'll be placed next to dad, already have a couple's stone. Just need another carving."

"I hear you," Darragh said. "But I owe you a debt and a service. You got me out of a place where my welcome was at its end."

Cap laughed. "Darragh, you had way more friends there than you know. But there were a few not as happy with you. Let's just say that we're all square. You answered a call for my mother, so for that, I'll be always grateful."

Darragh stood, and reached for the Carhartt coat. "Do you mind if I go for a walk? I'll be needing this coat of yours."

"Help yourself."

Darragh put on the coat, and extended his hand. As he and Cap shook hands, he said, "You know how we say farewell where I'm from?"

"Not a clue."

Darragh smiled. "Keep your lamps trimmed and burning."

Cap looked at him warily, and asked, "You are coming back, aren't you, Darragh? That's still a nasty wound under that eye that needs to be cared for."

Darragh turned his shot glass over and set it on the table. "Aye, I'll be back. You owe me that sail on the reach." He walked to the cottage door, then turned and said, "Don't drink all of that Aberlour while I'm gone. And Cap, keep those lamps trimmed and burning."

Printed in the USA
CPSIA information can be obtained
at www.ICGtesting.com
LVHW051239271223
767386LV00010B/664